SHADOWS OF IVORY

SHADOWS OF IVORY

Book One of The Godforged Chronicles
Copyright © 2020 T L Greylock
Published by Wraithmarked Creative, LLC

ISBN: 978-0-9991920-4-7

Cover Art by YAM
Cover Design by STK Kreations

T L
GREYLOCK

BRYCE
O'CONNOR

SHADOWS OF IVORY

THE
GODFORGED
CHRONICLES

BOOKS BY T L GREYLOCK

The Song of the Ash Tree

The Blood-Tainted Winter
The Hills of Home
Already Comes Darkness

BOOKS BY BRYCE O'CONNOR

The Wings of War

Child of the Daystar
The Warring Son
Winter's King
As Iron Falls
Of Sand and Snow

The Shattered Reigns

A Mark of Kings

For Laura.

She knows why.

Contents

PART III

Part
1

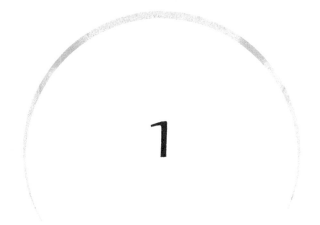

1

"You know how women are when it comes to pretty things."

"TECHNICALLY, I DIDN'T STEAL IT."

It was not lost on Eska that these were unlikely to be the best choice of words when faced with a pair of inspectors, the hot-breathed hounds panting at their heels, and the half dozen grunts wielding various instruments of violence just outside the alley. Not to mention the Iron Baron himself, fixing her with a steely glare. No, not lost at all, considering she was, in fact, holding in plain view the very object she was accused of stealing, an object quite dear to the belligerent baron.

"Nor was I going to keep it."

The inspectors glanced at each other, but it was the Baron's gaze that got under her skin, those condescending eyes, those furiously-angled eyebrows, that large chin which was offensive simply for being attached to his face.

"It's not worth what you think it is, you know."

This was patently false, but Eska never had learned when to keep her mouth shut, despite the numerous attempts made by more than one governess, and she couldn't resist a jab at the Baron's notorious lack of sophistication when it came to his home decor.

His face reddening, the Baron plucked the carved ivory and gold box from her hands and dropped it into the waiting arms of his valet, who stared at the ground as though it were the most fascinating thing under the sun.

"You're fortunate you carry the name of de Caraval, girl," the Iron Baron growled, forcing the words out through clenched teeth in a manner that reminded Eska of bones mistakenly placed in a meat grinder. The image pleased her.

"What would you do to me, Baron, if I didn't wear ancinni silk and have priceless jewels on my fingers? Cut off my hand? Sell me to the highest bidder? I hear you do quite the trade in such things." The rumor rushed off Eska's tongue as cheerfully as a waterfall leaps off a cliff.

The Baron went from red to white in a heartbeat, his cheeks fairly blooming with iciness. If the valet could have melted into the cobblestones, surely he would have. Instead, he picked absentmindedly—or perhaps with subconscious insight—at the ring of golden daggers embroidered on the upper arm of his velvet jacket.

"It's dark, girl, and no one knows where you are." The Baron leaned close. Eska smelled the wine on his breath. Sweet and sour. And cheap. "I could make you disappear."

Eska fought the urge to step back, but felt certain her heart was a moment from breaking free from the prison of her ribcage. "You forget yourself, Baron," she said, hoping she sounded unruffled.

The small dagger—hardly more deadly than a letter opener—strapped to her ankle would be of no use here, though the bone handle seemed to burn against her skin. She nodded over the Baron's shoulder at the inspectors. "These fine gentlemen know exactly where I am. In fact, I'm quite sure they'd be prepared to tell my father, the Vice-Chancelier, exactly how you laid hands on me, how you injured me, how you dragged me off to dispose of me."

The inspectors kept their faces still, well-schooled in such things, and Eska wondered how much the Baron had paid them. The hounds stared up at Eska with dark eyes, panting steadily, every muscle taut beneath their smooth coats, their teeth white in the moonlight. Then the taller of the inspectors broke the silence, his words bringing Eska more relief than she cared to admit.

"I'm sure it's all a misunderstanding, Baron." The inspector smiled thinly at Eska. "You know how women are when it comes to pretty things." He gestured to the ivory, glistening in the moonlight as it disappeared into the valet's satchel. "You have your property back. I think it's time we all go home."

The notion that Eska was like a crow when confronted with a shiny object irked her as much as the Baron's chin, but for once she held her tongue. Madam Mantua might have died of shock to see it.

The inspectors broke their shoulder to shoulder blockade, opening a path for her to leave the alley. Eska leaned over and patted the young valet on the shoulder. "The de Caraval household is always in search of good people," she said. Without a glance at the Baron, Eska swept past the inspectors, trying not to shy away from the hounds who sniffed her with more interest than she'd like.

"We don't bite," she called over her shoulder, "and I'm quite certain my father would never send you on such a ridiculous task in the middle of the night. And as you can see, I run my own midnight errands."

Despite the words of the inspector, the men outside the entrance to the alley did little to allow Eska easy passage. She managed to traverse the obstacle course comprised of their large booted feet, broad shoulders, and stout clubs without incident, but it wasn't until she had put several wide avenues between her and the Baron that she felt capable of slowing her pace. She crossed the expanse of the Decadronum, the clacking of the heels on her boots horribly loud on the white stone as she followed the line of sentinel columns across the ten-sided plaza, and only then, sinking into the familiar shadows of the Lordican's portico, did she allow herself to relax and breathe deeply.

The eerie water chimes at the far end of the Decadronum sounded the second song of the morning as Eska took a moment to wait for her heartbeat to return to normal. As the song faded, sending a shiver down her spine, she pressed the concealed release that unlocked one of the library's tall wooden doors and slipped into the dim interior. Cursing her shoes once more, she crossed the marble entryway, the unfortunate *clackety clack* ringing after her, and entered one of the grand reading rooms, the empty desks lined up like a flock of sleeping swans. Eska threaded her way to the rear of the reading room and pressed another hidden lever, this one disguised as the big toe on a statue of a man clothed in nothing but a sweeping cape and gesturing dramatically—with equally dramatic muscles—toward an unseen horizon.

Nothing happened.

The bronze studded door in front of her, which ought to have opened to reveal a passageway restricted to staff at the Lordican—and therefore the sort of door Eska should not know how to open—remained steadfastly shut.

"Really?" Eska cast a withering gaze up at the blank eyes of the statue. "Now is hardly the time, Lyndronicus."

The statue made no reply and Eska bent over to fiddle with the long-dead conqueror's toe. It was known to stick, a faulty mechanism, the staff claimed. Eska was inclined to believe the door's creator had deliberately made the latch tricky and susceptible to damp. If half the stories about the library's first and greatest patron, who also happened to be its designer and architect, were true, Eska would expect the statue's toe to crumble to dust at some predetermined future date—rendering the passageway useless. It was the kind of joke she was sure Giovanespi de Varetteau would enjoy.

"Perhaps," Eska muttered as she wiggled the toe this way and that way, ears straining for the faint click that would signal the alignment had been corrected, "a different appendage would be more appropriate. At least if I yanked it, I ought to get a response."

"That's rather vulgar."

Eska whirled around, nearly convinced the statue of Lyndronicus had finally answered her after years of one-way conversations. But the voice belonged to a slender man who had crossed the reading room far too stealthily, a stack of books pressing up against his chin as he cradled the tomes in his arms.

Eska sighed and pushed a strand of hair out of her face. "You are far too—"

"Quiet for my own good, yes, you've made me aware of that," the young man said. "Unfortunately, I have yet to discover my stampeding abilities."

Eska rolled her eyes. "I should fit you with an obnoxious bell, like a goat. Whenever you enter a room, it would warn the occupants that an insufferable know-it-all is in their midst."

"Good thing this know-it-all also happens to know that you need to be gentler with the toe. You'll never find the right spot if you bash it around like that."

Eska laughed. "What woman hasn't had to tell a man that at least once."

Blushing furiously, much to Eska's delight, the young man brushed past her, left his books on a desk, and, with a well-practiced flick of a finger, set the lever in place. The door swung open.

"Don't smirk, Albus."

"I never smirk." The young man performed the tiniest of bows before scooping the stack of books up once more. "After you, my Lady de Caraval."

———— ◦ ————

"That was the best you could manage? 'Technically, I didn't steal it?' I've come to expect so much more from you, Eska."

The library employee never looked up from the pages he was bent over, his gaze intent on the intricate, ancient script he insisted he could read.

"This is where you choose to interject? Not when I related my fear at being confronted by the Iron Baron and a host of lowlifes? A gentleman would inquire after my safety and ascertain if I was unharmed. You know the stories about Thibault de Venescu." Eska stopped pacing the length of the worktable where Albus sat. Her fierce frown, however, was lost on the librarian, who still had eyes only for his book.

"You've had your share of risky adventures," Albus said mildly. "You should take my lack of concern as a compliment on your abilities."

"Yes, well, that may be, but you might reconsider your assumption of my safety if you knew what was in my possession." Eska planted her hands on her hips, certain her dramatic air would at last draw Albus away from his text. The librarian seemed not to have heard.

"Albus."

"Mmm?"

"Don't you want to know what I have?"

"I daresay you're going to tell me regardless of what I might desire."

"By all the dead librarians, Albus, you really are horrible. Now get your nose out of that book and look at me."

Smiling faintly, the librarian lifted his gaze at last, but the humor vanished the moment he saw what lay in Eska's palm. Albus lurched to his feet, the book forgotten, his hands hovering over the pages.

"What is that?"

"I should very much like you to tell me. I don't suppose you happen to know what a long-dead queen stashed in a box that has been lost for centuries and no one knows how to open."

"Then you did steal something." The librarian seemed torn between rushing to examine the object Eska held and maintaining his composure.

"I must insist that technically I did not. The box containing it was handed to me. By a source I shall keep nameless."

"But you removed it from the box."

Eska shrugged, though the thrill of the moment in which she had discovered the box's secret sent her stomach tumbling over itself still— as though she were racing across the rooftop once again, voices careening after her, the ivory reliquary spilling from her grasp to land in a shard of moonlight. She took a steadying breath. "Someone had to."

"And the Baron?"

"I think he has no idea what, if anything, was in his precious box. To him, the ivory reliquary is merely a priceless relic of the Alescu dynasty. If he knew how to open it, he would have done so in my presence to ascertain the contents were safe."

At last Albus' gaze fixed on Eska, his face grave. "That was a risk. If he had opened it…."

The memory of that moment and the terror she had felt tightened like skewers into Eska's temples. "But he didn't." She swallowed hard and was glad that at last Albus could see what the evening almost cost her.

Their gazes remained locked for a long moment, the librarian's brown eyes full of concern.

"May I?" he asked at last.

Without a word, Eska extended her hand. Albus drifted silently around the corner of the long table. His fingers hesitated over Eska's palm as he took in the disc and the pattern of markings—thin lines of varying lengths and direction, interrupted here and there by dots and empty spaces carved into the metal and stained black—and then, hesitation replaced by scholarly purpose, he plucked the disc up by its edge.

"No, not like that," Eska said. But it was too late. The disc, strangely malleable despite the appearance of bronze, crumpled, folding in on itself like a threatened hedgehog until it resembled a large and rather lumpy twenty-sided die. The librarian stared at it in confusion and surprise. Eska couldn't resist a grin. "Now you've done it."

"How did you know?"

"Well, when one is in a hurry and trying to steal something, one is not often very precise about where one places one's fingers."

Albus frowned and looked Eska up and down. "How on earth did you transport it and keep it flat?"

"Wouldn't you like to know. And wouldn't you like me to tell you how to restore it?"

"It's unbecoming to gloat, Eska."

"I never gloat."

It was Albus' turn to roll his eyes, but so great was his impatience that he handed the strange object back to Eska without another word—and then proceeded to screech in horror as she placed it on the floor and brought the heel of her boot down onto it as hard as she could.

"I can hardly believe that's the proper method," Albus said, aghast.

"You are undoubtedly correct. But it worked, didn't it?"

Indeed the disc was once more a disc, gleaming up at them from the wooden floorboards.

"I don't think I want to know how you discovered that."

"In a fit of anger, naturally." And fear.

Albus sighed. "Naturally."

"I'm sure you were going to attempt to coax it back with some clever rhyme spoken in sixteen languages."

"Nonsense. Metal doesn't understand language, Eska." And yet the librarian, for all his seriousness, couldn't suppress the smile forming on his lips. "Though that would be a beautiful thing to see. You trying to sing to it in ancient Azarian."

"Ancient Azarian has no vowels," Eska said, eyes narrowing.

The smile grew. "Precisely."

Albus turned his attention back to the disc, frowned, then grabbed a shapeless chunk of grey rock from a shelf and knelt on the floor. As he held the rock over the disc, it leapt from the floor and clung to the grey stone. Looking up at Eska expectantly, he made a little shooing motion with his free hand.

"Go on. You know I can't work with you hovering over me."

"Don't shoo me, Albus. But don't you need to go home? Sleep? The water chimes must be moments away from sounding the third song of the morning."

"Home?" The librarian got to his feet. "Don't lecture me. I get far more done when the library is quiet. Why on earth would I waste that time?"

"I'd hardly call socializing, eating, and sleeping a waste of time. But," Eska said, holding out her hands to express her surrender as the librarian began to argue, "I know you'll never appreciate the charms of sunlight and friends that aren't books. But I want to watch you work. I want to be here. I'll be quiet. Promise. As still as a sail on a windless day. You'll never even know I'm still here."

"We both know you can't sit still for longer than it takes you to invent some hare-brained idea and insist you go galloping after it." Albus ignored Eska's scowl and looked nonchalantly at the disc, still dangling from the rock in his hand. "Besides, are you not due in court at an early hour?"

Eska gasped, her stomach plummeting through the floorboards.

"I'd hate to see you lose the Bourdillon-Leveque contract all because you can't keep track of time."

Eska rushed to Albus and planted a kiss on his cheek. Hastening to the door and the network of restricted passageways beyond, she called over her shoulder, "I hate you and love you, Albus Courtenay."

"Likewise, my lady."

2

"Do you enjoy sea bathing, your Honor?"

"As you can see, your Honor, in paragraph five of section two hundred and seventy-three of amendment sixteen," the man in black paused, frowned, and cleared his throat for what Eska was sure was the two hundred and seventy-third time that morning. "Forgive me, your Honor, I misspoke. It is paragraph six, not five, of section two hundred and seventy-three. Line twelve, just there."

The man jabbed a long finger at the parchment in his hand. The justice, seated on high in front of Eska and the lawyer, blinked back at him. "I shall read it for you," the man in black said. He cleared his throat once more and Eska tried to shift imperceptibly on her tall, narrow chair. In vain. Her behind was most certainly going numb.

"The rights of the aforementioned property holder, henceforth known as…"

Eska, feeling like her eyelids were being dragged down by the weight of Albus' heaviest books, could not tear her gaze away from the careful ringlets of hair cascading down the justice's shoulders, keeping herself awake by imagining him seated before a vanity, rolling each ringlet before tucking them all beneath a lacy—no, silk, surely—nightcap. Even the slightest movement, a heavier breath, a tilted shoulder, sent the tight curls shuddering. It was mesmerizing. She would die before admitting it to Albus, but her late night was wearing on her and she was in danger of taking a nap in court.

"...held in perpetuity according to the will and testament of the deceased..."

A fly buzzed in front of Eska's face and she went slightly cross-eyed for a moment before it flew onward, coming to rest on the justice's lace-trimmed sleeve. She watched it march its way up the velvet landscape before coming to rest near the closest tangle of ringlets, no doubt eyeing the massive obstacle looming in its path with fear and doubt. Or perhaps gumption and reckless resolve. Eska really couldn't say. Regardless, the fly, either brave, suicidal, or very dim, sallied forth, entering into the vast morass of brown curls.

"...as stated in statute ten of the Varadian Compromise..."

Eska wondered if the fly was finding crumbs, a bit of pastry from the justice's morning meal, or better yet: fruit filling. Unless, of course, whatever the fly was hunting was a cruel ruse, a clever trap. The poor creature, lured in by irresistible odors and the promise of a rare feast, only to seek and find nothing but waxy pomade scented with strawberries and figs. Then again, Eska supposed it was possible a fly could eat pomade. She would have to ask Albus.

"Lady de Caraval?"

Eska flinched, suddenly aware that the justice's gaze and that of the man in black had shifted to her. She had the sinking feeling they had been waiting some time. She stood, trying not to wince at the numb sensation in her backside.

"Is it my turn already? How the time flies," Eska said, smiling pleasantly. She wondered if the insect had buzzed in the justice's ear yet. She turned to the man in black. "Your arguments are most compelling, sir, and I compliment you on the case you have made." The faintest of blushes marred the lawyer's stern countenance as Eska turned her attention to the justice.

"Do you enjoy sea bathing, your Honor?"

The justice frowned. "A frivolous past time."

A lie. Eska had it on good authority that the honorable justice had spent each of his last six holidays discreetly ensconced in a villa at the seaside, hosting all manner of guests, savory and unsavory, invited and compelled, for all manner of debauched activities. No matter. She hadn't expected him to admit to it.

She also had it on good authority that he had bribed, threatened, and murdered his way into possession of that coveted villa. And if he had done all that for a bit of sand and sun, well, Eska could only imagine what he might have done to ensure his miraculous election to yet another term—an astonishing four terms in all—as a member of the esteemed Court Beneath the Sun.

Eska smiled again. "My mistake. You look like a man who enjoys the fine things the seaside has to offer. Seaweed wraps." Eska kept smiling. "Sand baths." She paused. "Pearl diving." The justice went pale, the ringlets quivering. "And who could forget the cuisine. The eels are so," Eska hesitated once more, "ravishing."

The justice nearly bolted out of his seat. "The contract, Lady de Caraval," he managed to say. "What have you to say about it?" To Eska's relief, the man in black had his nose stuck in a thick sheaf of papers and was oblivious to the justice's consternation.

Eska gave a wave of her hand and assumed a brisk tone. "Only that the site in question must be excavated or we risk losing it forever as the river bed continues to alter and the banks cave in. There is no one more equipped to manage the situation. While I am sensitive to the concerns of my colleague's client," she said, nodding to the man in black, "the site is of such importance that we must abandon protocol and precedent and learn what we can before it is too late. It is vital to our understanding of the world and all future archaeological endeavors"—this was perhaps something of an exaggeration—"that we undertake this project with the utmost haste and care." Eska drew in a breath, prepared to continue.

"Enough." The justice got to his feet, his face still pale, his hands clasped tight behind his back. "I have reached a decision." He took a deep breath. The fly emerged and circled the justice's head. Eska swallowed a smile.

The man in black cleared his throat and stood up straighter, chest puffed against the buttons of his stiff jacket, no doubt prepared to enjoy his moment of victory over the presumptions of Lady de Caraval, who had not even had the sense to bring a trained lawyer to argue her case.

"In the matter of the Bourdillon-Leveque contract, I find in favor of Lady de Caraval. All rights, duties, financial gain or loss associated therein are now the sole responsibility of Lady de Caraval and the Firenzia Company. The Court Beneath the Sun washes its hands of this matter once and for all."

The man in black gaped. Eska reached over, hand extended. "Well-argued, my friend. My condolences, it's truly a surprise," she murmured. The man, his eyes glazing over as he grasped her fingers weakly, let forth a strangled noise that would no doubt have been a lovely compliment if only he weren't choking on his disbelief. Eska gave his fingers a firm shake, withdrew and approached the justice, prepared to offer him the same meaningless pleasantries.

"Your Honor," she began, but the justice cut her off.

"I trust you are satisfied?" His voice was tight and low, his brows knitted together in a deep frown.

Eska smiled. "But of course, your Honor. Delighted, in fact."

"Then we'll hear nothing more of pearl diving? Nor the eels?"

"Whatever are you speaking of, your Honor? You yourself said you avoid the seaside."

The justice rose up on his toes ever so slightly, his heels clicking as they came back down to the polished floor in an attempt to regain his composure. "Just so. Exactly."

"But if you were to change your mind," Eska went on, as though heedless of the vein pulsing in the justice's temple and the crimson creeping into his cheeks, "my father knows a thing or two about property. I'm sure he'd be happy to advise you in your purchase."

"Good day, Lady de Caraval," the justice interrupted. Nodding stiffly, he spun away from her, his curls bouncing in retreat. As the double doors swung open to release him, a serving girl slipped through. She clutched Eska's belongings tight and dipped a curtsey.

"Your cape, my lady."

Eska smiled at the girl and dropped the cape over her shoulders, its slick fabric still speckled with the rain that had burst from the overcast sky on her way to the Court Beneath the Sun. "And the trunk?"

Another curtsey. "Waiting, as you asked, my lady."

"Very good. Tell the driver he may proceed and that I'll follow shortly. The transport will be waiting at the company wharf. He'll know what to do." The girl nodded and ran off.

"A vulture, you are," the man in black said, staring after the girl. As he turned his gaze to her, Eska could see his brain working out the fact that she had arrived at the Court Beneath the Sun with no doubts as to the outcome of the hearing.

Unruffled, Eska met his incredulous hostility with the cold stare her father had taught her from an early age. "Why, sir, if you mean to compare me to a strong, practical creature with a great talent for survival, then I must thank you."

The lawyer sputtered and shoved his papers into a too-small case, his hand a merciless claw of destruction. "My client will appeal," he said.

"As is your client's right, sir." Eska fastened the rain cape at her collarbone, clipping the green-eyed snake into the gilt beak of the hawk. "In the meantime, the Firenzia Company will begin digging. And I'll see that your appeal gets so lost and tangled in the courts that even the great Gordinian would be unable to extract it. Good day."

Interlude 1

"Did you have to slay a fierce two-headed river cat to get to it, Uncle?"

The man with the golden beard laughs and pokes the girl on the tip of her nose. "Kovuntuu river cats only have a single head, my dear."

The girl frowns, her eyes still on the jade egg balanced upright in her palm. "Just because you haven't seen one with two heads doesn't mean they don't exist."

Her uncle throws up his hands in mock defeat. "I stand corrected. As usual." He leans in close and their eyes meet, the jade egg between them, man and girl, equally delighted by the intricate carvings despite the years separating them.

"What do the carvings mean?" the girl asks. "Do they tell a story?"

"I'm sure they do, clever one. Here, I see a pair of large birds, and here, a figure kneels. I think it's a woman."

The girl turns the egg in her palm and studies the figures her uncle speaks of. "It could be a man."

"Certainly," her uncle says, grinning. "It could be whatever you like, my dear."

"Perhaps the birds have escaped. And he's sad to lose them."

"Perhaps. Or perhaps he worships bird-gods and is praying as they fly overhead."

The girl frowns again. "I wish you knew and could tell me. I should like to know." But then she smiles and meets her uncle's gaze, his nose hidden by the jade. The slightest hint of dust from his journey is smeared across his forehead. "It's beautiful."

"Then you like it?"

"Oh, of course, Uncle! It's perfect." Her smile flashes out from behind the egg, which she lowers before stepping close to plant a kiss on her uncle's cheek. "I shall keep it safe, right next to the diadem you brought me at the winter festival. There's room for it there."

The man beams. "Is it your favorite, then?"

"My favorite?" The girl looks down at the egg once more. "I couldn't possibly choose a favorite. All the gifts you bring are very dear to me."

"How diplomatic of you. Your mother would be proud." Her uncle straightens, standing tall over his niece once more. "Now, I must present the rest of the temple's treasures to the Archduke. I'm already late, but I couldn't resist bringing your gift first." He turns to collect the box that had once contained the jade egg, but the girl, bobbing up and down on her toes in excitement, stops him.

"May I come, Uncle?"

"To the Varadome?" He makes a show of thinking, his mouth serious, but the glimmer in his eye gives him away. He sweeps low in an elaborate bow. "But of course, my Lady de Caraval, I would be most honored if you would grace me with your delightful company."

The girl curtseys with practiced formality, then giggles as her uncle offers, and she accepts, his arm.

"And who knows, perhaps we'll spot a two-headed river cat on the way."

"Uncle, river cats don't live north of the Umoria highlands. Everyone knows that."

The man laughs, a sound as bright and golden as his beard. "I doubt that's a thing everyone knows, my dear, certainly not most children of nine years. And just because you haven't seen a river cat north of the Umoria highlands doesn't mean they aren't there. Someone very wise taught me that logic."

He laughs again and this time she joins in as they step outside into the waiting glare of a sun masked by a thin layer of cloud. An open carriage awaits, emblazoned with a pair of hawks fighting over a snake in their talons. Behind it stand three plain wagons drawn by teams of four horses, each wagon covered with a dusty sheet of canvas, the contents straining against the ties binding the canvas to the rails. And just beyond, barely glanced at by the girl, a troop of mounted guards lingers in the courtyard, shadowed by the eastern wing of the *house and the tall, wide oak that whispers there.*

"Is this all?" the girl asks, a small hand shielding her eyes from the bright light as she contemplates the wagons.

"Hardly," the man says, laughing once more. "Only the best and most valuable. The rest follows, but these are the pieces worth showing the Archduke immediately."

"Will you tell me all about your journey on the way, Uncle?" the girl asks as the man opens the carriage door and then lifts her up in his arms and deposits her on the forward-facing seat. "Was it dangerous? Were there bandits?"

He climbs in after her and signals the driver to depart.

The girl leans across the gap between the bench seats, her green eyes alight with excitement. "Did you have to fight a great warrior in single combat? Or answer a series of riddles to unlock the hidden temple? What are the Irgardians like? Do they really not eat meat? Do they ride in tall saddles and use only their feet to steer? Are they really afraid of water?"

Her questions do not diminish as the carriage lurches to life and rumbles along the stone drive. Indeed, they are as continuous as the clip clop of horse hooves that follow.

3

"To bring honor to the name of de Caraval."

ESKA CLOSED THE DOOR BEHIND HER WITH A LONG EXHALE, UNCOM-
monly glad to be within the sturdy confines of her family home—and
out of the rain, which was persistent in its desire to drench her.

She heard the feet coming, of course. The soft pattering step of
Nonetta followed by the heavier tread that signaled Roscoe was with
the maid. Breathing in one last moment of silence and stillness, Eska
turned and put a pleasant smile on her face just as Nonetta rounded
the corner from the servants' wing into the glass-walled garden entrance. If Eska was honest with herself, she would admit that seeing
Roscoe, broad-shouldered, burly-armed Roscoe, captain of the de
Caraval house guards, was not unwelcome, despite the man's overpro-
tective nature. She had noticed the figure tailing her home from the
Court Beneath the Sun fairly quickly. She had not realized there were
two until she had reached the Jordiene Bridge, a misstep she chalked
up to her sleepless night and the monotony of court—but no less dangerous for that. Not a word to Roscoe, of course, but his presence was
welcome.

The tails belonged to the Iron Baron. Most likely. Whether Thibault
de Venescu wanted to kidnap her in broad daylight or merely scare her
was up for debate. Then again, there were other reasons the daughter of the Vice-Chancelier of Arconia might be followed through the
streets of the city. Most of them not innocuous.

"A bath please, Nonetta, and tell Alize to begin packing," Eska said, as she handed her gloves and rain cape to the maid, who curtseyed and hurried off. She acknowledged Roscoe's bow with a nod and turned to mount the small iron staircase that would take her to her chambers above the rose garden, then paused when her gaze fell upon an obsidian-tipped walking stick staked unceremoniously into a potted fern by the door she had just entered. Eska turned back to the captain. "Where is he?"

"The kitchen, my lady. In search of pastry."

Eska smiled. "Naturally."

Valentin de Caraval was no longer searching, as it turned out. Eska, momentarily unseen as she waited at the kitchen's threshold, watched as her uncle made exceptionally quick work of a cream-filled bun, nary a crumb of flaky pastry lost to the floor or his beard. He turned next with relish to a chocolate and cinnamon concoction, his mouth conveniently full when Eska chose to speak up.

"You know, Mira would be outraged to see her creations demolished with so little regard for the genius and craftsmanship that went into making them."

Whatever quick retort Valentin might have fired back was lost somewhere between his molars and he had the grace to look marginally abashed as he chewed and swallowed.

"I would argue, niece, that the speed with which I consume Mira's work is a testament to that genius—perhaps the greatest testament."

Eska laughed and went to him. "Uncle." She kissed his cheek.

"Eska." He returned her greeting.

"When did you arrive?" Eska pulled up a stool and watched across the wooden work bench as Valentin took a slender knife and divided the remainder of the dessert in two. He pushed her portion down the bench.

"Just before you, it would seem. But unlike you, I was clever enough to travel in a closed carriage."

Eska raised a hand to her head and patted her damp, disorderly hair. Shrugging, she nibbled on the corner of the cake. "A little rain is worth winning the Bourdillon-Leveque contract."

"Am I to congratulate you?"

"Would it be so difficult to do so?" Eska asked, keeping her voice light and knowing the answer that will come next.

"It's a waste of time, Eska."

"Seeing as my time is my own, that is no great loss, then."

"Not just time, money and resources," Valentin said, his gaze hardening. "There is nothing to be gained from that site but broken pottery."

"Broken pottery can tell us a great deal, Uncle."

"And after it tells you its useless story? What then? Will the Archduke buy it and add it to his collection? Will the wealthy bid on it at auction? Will the Contessa de Elvain wear a broken shard of old clay around her neck?"

Eska took a deep breath, wondering if her hands were as unsteady as her heart. "Old broken clay taught us that the ancient city of Unor was evacuated before it flooded. That the Lanoaans knew how to build kilns long before we first believed. That red corithorn once grew here, in our own soil, before the first walls of Arconia were ever raised, when this land had a name we no longer know."

"Tales of red corithorn do not keep the Firenzia ships in sailing shape. They do not pay the wages of guides or excavators. They do not buy horses and equipment and all the countless other things we must have to maintain this company, to keep our competition at bay." Valentin paused. "To bring honor to the name of de Caraval."

Eska stood, the stool tottering behind her. Her uncle mirrored her movement, slowly, his forehead knit with uncertainty. It was only in that moment that Eska noticed the silver box tied with a gauzy white ribbon where her uncle's elbow had been resting a moment before. Her latest gift. There was always a gift. He no longer seemed aware of its existence and Eska quickly looked away and met her uncle's gaze.

"Is it so dishonorable to seek knowledge? Is it so shameful to my family that a broken pot is as much a treasure to me as a golden crown worn by some ancient king?"

Valentin took a step toward Eska. "I do not mean—"

"But you do mean it, Uncle. Perhaps you have not admitted those words out loud or even in the silence of your own heart, but they are there, within you, and I see them well enough." Eska knew he could hear the shiver in her voice, knew he could see the hurt on her face. What she did not know, as she left the kitchen, was whether there could be some truth to what he said. The de Caraval family stood at the right hand of the Archduke of Arconia, amid a glittering, ambitious horde who would seize any opportunity to supplant them. Old pottery did not win trade arguments. Scraps of burnt cloth did not skewer opponents and rivals. Broken things long forgotten did not inspire loyalty or grant power. And power, Eska knew, was the pendulum on which Arconia, and the world, swung.

——— ◆ ———

Eska sank into the copper tub and inhaled deeply, willing herself to relax but unable to shake the memory of the disappointment that had clouded her uncle's face. It was a conversation they had conducted on more than one occasion, each instance a variation on the theme, and each lasting only moments. Eska did not dare think of what might befall should their tempers truly take control and they speak words they could not undo. And yet each time they clashed over the future of the Firenzia Company, each time she reminded her uncle she preferred scholarly work to treasure hunting, Eska felt the sting of uncertainty and the pain of losing her beloved uncle's trust and affection all over again.

That sting had all but burned away the excitement of the result of the morning, leaving only the faint impression of fear that had tailed Eska, literally, from the Court Beneath the Sun. As she breathed in the steam scented with mint, she attempted to summon it back again, the promise of the unknown, the mystery of the excavation that awaited her—all hers, at last. She could feel the dirt beneath her hands, feel the sun on the back of her neck as she bent to her tasks, feel the tools in her fingers. Eska smiled a little to herself, content with that spark of joy, dunked her head under the water, and then summoned her maid to the tub.

"Alize, did you add the harrow root powder as I asked?" Eska brushed water from her face and leaned back, eyes closed.

The young woman's hands paused on Eska's scalp. "Yes, my lady." A reluctant answer for a task reluctantly performed.

Eska sighed. "I am not unsympathetic to your concerns. When I am old and grey before my time and my eyesight fails me and when all the things you dread have come to pass, then you may say you told me so and I will not argue."

Silence. Then: "You should smell it in a moment, my lady."

Alize spoke true. The bath water came alive, fizzing gently, and then the scent, rich and spicy, wafted up to tickle Eska's nostrils. She kept her eyes closed as the vapor grew, swirling so thick she could feel it on her skin, each inhale expanding Eska's lungs until she felt as though she could breathe in the entire sky.

She couldn't, of course. But the harrow root made enticing promises and Eska would step out of the bath feeling more revitalized than she would after a night of deep sleep. The sense of strength, of endurance, would linger for days.

As the vapor diminished, Alize spoke again. "I've packed the kelp extract, my lady. You should try to remember to use it. You know how the sun dries out your hair. And the new cream for your hands."

"I shall try my best, Alize," Eska murmured.

"The midsummer masquerade is not far off. Will you return in time to attend?"

Eska smiled. "I sincerely hope I am far too deep in a pit on the outskirts of Toridium to contemplate returning to Arconia for a masquerade."

"Surely the crew can do without you for a few days." Alize hesitated. "And surely you would enjoy a respite from the dust and toil."

"What is it you're not saying, Alize?"

The maid was rinsing a conditioning oil from Eska's hair. "I have heard rumors, my lady."

"What sort of rumors?"

"That Alexandre de Minos intends to return to the city in time to attend the masquerade."

"Oh?"

As it happened, Eska was uncertain if she wanted to know more. Alexandre de Minos was a complication she could do without, but there was no denying curiosity had welled within her. In the end, she was momentarily spared from framing any thoughts on Alexandre de Minos by the sudden invasion of the bath chamber by a young man winded from taking the stairs three at a time.

"My lady," he gasped at the same moment Alize began to berate him for his lack of decorum.

"It's all right, Alize. Bastien wouldn't be here if it wasn't important." Eska began to rise from the tub, the water level dropping to her collarbone, then thought better of it as the young man's face grew crimson with sudden embarrassment. Eska stayed put and gestured for the heavy robe draped over a stool.

The maid stepped between the young man and the tub with the rigidity of an officer at attention and spread the robe wide. Eska stood, letting the water cascade off her skin, and stepped out of the tub. As Bastien tried to find anywhere to rest his gaze that wasn't Eska, Alize wrapped the robe tight, cinching the belt at the waist as though her knot were the only thing standing between Eska and utter ruin.

"That's quite enough, Alize."

"But your hair, my lady."

"Is wet," Eska said, growing impatient. "And will have no impact on what Bastien has to tell me." She stepped around the crestfallen maid. "What is it, Bastien?"

"Barca Company, my lady," Bastien blurted. "They know. They're on the move."

Despite the warmth of the robe and the room, Eska's skin prickled as though chilled.

"How?" she murmured. "And what do the Barcas want with Onandyan pottery?" But these were not the questions to ask when time was of the essence. There would be time later to discover how Firenzia's fiercest rivals had learned of the secret contract and the judgment handed down at the Court Beneath the Sun that morning—and what Manon Barca thought was buried on the banks of the Alencio. "How long do we have?" she amended.

"They were casting off, my lady, when I left the docks. We're lost."

"Never say that, Bastien," Eska said. She reached back and twisted her wet hair into a knot at the crown of her head. "Alize," she commanded without turning to look at the maid. With a mournful noise, Alize went to work pinning the hair in place. "We are not lost so long as we have the fastest ship in the harbor. I will not have my legally won contract stolen out from under me." Eska was pleased to see her defiance and spirit bring a gleam of pride to Bastien's eyes and there was no room in his face for embarrassment as Eska began to undo the knot holding the robe closed. "Go. See that everything is ready. I will only be a moment." As Bastien turned to leave, Eska placed a hand on his sleeve. "We will catch the bastards."

As Bastien pounded down the stairs, the door to the bath chamber left wide open in his wake, Eska let the robe drop. "My traveling clothes, Alize." The maid was already there, knowing better than to give further voice to whatever anxiety she felt at the state of Eska's hair. Eska, her skin still damp from the bath, pulled on the loose white shirt, its billowy sleeves sticking to her arms, but this, it seems, was too much for Alize to bear.

"But your undergarments! The corset!"

"This is hardly the time to have whale bones sticking into my ribs, Alize." Eska pulled on her trousers and was so intent on buttoning the grey and silver embroidered waistcoat Alize had maneuvered her into that she did not notice the figure in crisp blue and white looming at the bath chamber door.

"My lady," Alize said, dropping into a curtsey.

Eska looked up. "Mama." Her fingers fumbled at the buttons. "I'm afraid I have no time," she said, but Arconia's Ambassador-Superior cut her off.

"I'm afraid you do have time for this." Eska's mother used her thumb to brush away a bead of water forming on Eska's hairline, then took a seat on the stool Alize had vacated. "You are headed to Toridium?"

Eska gave the briefest of nods as she fastened the final button.

"As is a ducal delegation."

It was a collision of the sort Eska had mostly managed to avoid: her archaeological pursuits for Firenzia Company and her duties as her mother's primary aide kept her busy but seldom interfered with each other. And yet this particular collision brought a wide smile to Eska's face.

Sorina de Caraval raised a dark eyebrow. "Am I to understand this pleases you? I had thought you might beg to be excused. I know how long you've been waiting for this contract."

"You would be correct, Mama, if not for the fact that a ducal delegation is exactly what I need right now."

The Ambassador-Superior's forehead wrinkled ever so slightly. "You know I can't allow you to use my position to further company dealings."

"And I'm not asking you to. In fact, I'm not asking you to do anything. All that matters is that Toridium will know of your impending arrival. And your august station demands that all other traffic in and out of the city must be halted. That in itself is enough." The image of the Barca ship held at bay, impotent, within sight of the city but unable to reach it, brought a grin to Eska's face.

Sorina smiled again as she rose from the stool. "I think it's better I don't ask what this is all about. Come, I'd hate to have to reprimand my own daughter for keeping a ducal delegation waiting."

— ◆ —

Eska did end up keeping the ducal delegation waiting, but not by choice.

She was halfway to Arconia's harbor when her carriage came to an abrupt halt, the horse's hooves skittering on the cobblestones amid the shouts of concern from her driver.

Eska put her head out the window but could see little other than a few mounted figures blocking the narrow street. The clattering of more hooves had Eska twisting and looking in the direction the carriage had come—sure enough, three more horses were approaching from behind, hemming the de Caraval carriage in.

"Alfonse, what is it?" Eska called. It was broad daylight, which made the strange quiet in the street all the more disconcerting.

"Lady de Caraval, won't you join me in the fresh air."

The deep voice had all the trappings of politeness, but Eska knew the face it belonged to. And that face had been pale with anger the last time it looked at her.

Her frustration outweighing her fear, Eska leaned farther out the window and put a smile on her face just as the speaker walked his horse into view.

"Lord de Venescu. How charming that we should cross paths."

Thibault de Venescu, the Iron Baron, sat astride a tall chestnut stallion. He took up more than a third of the narrow street and was flanked by a pair of mounted men who looked less vicious and yet somehow more competent than the thugs de Venescu had used to chase her the night before. They were dressed in black and each had a ring of golden daggers, the Iron Baron's symbol, sewn around the right bicep. Eska didn't need to look at the other three riders a second time to know she was surrounded by professional mercenaries.

"Most charming, indeed, my lady."

"I thought our business concluded last night." Eska glanced quickly at Alfonse atop the carriage's driving seat—and was not reassured. The older man had shrunk back against the wall of the carriage, making himself as small and unthreatening as possible.

"Perhaps in the eyes of the inspectors, but I am not in the habit of allowing thieves to go unpunished, even thieves with names such as yours." The stallion fidgeted under de Venescu's firm grip on the reins.

"But you have your property," Eska said lightly. He didn't, of course. Or not all of it, at least. But Eska was still banking on the Iron Baron's ignorance regarding his very pretty box.

"Even so. You breached my home. I do not take such a violation lightly."

Eska sighed. She could have absolved herself of some of the blame by telling the Iron Baron that she hadn't actually set foot inside the ugly monstrosity he called a home—that he ought to question his household staff if he wished to know how the reliquary came into her possession. But Eska had no wish to be responsible for the retribution such an admission would no doubt inflict on the unsuspecting staff.

"It seems, then, we are at an impasse. What is it that you want, my lord? Do you think to kill me in the street? Or do you simply delight in threatening people and seeing them tremble at your feet and beg for mercy?" Eska faked a gasp and put a hand to her mouth. "Oh, my lord, I think I begin to understand. You require cruelty and terror to perform."

As expected, Thibault de Venescu shoved his knees into his stallion, which surged forward until it was nearly snorting into the window of the carriage. Eska forced herself not to flinch back. The sound of carriage wheels and voices from up ahead helped her breathe again.

The Iron Baron heard it, too. "I'll have my way with you, bitch," he growled as he backed his horse away. "Consider this your warning. When you return to Arconia, you'll be answering to me."

Eska smiled. "As you say, my lord." She raised her voice. "Alfonse. Drive on."

To her relief, the driver stirred and did as she said, and the Iron Baron and his mercenaries did not follow. Even so, Eska's heart did not return to its normal pace until they reached the company wharf and the familiar masts of the *Argonex* came into view. And it was only once Eska felt the fresh sea air in her hair and the first salt spray against her skin as the ship sailed out of Arconia's harbor that she put all thoughts of Thibault de Venescu and his threats behind her.

4

"Pears, I think."

"T<small>HEY WON'T CATCH US</small>."

Manon Barca didn't take her eyes off the curving coastline and the stretch of blue water behind her ship, but the call of a gull made her wonder how high a bird would have to fly to see the Firenzia ship that was, whatever her brother might say, no doubt bearing down on them. Perrin had given up watching the horizon not long after the *Carribe* had slipped out of the crowded confines of Arconia's harbor. With his face tilted to the sun, his eyes closed, and his legs resting on the rail, her brother looked as though he did not much care if the Firenzia ship caught them. But then, Perrin was very good at looking as though he did not care.

"They will." The words seemed to loosen something within Manon and she dropped the hand shielding her gaze from the bright sun. For two days she had watched the horizon from sunrise to sunset; at last she turned away from the wake and settled her gaze on her brother instead. "Whether here on the waves or by the time we reach the walls of Toridium, they will catch us. Firenzia Company spares no expense."

Perrin made a noise of agreement. "How pleasant it must be to know the ship beneath your feet is one of the fastest in all the Seven Cities of Bellara." Though his eyes remained closed and his face betrayed nothing, Manon could tell her brother was thinking of their own expenses, paid for by loans they couldn't afford at crippling interest rates. And that wasn't even including the third mortgage Manon had taken out on the summer house at Isle de Gaustin, the only piece of collateral that still belonged to her family. Perrin remained innocent of that particular business transaction and Manon would rather cut out her own tongue than tell him of it.

"You could have that one day, you know," Manon said, her voice so soft she wasn't sure Perrin would hear. "You pretend otherwise, but I know Julietta de Raveux is fond of you. You could," Manon paused, "escape all of this."

"You know that's not true," Perrin said, opening his eyes. A false smile brightened his face and he swung his feet to the deck. Rising up, he slung his arm around Manon. "She's very rich. Very beautiful. And very busy with a horde of men asking for her attentions and her father's consent. Better face it, Manon, I'm not going to be able to marry my way out of our family's trouble. But," he went on as Manon began to speak, "I do wish you would tell me why this place of all places is so crucial. Why the race to Toridium? What lies beneath the dirt that is so important we must vie against the might of Firenzia Company for it?"

Manon felt her face tighten. It was not the first time he had asked, and Manon was running out of ways to keep him from understanding she didn't have an answer. "I don't know," she admitted. He'd find out soon enough—the moment, in fact, she directed the crew to start digging. "But my source tells me it's a complicated contract, and anything tangled that deeply in the courts must be valuable. Especially anything Firenzia wants. " She didn't go on to say what she knew they were both thinking: a significant discovery could be the life raft the fading Barca fortunes needed. Manon could not count the number of times she had prayed to gods she did not believe in that her gamble would pay off.

The look on Perrin's face, that hint of hope brightening his features, reminded Manon of Perrin's youth, of all the dreams he had once had, and it only strengthened her intent. She had to save him from the dark future smothering their family. At all costs.

"We ought to see the towers soon," Manon said, shrugging out from under Perrin's arm.

Her brother sighed and stepped away, that look of casual boredom he had crafted and perfected in such a short amount of time returning to his features.

"Are there any plums in the icebox?"

"Pears, I think," Manon murmured, straining her eyes to catch sight of something that wasn't yet there.

Perrin flashed a smile and took the stairs down to the ship's main deck, the sailors around him going about their business. As he disappeared below deck, Manon let out a sigh of relief, temporary though she knew it would be.

"Are you sure you know what you're doing?"

Manon turned so sharply she nearly lost her balance. The man who had spoken leaned against the far rail, sleeves rolled to the elbow, his sun-browned arms crossed over his chest, dark eyes burrowing into Manon.

Manon drew herself up, filling out the tall frame she so often disguised. "What is between my brother and I is none of your business. You will not speak of it again. Do you understand?"

The man was unperturbed. "The name of de Caraval is one not to be lightly crossed. You know who her parents are. Are you sure you want the full might of the Vice-Chancelier of Arconia bearing down on you?"

Manon crossed the deck until she was face to face with the first mate. He smelled faintly of soap, just as he had in her bed the night before—and more than once before that. The stubble on his cheeks was longer, and showed the merest hint of silver beneath his bottom lip. She regretted the moment of weakness that made her confide in this man and tell him of her fears. "What Perrin deserves is a life filled with every good thing the world has to offer. I intend to see that he has that."

"And what will you sacrifice in the hope of that?"

Manon's voice turned fierce and cold. "You presume too much, sir. You are nothing more than a pair of clean hands capable of stringing four or five words together. When we return from this journey, you will no longer have a place on this ship."

The first mate held Manon's gaze. "If we return in chains, none of us will have a place on this ship."

Manon waited, content to be still, to let the silence and the power of time bend the man to her will. At last he dropped his gaze, but he did not leave. Instead, those dark eyes fell on the shore and Manon did not have to look to know the daunting sea cliffs were shrinking, that soon the deep Toridium harbor would split the coast, that in moments the tallest of the five towers of that city would rise into view, its golden cap blazing. She didn't look ahead; instead, Manon glanced behind, sure she would see the Firenzia ship flying across the waves—but there were only gulls swooping low for fish and the foaming wake of the *Carribe*. She let herself smile ever so slightly as her heart began to beat a little faster in her chest.

"No, you may not have my pear."

Manon turned to catch sight of Perrin snatching his hand away from an overeager gull, pear protectively shielded. The bird hovered, white wings flapping at Perrin, who flapped back just as aggressively with his free arm. At last the bird went in search of easier targets, leaving Perrin to triumphantly brandish his unscathed fruit in its direction. He turned to Manon and grinned. She smiled back, though her mind raced with the notion that he might have overheard some portion of her conversation with the first mate.

"There, Manon, the towers of Toridium." Perrin pointed over her shoulder and Manon turned as the city glided into view. He joined her at the starboard rail, knife slicing deftly through the juicy pear. "Victor told me once the harbor has no bottom." His gaze dropped to the deep blue of the sea. "Threatened to drop me overboard, as I recall, the first time we came here."

Manon shivered at the mention of their older brother, unwilling to peel back that particular veil—at least not then, in that moment when she had a taste of victory, however small, over Eska de Caraval and Firenzia Company. It was the first good thing to happen to the Barcas in, well, in far longer than Manon cared to contemplate.

"I know," she said. "He wanted me to help him, but I told him you were too good at earning extra cakes."

Perrin scowled. "I'd hardly say extra. You and Victor always snatched them out of my reach before I ever got any. I had to go shed a tear in front of Olla to get my fair share."

The *Carribe*, under oar power by then, sails safely stored, began to turn into the narrow harbor mouth. Manon frowned as a small ship, approaching from the city, neglected to deviate from its path, choosing instead to hold the middle of the channel, oars flashing a steady pattern of forward and back, forward and back, to maintain position against the current.

"Manon...," Perrin said, voice drifting away.

Manon looked deeper into the harbor to see five other ships cruising forward to join the first, their bright red hulls—the Toridua had always been ostentatious—forming an ominous blockade.

"What are they doing?" Perrin asked. The gulls were the only ones to give answer.

Afterwards, Manon could not have said which came first, the thought flashing into her mind to order Captain Ivano not to halt the *Carribe* or the first mate's heavy hand on her arm, restraining her. If the latter, well, then the man knew her better than she liked. She looked over her shoulder, meeting his gaze, chest constricting, the spark that lived within her ribcage flaring, asking to be let loose so it might end the man's presumption in a manner that would sear, quite literally, the memory of his error into him forever. But in the end, it didn't matter which came first, because the words never left her mouth. Instead, Captain Ivano gave the order for the *Carribe* to slow, the oars grinding the ship to a hesitant stop. And Manon quelled the spark, turning it to ash, forcing herself to look away from the mate's eyes.

It was a foolish idea. Of course it was. The *Carribe* was large enough to damage the harbor patrol, but only at great cost to her own hull. Besides the fact that smashing through the blockade would result in her imprisonment—a rough guess told her that sinking ships and killing sailors was worth the rest of the years of her life—Manon could not risk losing the *Carribe*; it was the only asset left to Barca Company. But Manon had never been one to tolerate inaction.

A rowboat, neatly and efficiently lowered from one of the patrol ships, sliced through the gentle swell of the waves. Manon joined Captain Ivano at the rail.

"Captain?" Manon asked quietly.

The man shook his head, his grey eyes narrowed to slits as he watched the rowboat's approach. "They have no cause for this. None that I can name."

It was as Manon expected. The *Carribe* carried no illicit cargo. The sailors were all familiar to Manon—no criminals, no fugitives from the law. The Barca ship had as much right to be in the harbor of Toridium as any other.

"Perhaps it is something going on in the city, and nothing to do with us," Manon murmured, entirely unconvinced by her own words. Eska de Caraval was at the heart of this. Manon did not know how, but of that she was certain.

The rowboat came alongside the *Carribe* and Captain Ivano answered the hail from below, granting permission for a pair of harbor officers to climb up to the deck.

Like their red-hulled ships, the officers were clad in long crimson coats trimmed with black braid, buttons gleaming all the way to their chins. Each wore a sword at the hip, and the constellation of stars on the man's sleeve told Manon he knew how to use it, but it was the woman, tall and broad, who caught her attention.

The spark in Manon's chest came alive again, recognizing a cousin, though they shared no blood. Not a cousin of fire, no. Manon could not have explained how she knew, but she did. Water, perhaps. Fitting considering the woman's position.

The other Carrier met Manon's gaze, but if she, too, felt their shared connection, she gave no indication.

"The harbor is closed," the woman said. "No ships may enter."

"Why?" It was Perrin who asked and Manon watched the woman's sharp gaze flicker to her brother.

"Government business. That is all you need to know."

"And when will it be opened? We have urgent business of our own," Manon said.

The woman looked back to Manon, the sharp angles of her cheekbones and the length of her nose giving her every impression of an eagle contemplating an inferior opponent. "When it pleases the Vismarch to do so."

Manon drifted away, letting Captain Ivano and the harbor officers deal with the necessary exchange of information. She watched as the man took down the ship's name and purpose in Toridium—a purpose composed of bits of truth and glossed over with a rather large lie. The female officer glanced over at Manon when Captain Ivano named her as the owner of the *Carribe*. Manon met the woman's gaze but couldn't tell if the officer was merely curious or if the name of Barca was familiar to her.

"The Vismarch can go stew his own balls in wine," Perrin muttered. Manon shot him a warning glance, but her brother was prudent enough to have spoken so only Manon might hear. "What do we do now?"

Manon sighed. "We wait. We do as we are told." She turned away from the view of the harbor, suddenly very weary of the sight of Toridium. "Victor would have done something, he would not have allowed this delay," she said, only aware the thought had been spoken aloud when Perrin stepped close, his gaze lit with an anger she was not used to seeing.

"And in doing so, Victor would have gotten every last person on this ship killed," Perrin whispered fiercely. The anger fled in an instant, replaced so quickly by studied nonchalance Manon could hardly fathom the change. "Do you think the famous Toridium olives are in season? I should very much like to have some while we're here."

It was not a question Manon was meant to answer and as she turned her attention to the departing harbor officers, she found herself wishing, for the first time in four years, her father were there to take control—and then hating herself for that wish, that weakness.

Julian Barca could never help her again, nor did she want him to.

———— ◆ ● ► ————

The ships came with the dusk. A pair of them slipping along the coast, sleek and dark in the dying light.

"The Archduke's flag," the first mate said. He had stood watch with Manon, to her irritation, apparently having no duties to attend to. Whether he did so out of some misplaced sense of affection or because he wished to see her humbled after her harsh words to him, Manon did not know nor care, and she would have ordered him away but for the fact that doing so would leave her alone with Perrin and with her own thoughts, neither of which she wanted the sole burden of entertaining.

"That explains it then, an official delegation. Surely not the Archduke himself?" There was no lingering trace of Perrin's anger, a fact that was nearly as disconcerting as its appearance had been in the first place. "Nothing to do with us, at any rate."

"No," Manon said, for her gaze had shifted to the second ship, slightly smaller but no less impressive. "Everything to do with us." She gestured to the ships. "It might pretend to be a ducal delegation, but it's Firenzia. See that second flag? That bitch is using her family name to ensure she gains entry into Toridium before we do."

"Can she do that?" Perrin sounded more confused than irritated.

"She can't. But she has. The delegation would be expected. She knew it was her only chance. But she's mistaken if she thinks she'll get away with it. The Vismarch won't like knowing she flew the Archduke's colors for her own gain." Manon smiled. "If they discover it soon enough, they may not even let her into the city—or worse."

"You're wrong there." The first mate's words sent Manaon's lips into a curl. "It's no ruse." He handed her a looking glass. "Look more closely at the first ship."

Manon put the glass to her eye and scanned the approaching ship. Huffing her impatience, she removed the glass. "What am I looking for?"

"If I'm not mistaken, the woman on the aft deck is the Ambassador-Superior herself. It's a delegation all right, a real one. They'll be in the city before full dark and we'll still be floating out here at the Vismarch's pleasure."

Manon lifted the glass once more and adjusted it until she could see the woman clearly. She would have liked to have proven the first mate wrong, but she had seen the Ambassador-Superior from a distance often enough to accept that the tall woman, her dark-hair pulled back from her face in a regal style, her heavy cloak sculpting her into some sort of sea goddess of old, was in fact Sorina de Caraval. Manon swung the glass to the second ship, looking for the ambassador's daughter.

There. At the prow, leaning over the rail, pointing to the porpoises that had come to welcome the ships to the harbor—of course there were porpoises to announce her arrival. She was laughing with delight, oblivious to the *Carribe* and the harbor blockade, which was moving aside to allow them passage.

But then Eska de Caraval looked up.

She could not have seen Manon, not in the dying light and at that distance. But Manon would have sworn on the memory of her dead brother that Eska was looking straight at her, the laughter gone from her face, leaving behind a steady gaze—was that a smirk?—interrupted only by the strands of hair blowing across her features.

It was the steadiness that did it, Manon decided later, that look of composure, of knowing full well that she had won, that she was superior.

Manon threw down the looking glass and scrambled for the small leather case belted around her torso, her fingers fumbling for the clasps. She withdrew the copper device, the metal cold against her skin, and the silver vial, her hands shaking as she unscrewed the device's lower chamber.

"Manon! No!"

Perrin's voice broke through, but Manon did not dare look at him, did not dare contemplate the consequences of revealing her secret to the crew. Taking a deep breath, she steadied herself and unstoppered the vial, taking care not to breathe in the toxic fumes. She ought to be wearing gloves. She ought to be holding the device on a steady, even surface, not cradling it to her chest against the whims of the sea. Manon tilted the vial, inhaling sharply as the *Carribe* rocked and it nearly slipped from her grasp. She felt the sting of the fumes burn her nostrils and a small part of her wondered if she had inhaled enough to kill her. But at last her hands were steady as she poured the contents of the vial into the chamber, the particles, gleaming like ivory, whispering against the copper. Casting aside the empty vial, Manon stood, ignoring the warning shouts of the men around her. The ships were beyond them now, driving onward past the harbor patrol. Manon caught sight of Eska's figure at the rail once again, blurring into something shapeless as the toxic substance went to work on Manon's senses. She could feel the telltale tingling in her ears and the heat in her gums. Closing her eyes, Manon took the deepest breath she could manage, summoning the fire that lingered in her ribcage, willing it to occupy the air inside the chamber, to ignite the particles. A hand fell on her wrist, Perrin's or the first mate's, she did not know. She shrugged it aside.

Manon opened her eyes, aimed, released.

And missed.

Black smoke billowed in the air, but all that was left of the contents of the vial was a sizzle on the waves and a faint spray of salt water. The Firenzia ship sailed on, unscathed.

Someone was shouting. Not Perrin. The harbor patrol ships were closing on them, churning over the waves. Manon swayed, no longer able to focus.

"That's all," she heard herself murmur. "Could only afford…one vial." Manon sought Perrin's face at last, a blurry mask of distaste and sorrow greeting her there, and then she felt her knees give out. Her mouth was on fire, her limbs trembled wildly as she sagged against the rail. More shouting. A hand reaching for her. The ship rocked violently, her own convulsions, she realized distantly. And then she was overboard, the sea claiming her.

Interlude 2

Excerpt from Corin and Bravi's Genuine & Noble Bulletin

BARCA BANKRUPT!

In the wake of the Abrupt and Mysterious sentencing of Notorious fortune hunter Julian Barca—may he rot for one Thousand years—Scandal and Justice continue to descend on the Barca family. Barca Company, that foul bed of Corruption and Villainy, has been declared Bankrupt, having violated all Laws of Good & Honest business.

Unable to bear the Shame, Isoula Barca, Wife to that Madman, has fled the City, taking with her stolen Objects and abandoning her children to their Fate. Witnesses say she vowed Vengeance and spat Curses as she boarded a Ship with black sails. One Witness claims the ship disappeared into thin Air before sailing clear of the Harbor, but this Honest bulletin does not put Stock in Foolish notions.

5

"We make them immortal."

"So Manon Barca is a Carrier."

Eska nodded, her eyes on the black smoke dissipating behind the *Argonex*. Somewhere in her peripheral vision, she saw a woman fall, tumbling into the sea. Beside her, Firenzia Company's dig master gaped.

"Should we help, my lady?"

Eska scanned the water, watched as a man dove in after Manon Barca. The patrol ships converged, shouted orders and threats carrying over the waves.

"She could have killed everyone aboard this ship, Cedric," Eska said softly. "Not to mention my mother, had her aim been any worse. I will not weep if they do not fish her out. Besides, she may well be dead already. Carrier substances are notoriously toxic." As she finished speaking, a head emerged from beneath the waves, and then a second, this one limp and lolling, the man's strong arm around Manon Barca's chest. At that distance, as the *Argonex* pushed deeper into the harbor, there was no telling if she was alive or dead.

"So you knew?" Cedric Antilles asked.

"That she was capable of such things? I heard a rumor once, more than a few years ago now. But I never saw any evidence of it and you know as well as I that Carriers often keep their secret close. I'd have taken precautions if I'd known." Eska frowned and turned her attention to the ship ahead of her own, seeking the Ambassador-Superior's figure at the stern, then raising a hand to indicate to her mother that all was well. "What it doesn't explain is why she'd make such a ridiculous decision. Attack a ducal delegation in plain sight of the Vismarch's officers? That's tantamount to suicide. What could she possibly have been thinking?" Eska turned and motioned for the *Argonex's* captain, whose countenance was entirely free of any suggestion that his ship had nearly been blown up, to toss her his spyglass. She caught it with one hand and extended it as she brought it up to her eye. Scanning the Barca ship, Eska murmured, "Do relax, Cedric. No one is mourning her just yet." The woman did look very pale, though, and very still. A man, quite young, his fair hair askew as he knelt at the woman's side, clutched her hand. The brother, Eska was nearly certain, the younger one, though she could only remember seeing Perrin Barca once at a distance. Harbor officers swarmed over the rail of the Barca ship. No resistance was offered as every last sailor was taken into custody. Eska glanced to her right, smiling at the older man. "I doubt she'd appreciate your gentlemanly concern, but it is very touching." Cedric's droopy mustache did nothing to conceal the blush rising to his cheeks. Eska returned the looking glass to the captain. "At least we're rid of the Barca problem now. She's done us a great favor."

The remaining distance to one of the wide piers of Toridium passed without incident, and Eska climbed over the rail and dropped down to the pier before the *Argonex* had finished docking. A brief flash of her ducal badge got her past the pier master and his underlings, and she quickly joined her mother's entourage as it made its way off the pier and onto the Toridium wharf.

"What on earth was that, Eska?" Sorina de Caraval's question was voiced quietly but firmly. "Tell me you weren't expecting to nearly be blown out of the water by a Carrier?" The last words caused a shiver in the Ambassador-Superior's voice, a shiver Eska did not like to hear. Sorina absently touched her collarbone, below the high neck of her cloak, the place where the scars began. Eska looked away, knowing her mother would not want her to see the gesture.

"Expecting? Certainly not. I would never have knowingly placed you in danger, Mama."

Sorina straightened as the procession began to walk away from the waterfront. As was tradition among the Seven Cities of Bellara, the Ambassador-Superior would traverse the city on foot until meeting with the Vismarch, forgoing all loftier forms of transport. "Of course not, but you are related to your uncle and he has been known to neglect to think everything through. I take it you needed to arrive in Toridium before that ship—did you not think there could be consequences?"

"I am not so rash as my uncle, Mama," Eska said, struggling to keep her voice low. "But I can hardly be faulted for not foreseeing that Manon Barca would be so desperate as to act like an utter fool."

Sorina's eyes narrowed. "Manon Barca? I thought the Barcas were destitute, run out of business the moment Julian Barca went to prison."

"Four years ago, Mama. A great many things can change in four years." Eska had not intended to mention the name of Barca—she certainly did not intend for her mother to know that Manon Barca herself was the Carrier who had nearly killed them.

Sorina placed her hand on Eska's wrist, lightly, the touch barely felt through Eska's sleeve, but there was no mistaking the authority in that touch. "This delegation is important, Eska. I have allowed you to bring the company along, but these negotiations must be your priority. I will not tolerate interruption."

Eska tried to read between her mother's words—negotiations among the Seven Cities were always important and the Ambassador-Superior never took her duties lightly—but there was nothing to see behind Sorina's rigid exterior. "I understand, Ambassador-Superior."

———— ◆ ————

"Are you sure it's the right place, my lady?"

Eska surveyed the land before her, one hand shielding her eyes from the morning sun, still close to the eastern horizon and burning through the thick fog that lay below Toridium's walls. The slice of land she had won the rights to at the Court Beneath the Sun was an unremarkable place, dry ground nestled between the lazy waters of the Alencio and the gentle hills that rose up south-east of the city. Behind Eska, Toridium was strangely quiet, the city's morning bustle swallowed by the fog.

She had risen early, both out of eagerness to begin the work and out of necessity. Much of her day would be spent observing formalities before the Vismarch officially welcomed her mother to the city that night. These moments of fog and chirping birds would be all she could spend at the site that day. But Firenzia Company didn't require her presence to function. Cedric was already at work sectioning off the site, measuring it into quadrants that would later be divided into smaller parcels.

"It may not look like much, Bastien," Eska said, "but I believe this was once home to perhaps the largest seasonal gathering place of the Onandya clans. Imagine a vast herd of ponies, shaggy and sure-footed, drinking from the river, just there." Eska pointed across the site. "The chiefs would have vied for prime location, upriver from the ponies, close to the water, measuring their strength by the number of wolf tails they had strung to their staffs. They might have fought, if the hierarchy was in doubt and if the elders allowed it, but most of all this was a time of peace for the clans, when feuds were set aside as the chiefs came to honor the elders and the gods that granted the food they had spent the warm months hunting and gathering. This was the last place they would meet before retreating to their winter lands in the hills to the east and south, the last place of sun and dance and music before they faced the cold winds and deep snows of winter."

Eska smiled as she watched Bastien's gaze roam over the land, knowing he was imagining what she described.

"I wish I could have seen it with my own eyes," the young man said.

"That is why we do what we do, Bastien. Finding pieces of their lives, learning their stories, that is as close as we can come to living the life of another, transcending time, preserving history and knowledge and things otherwise lost." Eska met Bastien's gaze. "We make them immortal."

The words filled Eska's heart, as she knew they did Bastien's, banishing any lingering trace of her uncle's philosophy of fame and fortune. Here, at least, she had a crew who shared her dedication, who worked without thought of treasure or monetary gain—helped, naturally, by generous wages and contracts. Eska was not naïve. But though they all worked under the banner of the Firenzia Company, there was a vast difference between her uncle's favored crew and the one working diligently in the fog along the bank of the Alencio.

"Come," Eska said, "let us see what our fine engineer has to say."

With Bastien at her heels, Eska traversed the site to the river, where a man and his apprentice were contemplating the ground.

"Well, Master Gabriel?"

The engineer brushed curly hair from his eyes as he looked up at Eska's approach. "Can't say I'm terribly pleased, my lady. It's not unsafe, not at the moment, but this soil will be full of holes and hollow bits, and with the river so close, there's no way to predict how things could shift when we start digging."

Eska nodded. "Your recommendation?"

Gabriel spread his hands, a frown etched on his face. "We can prepare some timbers in anticipation of having to shore up the bank. But I would suggest you only give orders to dig close to the river if absolutely necessary."

"It's the river, my lady," the young apprentice spoke up. "It looks calm, but there's a nasty current below the surface."

Gabriel nodded. "Tia is right. Worst case scenario, the bank collapses and the river sweeps away half the site before we can blink an eye."

"Half the site and anyone unlucky enough to be standing in the wrong place at the wrong time," Eska murmured. She watched the smooth brown waters of the Alencio for a moment, then looked back at her engineer. "All right, make what preparations you can and if there's anything you can do to prevent such an incident, do it. Meanwhile, I'll have Cedric begin digging as far from here as we can. But I don't need to tell you, Gabriel, there's a strong chance the most valuable finds will come closer to the river. Water is life, just as much for the ancients as for us."

Gabriel nodded. "I understand, my lady."

Eska turned to Bastien. "We'll set up the tents and crew quarters to the north, Bastien, closer to the walls. I trust you can oversee that?"

Bastien nodded, but then his gaze drifted over Eska's shoulder, to the south. "A ship, my lady."

Several small boats, merchants, fisher folk, and a few travelers, had passed the site that morning, plying the waters of the Alencio on their way to Toridium, but there was something in Bastien's voice that told Eska this was no ordinary contribution to the river traffic. She turned.

Not just a ship, a beautiful work of art, a pleasure cruiser as unlike the utilitarian barges and wide-decked rigs common to the river as the Lordican was unlike a secondhand bookshop—as much as Eska liked a secondhand bookshop.

By then, others had gathered on the bank and voices murmured in admiration for the sleek craft headed north.

"Some sort of flag, my lady, at the stern. White and blue. Can't make out the emblem," Gabriel said.

"Three stars. Over crossed spears. Or so I imagine." For Eska was quite certain she knew that ship, or knew, at least, who would possess such a beautiful work of art. Gabriel gave her a curious stare but Eska could not take her gaze from the invaders.

Not invaders truly. The man on board the ship had no interest in Eska's site or whatever she might find in the dirt, of that she was certain. This was no Barca Company come to steal her prize. But nonetheless his impending presence had the feel of a hostile take-over, or at least a takeover of questionable intentions. Eska scowled at herself, trying to chase the apprehension from her stomach. Arch-Commander Alexandre de Minos was just a man, after all, and one she was well-practiced at handling.

Joined by the crew, all eyes watched in silence as the new arrival glided north before executing a graceful turn that brought her close to shore. The shallow-bottomed craft, built for river voyages, dropped anchor—and Alexandre de Minos made his entrance.

The figure standing on the railing, the hem of his long coat rippling in the wind, without so much as a rope or a helping hand, stepped off the ship rail as easily as one might step out of bed in the morning—at the same moment the river below him swirled and sent up a graceful arc of water that formed into a gleaming, liquid staircase. He took each step with infuriating poise and then, to the audible amazement of everyone around Eska, began to walk across the river, his boots showing nary a damp spot.

When he reached the shore, de Minos ascended the bank with ease and stopped, features utterly devoid of the smirking triumph any other breathing human wouldn't have been able to resist. And Eska hated him for it.

She approached slowly, matching his dignity and pace, until she came to a halt just out of arm's reach and equaled his steady, blue-eyed gaze.

"You've cut your hair," she said.

He had. This was true. No longer was his head covered in blonde locks. It was shorn close to his scalp, making a faint golden halo in the bright sun. The effect, when paired with his cheekbones and blue eyes, was quite striking. But in light of his entrance it was certainly the least remarkable thing on which Eska could choose to comment. And it worked. She saw the slightest twitch on his left jawline, just below his ear.

"You wouldn't really expect me to mention the obvious, would you?"

At last he spoke. "You never were one for the obvious."

"Sascha," she acknowledged, speaking the familiar youthful nickname for the first time in a very long time.

"Eska." A slight dip of his head, but his eyes never left hers.

"If I ask you to leave, will you go?" There was no harm in asking.

"No." Alexandre's answer was firm, but wary, as though he sensed a predator ready to spring.

Eska decided to smile instead. "Then in that case, you're going to need something to keep the sun off."

6

"That's a very green sort of green."

"I'M FAIRLY CERTAIN CARRIERS MOST OFTEN PRESENT AT AN EARLY AGE. Don't tell me you're some sort of anomaly."

Eska took a sip of wine and settled as far back into her seat as the stiff, upright camp chair would allow. They had taken refuge from the growing heat—and the eyes and ears of the Firenzia crew—in the shade of a sprawling willow, a pair of chairs hastily set up, wine brought, glasses filled—and then silence.

Not that head-scratching, eyes-averted kind, but the kind of silence between two people who once knew each other's measure and were assessing what, if anything, had changed.

Alexandre, his chair abandoned in favor of the ground and a cushion, his legs outstretched in an inconceivably elegant manner, had begun to relax. The Arch-Commander laughed. "His name is Oscar. At least, as far as I can tell it is. No tongue. He's been with me for two campaigns in the south, first against Nystrom and then when the Vothians made their foolish foray over the isthmus at the beginning of spring. He has a way with water." He took a drink. "You have to admit, it was far easier and swifter than lowering a boat."

Eska made a face. "That may be, but it seems a waste of his skill."

"Oh?" Alexandre's eyes flashed as he grinned. "Sudden sympathy for a Carrier? That's not like you."

"You'll find I can express sympathy for a great many things if it means a chance to chip away at your infinite sense of...." Eska trailed off, for once not sure of the word she was looking for.

"I believe the word you're seeking is style."

Eska couldn't argue with that. Or, perhaps, given a different situation on a different day, she might have argued, but the man did have style. It was military style at its core, as befit his occupation and rank, crisp and clean, yet effortless and with just the right amount of flair, whether it was in the cut of his collar or the angle of the sash on his hips or the hint of color at his cuffs.

"Still vain, I see," Eska said.

"Still unwilling to concede a point."

The words were said with laughter and good humor, but Eska was certain Alexandre felt them as deeply as she did, like a dull spoon prodding at old wounds and unwelcome truths.

Eska emptied her glass and stood to refill it, but he beat her to the bottle, getting to his feet with easy grace. He poured for them both and Eska wondered if he, too, took care not to touch her fingers when he returned her glass to her. Alexandre held her gaze for a moment before sitting once more, this time in profile as he leaned back against the willow's ample trunk.

"What are you doing here, Sascha?" Eska asked at last.

"The truth? Or something easier?"

And Eska found she did not know what she wanted.

"As it happens, I am innocent of anything nefarious, if that's what you're wondering. I had no prior knowledge of Firenzia Company's presence here. Imagine, to my surprise, the fog parting to show me none other than the Firenzia flag on a riverbank outside of Toridium. It seemed only polite to greet you."

"Polite. Yes." Alexandre's words were simple enough, and Eska had no reason to doubt the chance of their meeting. And yet there was something he did not say. "Not just Firenzia. My mother has business in the city. You'll hear of it soon enough, I'm sure."

The Arch-Commander raised an eyebrow and took a sip of wine. "Trade negotiations? The usual sparring?"

"I haven't actually been briefed yet myself. The trip was undertaken in a hurry and the circumstances of our arrival prevented much in the way of explanation."

Now Alexandre's curiosity was more than show. "Circumstances?"

Eska couldn't suppress the edge that crept into her voice. "Carrier work. Nearly sunk the *Argonex*."

"Very dramatic. I take it the culprit has been taken into custody?"

"Swiftly. The harbor patrol knows its business." Eska weighed her words for a moment, but de Minos would likely know the full situation soon enough. As one of the highest-ranking military officers in the Seven Cities, such knowledge was his right the moment he passed through one of Toridium's gates. "It was the Barcas. It seems Manon Barca has a talent for more than troublemaking. She tried to blow up my ship."

Alexandre leaned forward, properly intrigued. "Now that is quite the unexpected turn of events. You'll press charges?"

"Naturally. The woman put lives at risk, not to mention my property. She deserves to join her father."

Alexandre thought for a moment. "The Vismarch may want to hold and try her here, and would be within his rights to do so. Will you press to have her returned to Arconia? There's no telling what the Toridium courts will do. In Arconia, her family name makes her something of a known quantity."

Eska hesitated, then took a drink. "To be honest, I hadn't thought that far yet. It was only yesterday and I've been out here since dawn." She rose from her chair and went to the curtain of willow branches, looking out at the site Cedric was mapping.

Alexandre followed her there, his face turning serious. "I'm relieved you are unhurt, Eska."

The hand on her back was light, barely brushing her skin through the fabric of her shirt, and yet deliberate. Eska froze, startled by the unexpected touch, but did not look away.

She watched a shaft of light spread across his face as the willow shifted in a sudden breeze, and for a moment she was drawn into the past, into a time when everything between them had been easy and true and unbroken. There were so many things she once would have told him—of her ever-more-frequent arguments with her uncle, of her own doubts about her career, of her hopes for the excavation—but the past had never been easy or true or unbroken. She had learned that. Eska kept silent, unable to trust her tongue, hoping he didn't suspect what words might lie in wait there.

Alexandre held her gaze for a long moment and then sighed, his hand dropping away from Eska's back. "I'm expected in the city. I'll be here some days. I'm sure our paths will cross again." He made the smallest of bows. "Give your mother my best wishes."

Eska nodded, then watched as he pushed through the willow and strode back toward the river, the sun, having vanquished the fog, gleaming on his golden head.

◆━━━◆━◆━━━◆

Eska rubbed the erbore oil into her palms and then ran her hands through her hair, smiling at the subtle scent, then twisted it back and up into a simple style. Alize knew her work well, though no doubt the maid would be horrified at the sight of Eska. She had spent the day at the site, longer than she ought to have, seeing to the set up of the tents and equipment and keeping an eye on Cedric Antilles as the dig master mapped and sectioned the site, and had only rushed back behind Toridium's walls when the sun threatened to dip below the horizon. There had been no time to do more than splash a wet sponge here and there, and as for her hair—well, the lightweight oil was doing its best to tame the flyaways, but it still had a decidedly wild look that Eska did not have the time to help. At least she was dressed appropriately for the state dinner. If only she weren't still sweating.

"Are you ready?"

Sorina de Caraval appeared in the mirror over Eska's shoulder and Eska turned to face her mother.

"Do I look acceptable?" State dinners were matters of great import and formality. The tone set that evening would affect the negotiations between the Vismarch's chancellors and the ducal delegation.

Sorina smiled. "You look like yourself, which is to say, you look both like a windswept prairie and a goddess of legend."

Eska laughed. "I quite like the sound of that."

"You should. No one else will look like that tonight. And I'm counting on it." Sorina stepped close to her daughter and straightened the jewel that hung from Eska's neck. Then she paused. "On second thought, take that off. You're all the more alluring without it."

Eska reached up to undo the clasp. "Counting on it? You sound like you're trying to marry me off."

"It's important that we please the Vismarch tonight, Eska," Sorina said. "I want you to charm him."

"We all know the Vismarch isn't interested in women, Mama. My charms will likely go unnoticed." Eska set the necklace on her dressing table.

Sorina smiled again, her dark eyes twinkling. "That doesn't mean he doesn't have an eye for beauty. Besides, he happens to be a self-proclaimed expert on ancient artifacts. No doubt the two of you have much to speak of."

"Self-proclaimed." Eska sighed and put a hand to her heart in mock agony. "Mama, you know just how to torture me."

Sorina laughed. "Fair is fair. You used my ship. I'm using your brain."

"I understand and accept my charge, Ambassador-Superior," Eska said, sweeping low in a bow. "I'll have the Vismarch staring deeply into my eyes as we speak of the nuances in clay pot firing techniques utilized by the Evidorian civilization."

"And you'll enjoy yourself, though you might swear otherwise. Now, if you hadn't been digging in the dirt all day, you'd be better prepared for tomorrow's initial meeting with Chancellors Fiorlieu and Pelle, but you should know before going in there tonight that the Archduke has charged us with negotiating a better deal on the fees Arconian ships pay to use Toridium's harbor."

"They are exorbitant," Eska murmured as she bent down to adjust one of her shoes. "My purse is considerably lighter since arriving yesterday."

"Naturally nothing will be said tomorrow of ships and harbors. We'll begin by speaking to the Chancellors of grain transports—overland."

"Naturally. I take it that at some point an innocuous comment about the dangers to transports posed by bandits and other nefarious schemers will be voiced? They're so slow and large, after all, and difficult to protect. Not to mention the very poor state of the roads running to and from Toridium. Why, there must be a graveyard of broken wagon wheels and axles along the Tor road. Such a waste. It would be enough to make any prudent Arconian merchants look elsewhere to sell their goods."

Sorina smiled. "Exactly."

"Ambassador-Superior?" A skinny young assistant dressed in black poked his head into the dressing chamber in the suite of rooms Eska had been granted use of by the Vismarch. "Everyone is assembled."

Sorina nodded. "Good. Thank you, Hugo." She turned to Eska. "Do try not to let the Vismarch hear your stomach rumbling, my dear."

Eska flushed and was trying not to laugh as she and the Ambassador-Superior joined the rest of the ducal delegation in the wide, tiled hallway. They began to process to the Hall of the Lions, the great pyramid-shaped chamber that had been built by the old kings of Toridium.

She was still smiling when the Vismarch of Toridium took her hand in that pyramid—because the Vismarch of Toridium was wearing a very elaborate, very ornate, very ostentatious collar, a heavy thing of gold and gems and obsidian that lay across his collarbones in the abstract shape of an eagle, wings reaching to his shoulders, talons clutching a large emerald.

It also happened to be very fake.

Eska made the necessary gestures, the words flowing from her tongue with the ease of one who has lived her whole life in the sphere of the rulers of the Seven Cities. But her eyes never strayed long from the piece around his neck—meant, it was clear, to be a relic of the ancient Pharecian queens of the sweeping sands far to the south. It was a beautiful forgery. Made with skill and care. But for one error. The queens of Pharecia never put eyes on their eagles and this one had a pair of very gorgeous, very blue sapphires set in its golden head. Perhaps the craftsman had not known. Or perhaps the original owner, unsettled by the unnerving gaze of the sightless creature, had demanded the alteration. Either way, Eska wondered if the Vismarch was aware of the lie he wore with such obvious pleasure.

"You are all welcome to Toridium," the Vismarch was saying after Eska and her mother had greeted the high-ranking officials arrayed behind him. "And I honor you as I would honor the Archduke himself, as friends, allies, brothers and sisters, in recognition of the love I bear for my brother-in-rule." He clapped his slender hands together, his sleeves rippling just so. "Come, let us drink a toast in his name." Servants rushed forward bearing trays of sparkling wine and the Vismarch waited until each member of the ducal delegation, down to the youngest scribe, had a diamond-encrusted glass before continuing. He raised his own and Eska mirrored him. "To the great and good health of Valexi Arcturos de Vauquelin-Preux."

"Arcturos," Eska murmured alongside the rest of the Arconians, using the shortened name the Archduke permitted. They drank from their glasses.

"And to your health, my dear Vismarch," Sorina spoke up. "You are, as always, the most generous of hosts." She nodded her deference and the glasses were raised once more.

The Vismarch smiled and lifted his free hand. "Unfortunately, we do not dine alone tonight. I regret that our simple little supper party between friends has, by necessity, expanded into a larger affair." He did not seem very regretful at all. Eska noted the way the left corner of his mouth kept twitching upward—either it had a mind of its own or he had reason to be pleased by the prospect of the new arrangements. "Ah, I think I hear our new companions now."

It was Alexandre. Of course it was Alexandre.

Eska knew she could hardly expect that the Vismarch of Toridium would exclude the suddenly-arrived Arch-Commander of Arconia. Such things weren't done. And yet she hoped the extra dining couches she had noticed upon entering—greater in number than the delegation and the Toridium representatives—were part of the entertainment.

Alexandre de Minos entered the pyramid as he entered any other room, that is, he managed to own the Hall of the Lions from the moment he set foot in it without giving the appearance—or threat—of doing so.

His strides were strong and precise, with just a hint of the drill yard, his five-button coat outrageously simple for the occasion and yet just as outrageously refined, the polish of his boots rivaled the shine on the glass-infused tile floor, and four officers who had perfected the art of staring an opponent into submission acted as escort.

Alexandre bowed low before the Vismarch. "Please forgive our lateness, your Eminence."

Eska exchanged a glance with her mother, knowing they were of one mind. Though the dinner was a formal one, not meant to witness any true negotiations, the presence of guests from outside the delegation, most especially the presence of a war hero who ranked only just below the rulers of the Seven Cities of Bellara, rendered it nearly useless.

"You no doubt know your compatriots," the Vismarch was saying, and Eska became aware he was gesturing in her direction. Alexandre met her gaze without any hint of the hesitation she had detected by the river that morning.

"Ambassador-Superior." Alexandre stepped forward and bowed once more. "Lady de Caraval." Eska swallowed her grimace and found it was not difficult to match his poise and distance.

"Arch-Commander de Minos," she said, nodding her respect, eyes lowered. "What an honor that you are able to join us this evening."

"I assure you, my lady, the honor is all mine."

The Vismarch clapped his hands once more and the servants stepped in unison to their posts beside each dining couch. Eska's mother was granted the seat of honor on the Vismarch's right, Alexandre on the left, leaving Eska, once all the finely dressed officials of Toridium had arranged themselves, with a couch some four removed from the Vismarch. As she settled onto the cushions, she shared another look with Sorina, whose frustration was noticeable only to those who understood that her smile was just a touch too sharp. There would be little chance of Eska conversing with the Vismarch that evening, little hope of establishing a rapport the Ambassador-Superior could use to her advantage in the negotiations to come.

"That's a very green sort of green."

The voice came from Eska's left, the speaker a man who would have been counted as thin were it not for the decidedly rotund belly that protruded from his middle, entirely at odds with his scrawny frame. He perched on one hip and elbow and held out his hands one at a time for a servant to wipe clean as he looked at Eska's dress.

Eska glanced down at her gown and then back at her dining companion. "Why, I do believe you're correct, sir."

He frowned, clearly uncertain if she was mocking him, then shooed away the servant, who fetched a new cloth and came to Eska's couch. "What do you call it?" he asked.

"Well, I daresay green would do. But perhaps you'd prefer peacock."

This seemed to displease him. "Peacocks are far more blue in the feather, madam."

"Then surely it's jade."

His lips merged into a thin line and he merely shook his head at that suggestion, clearly unable to voice his extreme disagreement.

"What, then, would you call it, sir?"

He pursed his lips and thought for a moment. "Green."

"Ah." Eska would have given a great deal in that moment to be able to roll her eyes all the way up to the tip of the pyramid far above, but her grip on decorum was just strong enough—for the time being. "May I have the honor of your name, sir?"

The man sniffed as though the honor was very high indeed. "I am Antoni Cesare Beranaire, Master Clothier to the Vismarch himself."

What a clothier, however lofty, was doing at a state dinner was beyond Eska, but she smiled and nodded. "I am—"

"I know who you are." Beranaire sniffed again and turned his face away to contemplate, with not inconsiderable disdain, the plate of figs and tiny pickled fish set on the low table before him.

"How charming," Eska muttered as she, too, resolved to focus on her food for a moment before forcing herself to utter more pleasantries. Beranaire, apparently in conflict with the sneer on his face, did not give her the chance to do more than pick up a fig before speaking again.

"You Arconians have such limited taste in clothing, you know. You should look to others for inspiration." He gestured at Eska, a fish waggling between his fingers. "No structure. No artistry."

"Where would you suggest I look, sir?"

The clothier made his gesture larger, encompassing the entire pyramid. Eska half-feared, half-hoped to see the fish slip free and arc across to the dining couches opposite. "Look around," Beranaire said. "The Vismarch is an example of the highest degree. I dress half of his officials as well."

"Only half?" The disbelief was perhaps a bit too thick on her tongue, but Beranaire seemed not to notice.

"You are not unattractive, madam," he went on. "I would dress you in swaths of white."

"Swaths. Sounds difficult to walk in." Eska managed a bite of her fig. By all the dead librarians, she was hungry.

Beranaire looked at Eska as though she were speaking gibberish. "Walk? Are you meaning to make a pilgrimage from here to Teroa?"

"I am an archeologist, sir, and as such need a certain degree of mobility."

Eska did not think his expression of outrage could be greater if she had said the Vismarch was poorly dressed. The fish had still not made it to his mouth. They were both going to be insufficiently fed at this rate.

"You are a spider herder?" he spluttered.

Eska stared, decorum forgotten for a moment as she tried to

decipher the man's words. Perhaps he was under the influence of a great deal of wine.

"You mean an arachnidologist," Eska said, inventing the profession on the spot. "Unfortunately, sir, I do not work with spiders, much less have the rare ability to herd them."

His gaze narrowed, his incomprehension a palatable presence between them. Eska very desperately wanted to laugh or tell Albus—or both, preferably both. She could imagine earning a snicker from the librarian, for he would attempt to maintain his dignity, a snicker that would burst into tear-inducing laughter. She could have gone on, could have played on the man's complete ignorance and confused notions about spiders for the rest of the dinner—and gotten a great deal of amusement out of it. But her mother's presence four couches away held Eska in check and she kept her mouth shut, resolving instead to focus on the next plate lest she miss out on that one, too, provided Beranaire would let her eat.

He didn't.

By the time four courses had come and gone, Eska had managed to swallow no more than one fig, a single bite of a mushroom stuffed with onions, a tiny raw, jellied quail egg dipped in spiced oil, and a spoonful of cold soup—it hadn't arrived cold. Despite his obvious distaste for Eska, her city, and the shade of green she was wearing, Beranaire seemed determined to prevent either of them from having a moment's peace. She honestly could not have said which of them was more miserable.

Rescue came in the form of the Arch-Commander of Arconia. Were she not so absurdly grateful when Alexandre called over from his couch to ask her opinion on where the Archduke should build his latest palace, she might have resented knowing that Alexandre had been watching her predicament, no doubt with no small amount of amusement, and deemed her in need of assistance.

"The Bay of Heloi is the obvious answer," Eska answered promptly. "The white sands and cliffs will complement the black stone he has purchased for the project."

"Black stone?" The Vismarch leaned forward on his elbow. "From Cienna? Or Pharecian?"

"Pharecian, your Eminence. It is the finest black stone in all the world, after all."

The Vismarch smiled; clearly they were about to enter upon one of his favored subjects. "Indeed, the Pharecian queens had the finest of everything, save for the skill to keep power. This collar is Pharecian," he said, his hand coming up to rest on the eagle's outstretched, jeweled feathers, "though I'm sure you knew that already, Lady de Caraval. Your mother tells me you are quite knowledgeable about such things."

And there it was. A moment for Eska to make an impression on the Vismarch. Also a moment to nearly guarantee she wouldn't have to exchange another syllable with Beranaire, but that, surely, was not the reason Eska spoke her next words. Surely.

"I am, your Eminence. Which is why I feel I must tell you that collar you wear is a fake."

Interlude 3

A letter sent from the Lordican, dated two years ago, copied and kept in that institution's official record of correspondence

My nameless friend,

I hope this letter finds you. The instructions for reply do not inspire certainty in success, but I understand why you have undertaken these measures. I suppose I must have confidence that the vast forests of Licenza will not swallow up my response.

I understand, too, the risk you took in writing to me in the first place. As a scholar, you have my gratitude. As a man, you have my thanks for your trust and my sincere, fervent wish that no ill has—or will—befall you as a result of your letter or my reply.

Now to the matter at hand. This is an extraordinary thing you speak of. It will, perhaps, give you no comfort to know that never before have I heard or read of this ability you find manifested in yourself. I am aware of no record, academic or otherwise, of a person possessing the power to strip a Carrier of his or her gift.

I can, however, tell you that it may be related to the phenomenon known most commonly as Carrier fever, which is, like so many things, misnamed. When afflicted, Carriers do not experience a fever as you or I might. However, the symptoms experienced by the Carrier, poor vision, nausea, loss of hearing or sense of smell, physical weakness, and, of course, most importantly, the temporary absence of their power, align closely with what you say you have inflicted. Of course, given that you have achieved this intentionally only once, we must not leap to assumptions.

Forgive me if my use of the word inflicted feels accusatory. I cast no aspersions on you. The anguish and guilt you carry are clearly reflected in your letter. Understand, though, that if I am to assist you, I must attempt to approach this from a scholarly perspective for the sake of accuracy and intellectual integrity. And perhaps even for the sake of Carriers themselves. This is a grave matter. My understanding of the fever is that Carriers suffer greatly at the loss of their power—a devastating wound to the mind and body.

I'm afraid I can do no more without significant study and research. Please treat this letter as an invitation to the Lordican—at your convenience. We will assume responsibility for all expenses, including your travel and other needs. I am certain we can learn more about your condition given the opportunity. In the meantime, please be assured I will adhere faithfully to your request for secrecy.

I remain your humble servant,

Diomede Tulienne,
Master Librarian, the Lordican

7

"I am no jealous child."

MANON WANTED TO CRY.

The sensation was one she could not remember experiencing since childhood, perhaps after a scuffle with her older brother, Victor, or a forgotten promise by her mother. And yet in all the years between those childish moments and the one in which she found herself a day after the incident in the Toridium harbor, there had been plenty of opportunity for tears. Certainly opportunities others might have taken advantage of. But not Manon. Not when the creditors had come for her father, nor when she realized her mother was never coming home from Teroa, not even when she watched Victor breathe his last, though that had been a near thing.

But there within the walls of a Toridium cell, her younger brother's mournful face staring back at her from between the bars that divided them, his silent hostility boring into her back whenever she turned away, tears prickled in the corners of her eyes.

She didn't remember being put in the cell. By the time she had fully recovered from the effects of the toxic fumes, her world had shrunk from blue skies over the harbor and the vast sea at her back to three walls and fourteen iron bars—she had counted them more than once. A cot filled the length of one wall, one leg shorter than the others, causing the frame to list uncertainly at the thought of bearing any weight. She had been fed, twice actually, which was more than she thought likely upon first waking, and the stone floor, while dusty, wasn't covered in grime or unidentifiable filth.

Perrin remained silent. It seemed that since discovering she wouldn't die just yet, his concern for her health, a hazy thing she sensed as she swam in and out of consciousness, evaporated, replaced by accusation in his eyes and anger in the set of his jaw and the hunch of his shoulders.

"It's not as though I killed anyone," Manon said. It wasn't the first time she'd done so, nor did she truly think repeating it would soften Perrin. "They can't keep us here forever."

Where exactly here was Manon did not know, she realized. In Arconia, those suspected of crimes were kept at various locations within the city walls, while those convicted were sent to the Hibarium—remote enough to be out of sight and mind, close enough if the Archduke wished to invite any prisoners to dine. Not that he did.

But Toridium was another matter and the only thing Manon knew with any certainty, due to the lack of rot and salt in the air, not to mention the cell wasn't swaying about, was that they were not aboard a prison ship in the harbor. Captain Ivano and her crew were nowhere to be seen and Perrin hadn't seen fit to relent and answer her questions about them.

"I did suggest you stay in Arconia. Don't forget that."

Pettiness didn't suit her, she knew, but at least that got a response, though not a very productive one. Perrin turned his back on her.

"I know this isn't just about what I tried to do to that ship. You've seen worse. This is childish stubbornness because you think I'm keeping secrets from you. Victor was stubborn too, but at least he knew when to accept the judgment of another."

"Tell me it's not for Victor you do all this."

Perrin had not moved, did not turn to face her, but the severity—the maturity—in his voice startled her, a reminder that he was born and bred of the same father as Manon, though he so seldom exhibited any commonalities with Julian Barca that Manon had wondered about his paternity more than once. But in that moment, his slouchy demeanor replaced by perfect posture, his voice more commanding than she had ever heard, he was the very image of their father.

"Victor is dead, Manon," he went on, quieter, but no less firm. "Nothing you can do can change that."

"I know," she said at last. "But he would have wanted this. He would have wanted me to fight for his legacy, for something other than the future our father made for us."

Perrin was silent so long, Manon thought he had resolved to shun her once more.

"But at what cost." It was not a question.

Manon felt herself flush with anger. "Do you hear yourself? Do you think to convince me you are happy with this life? With using scraps and crumbs and handouts to keep the creditors at bay? With losing our dignity and the respect the name of Barca once demanded?" Manon was on her feet, pacing, the words flying forth unchecked. "Victor would not have suffered such a life. But you, you do nothing. Are you still a child, unable to measure up to the brother everyone loved?"

At last Perrin turned to face her. He stepped close to the bars of his cell. The anger was gone, replaced by sorrow, his face pale, and for a moment Manon thought he repented of his words. "You place Victor among the stars, Manon, but he is not worthy of the excrement I would shove down his throat if he were alive."

Not repentant. Manon found she could not speak, could hardly breathe, and that perhaps she did not know her younger brother as well as she thought.

Perrin wrapped his hands around a bar and leaned as close as the iron would allow, his gaze unblinking, his every word grinding through his teeth. "Victor was a liar. A man of base, immoral character, bereft of any shred of decency. A man capable of destroying lives without a thought, of taking what he wanted, be it life or livelihood, without compunction. He knew neither guilt nor kindness nor empathy."

Manon stepped back, aware of a trembling in her hands, aware of a spark in her ribs, a spark she had not felt since summoning it aboard the *Carribe*. It beckoned to her, asking to be set free.

"Would you use your talents on me, Manon?" Perrin asked, composed, resigned. "Simply for speaking the truth? You spared little thought for sacrificing lives to get what you wanted yesterday, what's one more now? I'm sure Victor would be proud."

Manon did not understand how he could have known the spark had flared, did not know how long they stood there, how long it was before she regained control of her heart and her body. But at last she broke free of her brother's gaze and stepped away.

"I would never hurt you, Perrin."

He disregarded this, though not, she thought, because he believed her.

"I can prove it, Manon. All of it. I can show you who Victor truly was. I am no jealous child."

For a moment, Manon wanted desperately to ask him to explain. The feeling passed quickly, trod down by approaching footsteps.

It was not Manon's cell the guards opened. It was not Manon they dragged forth with rough hands. It was not Manon's face they shoved into the stones of the wall or her wrists they bound with iron cuffs. It was not Manon's foot they stomped when faced with resistance.

"Where are you taking him?" Manon screamed. "What are you doing? I did it!" She threw herself against the bars of her cell. "It's me you want. I am the guilty one!"

Her pleas fell on deaf ears and she sagged to the floor of her cell as Perrin was hauled out of sight. And so she was alone when the tears came. Quietly at first, taking her unaware as her eyes brimmed with wet heat. But as they spilled onto her cheeks it was like the breaking of a dam. The sobs burst forth in great ragged gasps and she sank to the ground, curled inward, trying to hold the pieces of herself together. But the torrent raged on until at last she was nothing more than an empty shell.

When she could breathe, when the tide had been stemmed, she got to her feet. Taking a deep inhale, she forced away the thought that Perrin might be dead in a matter of moments. She forced away, too, his words and any thoughts of the brother she knew was dead. And in place of those thoughts, a vow formed. She would survive this place. She would walk free. And if she could do nothing else, if she failed in all her plans, at least she could ruin Eska de Caraval. Whatever the cost.

8

"Snails?"

Eska could not have asked for a more dramatic reaction if she played a part opposite the Vismarch in one of Theobald Heuerfabre's works—the playwright was known as the poet of the endless swoon for a reason.

The Vismarch frowned at first, as though Eska's words were incomprehensible, then went a bit red in the face as his latest bite of lobster pie got caught somewhere between his disbelief and his esophagus. When he recovered, he came to his feet in a tangle of robes—swaths, as it were—the fake eagle swinging ponderously as he found his balance. Now he pointed a finger at her—truly, he was the spitting image of the tragically betrayed Duke Penza in Heuerfabre's *A Rose in Death*—and spoke.

"How dare you impugn my honor so! Am I to bear such an insult? And from a guest I have welcomed into my home? Does the love between our cities, the love I bear for my brother-in-rule mean so little?"

Eska might have laughed, but she was acutely aware of the pair of crimson-cloaked guards standing vigilant at the door into the Hall of the Lions. They had not quite placed their hands on the hilts of their swords, but they seemed prepared to do so and had taken several steps from their post.

"I mean no insult, your Eminence," Eska said, keeping her voice calm and low. "I speak not as a reflection on you or your good taste or the love you bear for the Archduke. I speak as one who has made a life of identifying and understanding artifacts, but most importantly, as one who has a great respect for the truth, as I know you do."

Her words had the desired effect and the Vismarch had the sense to look less affronted, though the frown was still etched on his face, which was, incidentally, still quite red.

"You will come with me, Lady de Caraval. Now." And with that the Vismarch of Toridium turned on his heel and marched from the pyramid, leaving Eska to follow him to a door tucked in a back corner. She met her mother's gaze as she hurried past and couldn't help but look at Alexandre, who raised an eyebrow and grinned.

To her surprise, she found herself in a vast room, not quite as cavernous as the pyramid, but just as grand. Pillars of carved marble supported the ceiling, which bore painted scenes Eska could not quite make out in the dim light. One wall was made entirely of glass and a series of skylights were strewn across the ceiling like a constellation. The effect, as daylight spread across the room and illuminated the collection of objects housed within, would be quite stunning, Eska realized.

The Vismarch, quiet now, allowed her a moment to take in the room, then beckoned her to follow once more. They passed statues of bronze and stone, a fountain made entirely of gold, and cases displaying rare and ancient coins. The Vismarch stopped in front of a nude torso carved from black stone—Pharecian stone, Eska was quite sure. The figure was armless, legless, and headless, but what remained was exquisitely worked. And adorning it, resting just above the nameless Pharecian queen's breasts, was a true eagle.

It was identical to the one the Vismarch wore, down to the gem-encrusted tips of the wings, save for the absence of eyes. And yet that sightless gaze sent a shiver down Eska's spine. She looked at the Vismarch and saw he was smiling.

"I would not dare wear the real thing. It's far safer here than on my person," he said. "Besides, who am I to lay claim to the legacy of Pharecia?" He touched the forgery around his neck. "This is a piece of my power, my position. I am known as a collector of rare items and so I must be seen as such, a man who adorns himself with treasure."

"Why give it eyes?" Eska asked.

The Vismarch smiled again. "I didn't at first. But I found it frightened people. It seems our world today is not capable of bearing up under the powerful gaze of the queens of Pharecia."

"And no one knows it's here? Your outrage was not just for my benefit."

The smile grew sad. "Few people take the time to explore my collection. I doubt a single person in that hall is aware. You will honor my performance, yes? I would not have it known that the Vismarch wears forgeries."

"Your secret is safe with me, your Eminence." Eska hesitated, unsure how far she could extend the intimacy he was granting her.

"Go on," he said. "You may touch it."

Eska approached the statue, her heart racing. She had seen a Pharecian collar before. There was one in the Lordican. But that one was incomplete, missing gems, and she had never been allowed to examine it for fear she might damage it further.

She reached a hand up and let her fingertips gently trace the edge of one wing, following the feathers down to the talons and the emerald embraced there.

"It's beautiful," Eska whispered. "Though that word does not even begin to describe it or do justice to it. How did you come by it?"

"Pure chance, I'm afraid," the Vismarch said. "It seems one of the ancient kings of Toridium owned it. It was discovered a few years ago when a wall in the old, unoccupied part of the palace caved in. The workmen clearing the rubble found a dagger with a lion on the hilt. I knew I needed to see what else had been hidden in that wall. It's a wonder the Alescus never discovered it." The Vismarch paused and looked at Eska. "It would suit you."

Despite herself, Eska felt the heat of a blush rising to her cheeks. "You flatter me." She took her eyes from the collar and faced the Vismarch.

"I never lie about beauty, my dear Lady de Caraval. In fact, it would go very well with the green of your gown."

Eska couldn't help but laugh. "Your clothier would disagree, I'm afraid."

The Vismarch frowned. "Beranaire?" He cocked his head. "Was he at dinner?"

Eska nodded. "And quite underwhelmed by his dining companion."

"But what on earth was he doing there? I can't imagine who invited him."

"It was your dinner, your Eminence."

The Vismarch nodded ruefully. "Indeed. But I usually leave the details to my chamberlain. Perhaps we had an odd number and he was the lucky addition. You'll have to forgive me. From now on, you'll sit by my side." His nose wrinkled. "Or at least closer to me. I'm afraid even I can't place you above your mother or Arch-Commander de Minos."

Eska smiled, this time with genuine warmth. "You honor me, your Eminence."

"It's not every day I have a guest who can spot a forgery from across a sea of dining couches." The Vismarch made an expansive gesture around them. "My collection is at your disposal, my lady, if you have the time and inclination to explore it. And perhaps, in exchange, you might tell me of some of the more fascinating things you have seen and studied at your Lordican."

"It would be a great pleasure, your Eminence. Have you had the chance to visit the Lordican?"

The Vismarch gave a slow shake of his head. "Sadly, when one is ruling one of the Seven Cities of Bellara, one has fleeting amounts of time to spend at leisure. I intended to go, once. It was a long time ago, when I was newly invested as Vismarch. I was touring the cities. Parades every day. Banquets every night. Extravagant entertainment around every corner." The Vismarch chuckled. "Your city was last, and I was thoroughly sick of the whole affair. I made a plan to sneak away from the Varadome disguised as an acolyte of some temple or another. My aide found me a cowl and the appropriate half-mask and I was

moments away from escape when the previous Archduke was assassi-
nated." The Vismarch smiled at Eska. "There was no going anywhere.
And your Lordican has remained out of reach ever since."

"If I may be so bold, your Eminence, the next time you have occasion to come to Arconia, it would be my great honor to serve as your
escort should you choose to grace the Lordican with your presence."

The smile grew, the smile, Eska thought, of a man who has come
to accept that his life is not his own. "I should like nothing more.
Unfortunately, we've been gone rather a long time, and I wouldn't
want your mother to fret, considering the circumstances of our exit.
Come, let us return."

With one last glance over her shoulder at the Pharecian eagle, Eska
followed the Vismarch the length of the room once more as they returned to the Hall of the Lions.

"They will have continued eating without us," the Vismarch said as
he opened the door into the pyramid, "as is Toridua tradition. Food
waits for no man or woman in my city. But we should be in time for
the sweet course to finish off the meal."

Eska allowed herself a moment to mourn the lost courses, then
swept back into the hall, matching her smile to the Vismarch's, and
returned to her couch.

"A misunderstanding," the Vismarch said, waving away the heads
that turned to mark their entrance. And that was that. Not a question
was asked, not a remark was made. But Alexandre's gaze burned into
Eska from his place next to the Vismarch, and, after making her features carefully blank, she allowed herself to meet it. Let him wonder.

To her relief, Antoni Cesare Beranaire had withdrawn as far from
her as the parameters of his couch would allow, no doubt for fear
of being tainted by Eska's disruption of the peace. He sniffed as she
settled on her couch and shifted his gaze to the Arconian opposite
him. To Eska's delight, the man was wearing green and she watched
Beranaire's lips curl into a grimace as though the sight pained him.

The Vismarch had spoken true. The servants laid out dishes of sweet
confections, chocolate mosaics, iced cakes, and cream-filled pastries,

with not a hint of proper sustenance remaining. Eska sighed and nibbled on a lacy piece of chocolate in the shape of butterfly. At least her stomach had long given up on crying out for attention.

The dinner ended quietly, the Vismarch seeing his guests out with polite distance. Eska understood he was no longer the man she had spoken to in private, the man who had allowed her a glimpse of what lay beyond his public persona. He was the representative and protector of his city—and the morning would see the first official negotiations between his Chancellors and Eska's mother. Brothers-in-rule he and the Archduke might be, steady allies the cities of Toridium and Arconia might be, but there was a great deal at stake, his pride and power not least of all.

But amid all the polite murmurings between the representatives of the two cities at the grand doors to the Hall of the Lions, Eska noticed Alexandre in quiet conversation with the Vismarch. The Arch-Commander spoke earnestly but with the proper deference, leaving Eska to wonder what he needed from the Vismarch of Toridium.

Eska, tired after her day out in the sun, hastened her exit, bidding her mother goodnight before hurrying back through the Vismarch's palace to her suite in the wing granted to the ducal delegation. She withdrew gratefully into the darkness and silence, noting the pleasant scent of white miranna drifting in through the open windows from the garden below.

Tall white candles had been left for her, alongside two letters on the desk near the windows of the sitting room. Eska scanned them—a note from her father wishing her luck in all that had brought her to Toridium, and one from Firenzia Company's lawyer apprising her of a pending change in the excise laws of Arconia that would alter precisely nothing in the day-to-day operations of the company. The lawyer was brilliant, devoted, and tremendously good with detail, but Eska often found herself wishing he would keep such tedious nuggets of boredom to himself. And yet her uncle seldom bothered with such information, leaving Eska to feel obliged to do so in his place.

Eska drifted to the large bay window, the notes still in hand, and settled onto the amply-cushioned seat, her mind thinking ahead to the next day and how she would fit in a visit to the excavation site amid the negotiations. Not that Cedric couldn't handle everything without her. The dig master was fastidiously capable and the crew respected him even if they did laugh at his mustache. But she wanted to be there, wanted to see the soil samples, wanted to help direct the first exploratory trench, wanted to feel the earth beneath her boots and her tools in her hands. And if she was honest with herself, she wanted to be the first to uncover a piece of the pottery that had drawn her to Toridium. The crew held a friendly wager at each excavation, and though she would never collect the winnings, Eska always enjoyed the race.

The hand on her shoulder startled her from a sleep that had fallen so swiftly and so heavily she had no notion she wasn't awake. Lurching upright—no, sideways, as it turned out—Eska tumbled from the window seat and to the floor, her flailing arms catching at the figure she could not quite make out in the low candlelight.

The laughter, however, told her everything she needed to know.

"If you find it amusing to appear in a woman's private chambers in the middle of the night and frighten her half to death, Alexandre de Minos, you deserve to get kneed in a very unpleasant location." Eska rose to her knees, brandishing the pieces of mail, which were somehow still in her grasp. "And a thousand paper cuts."

Alexandre was on one knee in front of her, not even bothering to look contrite. "Forgive me, Eska. I only thought you might be hungry."

She was. Ravenous, in fact.

"Snails?"

"Snails? I ate a fig and a spoonful of soup for dinner and you offer me snails?"

Alexandre stood and held out his hand. "That's only the start. That is, if you're not too angry at me to eat."

Eska took his hand and allowed him to pull her upright, using the moment to consider if Alexandre de Minos might have a reason other than feeding her for coming to see her in the middle of the night. Not *that* reason. No, something perhaps to do with his discrete conversation with the Vismarch. She would find out if she could.

"Thank you. I suppose."

Smiling, Alexandre turned and went to the door. Opening it, he beckoned in a short parade of servants, each bearing a covered platter of things that smelled delicious. Alexandre looked around, then evidently decided the writing desk was no adequate dining table. With a flourish, he settled a square of blue, embroidered linen on the floor—the floor!—and a servant, apparently unperturbed by this turn of events, rushed forward to lay out plates, silverware, and delicate crystal wineglasses. Meanwhile, Alexandre found a cadre of suitable cushions and set them on two sides of the linen.

"Close enough to the Toridua style, don't you think?" he asked Eska, who could do nothing more than sigh, laugh, and shake her head all at once.

As though they were attending the Archduke in the Varadome, Alexandre extended his hand once more to Eska, bowing low. She accepted it and lowered herself as gracefully as possible to the cushions. Alexandre did the same opposite her and dismissed the servants with a gesture.

"That will be all. The lady and I are quite capable of serving ourselves," he said, already lifting the lid from one of the platters as the servants vanished with quiet precision. "Ah, these smell divine."

The snails did indeed set Eska's tongue to watering, but it was the swordfish that caught her attention and she helped herself to a generous portion, following that up with cold peas and radishes in a sharp dressing. For a moment, she ate in silence and Alexandre, wearing an indulgent smile on his face, let her behave like a starving urchin.

"You really ought to bring a proper chef on these expeditions. It's not as though the Company can't afford it." Alexandre spooned snails into a shallow bowl and placed it next to Eska's plate.

"Expeditions are for digging, Sascha, not eating. Besides, I expect most of my meals will be taken with the delegation, not with my crew."

Alexandre laughed and gestured to the manner in which Eska attacked her snails. "And yet here you are."

Eska made a face. "I blame my dinner companion. I swear, Sascha, I do not know the last time I had a more ridiculous conversation. The man thinks spiders can be herded."

Alexandre laughed. "I can only imagine how that topic came up."

"I'd have given anything for a meal under the stars with my crew after a hard day in the dirt. Better company, better conversation."

"Just admit it, you like the idea of roughing it. Sleeping under the moon, eating the same thing for weeks on end, washing your clothes in the river. Lets you believe you're actually working." The grin on his lips was genuine, but calculated to provoke as much as his words.

Eska leaned back, the food forgotten for the moment, her temper swirling. "You know how hard I work, Sascha. No one on my crew would suggest I do not pull my weight."

"Would they dare complain about anything the Vice-Chancelier's daughter does?" Alexandre laughed as Eska felt heat flush into her cheeks and he put his hands out, palms up, in mock surrender. "I jest, Eska, and only because you make it so easy to do." He turned serious. "You know the respect I have for you, your work, and the company you run so ably." He made sure she was looking him in the eye before continuing. "The same respect they have. You should be proud of what you have done."

The satisfaction Eska felt at hearing those words from Alexandre was stronger than she would have liked, but she managed to summon up a tart response. "I don't need you to tell me that."

Alexandre laughed. "Of course not." He pulled back the cloth covering a basket, revealing one of Eska's most-loved dishes: steamed peppered buns with pockets of crispy roast pork and tiny, just set quail eggs. She couldn't help but smile.

"Do you remember the last time we ate these?" The question was out of Eska's mouth before she had the chance to consider the consequences.

Alexandre looked up from his plate and set down the knife he had been using to cut his bun in half.

"How could I forget."

The words weren't angry. The voice wasn't cold. But there was an edge in the moment. And rightly so. The last time Alexandre and Eska shared steamed buns, they had just dodged a rainstorm, sprinting through the streets of a seaside village, hand in hand, laughing, seeking shelter in a tiny tea shop as the skies opened. Three days later, after a storm of a different kind, Alexandre asked her to marry him and Eska had refused. It wasn't a thing easily forgotten.

The conversation slipped into safer things. Eska took refuge in her work, speaking of the known history of the site along the river and the things she hoped to learn from what they unearthed in the coming days.

"The pottery alone ought to be quite revealing. Based on the techniques used—say, whether the handles were fashioned from separate pieces of clay and attached after the formation of the vessel, or whether they were shaped during the formation—we'll know if the Onandya people from this area had contact with the Bardonian culture to the south. And if we know that, well that opens up a whole host of possibilities about trade networks and language. It could throw Hevere's entire theory about the region off a cliff. And that's before we even get to the possibilities regarding the burial rituals." Eska looked up from the salmon and seaweed and saw Alexandre sitting back, no longer eating, watching her quietly. She smiled. "Am I being frightfully boring?"

"Not at all. But you know I wouldn't be able to tell the difference between Alescu silver and a worthless spoon fished out of the sea."

"Says the man who furnishes his home with priceless ancinni silk screens and uses only Norvichy iron on his ship—don't think I didn't notice this morning," Eska said.

Alexandre laughed. "What you mean is I have expensive tastes." He took a drink of wine. "But you were talking about Hevere's theories. About throwing them off a cliff, I think. That ought to satisfy you. You've had a bone to pick with him for as long as I've known you. Shame he's been dead a century."

"I'm not saying he's got it all wrong. And his work on the Forthinal peninsula was extraordinary." Eska held out her glass for a refill. "I just think his notions about the isolated nature of the Onandya peoples who populated the eastern plains are entirely wrongheaded."

"Exactly," Alexandre said, grinning. "Off a cliff. Don't pretend you're not relishing the opportunity to prove one of the most revered scholars of archaeology wrong."

"It would be an important contribution to the discipline," Eska maintained, keeping her face as still and composed as she could manage. "It's hardly my fault if no one else is bold enough to question the great Hevere."

Alexandre laughed. "Hardly," he agreed. "But what of the delegation? What concessions is your mother going to win from Toridium tomorrow?"

"You place a great deal of confidence in her capabilities."

"Come, Eska, we both know your mother is not the Ambassador-Superior of Arconia without good reason. She could talk a god into giving up his immortality."

Eska couldn't keep the pride from her face. "She could. But this is far more mundane. Fees, transport of goods. Quite boring, really. I'm sure your own business with the Vismarch is more interesting." Eska glanced at Alexandre over the rim of her glass as she spoke, half of his face in sharp relief, the other cast in a golden shadow of candlelight and crystal.

"Merely a courtesy visit." Alexandre did not look away, as though challenging her to press for more.

"Forgive me, Sascha, but the Arch-Commander does not make simple courtesy visits."

"You're correct, he does not. But I'm afraid I can't say more, Eska."

"Very convenient." They looked at each other for a long moment, Eska wondering if she looked as wary to him as he did to her. Once, this kind of sparring, while full of sharp edges, had been purely an exercise, humorous and with no real consequences. Now it was laced with undercurrents she could not quite identify. Or perhaps she was simply feeling the distance—the necessary distance—that had grown between them in two years.

"Did you speak of Manon Barca to the Vismarch?" Alexandre's question broke the silence.

Eska roused herself from the past. "That's the most pressing question you have about my private moments with one of the most powerful people in the Seven Cities?"

Alexandre shrugged. "I imagine if he were throwing you into a cage or having you silenced for your transgression, he would have done it already. Besides, I know you. You are never wrong. If you say that eagle is a forgery, it's a forgery. Either you convinced him of this or you didn't—either way, he has reason to keep quiet about it, which tells me he's a prudent man."

"You're not wrong." Eska took a sip of wine. "I quite like him. He's invited me to explore his private collection, if I have the time to do so."

"Then you said nothing of the incident in the harbor."

"I'd rather not play all my cards at once."

"Ah, then you'll be using his newly acquired fondness for you to Arconia's advantage in the negotiations to come."

"As is my duty."

Alexandre nodded. He would not blame her for acting thus, she knew, not when he would do the same. "Did your mother put you up to it?"

"Did she put me up to publically insulting the Vismarch so I could gain a private audience with him? She's good at her job, Sascha, but as far as I am aware, she cannot read minds. I was meant to establish a good rapport with the Vismarch, that's all. And I was hard-pressed to do so given my placement at dinner—not to mention your presence."

Alexandre laughed. "So I am to blame after all. I should have realized. I'll have you know I requested that the Vismarch host me and my officers for dinner tomorrow, specifically because I did not want to intrude on the work of the delegation." He spread his hands. "The decision was not mine to make."

"And yet you had to know the Vismarch would hardly keep one of the most celebrated men in the Seven Cities waiting."

Alexandre accepted this with a nod. "I am what I am." It was not an arrogant statement or a puffed up credential. Alexandre's ability to know himself and understand the effect he had on people, both those in positions of authority and those whose lives he could change with a word, was one of the reasons she had been drawn to him in the first place. "As are you." Eska looked away, half wishing he had not said that. His next words sent her heart into her stomach. "As were we together." She met his gaze for the span of a heartbeat.

They moved in unison, coming to their feet, though whether Alexandre was merely taking his cues from her or if he, too, felt the conversation was poised before an abyss the depths of which Eska was not sure she wanted to explore, she did not know. They stepped around the side of the linen and the spread of dishes.

"I'll send a servant back to fetch everything," he said. He stared down at her, blue eyes radiating something she couldn't quite name. Eska broke away from that stare and found herself gazing at her feet. When had she taken her shoes off? Alexandre's hand gently brushing a stray lock of hair behind her ear brought her attention back to his face. But something in that familiarity, in those eyes, woke the need to retreat from the edge of the unknown.

After a long moment, Alexandre nodded to himself and then made the smallest of bows, an ordinary gesture that opened a gulf between them.

"Goodnight, Eska." And then he was gone, the door closing softly behind him, and Eska was left to wonder if it would have been better if he had not come at all.

Interlude 4

A letter from Alexandre de Minos to Eska de Caraval, dated four years ago

Dearest Eska,

Did you know there is a species of whale in the far northern seas that has learned how to hunt seals in groups by using their tails to create waves, thereby rocking floating pieces of ice hard enough to send the poor seals—just hoping to catch a bit of sun and a nap—tumbling into the whales' waiting jaws?

I suspect you did—or at the very least you probably wouldn't admit it if you didn't—but I had to try, didn't I?

If you have surmised by now that our Eduin campaign is a heap of tedium mixed with a generous helping of squabbling officers, you would be correct. I'm afraid that without a change in the wind, so to speak, we shall have to retreat at the end of the season and strike out again next year. I'm of a mind to create aforementioned wind, though it is as likely to see me discharged dishonorably—if I survive—as congratulated for breaking the Eduin knot. But if I say more, you'll be as much at fault as I, and if either of us is going to come to ruin, it really ought to be me.

I was thinking, as I spent yet another day in my waterlogged tent listening to bored soldiers bet each other how long it would take their boot prints to fill with rain, about those days we spent sailing down the Alencio last year—and how neither of us could stand more than a moment without being busy at some sort of task or another. I can still perfectly picture the poor captain's face when he caught us taking knot-tying and sail-mending lessons from the second mate. And yet I would choose the monotony of an endless river over the sheer madness that comes with a siege. I swear I have lost half my mind already, and the other half has begun to trickle out of my ears with every drop of rain.

And then I think of you, laughing as the wind whisks your broad-brimmed hat from your head and sends it wheeling overboard. You, watching the riverbank for green herons and pointing out each and every bumpy log or rock that might have been a carrion lizard. You, smiling at me, your hair strewn across that pathetic excuse for a pillow, your touch burning my skin as we try—and fail—not to wake the sailors in the berth next door. And I know that I could be anywhere, Eska, besieging or besieged, and I would be content as long as you were there, too.

Dig well, my love. I hope you find a lost civilization—or at least an interesting tool or piece of pottery from which your remarkable mind can glean astounding things. I may be fighting for Arconia, but you are a far greater champion of our city and what we Arconians are capable of.

Yours, always,
Sascha

9

"I know that duty well."

"SOMETHING HE ATE, I THINK."

Eska looked down at the soil samples spread out on the worktable in front of her.

"Something he ate?" Cedric repeated. "But he was at the dinner last night."

Eska made a questioning noise but did not bother to raise her head. The soil in the tallest glass rod was a beautiful reddish-brown in the upper layer, transitioning to crumbly brown, then dull and sandy followed by chalky, sludgy clay, and, at last, black streaked with richly-colored silt.

"You ate that dinner, too, my lady. "

Actually, Eska hadn't, but rather than take the time to explain her dining companion and the late-night meal shared with Alexandre, she merely said, "And yet Chancellor Fiorlieu is ill and the rest of us are not." Eska finally looked up and shrugged at her dig master's droopy mustache and skeptical eyebrows. "Cedric, let us take advantage of the fact that I am not needed in negotiations today due to the state of the poor Chancellor's bowels. We have a lot to do. Now, tell me, the deepest sample came from where, exactly?"

As Cedric pointed out on his map of the site where each sample had been taken, Eska was already thinking ahead to the dig plan for the day, making minor adjustments to what Cedric had relayed to her.

"We'll want to aim for just below the clay, I expect," Eska said when Cedric had finished speaking. The dig master nodded in agreement. "We'll start with a test trench running south-east from here to here," she drew a line with her finger on the map, "taking these quadrants on an angle. And then repeat that here." Another line. "But in addition to the two trenches, I want to try digging a series of probing holes here and here." This time she pointed to the southern-most quadrant, away from the river. "It'll be a good task for the new recruits, give them some experience, and if we're lucky, they may stumble across a refuse pit. The Onandya often placed those to the south of their gathering sites."

"Very good, my lady. Shall I see to the set up of your work tent?"

"I'll do that, Cedric. You may direct the crew to begin."

Eska's tent was, on the outside, not unlike the rest of the Firenzia tents. Three-sided when the door flaps were pulled aside, made of thin canvas, and smelling faintly of the starflower oil that was lightly brushed over the tents between expeditions to protect the material from the elements. Eska's tent featured a large worktable that occupied the entire length of one side. A cot rested at the back wall, draped with a simple, striped blanket. A trunk containing books, rolls of blank drafting paper, and a hodgepodge of miscellaneous pieces of equipment sat at the foot of the cot. Her tool case had been placed on the worktable and three straight-backed folding camp chairs leaned against the tent's center post.

Eska went straight to her tool case. She unbuckled the sturdy leather straps and undid the metal clasps, then lifted the lid, revealing neat trays of brushes and metal instruments of all shapes and sizes, and a set of knives on the top layer. Grasping handles at both sides of the trunk, Eska lifted the trays up and out, extending them over the worktable. Below, Eska kept drawing and writing materials, her favorite spade and pick nestled in protective cases, more brushes—one can never have too many—for sweeping away loose soil and cleaning artifacts, as well as a small obsidian sculpture that traveled everywhere with her.

Eska unwrapped the black fox from its fleece nest and smiled. It had been a gift from her uncle for her eleventh birthday and it had accompanied her on every expedition she had led on her own. Slightly abstract in design, the angled planes of its form gloriously smooth to the touch, the fox was the animal disguise of the ancient Mehathuen god Nehar. After receiving the fox from her uncle, Eska raced to the Lordican at the earliest opportunity to learn about it, finding, to her unending delight, that Nehar was a god of knowledge and discovery, a wanderer who explored the world.

She visited Mehatha once, or the place it had become, known to the world now as a small principality under the watch of its larger, more powerful neighbor, Irabor. Not quite independent, not quite a province, Mehatha was still a place proud of its once prominent position. Everywhere she looked, the old gods were remembered, though now placed below the Iraborean triumvirate, and the ruins of palaces, temples, and monuments from the golden age of the Mehathuen empire were still visible, a reminder of a time when Mehatha had ruled a vast stretch of land that nearly reached as far northwest as where the walls and towers of Toridium now stood. The wanderer god of Mehatha would have seen much indeed.

Eska brushed her thumb over the fox's face and then placed it on her worktable where the god could watch over her labor. Returning her attention to her tool case, she withdrew a blank sheet of paper, a bottle of ink and a pen, and the tray containing her most-used brushes and metal tools, and then closed the case up and placed it beneath the table. Unfolding one of the chairs, Eska took a seat to compose a letter to Albus.

There was little to report—especially if she decided not to mention Alexandre de Minos' presence in Toridium—but she would add to the letter over the next few days of excavating and send it back to Arconia once she filled a few pages. And there was, of course, the incident in the harbor. Albus might claim to only be interested in the findings Firenzia Company would make, but even he couldn't resist the allure of the feud between the rival companies and a riveting, and possibly slightly embellished, account of Manon Barca's attempt to sink the *Argonex*. Eska happened to know, though she would never tell him, that Albus sometimes read her more exciting letters to his fellow librarians.

After she finished writing a dozen lines, Eska put the pen down and leaned back as far as the stiff chair would allow, her mind turning to the object she had obtained from the Iron Baron and left in Albus's care. The strange bronze disc with its pattern of markings and hedgehog tendencies tugged at Eska's imagination. She had yet to formulate any realistic theories about its origin or purpose, but it had been hidden inside a reliquary once belonging to the Alescuan dynasty, a reliquary that was as famous for being difficult to open as it was for being one of a set of six lost after the fall of the dynasty. That alone was reason for excitement and speculation, and Eska never imagined, when she deduced that the Baron might possess one of the reliquaries, that it might contain something so unusual and unexplained. She hoped Albus had made some discoveries about the disc in her absence—and that he would relay them to her in writing.

As for her own letter, her progress was interrupted by a deafening explosion in the distance.

The blast startled her so thoroughly she bit her tongue. Springing from her chair, Eska tasted blood as she rushed out of the tent.

A cloud of dirt drifted away from the eastern edge of the site, where work on the first trench had begun. Dirt and dust that was a strange green color hung like a haze. Shouts filled the air. Even from a distance, Eska saw two, maybe three, figures on the ground. A fourth was on hands and knees.

Eska ran. Others followed. She was aware of Bastien at her side, of Cedric a step behind.

She got there in time for the second explosion.

The force of it threw Eska into the air, hurling her into the tall grass. She landed hard on her right side, all air escaping her lungs, wrist twisting torturously beneath her, head ringing with a terrible silence. Still unable to draw a full breath, she tried to lurch upright but found she was too disoriented to do anything other than lie with her face in the ground. Her heart thundered away in her chest, the only sensation she was truly aware of, but at last other sounds came to her, voices—distant, murky, indistinct—and a hissing sound she found she could not name but which instilled fear in her nonetheless.

A hand on her shoulder. A voice in her ear. Words, words she could not understand. A face thrust into her vision, blurry and gone as quickly as it had come. Then two hands cradling her shoulders, turning her so she lay upon her back. More distant shouting, still faint but shaping into something Eska could almost believe to be words.

Her hearing came back to her in a roar.

"My lady?"

The face belonged to Bastien. Blood trickled from the side of his head. Behind him, the air wobbled, like heat rising from a desert. No, no, that wasn't right. Couldn't be.

"Can you hear me? Are you badly hurt?"

Eska struggled to sit up and Bastien steadied her as she shook her head.

"Fine." Her mouth formed the word reluctantly. "I'm fine." Eska remembered the hissing sound she had heard and she struggled to convey her fear. "Do you," she paused, her head spinning, "do you hear that?" Eska grabbed Bastien's hand. "Air escaping," she managed. "There might be more." She tried to push at Bastien, tried to make him understand, but her hand swiped uselessly at his chest. "Get everyone away!"

Bastien frowned, but then Gabriel's voice cut through the chaos as the engineer echoed Eska's words and ushered everyone back. Bastien got Eska to her feet and together they made their way to a safe distance, Eska leaning on the young man for balance, Bastien clutching her arm as he hobbled in obvious pain.

The third explosion was quieter and smaller. The earth shuddered under Eska's feet, but far less dirt was flung in the air and when the dust settled, the ground no longer hissed.

But there was no sigh of relief escaping from Eska's lips. Not while she had eyes to see the prone body, limbs askew, that lay where it had landed after the first explosion.

She was not the first to reach him. Several crewmembers got there first, and for a moment Eska looked down on the dead man from over their bent heads, her skull still ringing, her wrist throbbing with pain. And then the crew parted and Eska knelt, hand reaching out to hover over the caved in chest, the tangle of organs. Behind her, voices murmured in sorrow. Nero. His name was Nero.

Forcing herself to rise, Eska searched out Cedric. The dig master was covered in a faint layer of dust, but appeared unhurt. He hurried to Eska's side.

"Are there others?"

He shook his head.

It did not make Eska glad. "The injured will need tending," she said. "Those with the gravest injuries must go straight to the city. The Vismarch will help."

The dig master nodded. "Your wrist, my lady."

Eska looked at it for the first time, trying to think beyond the pain and assess the extent of the injury. "I'll be fine." She swallowed. "We'll need to prepare Nero's body for burial."

"Of course, my lady." Cedric moved away to take a count of the injured.

Eska, still looking at her wrist, called for the engineer. Her voice was weak and cracked, but Gabriel appeared quickly.

"Air, my lady, pestilent air. Trapped beneath the earth. Not hidden very deep, and seems to have caught a spark while Nero was heating the rods for the soil samples."

Eska nodded. She tried to take a deep breath and found she could not. "We must know if there is more."

The engineer nodded his agreement. "I will do what I can."

Eska looked Gabriel in the eye, hoping to find comfort and seeing none. Turning back to the scene of the explosion, Eska was relieved to see Cedric had moved the crew away, back toward the tents. All but one walked under their own power. Two crewmembers wrapped Nero's body in canvas. The air was very still and quiet.

"We are fortunate, my lady," Gabriel said quietly. "In a matter of moments, another ten crewmembers would have been working on the trench."

———— ◆ ————

The visitors from the city arrived quickly, as she had known they would. Eska stood just outside the medical tent, far busier than it had ever been on any of her previous excavations. The wagon bearing the four most grievously injured crewmembers had departed moments before, crossing paths with the two riders from the city as they neared the site.

Eska answered the questions of the Toridua officials as best she could. No, it was three explosions. No, she did not know if the site was safe. Yes, they were working on it. No, they could not have known there were pockets of lethal air beneath the surface. No, there was no fault, no blame.

Except Eska did find fault—with herself. As the officials returned to the city, satisfied for the time being and promising to send assistance, Eska looked at her injured workers, men and women under her care, and knew guilt and shame.

"I know that look."

Alexandre's voice, soft and full of understanding, came to Eska from over her shoulder. She hadn't seen him arrive.

She didn't want to turn, didn't want to look him in the face and bear the weight of his compassion. But she did.

"You must not blame yourself, Eska."

She ought to answer him, ought to accept what he said, but she could not muster any words.

"I know you. I know that it would be fruitless to tell you that you could not possibly have prevented this. I know that now, in this moment, is when your logical mind fails you." Alexandre took a small step closer to her, almost close enough to touch her. "Don't eat yourself alive, Eska. Please." When still she said nothing, he gave a small nod.

"My men are at your disposal. I have already asked some to help with the wounded, but whatever you need, it is yours."

He turned to go and at last Eska summoned her voice. "Please stay." The words came unbidden. She had intended to thank him. She had intended to do so calmly and without letting him glimpse the storm that raged in her. Instead, she felt hot tears fill her eyes, felt her breath hitch in her lungs. And then she felt, as though from a great distance, Alexandre take her by the hand, the left one, and lead her to her tent.

His innate sense of what she needed might have irritated her under different circumstances, but her exhaustion and the touch of his skin on hers drained her of the last of her resistance. As they walked, Eska let Alexandre keep ahold of her hand. They ducked inside her tent and Alexandre lifted her onto the worktable. He left for a moment, returning quickly with two rolled bandages. After instructing Eska to hold out her wrist just so—earning him a string of curses for the pain—he wrapped it first with a delicate linen and then with a sturdier, fibrous material. When he finished, Eska experimented and found she could make only the tiniest movements.

"Well you've succeeded in trussing me up." It felt wrong to speak such lighthearted words, but she did not trust herself to broach what was truly on her mind.

"That's very dramatic," he said, laughing. "You're hardly a pig being sent off for slaughter." He examined his work, deemed it satisfactory, and glanced around the tent. "Would you like something for the pain? Where is that bottle of brandy you always keep around?"

"There's harrow root powder in my trunk," she said without thinking.

Alexandre turned sharply. "You said you would give that up."

Eska closed her eyes and stretched out on the worktable. "And you said my love was more important than your pride. But that turned out to be false as well." He didn't deserve such condemnation, of course. But for a moment Eska was able to direct her resentment at a target other than herself—and it felt good. She heard rather than saw the change in him. A subtle shift in his posture, the soles of his boots brushing through the dirt as he drew himself up and squared his shoulders. The whisper of his sleeves against each other as he put his hands behind his back. The uneven exhale he could not disguise. If she looked at him, he would be every inch the soldier: stiff, uncompromising, and, well, proud. Eska chose not to look.

To his credit, and despite her harsh words, Alexandre did not leave. He remained by her side throughout the afternoon, helping as he was able, writing up her dictated report of the incident for the Vismarch's officials and a second copy for the Firenzia records.

And when twilight came and the crew gathered to bury their fallen comrade some distance away from the river and site, under a copse of trees in the shadow of the hills to the east, he was still there.

"All speed, Nero."

Eska spoke the words and heard the crew echo them back to her. A few invoked a god of their choosing, or the spirits of their ancestors, asking to bring the dead man peace or to help him gain his next life, but the rest chose to keep whatever thoughts they had for their fallen comrade to themselves. Nero, his face grey, his fingers wrapped around a spade marked with the Firenzia crest, lay in a deep grave at their feet, and one by one the members of the crew tossed a handful of dirt over him.

Her injured hand trembling so badly she could not hide it or the pain it caused, Eska reached for a shovel, but a hand on her arm brought her up short. Alexandre took her good hand and nodded at one of his soldiers to claim the shovel, then tried to lead Eska away from the grave.

"I can do it." Eska's protest was weak and pitiful. She tried again, though her very bones longed to do nothing more than sink to the ground and sleep. "Let me do it, Sascha."

"You're hurt, Eska. There are plenty of hands for this task."

"But only mine are de Caraval hands," she said. Grief and the weight of responsibility, of her father's name and her family's company, injected strength into her voice at last. "It is my duty. He lost his life in service to my family."

Eska tried to pull away but Alexandre would not relent. Using both arms, he tucked her against his chest.

"I know that duty well," he murmured into her hair. "But if you pick up that shovel now, your wrist will take longer to heal than you have the patience to withstand. Your tools will be clumsy in your hands. You will grow irritable and morose. What then will you be? What will you be to them?" He waited a moment. "They need you, Eska. But they don't need you to do this."

At last his common sense permeated the brittle, angry shield she had carried around herself since the accident. As though he could feel her anger begin to seep away, Alexandre released her from his embrace, taking hold of her elbows instead. He smiled.

"I am expected in the city, but I will stay if you want me to."

Eska shook her head. "You have done enough. I cannot keep you."

He accepted this with a nod and squeezed her elbows.

"Thank you, Sascha," Eska said, at last.

And she meant it. By the time she went to her tent and slept, Eska had managed to separate the burden of Nero's death from her mind. Not to be forgotten, not to be ignored. But so she could remain focused on what was ahead of her, not what lay behind. Alexandre was right, after all. The crew needed her to be at her best.

But acknowledging that Alexandre was right did not stop her from burning a sachet of harrow root powder that night, and Eska went to sleep with the spicy, intoxicating scent swirling over her head, each breath drawing the vapor deep into her lungs, each breath filling her blood and heart with ideas of strength and washing away the raw pain of the day.

10

"You probably want to eat my books."

ALBUS COURTENAY HATED SHIPS.

He hated the smell of the sea air. He hated the sounds of the gulls—so happy! so carefree!—wheeling overhead. He hated the confines of starboard and stern, whatever those were. He hated how the damp damaged paper. Most of all he hated the way ships seemed to *know* just when to pitch about and unsettle him.

The academic in him argued, stoically and with the most irritating superiority, that ships couldn't possibly *know* anything, and yet, as Albus raced to the railing to empty the contents of his stomach—which was already quite empty, thank you—he felt he had a most compelling counter-argument.

"The things I do for you, Eska de Caraval," Albus muttered to the wind as he straightened at the rail, his hands clenched tight around the wood. "This better be worth a large donation to my private book collection." A gull flapped overhead, circled, and landed unnervingly close to Albus. He shooed at it, to no effect. "You probably want to eat my books."

Albus tilted his face to the sky and sighed. As a librarian accustomed to spending countless hours alone in the expanse of the Lordican, he frequently talked to himself. Discussions about the properties of the water found in the great salt lakes, for instance, or a cordial debate about the relevancy and proper incorporation of works of popular history. These conversations were calm—mostly—and thoughtful. But he had to admit that he was neither calm nor thoughtful and the ship and the sea and the gulls were only partially to blame.

The true source of his anxiety lay in a hidden pocket sewn into the lining of the small case he had hastily packed with more parchments than clothing. The item itself was innocuous—a single sheet of paper—but Albus could not say the same for the words on the paper or the man who had recently become aware of its existence, and Albus' existence as a result. The thought was not at all comforting.

Sylvain de Ulyssey was not a man to meet in a dark alley. But that was because he had people to go into dark alleys for him. De Ulyssey's alleys were the private balconies of the Varadome's spectacle hall, the counting houses of Bartok Row—six of eight, or so Albus had heard—the ballrooms of the merely wealthy, and the gold-plated pleasure ships of the exorbitantly rich. He prowled not in the dark of night, striking fear into the hearts of even the most vicious criminal by means of brute force and brass knuckles, but in the brightest light of day, yanking the fortunes out from under both unsuspecting fools and those who ought to know better. Albus didn't really know how he managed this, never having been subjected to it himself. Knowledge, he assumed. In the right hands, information was better than any currency. Eska had taught him that. Yes, Albus concluded, knowledge and the precise tightening of some very painful metaphorical screws. Perhaps even some actual screws. It was said that everything de Ulyssey did was legal, that men and women in their right minds signed away their lives—on pages seven, nineteen, and eighty-three.

But it was all whispers, whispers Albus had caught wind of once or twice and thought nothing of. Sylvain de Ulyssey was, after all, a patron of the arts, a lord of impeccable lineage, and a close confidant of the Archduke. Surely such whispers were the work of jealous enemies. He was nothing like the crude aristocrats who gained wealth as dirty as their reputations—say, for instance, like Thibault de Venescu, the so-called Iron Baron who fancied himself the linchpin around which the underbelly of the Archduke's city revolved. For all his strutting, the

Iron Baron was an annoying insect Sylvain de Ulyssey could crush with a word.

And yet it just so happened that Albus and Lord de Ulyssey had both recently come into possession of one small, astonishing, very secret bit of lost knowledge, eclipsing the letter he had sent to Eska in Toridium.

It was enough to get Albus on a ship.

Interlude 5

Letter from Eska de Caraval to Valentin de Caraval,
dated fourteen years ago

Dearest Uncle,

I have met the most wonderful boy. Some might find him odd, because he would rather read a treatise on linguistics than play at soldiering or sailing, and I'm afraid he might not like me at all, but I do hope to see him again soon. His name is Albus, Albus Courtenay, and he's apprenticed at the Lordican.

Did you know the Lordican has apprentices? I should like that very much. Perhaps I will ask Mama and Papa if I might be allowed to undertake such an apprenticeship. I think I would choose to study under Matteo. He laughs so well. No, perhaps Lucrea. She's the finest scholar on the Pharecian queens, no matter what that odious Gilvais says. Oh, Uncle, it would be so difficult to choose! Perhaps I can convince them all to let me study under each in turn.

Albus says he will be a Master Librarian some day, and I do not doubt him, though some would say he is young to think so highly of himself. He's very determined, I can see that already, and clever. I think you would like him very much, Uncle. We are very close in age, though I am taller. He left home—a village outside Arconia—three years ago, just before his tenth birthday, though he won't tell me why. He said I was prying, and I suppose I was, but you taught me to ask questions.

But enough about me. How I long to hear of your adventures in Ira-bor! Please write to me soon—and take me with you next time! I am bored to tears with my latest governess. She insists she is fluent in Mallerean, but she has yet to catch on when I weave Mycrini insults into our conversational practice sessions. Save me, Uncle!

All my love,
Eska

11

"He means nothing to me."

MANON DREAMED.

She knew this because her father, her dead brother, and her mother were all in a room together. Not just any room, a room that looked very much like the captain's quarters in the sunken ship she had explored in Lake Tuomo. Lake grass grew up through the floorboards, laying claim to the rotten desk, and freshwater urchins lived in the rusting remnants of the iron chandelier. All as she remembered from that dive on a summer's day three years ago—desperate for coin and willing to work for anyone to get it. And yet in the dream, there was no water, and her family members, one in prison, one dead, and one across the sea, gathered as though waiting for her.

It occurred to Manon that perhaps she was dead, that they were all dead, and this was where the Barcas were meant to spend whatever comes after life. It was not inconceivable. After all, Victor was already in the family mausoleum, Julian Barca was left to rot in the Hibarium four years before, and Isoula Barca had disappeared on a ship not four days later.

And for a moment, Manon wished it might be so because her father was smiling at her, his true smile, not the one he showed to the men who came to the Barca home late at night to discuss business behind locked doors, not the one he kept for audiences with the Archduke, and not even the one he used for Manon's mother. She missed that smile.

Julian Barca opened his mouth to speak.

But it was not his voice that emerged.

"It's him, sir."

And with that Manon woke, her father's smile, the smile she told herself she could never trust again, lost.

"Are you certain?" A second voice, stilted, hesitant. "The Lady de Caraval named the sister."

Manon lay still as she cracked her eyelids at the mention of the de Caraval name. The voices were quiet, not directly outside her cell, but she made no movement, not wishing to draw their attention, even though she longed to crane her neck to try to catch a glimpse.

"The lady is mistaken, sir. We know what we saw. The brother is the guilty one. He attacked the ship. He is the Carrier."

Horror froze Manon, breath hitching in her throat, mind screaming. Perrin. Perrin was innocent. How could they be so mistaken?

"He claims he has no such skills." The second voice again, still hesitant.

"Who would do otherwise, when faced with such charges?"

"If you're certain."

"Completely, sir."

"Very well. She's sleeping?" Silence. "Wake her. Bring her before the Vismarch."

Manon shut her eyes as one set of footsteps retreated and the other approached her cell. She allowed the man to call her name twice before stirring and then slowly came to her feet at his command.

"Where is my brother?"

The man ignored her as he opened the cell door. He was one of the two officers from the harbor patrol, the one with the sword.

"Where is he?" Manon asked again.

The officer indicated she was to walk in front of him. Manon stepped from her cell.

"Where are you taking me?"

Blank eyes stared back. "The Vismarch must not be kept waiting."

They emerged from the cells below ground via a wide, curved stone staircase, which spilled out into a nondescript, unadorned corridor. From there they traveled up again, then through a hall undergoing some kind of renovation and a second hall, this one narrow and lined with mirrors. Manon caught a glimpse of herself—pale cheeks, dark hair falling from pins, eyes that belonged to a cornered animal—before they emerged at last out into a three-sided courtyard with the fourth open to a long, still pool lined with hedges.

She saw Perrin first, though he did not see her. His head drooped to his chest, limbs stretched out by ropes and strung to a frame, his entire body suspended a short distance from the ground. Around him stood a few Toridua in officer uniforms and a crowd of curious servants.

"What is this?" Manon asked, trying to keep her voice calm though she longed to scream and lash out. The officer at her back said nothing. "What are they doing to him?"

"He has refused to speak." This was a new voice, a woman. No, not new. Manon turned and recognized the woman who had boarded the *Carribe*, the one who Carried. Though now, without the waters of the harbor around her, Manon could scarcely detect the woman's abilities. "He has refused to admit he is a Carrier. But he will show us. They all do, eventually."

Cold terror crept through Manon as she stared across the courtyard at her brother, her mind racing to think how she might protect him from whatever pain was coming.

She forced herself to turn back to the woman, forced herself to breathe normally. "My brother is no Carrier. I am." And with no more than a flicker of her thoughts, she summoned sparks to her fingers. They showered harmlessly to the ground, but the male officer had her on her knees before she could draw a second breath, her arm bent painfully behind her, his fingers tight enough on the back of her neck to tell her that it would go badly for her if he had cause to squeeze. The woman stood over her, having done nothing more than blink. Manon twisted in the man's grasp. "See," she hissed. "I am the one

who Carries. I have the gift. I could burn you where you stand." An exaggeration. Without an enhancing substance, Manon could probably
only manage to set a sleeve on fire.

"Manon!"

It was Perrin. She craned her neck in the officer's grip just enough
to see her brother's face. He looked unhurt and he strained against the
ropes that held him. He repeated her name, calling out, his concern
clear.

The whip cracked, ripping Manon's gaze away. It split the air a second time, wielded by a bare-chested man. He tested it a third time, the
noise causing the crowd to flinch and Manon's heart to drop to her
stomach where it pulsed in angry, heavy beats.

"Manon!" Perrin cried again. He paid no mind to the whip, and the
fear in his voice was for her.

"Call that fire and he dies." The woman knelt before Manon, her
blue eyes and sharp cheekbones so close Manon had to blink and try
to lean away. Again she twisted to catch site of Perrin.

"Manon! What is this madness?"

Manon looked back at the woman, willing the next words she must
speak into existence. "Why would I do that? Look at him. He is weak.
He cannot even save himself. See, see, I have told you the truth. He
does not Carry." Manon raised her eyes to Perrin one last time. The
anguish in his face twisted at her heart, but it was the trust she saw
there that she would remember. Putting iron in her voice and speaking
loud enough for all to hear. "He means nothing to me."

Perrin cried out.

The man with the whip closed in on him. The arm drew back, the
whip poised like a scorpion's tail. And then a voice, the speaker unseen,
said a single word and the whip was lowered to coil on the ground.

Before Manon could see more, she was wrenched to her feet and
forced to walk back toward the Vismarch's palace, and as she stumbled, movement from the shadows in the side of her vision caught her
attention.

A man stepped out from the pillared portico of the courtyard, his arms crossing in front of his chest. He met Manon's stare, clearly not caring that she saw him. Manon knew that face, knew that close-cropped hair, knew the Arconian badge on his coat, but could not put the name to them. But she shivered with the sudden instinct of prey who has seen the predator and understood with a rush of clarity that whatever had just happened in that courtyard was a game for which only he knew the rules.

Interlude 6

Excerpt from a treatise on Carriers, their history and abilities, by Lumiro Papilloni and Carminina Estavilla, both of the Lordican

The terms 'Carry' and 'Carrier' were first recorded in Arconia roughly forty years after the City's founding and during the term of the Tribune Eracomo Volanta, though they appear to have evolved perhaps a decade earlier in Toridium and Cancalo and those cities' surrounding regions. Earlier terminology was less consistent and often reflected local beliefs, customs, and incidents.

Documentation from these early days of the City is scarce, and nearly nonexistent throughout Bellara prior to the birth and spread of what we now know as the Seven Cities—however, evidence suggests our ancestors were initially inclined to believe Carriers to be marked somehow by divinity. At the time, the Smith God Erasmo, along with his consort Via, Goddess of the Hearth, was the dominant spiritual presence in these lands, with smaller segments of the population following either the Twins, Toora and Taalo, or Beron, the Moon Warrior.

We will delve into further detail later on the place Carriers held in these various populations and their social hierarchies. It is sufficient now to note that under Erasmo and Via, Carriers whose talents lay with fire were highly regarded, perhaps even thought to be, in rare cases, children of the deities, while those who shaped water were considered malignant and untrustworthy, possibly in connection to the belief that a great flood, the natural enemy of any fire and therefore the enemy of deities of forge and hearth, was foretold. For those who followed the Twins, Carriers appear to have occupied a position of neutrality, though there is evidence they were thought to possess, thanks to their gifts, inhuman insight and perception. As a result, there are some scholars (de Maris and Chiara, for example), who believe the first Wisdoms of Onaxos were Carriers. This is much debated and beyond the scope of this work. As for adherents to Beron the Moon Warrior, those who Carried were scorned and mistrusted and the source of a great deal of violence, whether born from fire or water.

The origin of Carrier abilities is unknown, as is the manner in which they manifest. There is no discernable link from parent to child, indeed a family might exist for generations without producing one or might never produce one at all. Nor is there evidence that a child's environment affects the emergence or strength of the abilities. Strength is, however, the one aspect that can be reliably observed, tested, and studied. We will examine this and the scholarly works that preceded us in section three.

As Dionnaro demonstrated and has been replicated by several noted scholars since, some Carriers have been found to possess the ability without knowing it exists within them. Equally unreliable is the age at which a Carrier's abilities emerge. An inconclusive—and imperfect—study undertaken by Arenault and Indomicus attempted to prove that exposure to severe stress, pain, or traumatic events, either direct or as a witness, could trigger the development of the ability within a person. We will discuss these parameters, both known and suspected, in greater detail in section four, but the general conclusion that must be made is that our understanding of Carrier abilities remains limited.

To date there is precious little information—beyond anecdotes and legends—regarding Carriers whose abilities lie with neither fire nor water. Without evidence to support these theories, we will leave them to the playwrights and artists and those who might wish to frighten small children into good behavior. The most recent anecdotal evidence from our Seven Cities stems, naturally, from the mystery and fear surrounding the Alescuan dynasty. We will note simply that claims have been made in support of Carriers who can create and control metal (be it common iron or the purest gold), air, and, most disturbing of all, blood.

12

"He's a bit of a bore, though."

"Is Firenzia taking in strays now?"

They were, perhaps, not the kindest words to ever come out of Eska's mouth, but in her defense she was hot, sweaty, and waist deep in a hole in the ground. She held a hand up to shield the sun from her face and looked up at Alexandre with an expression she hoped was more steely than squinty.

"What am I to do with him, Sascha?"

She looked past the Arch-Commander to where Perrin Barca stood just beyond the edge of the dig site, the bright sunlight flaring over the tall grasses surrounding him. Though he was little more than a silhouette, she could see his head was down, gaze fixed firmly on his feet. Despite herself, Eska was reminded of a contrite dog.

"He's harmless, Eska, and he has nowhere else to go." Alexandre reached down to offer a hand to help Eska out of the hole. Sighing, she abandoned her spade—which she had been wielding rather uselessly given the injury to her right wrist, though the harrow root had done its work—and accepted his assistance. Brushing dirt from her hands, she looked once more at the Barca Alexandre had brought to her.

"Take him back to Arconia with you," Eska said.

"I would, but I'm not going back to Arconia. Not yet anyway. Besides, I will have his sister in my custody."

Eska looked sharply over at him. "The Vismarch released her to you?"

Alexandre nodded.

"Why?"

"Because I asked him to."

Eska tried to read whatever was hidden behind Alexandre's eyes—and failed. "Why not take them both, then?"

The Arch-Commander of Arconia studied Eska for a moment. "After the Barcas were taken into custody, I received word of something curious from the officers who made the arrest. One is a Carrier and she had an interesting story to tell. Come, let's find some shade."

For a moment Eska considered stubbornly insisting that any story he had to tell could be told right there, but Eska knew Alexandre and knew he was not just seeking shade—he sought privacy. Whatever he had to say was not for the ears of the Firenzia crewmembers working nearby. She glanced back at Perrin and watched as one of Alexandre's officers handed the youngest Barca his few possessions, no doubt confiscated upon his arrest. Perrin received them without a change in demeanor, the knife sliding onto his belt, the long coat slung over one shoulder.

Eska looked back at Alexandre, then nodded and they traversed the site to a small tent, a water station. Two barrels of cool water waited there and Alexandre used the copper dipper to fill a pair of cups.

Eska drained hers quickly, filled it a second time, and poured the contents down the back of her neck. "All right, tell me this story." She brushed a tendril of sweat-dampened hair behind her ear.

"As you know, Manon Barca breathed in the toxic Carrier substance she used to try to put a hole in the *Argonex*. She fell ill and her brother, naturally, was distraught. The officer swears she saw Perrin Barca," here Alexandre paused, searching for words, "try to draw the toxins from her body." He met Eska's gaze and waited.

Eska frowned, not understanding. "That doesn't make sense. It doesn't work like a snake bite."

"I don't mean like a snake bite." Alexandre ran a hand over his scalp. "I mean like a Carrier might draw water from the sea or fire from an ember."

Eska felt her frown deepen.

"The officer thinks Perrin Barca Carries, Eska, though she's quite certain he is ignorant of this himself. She thinks in that moment of fear for his sister, Perrin's instincts took over and he tried to save her—unbeknownst to him and certainly unbeknownst to his sister."

"Is that even possible? Could a Carrier draw poison out of a wound, out of the blood?"

Alexandre spread his hands, palms up. "I don't know. She says she heard a story once about something similar."

Eska turned away and paced a few steps out of the tent. She stared across the site, but wasn't truly seeing it. "And this is supposed to make me want to take him in?"

Alexandre joined her in the sun. "I know what I'm asking of you. But let me finish. This morning, I performed an experiment. I let Manon overhear talk that it was her brother who Carried, not her, and that he had made the attempt on your ship. I then let her see him appear to be moments from being tortured for refusing to admit he Carries. And I let him see her. And in that moment, when fear and adrenaline and love for his sister might have elicited whatever skills he possesses, he did nothing. Manon cursed and made threats and sparks, as you would expect, but Perrin made no attempt to save himself or his sister."

Eska looked hard at Alexandre. "So you don't think he Carries."

"I think he's harmless," he said, which was not exactly an answer. He took a drink of water. "That's not all that happened. Manon, for a reason only she understands, said she would make no effort to save him. That he was weak. That he meant nothing to her. And she said it loud enough for him to hear. She broke him, Eska. He is a shell, a husk, a depleted spirit. What I am asking is that someone show him a little kindness."

Eska was quiet for a long moment as she tried to sort through the conflicting thoughts and emotions that whirled in her mind. "And I suppose sending him away on the Barca ship is out of the question?"

"The captain and crew have been released. But the ship has been confiscated. Retribution for endangering Toridua officers." Alexandre sighed. "Look, Eska, it's true, he could travel overland with the crew. He could be back in Arconia in a matter of days. But think of what he has to return to." He looked over at Perrin, still as a statue. "Nothing. The Barcas are nearly penniless. His father is in the Hibarium, never to breathe free air again. His mother has abandoned the family. His brother is dead. And now his sister is a criminal and, worse, has severed the ties of shared blood, disowned him."

Eska looked down at her right hand and picked at the stiff bandage, trying to find a reason to say no. Alexandre's hand came to rest on her forearm.

"I have not forgotten what happened to your mother those years ago. I know the reasons you have to distrust those who Carry, I know what hardened you against them and I respect that. But I also know that you are equal parts logic and compassion, that your heart holds both, that they join forces to make you the extraordinary person you are. And I would never ask this of you if I did not know that heart."

His words flowed over Eska like smooth silk and she was quite certain that nothing but his blue eyes existed in that moment. "I suppose I should be angry that you know me so well—perhaps better than I know myself."

Alexandre's answering smile was easy and intimate and exactly the smile that haunted Eska's dreams after she turned down his offer of marriage.

"It's really quite irritating, Sascha, how good you are at getting what you want."

Alexandre laughed. "I learned from the best." But then the man she had loved leaned close and whispered, "You need only say the word, Eska, and Manon Barca will never make it back to Arconia." The eyes that sought hers were filled with deadly promise.

Eska hesitated, not because she truly wanted Manon Barca to suffer an unlucky accident, but because she had forgotten what it felt like when she and Alexandre once vowed to take on the world together.

Eska forced herself to smile with a nonchalance she didn't feel. "I won't have you turn into some sort of rogue assassin on my account. You aren't cut out for that kind of work."

"No?"

She patted the Arch-Commander's cheek. "Assassins work in the dark, Sascha. But you, you are a creature of the light. And I know how fond you are of seeing your name crowned with glory." Eska smiled at the faint frown of disagreement that passed over his face. "How many names are you up to?" Eska began to walk back to the trench, suddenly eager to put her mind to work on something other than Carriers and Perrin Barca. He followed. "Protector of the Seven Cities, Knight of Arconia," Eska said, ticking the titles off on her fingers. "Scourge of Eduin, Celestial Knight of Bellara—goodness, that's two knights—Guardian of Verdienne, Silentspear. Not to mention Arch-Commander de Minos." She leaned close and lowered her voice to a conspiratorial whisper. "He's a bit of a bore, though."

"Never heard of him," Alexandre said.

Eska shook her head with mock pity. "Shame. You'd get along." Eska drew up short, her hand on Alexandre's forearm, her gaze settling onto his familiar features. Whether driven by the pain in her wrist or the influence of the harrow root or the way he was looking at her, Eska could not be sure, but even she was surprised by the next words out of her mouth. "He's not a bore, not really. He's loyal and brave. He's kind and decent." She hesitated. "He's a very rare sort of man."

Alexandre broke eye contact this time. "Do you know, Eska, he also thinks you've been out in the sun too long."

Eska shrugged, glad to be the one to make him uncomfortable for once. "Well, if I'm to take in a foster, you'd better send him over so we can be properly introduced."

———— ◄ ● ► ————

"How long does it take a man to starve to death?"

In the distance, Perrin Barca sat unmoving, legs crossed, head down, looking no different than he had when arriving on Alexandre's heels that morning.

Gabriel shuffled his feet. "Depends, my lady. If properly hydrated, a healthy man could go from new moon to full. But without water—"

"It was a rhetorical question, Gabriel," Eska said while flexing her wrist in its heavy wrappings. "But the Arch-Commander said he has eaten nothing in a day and the fact remains I don't want him dying on me."

"Perhaps if you talked to him, my lady?"

"I very much doubt he has any wish to talk to me. And I'm afraid if I try, I'll be eating my words, and he'll stay hungry." And yet Eska sighed and began to make her way to the piece of riverbank Perrin Barca had claimed north of the camp, far enough so the sounds of the excavation site grew faint. If Eska was honest with herself, adding Perrin Barca to her list of burdens was something of a relief. If nothing else, it kept her from thinking too much of Nero's death or the possibility of more pockets of deadly air lingering below the surface of the site. The work that day had progressed smoothly, though, and the engineer's testing had suggested the danger was passed.

Eska came to a halt several paces from Perrin. The young man—younger, even, then Eska had first thought—gave no notice that he was aware of her presence.

"The sun will be hot today." Ridiculous. The sun was hot every day in that place. Eska had hardly seen a cloud since they arrived. She soldiered on. "You should be sure to drink plenty of water."

Perrin Barca stared out at the river, though Eska was certain it was not the brown swirling waters he saw. More likely his mind was full of the moment his sister abandoned him.

"I hold no grudge against you," Eska said, changing tactics. "Or your crew. Your sister acted on her own. It is she who will go before the Archduke's tribunal. Not you."

Still the young man was silent, as though he had one foot in death already.

Eska felt her patience thinning. "I suppose you think dying in my custody would be a great inconvenience to me. I assure you it would not. Nor will news of your death cause any great disturbance to the world. Your family was never more than over-reaching smugglers and grave robbers. It does not matter to me if you never make it home." Eska turned to go.

"Home." Perrin Barca's laugh was dry and hoarse and bitter. "There is no more home." He continued to stare out at the river. "She thinks it a secret, but I know about the third mortgage on the house at Isle de Gaustin. Once they learn of this, the creditors will descend on it first. Prime location. The right neighbors. But they'll go after the rest soon enough. They know we're ruined." He looked at Eska for the first time. "And you're right. I come from a long line of over-reachers. It is, perhaps, what we do best."

Eska came a step closer. "Why? Why risk so much? All for this Onandya site? I'm looking for pottery, Perrin, not treasure. Why?"

"I no longer pretend to understand my sister's mind. She has always been a risk-taker. Bold, determined, single-minded. Every breath she takes is for the Barca fortunes and legacy. But this, this was different." A ghost of a smile played across his face. "This was beyond reckless, beyond reason, and I once saw my sister ride a horse through a herd of stampeding buffalo."

Eska didn't echo his smile. "You'll excuse me if I don't find the Barca tradition for reckless behavior amusing. Your sister could have killed my entire crew. My mother."

Perrin Barca hung his head. "I know," he said. "I also know my apology means nothing to you, but you have it nonetheless."

Eska was quiet for a moment, unsure how to bridge the long-standing enmity between Barca and Firenzia, unsure if she even wanted to. She was aware, too, that some part of her was trying to detect the Carrier blood in him, as though it might appear at any moment in his voice or his eyes or the way he plucked at the grass he sat on. A foolish notion. She tried to put a note of sympathy in her voice. "Do you really intend to starve to death out here?"

To her surprise, Perrin Barca began to laugh. Not the bitter sound that had burst from his lungs moments before, but a full-throated laugh of genuine amusement, so forceful it bent him over until his head was tucked between his crossed legs. When he resurfaced, it was to wipe tears from his eyes, and even then it took him several attempts to speak.

"I had thought," he said at last, "that perhaps I should do exactly that. Probably what's expected of me. But this morning, I found this in my pocket," he said, withdrawing a small drawstring linen bag from inside his waistcoat, "and before I knew it, I'd eaten the lot of them." He opened the bag and showed Eska a dozen or so date pits. "So I gave up on the whole starve yourself for your family's honor idea."

Eska couldn't help herself. She and Perrin Barca, who she would have considered a sworn enemy but a day before, laughed together until they both had tears streaming down their cheeks. All over a sack of dates.

In the end, there was something more than humor in those tears and when at last they dried their eyes, Eska saw the grief and sorrow in Perrin's face. She wondered what he saw in hers.

Offering her hand, Eska helped Perrin to his feet. "You are not like the other Barcas I have known."

Sadness and humor twisted together on Perrin's face once more. "I was always sure I was a disappointment," he said as he brushed dust from his pants. "Not enough interest in digging in the dirt for old junk. But tell me, how many of my esteemed family members have you encountered?"

"Too many. Your father, of course. I'll never forget seeing Julian Barca descend upon the Varadome towing the great frieze of Parnasscus on seventeen carts—on the same day my uncle received a commendation, of course. And there was your aunt. Leandra? She told me once when I was quite young, when my father and I were attending a lecture on Theodoria's philosophical works at the Lordican, that she'd reported my father for corruption. I had nightmares for half a year of my father getting dragged off in the dead of night, never to be seen again. And then there's your sister. A perfect marriage of your father's daring and your aunt's cunning."

Eska glanced at Perrin to see if she had gone too far. The young man was frowning, but not at her.

"And my brother? Victor?"

Eska shook her head, curious as to the origin of the sudden intensity behind Perrin's eyes. "Never in person."

Perrin nodded once, absentmindedly, and then his face smoothed over into a smile. "Dates, it seems, are not very filling. Could I beg you to show me where to find something of greater sustenance? In exchange, I promise not to mention the name Barca unless you bid me."

Eska laughed. "The name isn't the problem. It's the people attached to it. Come, the crew tells me the fishing was good this morning."

As she led Perrin back toward the camp and the excavation site, Eska's gaze wandered to a small barge floating downriver, the crew lazily poling their way through the shallower waters—except for one man. Eska froze as Perrin went on ahead, her attention fixed on a lone bearded figure standing at the aft of the barge. He seemed as intent on Eska as she was on him. She was meant to see him, to feel the weight of his gaze. And if she was not mistaken, he had a badge of golden daggers sewn onto the sleeve of his black jacket.

Eska trailed behind Perrin after the barge floated out of sight. She told no one that Thibault de Venescu, the Iron Baron, apparently wasn't satisfied with restricting his threats to narrow streets in Arconia—he was sending out shadows to stalk her.

13

"I fear I will fail that task."

"MY DEAR CHANCELLOR, YOU DON'T LOOK AT ALL WELL."

The Ambassador-Superior of Arconia's voice conveyed sympathy, compassion, and not even a hint of awareness that perhaps poor Chancellor Fiorlieu was suffering just as much from her negotiation tactics as from his stomach ailment.

The morning had begun politely enough—an exchange of gifts, ceremonial tea, a moment of silence at the large round table. There had even been birds singing in the hedges outside the windows, filigree shutters flung wide to let in the soft light and the smell of earth dampened by the rain that fell from the stars the night before. But then Eska watched her mother disarm, dismantle, and dismember—metaphorically speaking—Chancellors Pelle and Fiorlieu, leaving the latter grimacing under the weight of her devastating logic, unparalleled rhetorical eloquence, and charming smile. It wasn't even time to break for the noon meal and Sorina de Caraval had already gained concessions about the shoddy state of the roads branching out from Toridium, roads the Vismarch was obligated to maintain, and caused Chancellor Pelle to admit his government had been withholding information on known bands of renegades who preyed upon travelers of said roads.

It all left Eska with little to do but admire her mother's skill, and she longed to return to her work by the river.

"I assure you, I am well enough, Ambassador-Superior," Chancellor Fiorlieu managed, his jaw working beneath the short, thick beard he wore. He was the tougher opponent, Eska quickly realized, and had not bothered to hide his annoyance at Pelle's misstep. On his own and unbothered by a pain in his gut, he might be formidable. But the Vismarch had named them equal partners in the negotiations, Eska knew, and Fiorlieu would have to make what he could of the arrangement—and the Arconians would do what they could to drive the wedge between the Chancellors deeper.

"Perhaps a brief respite," Sorina de Caraval said, smiling gently. "The room has grown quite warm, has it not?"

Fiorlieu agreed with a begrudging nod and snapped his fingers, summoning a pair of servants with a cart bearing pitchers of refreshing beverages. They began to pour, the sound of ice clinking against silver and crystal filling the room. Eska rose from her chair and went to a window, finding her gaze drawn to the south. Towers and rooftops and air gardens—not to mention a large wall—stood between her and the excavation, but that did not stop her from looking. A whisper of fabric at her elbow alerted Eska to her mother's presence.

"Don't make me ask you if your mind is fully engaged here in this chamber." Sorina kept her voice low, unthreatening, excessively mild. It made Eska long for a pair of wings like those of the sparrows chattering below the window, wings that could carry her out of the city.

"I assure you, Mama, I will do my duty." Eska turned a carefully composed face to her mother and the older woman studied her for a long moment. Quiet conversations in the room behind them went unheeded.

"You see, Eska. There, right there. You have everything it takes to do what I do, what your father does. Your face right now is truly a wonder. I know that deep inside you, you clamor to be let loose, you chafe against the obligations that keep you here. But I only know that because I am your mother. You can fool everyone else in this room, perhaps even in all the Seven Cities and beyond."

Eska could think of one or two individuals who could likely see through any façade she might put up—and both their names happened to begin with A—but she kept this to herself.

"You cannot always be torn in two, Eska," Sorina murmured. "Some day you will have to choose between serving your city and running your uncle's company. And though you may be loathe to admit it, it will not be an easy choice for you in the end."

Eska was saved from having to acknowledge the truth of her mother's statement by the dismissal of the servants. Chairs scraped back, bottoms lowered to begin the process of going numb once again. And Eska took her seat having resolved to think no more of the excavation—at least not until she stepped foot outside the negotiation chamber at the end of the day.

The Ambassador-Superior took charge once more. "Now, Chancellors, if we may, might I suggest we take a momentary break from discussing the Toridium roads and turn our attention to the fungus that has affected Arconia's lumber production?"

It was a masterful stroke, a sudden change in tactic that would blind the Chancellors to the ambush being prepared for them. Rather than continue to enumerate Toridium's deficiencies, Sorina de Caraval was turning attention to her own city and feeding the Chancellors an opportunity to find their footing and express a momentary superiority. Never mind they were standing on quicksand.

Chancellor Pelle pounced. Very predictable. Eager to make up for his mistake, the younger official expounded at length about the dearth of lumber and demanded to know how the Archduke meant to make up for it.

After some back and forth, during which Eska provided a few key financial details, the Ambassador-Superior of Arconia was forced to concede to a reduction in the price of lumber, to be revisited in three years.

Pelle was triumphant. He tried not to smile, tried to maintain his decorum. It turned his usually pleasant face into something that looked like it had half-swallowed an eel. For their part, the members of the Arconian delegation went into the midday break between sessions wearing suitably distressed faces. But it was Fiorlieu Eska watched as the chamber emptied. The older man was either truly ill or suspicious of the minor victory his colleague had won. Likely both.

Eska approached him as he gathered his sheaf of papers. "Chancellor." They were the only people left in the room. "May I offer a suggestion?"

Chancellor Fiorlieu glanced up from below greying eyebrows. "That depends. Is this suggestion made in an official capacity? If so, I cannot and will not hear it, not until we have resumed."

"Very unofficial, I assure you."

The Chancellor frowned. "Then I suppose I cannot stop you."

He was certainly determined to be obstinate. Eska was tempted to swallow her well-meaning advice. Instead, she offered a slight smile. "Eldergrass." His frown deepened, if that was possible. "Eldergrass and finallian root. Brewed like a tea. For your stomach pains."

Though she was certain his persistent frown was caused at least in part by unrelenting pain in his belly, she half expected him to insist he was experiencing no pain. Instead he grunted. "Sweet and soothing is it? Sounds as useless as honeywater."

"Actually, it's really quite unpleasant," Eska said mildly. "Eldergrass ferments in the presence of hot water and the starch in the finallian root. And it will sting your throat all the way down." The Chancellor's grimace altered ever so slightly. "But it's a touch more effective than honeywater, I'd say." She swept from the room without waiting for a response. Either he'd try it and be grateful, thereby earning the Arconians some good will, or he would refuse it out of spite, the pain would not improve, and he'd lash out as a result. Arconian or Toridua, it made no difference at whom he lashed out. Either way, her mother would use his anger against him.

———— ◆ ————

Eska took her meal in the Vismarch's treasure hall. Rather, she stashed a cheese-stuffed roll in the pocket of her trousers, plucked a pear from the overflowing fruit bowl laid out for the negotiators, and slipped through the still, cool halls of the palace.

The treasure hall was guarded, of course, and Eska contemplated a not insignificant number of stories to explain her request to enter—some more plausible than others. She settled, just for the fun of it, on telling the guard on duty that she had been sent to measure the golden abdominal muscles of the statue of Helionicus—the mythical figure who, well, was mythical precisely because of his muscles—for a portrait of the Vismarch's paramour. In the end, she didn't have to say a word. Evidently the Vismarch had given notice to allow entry to a young woman sporting a hint of sunburn on her cheeks.

Eska entered the treasure hall quietly, chewing a mouthful of pear as the door closed with a muted click behind her.

Unlike her first visit, the hall was lit brilliantly by the sun and the Vismarch's collection quite literally sparkled and gleamed so brightly, Eska had to blink twice before she could take it in. It was hard to know where to look first. She settled on the chiseled statue of Helionicus because the ancient hero was on her mind.

From him she moved on to a ruby the size of a goose egg, then the splintered shield of Kyr—well and truly splintered, and the amulet of the prophet Xenia. The amulet gave her pause, for it was of the same smooth obsidian as her fox sculpture. It too had its origins in Mehatha, but where the fox was a symbol of the god Nehar, Xenia was the priestess who had foreseen the end of the Mehathuen empire and the rise of Irabor. The amulet and its beaded chain lay on black velvet, the obsidian stone sucking in the light around it. Eska reached out a hand, wanting to feel the smooth planes of the amulet's many faces, wondering if Xenia had welcomed the truth of her prophecy or if she had wept for what was lost. Hers was a shadowed story, pieces of a life cobbled together only after her name became a permanent part of Mehathuen history, no doubt made of as many lies invented by her enemies as truths known to her friends. Eska could not help but wonder who she really was and what she had wanted from life.

Eska wandered from display to display after leaving Xenia's amulet behind, but her mind was unfocused, her thoughts on the long-dead priestess and her mother's words about Eska having her own choice ahead of her. The Vismarch's treasures offered no answer. They were beautiful, they were rare, and they were clearly adored and protected. But they were not studied, not as Eska would if she had possession of them. They were only there to be seen, admired, but not understood. The Vismarch, for all his attention to detail, was not very different from Valentin de Caraval.

A vision of her uncle prowling that hall brought Eska back once more to the question her mother had posed, but the passage of time saved Eska from allowing herself to ponder whether her future lay with Firenzia Company or in the governance of her city, and she left the treasure hall behind to return to the negotiations.

So lost in thought was Eska that she nearly ran into the grey-haired woman kneeling in the middle of the vast floor of the Hall of the Lions, directly beneath the point of the pyramid. She begged very many pardons and the woman smiled.

"You're not the first I've seen to leave the Vismarch's treasure hall in a state of wonder." There was an accent on her tongue that Eska could not quite place.

"Have you seen it yourself?" Eska asked, trying to think why the woman had been kneeling in the empty pyramid, praying to no one, beseeching only the polished tiles.

The woman shook her head. "The Vismarch does not let me enter, though that is the sole purpose of my presence in this city."

"What do you mean?"

The woman sighed, waved away Eska's offer to help her stand, and spread her hands on her thighs. "Every day I come here to seek an audience with the Vismarch. Some days he speaks with me. Most he does not. It's not that he's unkind. He is polite and respectful. But he refuses to hear my request. We do not even speak of it."

"Your request?"

"Behind that door is an artifact that belongs to my people, to the land I come from. It is valuable, yes, but it is more than the gold it would take to buy it, indeed, if such an amount exists. It is part of the story of my country, our heritage, our hearts, the blood we have shed." The woman glanced up at Eska, her hands raised as if in supplication. "And it belongs with us." At last she got to her feet, the top of her head coming no higher than Eska's chin. "Perhaps you have seen it? A stone black as night on a chain of silver beads."

"The amulet of Xenia," Eska breathed. "You are from Mehatha."

The woman nodded solemnly. "I am. And each day for thirty years I have risen with the sun and come to the Hall of the Lions to ask the Vismarch to return it to us."

"Thirty years," Eska repeated, unable to fathom the single-minded dedication it would take to live such a life.

The woman nodded again. "I was a young woman when I came here. I had dreams and a man I loved and who loved me. But I came to do my duty. Thirty years away from my homeland, my people. Thirty years speaking a language not my own. Thirty years with one task on my shoulders." She sighed, sadness creeping into her face. "My bones grow weary of kneeling on this floor. My joints are stiff from years of supplication. My hearing is not what it once was. I fear I will fail that task." She turned away from Eska and began a slow, lonely procession to the towering doors of the pyramid.

Stunned, full of questions, but able to put words to only one, Eska called after her. "What is your name?"

The woman stopped and looked over her shoulder. "Why do you ask?"

Eska shook her head. "I don't know."

The woman turned to face Eska fully, but did not speak for a moment. At last she touched her fingertips to her forehead before extending her hand out from her torso, the traditional Mehathuen greeting.

"I am Parisia of Mehatha."

She turned on slippered feet and walked silently from the pyramid, leaving behind only the weight of her sadness.

———◆———

The afternoon session of negotiations, as it turned out, never commenced.

Chancellor Pelle greeted Sorina de Caraval, Eska, and the rest of the Arconian delegation outside the chamber with the round table and the filigreed shutters. Bowing slightly, he informed them that Chancellor Fiorlieu had taken to his bed once again. He acknowledged that the Ambassador-Superior could choose to demand the work continue, with or without Fiorlieu, but begged that she might consider breaking official diplomatic protocol—which stated that a strict negotiation schedule must be followed—and grant a recess of a single day. Sorina de Caraval—let no one call her ungracious—agreed.

And Eska, well, upon finding herself with the afternoon unexpectedly at her disposal, she left the city in short order, taking a horse from the Vismarch's stable and discovering a squashed cheese roll in her pocket halfway between Toridium and the Firenzia site.

It was, therefore, with said roll in one hand and a small brush in the other, that she acquired the attention of the three newest crewmembers over the hole they had been digging.

They had, to her delight, discovered the very refuse pit she hoped they might come across, and a number of small, broken objects had already been pulled from the dirt.

Eska swallowed the last of her cheese roll, crouched on the ground, and picked up one of the objects. "See this, Dea?" Eska brushed soil from the thing in her palm. Dea, a skinny girl from an orphanage in Arconia, squatted next to her in the dirt. "It's marvelous. I've seen them before, but usually cracked and broken. This one is quite well-preserved."

"What is it?" The girl was on her first contract with Firenzia Company and likely on her first journey away from home.

Eska set the slender wooden cylinder in Dea's hand. Unskilled she might be, but the girl had shown more than a spoonful of curiosity. "See the grooves?" Eska pointed to the three slight indentations that encircled the smooth wood. "And just there. That fiber." Eska pointed again, this time to a single rope fiber embedded in a tiny crack in the wood.

"It looks like a hair. From a dog, maybe."

Eska laughed. "You're not far off. It's goat, most likely. Imagine now three slim ropes made of that hair tied in each of these grooves. They're delicate." Eska reached over and pinched a small lock of Dea's hair between her thumb and forefinger. "No bigger than this."

"What was it for?"

"The Onandya people traded a great many things with their neighbors. Animal skins, pottery, woven baskets. In exchange, they would receive many goods they could not make from the materials native to their lands. One of the items they treasured most were beads of all colors and sizes. It's believed that these," Eska tapped the piece of wood in the girl's hand, "were created to display a prized collection, the beads arranged, perhaps in order of size or shape or material, on the little ropes. A very great collection might even have been able to make a distinct pattern, for this would indicate that the owner had so many beads, he or she could pick and choose which to display. What's difficult to make out is why this was put in the refuse pit. It's not broken. And if I'm not mistaken," Eska said, gaze narrowing as she leaned in close, "it may even bear traces of pigmentation—ochre. Painting, you or I would say, for decoration," Eska went on to explain, noting the girl's furrowed brow. "Very curious. This was an important item. The Onandya did not throw things away lightly."

Eska straightened and rolled her neck to work out the stiffness in it, leaving Dea to contemplate the object further. At least there in the hole, with her tools, Eska could forget, if only for a moment, the Mehathuen woman and her thirty-year ordeal—not to mention her own discomfort at the niggling thought that Firenzia Company had contributed to, no, caused, uncounted situations just like that of Parisia and Xenia's amulet. Around her, the site hummed with activity. The trench progressed nicely and a second was being marked out for digging.

"It's a far cry from my father's dig sites." Perrin Barca, standing at Eska's elbow, had hovered over the work since her return. "Where he knew only speed, here there is structure and precision. I can't imagine my father taking delight in anything someone else chose to throw away." This last was said with a smile, which Eska mirrored.

"It comes with the territory, I'm afraid. The scholars of the Lordican taught me to respect my work and the sites I was privileged enough to be responsible for. It's been hammered into my very bones that I should cherish intellectual gain as much as material." Eska moved to the water shelter erected close to the refuse pit. She reached for a tin cup and ladled clear water from a barrel into it, then handed it to Perrin before filling her own.

"It's admirable," Perrin said. "So many succumb to the promise of a tremendous payout. My family chief among them."

Eska took a drink and made herself meet Perrin's eyes over her cup. "Mine too," she said. She went on, though she could not have said what prompted her to admit such things to a Barca. "My uncle places more value in the object he unearths than in the story of how it got there and to whom it once belonged." She turned her profile to Perrin and filled her cup once more. "I should not speak ill of him."

"I think anyone who never speaks ill of a loved one is lying. To themselves and to the world." Perrin's voice was quiet but tinged with just enough good humor to elicit a smile from Eska.

"Has the de Caraval family ever known Carrier blood?"

The question, unexpected and accompanied by a sudden intensity in Perrin's eyes, caught Eska off guard. She took another drink of water. "It has." She made no attempt to disguise the edge in her voice.

Perrin Barca seemed unperturbed. "But not recently."

Eska was quicker with her answer this time. "Not in the past five generations."

"Manon was the first," Perrin said, his gaze distant, the intensity gone. "First known Carrier in my family, that is. But we do not trace our family history back so far as that of de Caraval. Perhaps I have grandmothers and grandfathers many times removed who Carried. I have no way of knowing. If so, they were fisher folk and weavers, their skills turned to common tasks." A hint of a smile turned up the corners of Perrin's mouth. "Most likely a pirate or two in the mix as well.

We always were a disreputable lot." The smile vanished. "I sometimes wonder what might have been different if Manon had not been born with such a talent."

Before Eska could respond, she spotted Bastien hurrying to her, a piece of paper in his hand. Dreading a summons back to the city, Eska sighed.

"My mother?" she asked.

Bastien shook his head and thrust the paper at her. "From the Lordican, my lady."

Eska brightened. "Albus. Delightful." She glanced at Perrin. "If you'll excuse me." Wiping her hands on her trousers, Eska took the letter. She didn't make it more than five steps in the direction of her tent before a startled gasp drew her back. Retracing her steps, Eska bent over Dea, who, white-faced, fingers trembling, was reaching into the hole.

"Don't!" Eska said. The girl froze. "Not with your bare hands. It's far too delicate. Let me show you." And so Eska, Albus's letter forgotten, her right hand aching with the effort, demonstrated before half a dozen watching faces, the proper technique for extracting a piece of bone from the earth.

———— ◆ ————

"It's human."

The sky was dusty pink by the time Eska was able to contemplate the discovery in the lantern light of her tent. Cedric, Perrin, and Gabriel stood around her worktable, all eyes fixed on the pale pieces of bone spread out on a sheet of linen on the table. Five in all, three of them meant to fit together. Others would come, Eska was sure, but this was what they had taken before running out of light.

"How do you know?"

It was Bastien who asked the question, though he was meant to be eating the evening meal with the rest of the crew. The young man, hands folded in front of him sheepishly, stepped into the lantern light from where he lurked at the entrance. Eska was too excited to reprimand him.

"It's a knee joint." She pointed with a gloved hand to the three pieces set close to each other. "Male, I think. And damaged. The two shards are harder to identify, though likely from the shin bone. We'll know more when we find the rest."

"The rest." Perrin this time.

"Surely you don't think we've found a single knee joint and nothing else? There's a skeleton waiting for us down there." Eska stripped the gloves from her hands.

"The location is strange, my lady." Cedric hunched over the table for a closer look.

"Agreed. The Onandya did not place human bones in their refuse pits. Another question we can only hope to answer the further we dig." Eska rubbed the back of her neck. "Cedric, I don't know if I'll be called to the city in the morning. If I am, your sole task tomorrow is to uncover as much of our mystery skeleton as you can. I am entrusting it to you." The dig master's mustache quivered as he accepted with a bow. "Gabriel," Eska went on, turning to the engineer, "that makes you responsible for everything else. And finally, Bastien, I want you to take a message to Arch-Commander de Minos in the Vismarch's palace. I have need of his opinion."

Bastien hesitated as he glanced first to Cedric and then back at Eska. "My lady, the Arch-Commander is gone. He came to the site earlier, but when he learned you were in negotiations and unavailable, he did not wait."

An inconvenience, that was all. He was not the only person who could tell her if the knee joint might have been smashed by a blunt weapon. And Eska wasn't irked by the fact that she hadn't seen him one last time. Certainly not.

"No matter. Take a message to my mother instead. Tell her I won't be spending the night in the city. If I am needed come morning, she knows where to find me. I mean to spend every moment I can with these bones."

The Firenzia tents were quiet by the time Eska turned her lanterns down and straightened from the hunched position she had occupied for far too long. Wincing as her back and neck uncurled, Eska put aside her magnifying glass and tools and blinked rapidly, forcing away the dryness that had laid claim to her eyes as she worked.

Turning away from her worktable, Eska frowned at the tray of food—cold meat, bread, fat green grapes—sitting on her cot, unsure when it had arrived or who had delivered it. Cedric, most likely. Sighing, Eska poured herself a glass of pale wine, drained it quickly, and refilled it to the brim, her parched throat clamoring for more liquid. She lowered herself to sit on the cot, thought better of it, shifted the wine to the crook of her elbow, and balanced the tray precariously between her ribcage and her forearm.

"This won't go badly at all," Eska murmured to the empty tent. Taking up one of the lanterns with her free hand—sloshing wine onto her sleeve in the process—Eska slipped out of the tent and made her way to the river. A gently flickering light in the distance—south and east across the excavation site—assured her of the presence of a crewmember on watch. Pleased with herself for not spilling a second time, Eska set her tray down among the roots of the willow under which she and Alexandre had sought escape from the sun—was that just two days ago?—and leaned back against the trunk.

The night was cool and clear, the stars twinkling behind the willow's branches, the river rushing by in the dark in that quiet way rivers have. Eska breathed deeply, relishing the stillness, and smiled. She had been to more excavation sites than she could readily count, but while they were all marked by the same sights and sounds and smells, she could remember them all and each of them was as unique in her mind as the snowflakes she had caught on her tongue in the Vachon Valley as a child.

"What will define you?" Eska asked, her question weaving among the willow branches. "Let it not be death," she said, her mind turning to Nero. She rested a hand on the root at her side, as though the earth could hear her plea. "Porcini had the eagles. Armexes the mud. Urilla the mineral-rich smell of the hot pools." She took a deep breath. "Let Toridium and the plains of the Alencio not be remembered only for death."

She could, perhaps, upon later reflection, be forgiven if she had succumbed to the belief that a vengeful deity or the spirit of the Onandya people was working against her. After all, when one speaks of death and then, less than a heartbeat later, nearly loses an eye—and a life— to a knife hurtling out of the darkness as though cast by an invisible hand, well, one can be inclined to believe any number of things.

For better or for worse, Eska was inclined to believe that knives could not be thrown by invisible hands.

She threw herself to the ground, sending the wine spilling across the earth, her heart pounding in her ears, the knife lodged in the willow's trunk without so much as a quiver. Her face pressed against the ground, Eska tried to seek any sign of movement, any whisper of sound to betray the assailant's position, but the willow merely whispered around her and the river answered with its endless song.

North. The attacker had to be to the north, along the riverbank, given the angle of the knife's approach and subsequent impaling of the tree. Eska cursed silently at the friendly glow of her lantern, just at the periphery of her vision. She did not dare move to snuff it out, but nor could she allow her vision to be hampered by it.

She also could not linger. Not when every moment gave the assassin the chance to approach and strike a deadlier blow. This thought jabbed repeatedly at her mind, harsh and insistent, until at last Eska, her fingers scrabbling at dirt and grass, forced herself to crawl on her elbows, her body a useless weight behind her.

Her progress was torturously slow, made all the worse by the fact that she could not move silently. Sure she was as obvious as a wounded, fat wood pigeon fluttering in the brush, Eska emerged from behind the willow's curtain and began to drag herself toward the tents, desperate to believe there was safety to be found there.

She did not cry out, not when the distance between her and the nearest tent was so great. Calling for help seemed a sure way to attract a second knife, this one thrown true.

It was not, in the end, a second knife she needed to worry about.

She heard the bounding footsteps, scrambled to her hands and knees, lost all breath as the man's weight forced her back to the earth, the impact sending a spasm of pain through her chest and the wrist she had injured in the explosions.

She fought. Of course she did. Writhing, flailing, her free hand reaching back for the face she could feel pressed against her neck and shoulder as the man waited for her to tire, his solid bulk a bastion of certainty, one arm a vice around her torso. Eska lifted her head to cry out—a mistake. Her assailant's other arm snaked around her neck, clamping her jaw shut, cutting off her scream before it could leap from her throat, and Eska felt panic rise from her stomach and flee through her limbs.

"Quit struggling, or it'll hurt more," the man growled quietly into her ear, his beard brushing against the hollow under her jaw. The words, the tangible proof that this was merely a man, did what her fear could not. Eska went still, her breath coming hard and fast through her nose, aware suddenly of the smell of soap on his forearm, of the way his feet were rendering her legs immobile, and, yes, of the object pressing into her side, the object that had the shape and feel of the hilt of a knife.

Not that this knowledge mattered. She couldn't reach it. Suddenly she very much wished she had taken the knife from the willow.

It was as Eska berated herself for this oversight that she felt the man's grip on her torso relax.

For a moment she thought she imagined it, but when that moment spawned a second, and then a third, Eska knew, with as much certainty as an archaeologist who had never before been in a grappling match for her life, her opportunity was close—and close enough to pass her by as swiftly as an owl in the night if she didn't seize it.

"That's it," the man said. "The Iron Baron will be pleased to know you went quiet like." He began to slide his arm out from under Eska's stomach, his weight still heavy on her, but his attention—Eska could feel it—on the knife at his belt.

Bucking her hips, Eska twisted in his grasp, her fingers tearing at any part of him she could reach, the Iron Baron's cold eyes flashing before her. Using the fraction of space she had earned for herself, she brought her knee up into her assailant's groin as hard as she could.

The awkward angle did not achieve the satisfying impact she had hoped for. It was enough, however, to make his eyes roll back and the sound he emitted was rather like, she realized later, an angry camel. Most importantly, his grip slackened and Eska seized her chance to scramble away.

No sooner had she stumbled to her feet, her voice croaking for help, aware of movement behind her, than a dark shape hurtled out of the night and tackled her assailant, sending both men sprawling across the earth.

She had expected Gabriel.

The engineer was a strong man, courageous and quick to act. She had seen him spare little thought for his own safety for the sake of others.

The sight of Perrin Barca on his knees, snarling at Eska's assailant, his features twisted into something wild, a knife flashing in his hand, while her attacker bled from a gash across his chest—it was something Eska knew she would never forget.

With a scuff of dirt and a whisper of grass, the two men got to their feet, each prepared to strike, each with eyes only for the other. The hesitation in both was borne of calculation as they shifted their stances and grips in preparation for the other to attack.

The assailant moved first, lunging for Perrin. The younger man twisted aside nimbly, his feet quick and sure, and countered with devastating speed, knife slicing into the stranger's elbow. The man grunted, his hand dropping to his side, pain marring his face. He grasped the bleeding joint with his free hand, forearm dangling uselessly, gaze narrowing in surprise.

They never had the chance to test each other again. Voices among the tents broke the deadly silence. The man risked a quick glance at Eska and then he was gone, racing through the darkness, disappearing as quickly and quietly as he had come.

Perrin was at Eska's elbow before she tore her gaze away from the empty night.

"Are you hurt? Eska?"

She found Perrin's face, saw the wildness fade into worry, saw the knife drop to the ground as he took her forearms, his gaze searching over her for signs of harm.

"I'm all right," she heard herself say, her words undermined by the shaking of her hands.

And then Gabriel was there, Cedric, others, faces alight with lantern-forged shadows, voices rippling with concern and questions. She relayed what had taken place, the words a poor echo of the experience. Gabriel ordered for the watch to be tripled, and for each crewmember to be armed, as Cedric fretted about who would order such an attack.

"Thibault de Venescu," Eska said, her voice stronger and clearer than before. She looked into the darkness where the man had disappeared. Gabriel muttered an insult. "He was sure of himself, sure of success, admitted the Iron Baron had paid him well," she said. "I imagine he will pay just as well for his failure."

"Should we go after him?" Cedric asked. "Search for him?"

She wished for Alexandre in that moment. Wished for his experience and decisiveness. It was Perrin's eyes that steadied her.

"No," she said. "It would be a waste. He will be long gone. It is enough to know who paid him."

If Eska slept that night, it was a fretful and fleeting sleep. After the crew dispersed, hushed voices trailing into what remained of the night, she lay on her cot, eyes staring up at the canvas overhead, her lantern flickering diligently on her worktable until it burned up the oil, leaving her in darkness. Eska closed her eyes, willing herself to find sleep, but within moments she was up, first pacing around her tent, then drawing aside the flap and staring out at nothing.

In the end she spent the night at her table. She wrote an account of the attack, copied it onto a second sheet of paper, then signed and dated both, leaving room for Cedric to sign as witness to the events.

They would be sent to her father and the Firenzia Company lawyer as proof of what had happened. She added a note to the lawyer's copy requesting that he begin researching the private and business dealings of Thibault de Venescu—quietly, of course. She did not want the poor lawyer to earn himself a share of the Iron Baron's wrath. But if she wanted to bring him to justice, if she wanted to build a case against him that would overpower the blackmailing and bribing and violence he would enact in self-preservation, she needed to sort out the rumors from the truth. And the rumors were myriad.

She also needed to follow the law to the letter. It wouldn't do to have her case shredded because of misplaced paperwork or a failure to comply with the most obscure regulations. But Eska wasn't concerned about that. Pierro Gustini was nothing if not meticulous, scrupulous, and possessed of one of the finest legal minds in the Seven Cities of Bellara.

Eska emerged from her tent at the first hint of dawn, finding strength in her resolve to reveal the Iron Baron as the criminal he was whispered to be. But there was another strength she could avail herself of—if he would agree to help.

She was not surprised to find Perrin Barca awake. Nor was he startled by her appearance at the flap of his borrowed tent. He sat on his cot, still fully dressed, shirtsleeves rolled to his elbows, waistcoat unbuttoned, boots unlaced but not removed, hair decidedly ruffled. He seemed older than the young man she had met. Worn.

"Are you all right?" Perrin stood and went to the bottle of wine waiting on his small table. "Wine?"

It was either very early or very late for wine, but Eska found she did not much care. She nodded and waited until Perrin placed a glass in her hand before speaking.

"I did not expect you to," Eska began, then trailed off. She smiled a little. "I did not expect you, I suppose is what I mean."

"I was closest," he said.

"And I believe any member of my crew whose tent was closest would have acted as you did. But I would not have believed that a man who was very nearly a stranger a matter of days ago, indeed, a man who might have cause to despise my family, would have acted as you did."

Perrin gave a shrug, the dismissive kind that showed his discomfort. His gaze dropped from Eska and shifted to a knife on the table, the knife he had been prepared to use in her defense. "I am not unfamiliar with men who use knives in the dark," he said. Eska waited. Perrin emptied his wine glass and sank back onto his cot. He dropped his head into his hands, his fingers spidering through his hair—as, Eska was suddenly sure, he had done throughout the night. At last he looked up at her. "I learned from my brother. Victor was a good teacher and I a better student than either of us expected. When I understood this, I tried to hide my growing skill from him, but it was too late. I had become a tool, and Victor excelled at using people as tools." For a moment Perrin looked as though he might say more, but then he offered a smile instead of the story that lurked behind his face. The smile washed away the worry and wear Eska had seen on his features. He looked young again, and carefree. "At least my skill was used for good last night. I am glad I was able to protect you."

Eska went to the side of the cot and sank down to her knees so she could look him fully in the eyes. "I have an enemy, Perrin. A vicious enemy whose anger will not fade with time. But time is what I need, time to ensure I can expose him and have him sent to the Hibarium for the rest of his life. I am afraid, for my life, yes, but also that I might not live long enough to see this done." Eska placed a hand on his knee. "Teach me, Perrin. Teach me how to survive knives in the dark."

Interlude 7

Excerpt from Corin and Bravi's Genuine & Noble Bulletin

DIVINE CANERO SHINES AGAIN! TRAGEDY AT THE RACES!

It comes as no Surprise that our beloved Archduke, whose Stables are second to None in all the Seven Cities, received yet another grass Crown—his Fifth in the same number of Years—in the winner's Garden after the Champion's Race. His stallion, the Temperamental and Superb Canero, raced as though he had Wings instead of hooves, effortlessly showing his Superior breeding and training. He Soared to an easy Victory, doing Honor to his Namesake, the Celestial Knight Salvatore de Canero, who Slew the last Alescu Tyrant. The rest of the Field ought to be Ashamed for even being in Canero's Presence, though the Archduke was Gracious in his Praise of these inferior Nags.

After the Race, the Horse belonging to Thibault de Venescu, which came in third place, was involved in a terrible Accident, causing both beast and rider to Die. This Bulletin has been told the horse, suddenly Crazed, bolted and Threw the rider, who had the Misfortune of being Caught by the stirrup and Dragged for some distance. We apologize to our Dear Readers for the Violence we must describe—but we have Vowed to always report the Truth and so we Must: the Rider was found with his Skull caved in and the Horse broke Two legs after becoming tangled in Unspecified material. The Horse was relieved of its Misery, some say by the Iron Baron himself. We give our humble Condolences to the Virtuous and Most Courteous Owner, who is a Patron of this very Bulletin.

14

"People with power rely on bribes and threats and call it justice."

"This is not the way to Arconia."

Manon Barca was no sailor, but she had been on enough sea voyages to know a thing or two about headings. Besides, the coast had been shrinking away behind them—slowly, so slowly Manon had watched the sun cross a quarter of the sky before she was certain. The ship, a great three-masted vessel from the Archduke's fleet, was headed west, yes, toward Arconia, but on a course that was angling them, bit by bit, away from land.

Her statement fell on no ears, for she was alone at the rail. Not quite a prisoner, not quite free to roam the ship at will, she had been allowed on deck after they cleared the Toridium harbor. No bonds restricted her movement and below deck she had been given a small, clean cabin. But the soldier who mirrored her movements as though a tether connected him to her made Manon's circumstances clear enough. The soldier was quiet, unobtrusive even, and his hand never strayed anywhere near his sword, but he also never took his gaze from her, never yawned or lost focus. Indeed, every man and woman aboard that ship was a model of precision, both in conduct and appearance. Manon had never seen the like.

She attributed it to the identity of the man commanding the ship, though whether everyone, from first officers to cabin boys, acted as they did out of fear or loyalty or something else entirely, Manon did not know. What she did know was the name of that man, the name that had escaped her in the Vismarch's courtyard.

Arch-Commander de Minos had not spoken a word directly to her. She had been put aboard the Arconian ship the day before, directly after the incident in the courtyard, left to float in the Toridium harbor, to wonder if she would ever see her brother again. She had done what she could, of course, to save him, to be certain all blame for her attempt on the de Caraval ship fell on her. She did not know if it had been enough.

The ship, a behemoth called *Horatio*, had come to life early that morning. Manon, in her cabin, could hear but not see the activity and had assumed that she would experience whatever voyage the *Horatio* was about to undertake from within her cabin. To her surprise, not long after the ship was underway, a young officer had rapped smartly on her door—a polite gesture only, the door was locked from the outside—and then entered and informed her she was at liberty to go above deck. Manon had accepted—more eagerly than she would like to admit. Closed, windowless chambers, however comfortable, had always made her uneasy and the fresh sea air that whipped through her hair the moment she emerged on deck had brought immense relief. The young officer—irritatingly polite—had glanced away, her own hair cut short in a practical manner that defied the wind, allowing Manon the idea of privacy as she let out a deep exhale and closed her eyes for a moment. The officer then told her she could walk where she wished, introduced her to her new shadow—Jourdain, was it?—and then disappeared below deck once more.

And so Manon stood at the rail, Jourdain a very precise distance behind her, watching the waves, watching the sun, watching the gulls, watching porpoises dart around the ship—watching and wondering where the *Horatio* was headed.

"Parnaxes, if you'd like to know."

Manon stiffened at the voice behind her. The tone of that voice could be mistaken as nonchalant, conversational, friendly even, but the experience in the courtyard with Perrin had quickly taught Manon that the Arch-Commander of Arconia was not likely to make meaningless, pleasant conversation with her.

She released the rail, which she realized she'd been gripping far too firmly, and allowed herself to turn to face him. "Why?" She hoped her tone matched his as her mind sought to explain why they were going to one of Arconia's sister cities.

Alexandre de Minos watched her for a long moment, watched as the wind continued to swirl Manon's hair about her, watched as though he was waiting for her heart rate to increase under that stare. He was exceptionally good at watching, she realized, his face betraying nothing. He exuded, if such a thing was possible, the combined sum of all the precision, manners, efficiency, and order that Manon witnessed aboard the *Horatio*. And something more. The predator Manon saw in his gaze in the Vismarch's courtyard lurked just below the surface, shifting, stretching, like sunlight on water.

"Orders," he answered. From the Archduke, then. This man took orders from only one person. "It'll be a short visit, no more than a day. We'll be in Arconia in seven days."

"And then? Is it the Hibarium for me? I'm sure Eska de Caraval would like to see me rot alongside my father." Manon did not bother to—could not have if she tried—mask the venom the name of de Caraval spawned within her.

The Arch-Commander was unperturbed. "Then you don't know Eska de Caraval very well. She puts her trust in the law courts of Arconia. She'd want you to be tried fairly."

"Fairly." Manon spat out the word. "Her father is the Vice-Chancelier of Arconia and her mother is Ambassador-Superior. They have the ear of the Archduke. People with power rely on bribes and threats and call it justice."

"If that's your opinion, then perhaps you'll be glad to know there won't be any trial." He tossed that statement at her as casually as a butcher tosses a bone to a dog.

Manon felt fear grip her insides and wondered if her face showed it. She tried to draw herself up, tried to square her shoulders. "Are you trying to frighten me, Arch-Commander? Do you think to make me beg for my life and my freedom? Perhaps you like the sight of a woman on her knees in front of you, wholly at your mercy."

The Arch-Commander's lip curled in disdain at Manon's suggestion. "There won't be a trial because you are under the Archduke's protection."

It took a moment for the words to sink in. "Protection. What for? What does he want with me?"

"I'll let him be the one to tell you." The Arch-Commander turned to go, then paused. "A word of advice, Manon Barca. You are not a prisoner now, but if you refuse the Archduke, you will be."

Manon scoffed and pointed at her shadow. "Not a prisoner?"

Alexandre de Minos shrugged, the gesture infuriatingly dispassionate. "Think what you like. But I suggest you find a way to keep that temper of yours in check by the time we return to Arconia."

Manon watched him walk the length of the ship, flanked by a pair of officers, to join the helmsman at the wheel. His words chilled her and she brushed angrily at the hair in her face as though she could brush away the effect he had on her. But it was what he had not said that gave her pause as she leaned over the rail once more. Not to her, no, but what he chose to say and what not to say to the Vismarch and Eska de Caraval, who were undoubtedly under the assumption Manon was a prisoner returning to Arconia to face justice. Alexandre de Minos, Arch-Commander of Arconia, had lied.

Interlude 8

Customs Form
#8757-90

Company Name: Barca Company
Ship: Evina
Captain: Roland Realmuto
Port of Origin: Arconia

Ports Visited: Parnaxes, Covinus, Alsara

Contents of Hold: Items from the Temple of Sunnil, Alsara

Five (5) jade figurines
Seventy (70) silver vases
Sixteen (16) stone statues, various poses
One (1) iron horse, headless
Twenty-nine (29) gold-filigree crowns*

*I am instructed to note that the thirtieth crown was left behind to appease the despot who has recently taken power in Covinus. – G.B., clerk, harbor office

Addendum:

Barca Company has filed for financial compensation from the Treasury of Arconia due to the loss of the thirtieth crown as well as for time lost and damages, physical and otherwise, sustained by five members of the crew during the uprising in Covinus. Hearing pending. – A.T., clerk, Varadome, Treasury Division

15

"I imagine that will put an end to our negotiations."

THE SUMMONS DIDN'T COME FROM THE CITY UNTIL THE SUN NEARLY reached its zenith. Eska was loath to answer it.

She and Perrin had worked from dawn until the morning meal, then again until she had a rough understanding of the grip Perrin suggested she adopt, as well as stance, the balance of the knife in her hand, and the footwork that might keep her alive. Eska began their practice with one of the knives she carried among her tools, tucked away in the chest, but Perrin insisted she use his, a piece meant for deadlier pursuits than opening letters. He showed her how the blade was balanced for his hand, and told her she should have one—or better yet, a pair—made to her specifications.

"I can recommend a good bladesmith in Arconia," he had said as they paused for a drink of water. "But I am not familiar with Toridium. Perhaps I can inquire on your behalf." Eska had agreed to this and rebuffed his suggestion that they had done enough for one day. More than a few pairs of eyes had lingered on them over the course of the morning, though Cedric was quick to direct the crew back to their tasks. For Eska's part, she had expected to be distracted by the bones she knew the dig master was unearthing. But she found the sharpness of the blade in her hand and the memory of the man springing from the darkness were enough to keep her undivided attention on her new teacher. Albus would have been surprised.

The summons alone was enough to break her concentration. She was sweaty and far from presentable, and the water she splashed across her face and neck as the messenger retreated back to the city did little to help the matter. Brushing water from her face, Eska thanked Perrin, who offered a tight smile, then took a moment to check on Cedric's progress.

The dig master had succeeded in assembling the skeleton nearly to completion. Eska surveyed the work and listened as he dictated notes to Bastien about the soil in which the skeleton had been found, the depths to which they needed to dig, as well as the distances between various bones and how they were situated in the ground relative to each other. Her mind, as though working to make up for her absence, raced through the information, but she refused to contemplate any theories—not yet. She had learned long ago to shut off that part of her mind during such a task, focusing instead on recording the relevant data so that she might later bring the full weight of her mind and the information gleaned to theorizing. Still, the question Cedric had posed upon the initial discovery—what it was doing in a refuse pit—nagged at her.

Her wrist nagged her, too, though she did not want to admit it. More than nagged, really, the injury rearing its head in the wake of the attack. Though she would rather remain at the dig site, Eska knew an afternoon at the negotiation table rather than in the dirt would be beneficial.

After leaving Cedric with further instructions and the letters to her father and Pierro Gustini, Eska made the short journey back to Toridium and cleaned herself up as best she could. She was traversing the way between her suite and the negotiation chamber and lamenting the fact that she did not have time to find a meal, when loud voices approaching from the other direction hurried her steps. She rounded the corner to find an ashen-faced Chancellor Pelle, attended by a flock of officials, striding toward her, robes billowing in his haste.

"Lady de Caraval," he began, voice hoarse with emotion.

"Chancellor, what is the matter?" It was the Ambassador-Superior, coming up behind Eska, her own entourage at her heels.

The man clutched his hands. "Chancellor Fiorlieu, he's dead."

"Not just dead." The new arrival at the far end of the corridor spoke loudly, authority clear in both her voice and the way the armed men followed her. Her face had none of Chancellor Pelle's grief or distress. Eska felt more than saw her mother tense at her side. The Ambassador-Superior took half a step forward, placing herself and her own authority in full view. The newcomer, a tall blonde woman in a red cloak, came to a halt fifteen paces away, the men spreading their ranks to fill the corridor. "Poisoned."

"Poisoned!" Chancellor Pelle's voice caught in his throat and his hands fluttered to his mouth.

"Poisoned?" Sorina de Caraval repeated the word, the picture of dignity, of calm. Only Eska saw the pulse in her neck. Only Eska knew the Ambassador-Superior was as taut as a bowstring. "Is it certain?"

"Unmistakably." The blonde woman's gaze shifted to Eska. "Eska de Caraval, I am here to place you under arrest for the murder of Chancellor Fiorlieu."

"Murder?" Eska wanted to laugh at the absurdity of it, but some instinct that valued survival told her not to. It also told her that countering this accusation with a story about knives in the dark and the Iron Baron, however true, would not be to her benefit in that moment—or her mother's benefit. The attempt on her life would have to remain a secret. The irony, however, that the Chancellor might have been murdered mere hours after her own narrow escape was not lost on her. "I merely suggested a remedy for the Chancellor's ailment," she said.

"Eska," Sorina muttered, "quiet."

"Eldergrass and finallian root are not a recipe for murder," Eska went on. "The idea is preposterous."

The blonde woman's eyes gleamed. "You admit you have knowledge of this."

Eska opened her mouth to protest but Sorina urged silence a second time and she had the sense to obey. The Ambassador-Superior stepped directly in the line of sight between the woman and Eska.

"Commander, I invoke my diplomatic rights to speak with this citizen of Arconia in private."

The commander smirked. "Granted, but unnecessary. I have orders to confine Lady de Caraval to her chambers for the time being."

"And I may enter freely?"

"You may, though your time will be limited."

Sorina gave a curt nod. "Agreed."

The commander marched around Sorina and grabbed Eska's upper arm in a cruel grip. As she was propelled back down the corridor, Eska, her heart beating in her throat, fought the urge to try to shake free of the woman, not wanting to give her the satisfaction of knowing the pain she inflicted. When they reached Eska's suite, the woman made a cursory inspection of the outer chamber, as though looking for a vial of poison left out in the open, and then, upon admitting Sorina, locked them inside.

Sorina, shaken but not beyond anger, stared hard at her daughter. "What did you do?"

"Mama," Eska cried, "you can't believe I killed him."

Sorina raised her eyes to the ceiling. "Don't be ridiculous. Of course not. But you did something. How else could that commander have your name up her sleeve?"

Eska turned and paced away. "I told the Chancellor to take a tea of eldergrass and finallion root for his stomach pains. You know as well as I do that eldergrass and finallian can't kill."

"That may be, but the Chancellor is dead, apparently after taking your advice." Sorina let out a harsh laugh. "I imagine that will put an end to our negotiations." The Ambassador-Superior sighed and caught Eska by the shoulders, bringing a halt to her pacing. "It will all be cleared up. You're innocent. The man might have died of natural causes. I will go speak with the commander, with the Vismarch if needed. Everything will be fine." She waited until Eska gave a nod, then placed her palm on her daughter's cheek. "I'll return as soon as I can. Try not to worry." And then she was gone, leaving Eska without a chance to tell Sorina of the attempt on her life.

The sudden turn of events, Eska realized with a bitter laugh as she went to her window, at least gave her something to dwell on other than the memory of the night before. Instead of remembering the weight of the man, the sound of his voice in her ear, the helplessness she had felt—instead, she could fume over the time taken away from her work, ponder how a man suffering from a minor ailment might die less than a day later, and, most of all, wonder what the punishment might be if she were declared guilty of murdering one of the highest-ranking officials in Toridium.

◆ ◆ ◆

If the Toridua commander wanted to torture Eska into a confession, she could not have chosen a better method. That is, if Eska had anything to confess.

As it was, she spent her solitary confinement alternating between pacing from chamber to chamber, fidgeting at all of the windows, and composing a letter to Albus in her head—while pacing, naturally. His letter, forgotten in her haste to return to the city, lay unread in her tent.

No.

His letter was unceremoniously folded in her coat pocket, the same long, dusty coat she had pulled on that morning before leaving the dig site.

Seizing on anything that might distract her from her situation, Eska nearly tore the folded pages as she pulled out the letter and broke the seal of the Lordican. Suddenly aware she was parched, Eska poured herself a glass of lemon water and settled into the window seat to read Albus's neat, flowing script aloud.

"'*My dear Eska. I won't say I hope this letter finds you well as I know you enough to know that simply digging in the dirt is the same as being well in your mind—therefore, you are, I am sure, incandescently happy. As it is my chief pleasure to be among my books, it is yours to be sun-beaten and dirty.*'—I'm not that dirty, Albus—'*But now it is my turn to remind you to stop and consume something*

resembling food, just as you have so often counseled me.'" Eska
smiled, the letter so at odds with the reality of her situation that she
could not help but find some joy in imagining the librarian hunched
over a writing desk, absent-mindedly penning the opening lines, his
thoughts flitting back to whatever treatise he was currently engrossed
in.

"*'Your esteemed father has given a speech in favor of amending
the trade agreement with Parphea. Naturally I was not in attendance as I can't imagine a more tedious way to spend a morning
than in the company of political manipulators and over-stuffed bar-
ons—though several of my colleagues did attend.'"* Eska paused for
a moment, the comment about Parphea earning a moment of study.
Though Parphea was not one of the Seven Cities of Bellara, the kingdom had been on good terms with the Seven for generations. "First
new negotiations with Toridium, and now Parphea?" she mused.

She took a sip of lemon water before continuing. "*'But it seems to
have made quite the stir, being the first indication from any of the
senior government officials that action might be taken. I do wonder,
Eska, what your mother might have to say on the subject given the
years she served in Parphea. That reminds me—I should like to ask
her about the friezes in the undercity, not yet having had a chance
to see them myself.'* Yes, Albus, I'm sure my mother spent her spare
time examining underground friezes. Honestly, one might think you
imagine librarians are the only people capable of putting in a full day's
work."

Eska rolled her eyes and nearly tossed the papers to the ground,
the turn of Albus's attention no longer serving to distract her own,
but a shift in the librarian's handwriting at the top of the second sheet
caught her eye and she snatched at the half-escaped pages.

"*'My dear Eska,'"* she read, the words tumbling faster now, "*'two
days have passed since I began this letter to you and I can hardly begin to formulate the words that will adequately convey to you what
I have come to understand since yesterday afternoon. You must forgive me if my thoughts seem out of sorts, but I scarcely know where*

to begin. But in short, the item you left in my care has defied most of my expectations and proved to be even more interesting than I could ever have imagined. You, with your infinite capacity for imagination, likely thought of this scenario and half a hundred more just as unlikely.'" Here the letter was interrupted by several marks of ink, as though Albus had hesitated over the paper, setting the pen to the page only to change his mind more than once.

"'Eska, I don't know what made you want to take a peek inside the Iron Baron's ivory box, but I fear this curiosity will either carry you to immortal fame or be the death of you. How this object got to be in one of the six famed celestial reliquaries from the Alescu era is quite beyond me, but it is a truly remarkable thing, not merely made of metal. Strange as it is to say, the item's most extraordinary feature is <u>not</u> the metal's ability to compress, to fold and reshape itself as you so ably demonstrated. No, stranger still is that the metal is somehow knit together with the faintest hint of diamonds—and a second substance I cannot name. Though my hand trembles to write the words and I might, for the first time in my career, wish to be incorrect, all my research indicates that this is a god disc.'"

Eska's hands dropped slowly to her lap. Her mouth hung open, not having recovered from speaking Albus's words. A god disc. One of the Hands of Fate. Albus gave her far too much credit—of all the imaginative scenarios she had conceived, this one had never crossed her mind. To presume she might have found a god disc, an object so mysterious, so mythical most scholars doubted its very existence, was the very idea of hubris. She returned to the last paragraph of the letter.

"'If you have recovered sufficiently, I'm afraid I have one last piece of news. I believe I know where another such disc is. You must go to Cancalo, Eska. And you must find a way into the sunken vault at the bottom of Lake Delo. You know the stories about the Hands of Fate better than I.'"

For a moment, Eska forgot all about the locked door, about Chancellor Fiorlieu and his unfortunate demise, about her own uncertain future. For a moment, her mind was elsewhere, on the shores of Lake Delo, the water sparkling in the sun. The lure of the vault was so strong that Eska came to her feet—and then everything came back to her.

Her hands trembling, Eska folded the letter, neatly this time, and set it on the desk. Better to put that aside. Better not to dream that dream. Not yet, not like this. Not while an over-eager commander had her under lock and key.

She began to pace once more.

———•►———

As the time dragged on and her mother still did not return, Eska's resentment and anger faded, as did her ability to occupy her mind, replaced by a true sense of fear—fear made all the more palpable by the assassination attempt. And so it was that when Sorina de Caraval was readmitted, she found Eska cross-legged on the floor, hunched over herself, her face in her hands.

Sorina rushed over and lowered herself onto the floorboards, her hands reaching for Eska's. "My darling," she said, her voice hushed and gentle.

Eska raised her head and met her mother's gaze. She knew immediately Sorina did not bring good news.

"The Vismarch did not see me," Sorina began. "I spoke with the commander and Chancellor Nevolis, who oversees the prosecution of crimes in this city. I demanded to know what evidence they have." She hesitated. "I saw Fiorlieu's body. They wanted me to see proof of poison." Sorina squeezed Eska's hands. "I do not know what killed him, but he did not die naturally. The poison strangled the life from him." She took a deep breath. "They showed me the remnants of what he took. I could smell the eldergrass and finallian root, just as you said, but there was something else. And they let me speak with a servant who said the Chancellor had asked him to prepare the tea on your instructions."

"A child learning logical arguments can see the holes in this theory of theirs," Eska said, her voice bitter. She stood abruptly and went to the window.

Sorina was quiet for a moment. When she did speak, the lack of resistance in her voice, the absence of fierceness, scared Eska more than the words that followed.

"Things are not," she paused, "well between Arconia and Toridium. The Vismarch speaks of love between brothers-in-rule, but it is a falsehood, propped up by both rulers so long as the status quo suits them. I only know this because your father sought to warn me. I am afraid the Vismarch may see this as an opportunity to chip away at that falsehood, to shift the status quo."

Eska turned, frowning. "Perhaps if I spoke to him. The Vismarch. Remind him that I am an archaeologist, not a poisoner."

Sorina shook her head. "I'm afraid a few moments in your company, no matter how charmed he was, would not be enough to combat years of enmity between him and the Archduke. He wouldn't even see me, Eska. I think we will find him quite inflexible in this matter."

"This matter." Something shattered within Eska and she lost control of the tension that had been building within her. "Is that how you would name it? This is my career we are talking about, Mama, perhaps my life." A weight on her back, a cold voice in her ear. Knives in the shadows. Eska suppressed a shudder. "And you speak of it as you would a squabble between children."

The words weren't fair. She knew they weren't. Especially when her mother was ignorant of the attack she had fought off the night before. Eska crossed her arms and balled her fists, aware, for the first time, of tears threatening to spill down her cheeks.

Sorina's voice was more frail than she had ever heard it, more frail even than in the days she lingered between life and death after the incident that had given her the scars that covered a third of her body.

"If I speak of it thus, it is because I am frightened, Eska. And I would do what I could to keep that fear at bay. To keep myself from succumbing to it. Because if I let it take hold, I will not be able to fight for you."

The tears and the sob slipped silently from Eska then. Her chest heaved, her shoulders shook, and then her mother was beside her, enveloping her in an embrace, her hand stroking Eska's hair.

"But I will fight for you," Sorina whispered. "I will make this right."

Eska nearly admitted all in that moment. The words sat in her throat, the memory of the night before burning on her tongue.

The heavy knock on the door broke them apart and whatever Eska might have said vanished like a candle flame in a strong wind. Sorina smiled as Eska wiped at her tears.

"I would tell you to be strong, my dear, but you have more strength than a lioness. And so I will tell you to wait with all the patience you can muster."

Eska nodded, not trusting herself to speak. She certainly wasn't about to admit that in that very instant, she realized she had no intention of waiting—not while she was innocent, not while her accusers were building their case against her, not while the Iron Baron knew where she was.

And certainly not while the memory of holding a god disc in her hands—and the possibility of finding a second—sent a thrilling chill across her skin.

———◆———

When one chooses to escape from the Vismarch's palace—via a window and a willingness to climb (fall, really, with many scrapes to show for it) down to a ledge and from there shimmy down a very stern looking statue of a Toridua statesman of old—then slip into the back of a wagon leaving the city and hide between layers of not-quite-dried shark skin while the night guards at the gate made a very lazy inspection, then tumble from said wagon at an opportune moment that also happens to be while the wagon is passing through a very muddy stretch of road—well, when one chooses to do all that, one is not often left in the most discerning frame of mind.

It was Gabriel's tent Eska had slipped into, having waved off—more severely than she ought—the sentries she passed at the edge of the site. Gabriel's because Cedric, for all his many excellent qualities, would gape at her, his mustache working furiously over his upper lip as he tried to rearrange his sensibilities, and she didn't have time for gaping.

Of course, waking Gabriel meant waking Cosimo, but the engineer's partner was a sensible sort of man and capable of not gaping.

To his credit, Gabriel had awoken swiftly and taken in Eska's disheveled, muddy appearance with equanimity. He had then carried out each and every one of her orders efficiently and quickly without even a single question passing his lips, though she could see them burning behind his eyes. Cosimo had made himself both scarce and helpful.

As the engineer had made the necessary preparations and woke the necessary crewmembers, Eska had taken a moment to wash the worst of the filth from her body, using a dipper and a liberal amount of drinking water from a barrel. She had then changed into clean clothes and packed her own belongings, not all of them, of course, but some necessary things.

It was in that moment, of deciding what should stay and what should go, that she made two decisions. The skeleton was the first one. It seemed cruel to leave it unfinished, its story undiscovered. And if she had to abandon the whole site, this at least she could take with her. She had then written a note for Cedric, to explain her sudden departure. He would be tasked with bringing the majority of the crew and equipment safely back to Arconia aboard the *Argonex*.

The second decision was even stranger and more abruptly made and acted upon—before she could change her mind.

As Eska had packed the last of her things, her gaze had fallen on the fox sculpture, its black form nearly golden in the lantern light. She picked it up.

"I've never been one for gods of any sort," she had murmured while stroking the fox, "but if there ever was a god for me, I'd like to think it'd be you. I won't say you've guided me, but you've been here with me, you've been part of every step of my journey. So perhaps I'm trying to say thank you. And goodbye."

And so it was that Eska stood watching Bastien gallop back to Toridium, a dark shape disappearing into a moonless night. He carried two objects with him: the fox sculpture wrapped in linen, the folds pinned closed with a silver hawk clasping a snake in its talons.

"Parisia of Mehatha," Bastien had repeated, nodding to show he understood what was being asked of him. "Who is she?"

Eska had smiled. "A woman with thirty years of determination. She will know what to do with this."

Bastien had nodded once more and tucked the precious cargo in his satchel, then vaulted up onto the horse.

"And Bastien," Eska had said, "say nothing of who you are or of Firenzia Company. Don't linger in the city. Cross the river at the Iluvian Bridge. Ride hard to the southwest. You'll find us before long."

Eska turned away when she could no longer see Bastien. She did not permit herself a final look around the abandoned site, did not allow herself to think of the Onandyan pottery that she might now never uncover.

She nearly ran into Perrin as she passed between two tents.

"What's going on?"

She hadn't forgotten about him. She had merely been unable to decide what to do with him.

"I have to leave. Urgent business elsewhere."

The light of a lantern burning inside a tent exaggerated Perrin's frown. Eska made to move on, but Perrin put a hand on her arm.

"Take me with you," he said.

The light was certainly not exaggerating the note of desperation in his voice.

"Perrin," Eska said, shaking her head. She hesitated. "I can't." She thought of what Alexandre had told her, of the agreement she had made to look after Perrin. But most of all she thought of the training they had done that morning and the look on his face when he was prepared to take a life for her.

Perrin released her arm and his gaze dropped to fix somewhere around Eska's navel. "Please," he murmured. "You asked for my help.

Don't tell me you don't need it now more than ever."

He looked a little like his sister in that moment, but not as Manon had ever appeared to Eska. The night darkened his fair hair to look like hers. There was something in his posture, both proud and broken, that reminded Eska of the other Barca. And when he looked up at Eska once more, the eyes were the same, and yet held a look Eska had never seen in Manon's: loneliness.

It was that look that made her agree, not her promise to Alexandre, not even the events of the night before.

"Perrin," she said quietly, "understand that this is more than the Iron Baron. This is something I do not understand and do not yet know how to fight. Knives may matter little here and it may be that I will be unable to protect you from what follows. To be associated with a de Caraval may become a dangerous thing in the coming days."

Perrin was quiet for a moment, the loneliness in his face replaced by something she could not quite read and Eska began to think—fear— that he had changed his mind.

"I can think of little our families have in common, Eska," he said, "but perhaps it can be said that our names do not go hand in hand with a simple life." He stepped close, reaching out as though he might take her hand, but then he lowered his gaze and made no further move- ment. "My family has a way of abandoning each other," he went on, his voice very quiet. "I do not wish to be like them."

It was Eska who took his hand, who waited until he lifted his gaze once more. She squeezed his fingers and nodded. "I have all the proof of that I could ever need," she said.

Making her way to the two wagons Gabriel had prepared, Perrin following, she looked over the six sleepy-eyed crewmembers who awaited her there. Gabriel gave her a nod to indicate everything was ready.

"I know you have questions," Eska said, shifting her gaze from face to face. She could see little of them but their eyes. "And you will have answers. I promise you that. For now, we must make haste and I must trust each and every one of you. What lies ahead is unknown to me. It may be dangerous. If you would rather stay and sail back to Arconia tomorrow, you are free to do so."

No one moved. Gabriel crossed his arms over his torso, as though daring anyone to back down.

Eska smiled, excitement building in her chest, assassins and accusations pushed to the corners of her mind by the thrill of the journey they were embarking on.

"Let's hunt a myth."

Part
11

16

"Swords negate logic."

Albus had discovered something he hated more than ships.

The rational part of him argued that without ships, this new terror would not exist. Therefore, it was only logical that ships were still at the heart of the matter. But when staring down the length of a very sharp, very pointed cutlass in the hand of a very fierce, very blood-thirsty pirate, well, Albus was inclined to find pirates the greater of two evils.

If Albus were a seafaring man, an experienced sailor or captain who ought to have been alert for these sorts of things, he would have been embarrassed for the ease with which the pirates had taken the small trading vessel, stealing aboard before dawn and silently slit-ting the throats of the two sailors on watch. And when the crew of Albus's ship had stirred into wakefulness in search of breakfast, they had found thirty pirates, steel drawn, unpleasant smiles on their faces, waiting on deck. But Albus was not a seafaring man. Instead he was merely embarrassed by a moment of foolish delusion, a moment that saw Albus, whose most prized skill was his ability to read eighteen languages, attempt to fight back. His chosen weapon: a book. A trea-tise, to be precise, on the battle strategies of Emeric Montreux, the Conqueror of Calviza. The irony was not lost on Albus.

To be fair, the book was a hefty one—Montreux being a prolific wager of war and the city of Calviza being a particularly tough nut to crack—and Albus, after cowering unseen for a moment, had glimpsed an opportunity to deliver a mighty blow to the back of an unsuspecting pirate's head. His efforts, however, were rewarded with a cutlass pointed at his sternum, the book, its binding slashed, pages bleeding from within, cut down to lay in ignominy at the pirate's feet. And so Albus was left to watch the pirate captain, gold earrings gleaming, dark braids clinking—were those teeth?—exchange terms with the captain of his vessel.

The particular pirate in possession of the cutlass poised to carve Albus's heart from his chest had more interest in scouring Albus for anything of value than in listening to the two captains. Without warning, he thrust his free hand into one of Albus's pockets, startling Albus into yelping and leaping backwards.

"That's hardly necessary," Albus said, trying not to imagine his blood staining the blade. "I'll gladly give you the contents of my pockets, if you would just ask."

The pirate stared at Albus as though he had just offered up the Archduke's celestial staff and a year's worth of breeding fees from the Varadome's prized stallions.

"Well, it's only a few scraps of paper." Albus rummaged in the coat pocket in question. "Ah, a bottle of ink." He held up the square bottle, trying in vain to listen to the captains. The pirate captain was saying something about their cargo. She did not look pleased.

The ink did not impress the pirate. "That's only because you don't know any better." Albus waggled the bottle. "This is expensive. Very fine," he said. Though he very much suspected he ought to keep his mouth shut, the words seemed to be stemming from a fountain with an eternal source. "Ah, yes, and I have a handkerchief. Good stitching. See my initials there?" The white cloth twitched in his hand. "Only it's very dear to me as it was given to me to commemorate my first year of study at the Lordican." Albus suddenly clutched the handkerchief close. "Actually, I'd rather you didn't take this."

Only then, as Albus wondered if he was about to die for a handkerchief, did the librarian notice the silence. And then, no doubt the cause of the silence, he noticed the face of the pirate captain, lips pressed together in stern disapproval, her braids no longer clinking, just off his port side.

If Eska had been there, she would have congratulated Albus on learning his port from his starboard.

This foolish thought vanished as quickly as it had come. Eska was not there. Albus was alone. He wondered if she had felt, as he did now, her heartbeat pulsing in the pit of her stomach as she faced the Iron Baron in that dark alley. Certainly not. But Albus was exceedingly aware of the bodies of the two unlucky sailors behind the pirate captain, their shirts dark with blood, their empty eyes staring at nothing.

The woman freed the handkerchief from Albus's fingers and let it flutter to the deck. She then pried the bottle of ink from his other hand, examined it in the sunlight, and let her gaze drop to the unfortunate remains of the Conqueror of Calviza's brilliance. She prodded at the book's splayed spine with the toe of her boot.

"Scribe?"

Her voice was heavily accented, thick with the tones of the kingdom of Seycherra. Albus might have paused to determine if she were from the coastal marshes or the inland lake region of that distant land were it not for her choice of word.

"Scribe?" Albus squared up his thin shoulders and continued in her native tongue. "I am a librarian of the great Lordican of the city of Arconia. I am a scholar, not a scribbler."

Though her crew muttered and hissed, the pirate captain's surprise at hearing her language came and went quickly and she eyed Albus with a newly calculating expression he did not much care for.

"Very well, scholar," she said quietly, a hint of teeth emerging as she grinned. The pirate captain shifted her weight and addressed the assembled crews. "Negotiations have changed. He," she shrugged a shoulder in Albus's direction, "will be the decider of fates."

"Unacceptable!" The captain of Albus's ship burst to life. "Negotiations are done captain to captain. Surely even a pirate honors that code."

The woman's grin widened. "I am bored. The code is boring."

"I won't accept this!"

The grin disappeared and her blade, flashing forth with such speed that Albus winced, came to rest just between the captain's eyes. "You will," she said. "Or you'll watch what follows with my blade up your ass." When she was convinced the captain meant to hold his tongue, the pirate raised her voice for the benefit of all.

"Your captain tells me you have only bricks and wool in your hold." The pirate shrugged. "We will see soon enough. Either he lies or he has wasted my time. I do not like liars. And I do not like men who waste my time. To make it up to me, you will play a game. He," here her sword cut a lazy arc through the air until it was aimed at Albus, "he will play a game."

The silence that followed was broken by a single voice. His voice, Albus realized.

"I'd rather not."

This was, it seemed, hilarious. But then, Albus supposed it was better to make a pirate captain laugh uproariously than make a pirate captain stab him in the belly. Further protestation seemed likely to encourage the latter, so, as the pirate crew began to herd the captives into an orderly huddle, Albus kept his mouth shut.

"The rules are simple," the pirate captain called out. "It is a game of questions. I ask," she looked to Albus, "you answer. Answer wrong, someone dies. Answer wrong three times, everyone dies, you last of all."

Fourteen pairs of eyes stared across the deck at Albus. Some were resentful, some fearful. All were making it abundantly clear that they did not trust Albus with their lives. And why should they? He was not of their crew. He was a stranger, a temporary passenger. Worst of all, he preferred the company of books to the company of people. Albus could hardly blame them.

"Understood?" The pirate captain was waiting for an answer.

Albus tried to draw himself up as he had seen Eska do so many times. She made it look easy. He felt no better for it. In fact, he felt

rather like a small bird puffing out its feathers, attempting—and failing—to look intimidating. It didn't help that the pirate captain was
watching him with a knowing grin.

"And if I answer correctly?" he asked.

"Each correct answer is a life spared."

"Given the earlier parameters," Albus said, "logic dictates that three
correct answers equates with freedom for all." The resolve he heard in
his own voice was something of a surprise.

The pirate captain's gaze narrowed. "Swords negate logic. I set the
rules. I say when you have won your freedom."

Albus hesitated, desperately trying to come up with a means of
making a better deal. He never had been good at haggling over the
price of fish or ink. Impatient, the pirate captain strode toward the
huddled crew. Before Albus could speak, before he was even aware of
the danger, a knife slid between the unsuspecting ribs of a sailor.

Stunned, jaw gaping, Albus stared as the man looked down at the
blood streaming from his chest. He put a hand to it, his face creasing in shock and confusion. When he dropped to his knees, Albus
flinched, unable to look away as the man's life drained onto the deck
of the ship. Three bodies. As easily as shooting a stag or gutting a fish.
It seemed incongruous that Albus had been sleeping moments—mere
moments!—before.

"Well, scholar?"

Albus forced himself to remove his gaze from the dead man. He
met the woman's eyes and understood that she had been watching his
reaction intently. He knew, also, that she had left him without a choice.

Albus swallowed, his heart hammering in his chest. "I accept."

———— ◂•▸ ————

It was all very formally done.

A strange thing, to sit at a small table, the pirate captain across
from him, as though they were discussing a business deal, not playing
with lives.

She leaned back in her chair, one arm slung casually across the back, her dark eyes never leaving Albus's face. Space had been cleared around them, a ring for the chosen champions to grapple in. The dead sailors had been tossed over the side. The pools of their blood, smeared ever so slightly and darkening with exposure to the air, were the only evidence of violence. Albus avoided looking at it, though he knew not if this was out of cowardice or a desperate need to keep his mind clear for the game ahead of him. He supposed they were perhaps one and the same.

The pirates watched with smug expressions, anticipating bloodshed. The sailors waited, mute and terrified. Albus rather hoped one or two of them might be formulating a means of fighting back, of breaking free and rebelling against their captors, but they did not strike him as an enterprising lot. The captain, who Albus might have expected to rally his crew with words of encouragement or, at the very least, stoic resilience, had shuffled to the back of the pack, his face a sickly shade of grey.

"What is your name, scholar?"

Surprised, Albus did not answer.

"I am Keleut, daughter of Nestor, and it is customary among my people to know the names of those we meet in single combat."

"Combat?" Albus noted that she was still armed, though the knife that had so recently spilled blood had been cleaned and returned to its home on her hip. Her sword, blade bared, had been placed between them on the table borrowed from the captain's cabin.

"A skirmish of the minds, if you prefer. Your name, scholar, or another one dies." Though he had just witnessed her dispatch a life with casual competence, the ease with which those words rolled off Keleut's tongue sent a chill down Albus's spine.

"Albus. Albus Courtenay."

"Very well, Albus Courtenay, here is your first question. But first," she gestured to a thickly-muscled pirate with a patchwork of scars on his forearms, "you will look into the eyes of the man whose life is now in your hands. Ichero, choose one."

The scarred pirate dragged a sailor from the group, a young man, fair-haired and frightened. Ichero shoved him to his knees in the empty ring, the puddle of blood his only companion. To his shame, Albus realized he did not know the sailor's name.

"You speak my language, Albus Courtenay, let us see how well you know my culture." Keleut suddenly leaned forward, her elbows on the table between them, her eyes alight with interest. "Once a year, at the breaking of the cold season, people across Seycherra hold a ceremony to honor their ancestors. It lasts for days. We feast, we dance, we race by boat and by foot. We dig up the bodies of our grandfathers and grandmothers and dress them in new robes. Tell me, Albus Courtenay, what do we whisper to their bones before we return them to the earth?"

Albus allowed himself a small smile. "Your people believe the dead make their home among the stars, specifically in a constellation you call the Spider's Web and we call the Shield of Domitarion. You whisper the way home to your dead, so they cannot get lost in the darkness between the stars. You whisper the path they must take, constellation to constellation, from the northern horizon to the Web."

Keleut nodded, neither visibly pleased nor displeased that Albus was right. "You speak correctly." She glanced to Ichero, who released the trembling sailor and directed him across the ring where he was left to stand alone, unguarded.

"Your second question. Your Alescu dynasty took countless treasures from my people when they rampaged across our land, yet were compelled to return one item. What was it?"

"The slippers of the hermit Corvalde, which bore traces of a disease the people of the Seven Cities of Bellara had little ability to withstand in that time, having never been exposed to it before." Albus settled into his chair, relaxing just enough to become aware of the sweat sliding down his neck. "I should note that the intervening years have seen an end to that particular problem."

"Shame," Keleut said, her voice cold. But Albus had the fleeting sensation that she was more than a little pleased with his answers.

A second sailor joined the first, this one making fervent signs of thanks to his ancestors. Albus rather thought he, too, might have earned some measure of gratitude, but the sailor did not so much as glance his way.

"When the city of Rhia attempted to break free from the yoke of Bellara and reduce the Seven Cities to six, who led the rebellion?"

"The disgraced Celestial Knight Vimicus was the face of Rhia's rebellion," Albus began, then raised his voice and pressed on as Keleut's eyes gleamed and her fingers flicked toward Ichero. "But later evidence proved his wife, a woman of Seycherran descent, was the true leader."

The pirate's fingers stilled, but the gleam in her eye didn't diminish. "You have a firm grasp of history, Albus Courtenay. It has saved three of your comrades. Answer one final question and I will let the remainder go free as well." Keleut gestured to the sword set between them. The blade, reflecting the sun into Albus's eyes, was nearly too bright to look upon. "A pretty thing, no? Tell me, scholar, why do all true Seycherran blades have no more and no fewer than thirteen pieces of ivory inlaid in their hilts?"

Albus's tongue went dry in his mouth, which, he was vaguely aware, was hanging open. Keleut watched him, expectant, the slightest quirk in her lips showing her pleasure in light of his silence.

"Come, Albus Courtenay, three times your answers have rolled off your tongue. Where are your words now? Where is your learning?"

Albus racked his memory, his traitorous gaze sliding from the pirate's face to the faces of the sailors whose fate hung on his next words. He swallowed, though his sudden dearth of saliva made it a painful experience, and forced himself to keep his eyes on Keleut and the sword, as though focusing on them might focus his mind.

Thirteen. Thirteen demons in the Poem of the Eid. Thirteen islands off the Onyx Coast. Thirteen diamonds stolen by the god Elontis—but that was a tale from far away Parphea. Thirteen ships burnt by Kora the Avenger. His heart pounding faster with each shallow breath he managed to drag into his lungs, Albus could think of no reason thirteen would be a number cherished by the Seycherrans.

"Time is up, scholar. An answer must be given." A breeze rustled the sails above Albus's head. He could hear—no, feel—the fear of the crew. The ship creaked beneath him, as though protesting what was to come.

"I...," Albus began, his hands shaking as they came off the table. His fingers longed for a book. But no book would save them. "I do not...."

"Very well." Keleut reached for the sword. Ichero was already pulling a screaming sailor from the herd. The blade flashed, whispering in Keleut's practiced hand as she came to her feet. The sailor whimpered.

"Thirteen rulers!" Albus blurted. The sword went still. "Thirteen rulers in the Alescu dynasty." He shoved himself up from the table, dizzy with the certainty that he was wrong, and found Keleut's gaze. "Thirteen men and women who drained Seycherra dry."

The sword hovered. Albus listened to the pounding of his own heart and was sure he could hear the heart of the man marked to die echoing his own. And then the sword was lowered.

"Release them." Keleut's voice was quiet but went unquestioned. The pirates stepped away from the crew of sailors. Albus let himself breathe. "Take him."

Ichero had hold of Albus's arm before he could comprehend the pirate captain's words. The scarred man's grip chased the protest from his mouth, leaving him to stare in utter incomprehension, first at Keleut, and then at the crew whose lives he had just saved. As they watched pirates climb over the rail and down the rope ladder that waited there, not a sailor, not even the captain, ventured to meet Albus's frantic gaze. But at last, as Albus was led to the ship rail, he found some words.

"What is the meaning of this? I answered correctly! Every question! You promised our freedom." Albus strained against Ichero's muscled form, a dry husk of wheat battering uselessly against the indomitable north wind.

"I made no such promise, scholar." Keleut stepped close, her dark eyes no more than a hand's width from Albus's, and spoke in her native tongue. "That answer earned your comrades their freedom. I never said a word about you."

17

"I don't threaten people, my dear, I kill them."

"Wine?"

Manon stood within the Archduke of Arconia's garden—one of a multitude, no doubt. And though the garden had the semblance of a private, personal space, made cozy by stone benches tucked into nooks within the hedges, statues serving as whimsical sentinels, and even a small plot of vegetables as though the Archduke himself might kneel in the dirt and tend squash, carrots, and curling tendrils of peas—not likely—it was, Manon was quite certain, all constructed to appear just so.

The appearance of it all, in fact, was one reason she was having difficulty adjusting to the fact that she was alone with the Archduke of Arconia and that he had begun what was likely the most important conversation of her life by offering her wine.

The other reason was that the journey to that garden within the walls of the Varadome had been both a whirlwind and a lesson in patience. The stop at the island city of Parnaxes, the most northwestern of the Seven Cities of Bellara, had been as brief as Arch-Commander de Minos had promised. Her visit had been confined to a view of the Parnaxes port taken in while she was given leave to walk the deck. They had arrived at dusk and were gone before dawn—and all Manon knew of the visit was the unknown commotion in the dark, deep black of night. The noise had woken her, loud voices and heavy footsteps on the main deck, perhaps even a crashing object, Manon couldn't be sure, and it was some minutes before silence reestablished itself. Naturally, when Manon was allowed out of her cabin in the morning, there was no sign of what had been brought on board, or what had caused the disturbance.

She had tried fishing for information, more out of habit than anything else. Jourdain was speaking to her by then, less of a shadow and more of a companion. Not that she ever thought she might somehow win his loyalty. That was clearly out of the question where the Arch-Commander was concerned. After unexpectedly discovering a shared appreciation for a particular breed of hunting dog, they had spoken here and there of safe things, harmless things.

But that morning, with the port of Parnaxes behind them, in response to her casual comment about not sleeping well and the headache she was sure to get as a result—nothing wrong with the sympathy play—Jourdain said he had slept as soundly as a dead man.

She didn't think it was a threat, not really. But it soured her on making further attempts at conversation, which, she realized, was likely the point.

They'd arrived in Arconia's harbor a day early, a boon from favorable winds the Arch-Commander had told her in that not-quite-conversational way of his as the *Horatio* was moored some distance away from the wharfs due to the vessel's immense size.

They had traveled to the Varadome together, Manon and the Arch-Commander, first by rowboat, then by carriage, but the man said nothing further, apparently his capacity for warnings, threats, and advice fully depleted. At another time, his obvious preoccupation would have sparked Manon's curiosity. As it was, every turn of the carriage wheel that would bring her face to face with the Archduke was all she could think about.

She had been escorted by a herald to the stone arch—carefully and artfully ruined—that led to the paths within the garden's walls. The herald had gestured for her to enter on her own and Manon had crossed the threshold and wound her way within the shrubbery and past a fountain before she saw evidence of another person. A gardener was at work wielding a large pair of shears, trimming the tail on a lion-shaped bush. And yet, as Manon approached and passed by, he snapped his shears repeatedly at the same branch that was decidedly not in need of further trimming. Not a gardener, then. Manon wondered if he had a knife tucked in his boot and then decided the shears were probably deadly enough. The Archduke's elite guards were known to be efficient and proficient.

And now she stood in a grove of lemon trees as the Archduke of Arconia offered her a glass of wine.

"I have a strong red from Deios. Full-bodied. Smoky." The Archduke studied Manon as he spoke. "The white is Sarentian. Sweet but not sickly. Very crisp. Or if you prefer, I have a rosé. Silky, and just enough mineral quality to make it interesting. Quite elegant, really."

Manon had the distinct impression that her choice would matter a great deal to the Archduke's opinion of her.

She had met Valexi Arcturos de Vauquelin-Preux, Archduke of Arconia, face to face once before, had knelt before him and pleaded for mercy for her father, had begged him to consider Julian Barca's contributions to Arconia's coffers and prestige and find in his heart the clemency to grant a lighter sentence. He looked much the same as he had that day, though the guards were now replaced by lemon trees and he was offering her wine instead of tears. Dark eyes, dark hair, an elegant touch of silver at his temple. Black coat suggesting a plainness countered by the staggering size of the emerald on his left hand. He had worn a sapphire, Manon remembered. She had grasped that hand, nearly blind with tears, his fingers smooth and firm and cool beneath her desperate, hot touch. And he had not withdrawn his hand. He bore the discourtesy with silence and dignity and then he spoke words that seemed to shatter like cold crystal in Manon's chest. Manon had no doubt that he remembered that day as clearly as she did, that it was playing through his mind even as it flashed through Manon's. But in that moment he gave no indication he cared about anything other than her choice of crushed grapes.

"I am satisfied to have you choose for me, Commendatore."

The Archduke seemed disappointed with this answer, but he turned and beckoned to a serving girl who had been waiting at the foot of the nearest statue. She trotted forward and gave a quick curtsey.

"The Taracini rosé. Two glasses."

The girl raced off and the Archduke turned back to Manon, his arms folding in front of him, his hands clasping each other lightly. He proceeded to gaze at her with a disconcerting lack of calculation, intensity, or even apparent concentration. But not once did he look away—nor did he speak—until the girl returned, decanter and glasses set upon a gilded porcelain tray. By then, Manon, despite her best intentions, felt entirely undone and depleted.

"It took me more years than I care to admit to learn to appreciate wine." Valexi Arcturos de Vauquelin-Preux handed Manon a glass, then raised his own. "To your health."

Manon managed to utter the expected reply. "To yours and to Arconia's, Commendatore."

They both drank. The rosé was exquisite. But, then, of course it was.

"As I was saying," the Archduke went on, "my intolerance for fermented grapes was amusing at first, but beyond the age of sixteen, my parents found it embarrassing. They made excuses for me not to attend dinners with ambassadors, preferring to parade me about on the hunting grounds or in the music hall instead—anything but the dining hall where I might make a face over my goblet."

He was smiling. Manon swallowed.

"I remember traveling to our sister city of Cancalo. My first visit. I longed to see the waterfalls and take part in the regatta on Lake Delo. But our first night there, I attended the formal dinner. It would have been exceedingly rude not to. As it happens, it was ruder still to surreptitiously pour my wine on the floor under the table, especially when the puddle grows large enough to stain the silk slippers of your dining companion." The smile grew, crinkling the corners of his dark grey eyes. "I was sent home the next day under the pretext of a sudden and highly contagious case of vine fever."

The Archduke watched Manon expectantly. When she failed to find the response he was looking for, he sighed, the smile disappearing. "Vine fever. Ironic, yes?"

Manon nodded, understanding that she was proving to be a great disappointment. "Yes, Commendatore." Unbidden, the image of Eska de Caraval materialized in Manon's mind. No doubt the de Caraval woman would be comfortable drinking wine in the Archduke's garden. No doubt she would know what to say, when to say it, and what artful gesture ought to accompany it. She belonged amid these vipers of the Varadome. The sudden spiteful thought must have shown on Manon's face for the Archduke's eyes showed the first flash of something that wasn't mundane. Manon rearranged her features as quickly as she could, determined to play the game—whatever it was—to the best of her ability.

"Do you like it?" The Archduke nodded his head at the glass in her hand.

"I've never tasted anything quite like it."

"It's a particularly good vintage. Taracini rosés are pleasant enough, but this one is special. Would you like to know why?"

Manon was ready with her answer this time. "I'd be delighted."

The Archduke took a sip. "Lightning storm. As though every god ever invented by the minds of men was casting thunderbolts down to the island. Or so the story goes. Only a few residents of the island are old enough to recall it. But there can be no doubting the superiority of the wine that year. I bought all of it." Another sip. "Perhaps a bit of lightning is the answer to everything."

This was, Manon was certain, intended to have a double meaning. Or perhaps she was only meant to think it did.

"Please forgive me, Commendatore, may I ask why you have summoned me?"

The Archduke drained his glass but said nothing until Manon did the same. He refilled both before answering.

"I hear you recently made a journey to our sister-city of Toridium."

"You are well informed, Commendatore." A foolish thing to say. If there was someone in Arconia better informed than Valexi Arcturos de Vauquelin-Preux, Manon did not know it.

"I also heard Eska de Caraval was there."

Manon managed a nod. The smile was returning to the Archduke's face. She desperately wished it to be a cold smile, or a smile meant to signal his superiority, but it was the same smile as before.

"Do you have any plans for the next season?"

The question was entirely unexpected. Manon attempted to hide her surprise by taking a drink of wine, but she did not believe the Archduke was fooled.

"I prefer not to say, Commendatore." A bold answer, at last. Manon plowed ahead. "These things have a way of getting out. You know as well as I that secrecy is important in my profession."

The smile didn't waver. "Indeed. I won't insist, then. But you know what else has a habit of getting out?" He waited. "Financial," he paused, letting the next word escape his lips as though he truly enjoyed the taste of it, "difficulties."

Manon did not want to think about the state of her facial expression.

"Come now, it's not something to be ashamed of." The Archduke's voice suggested precisely the opposite. "It happens, even to those who deserve better." Manon had the distinct impression that he did not count the Barcas in that category. "Besides, you can hardly be surprised that I might know a thing or two about it."

No, no, she certainly was not, but it was the closest the Archduke had touched on the subject of her father and it made her heart beat all the faster.

He switched tacks again, just when she thought she knew what might be coming next.

"How long have you known you were a Carrier?"

Manon took a sip of wine, but there was no composure to be fished out of the bottom of her glass. If anything the rosé was working against her, feeding off the too small meal she had eaten that morning aboard the *Horatio*.

"I don't remember a time when I did not know it, Commendatore."

"Fire, is it?" He knew even more than Manon could have imagined. As though sensing her deep discomfort, he adopted a conspiratorial air and winked. "Though I don't pretend to understand why you Carriers guard the particulars of your abilities so closely, never fear, your secret is safe with me." A preposterous thing to say. Carriers had been distrusted and feared and ostracized ever since the overthrow of the Alescus. The persecution had lessened over time, and the harbor officer in Toridium was but one example of many of Carriers earning respected, honored roles in society. But just as Manon did not remember a time when she didn't know she Carried, so too did she not remember a time when she did not understand her gift was to be kept secret. But the Archduke was not one to fling words about without thought or care. He took a swallow of wine, his eyes never leaving Manon. "And your brother? The remaining one, I mean."

Manon felt the jab at Victor, as she was meant to, but the deeper pain was the memory of Perrin's face in the courtyard at the Vismarch's palace. "Perrin does not Carry."

"Odd, don't you think, that it was the male Carriers who were so feared during the revolutionary years. The strongest Carriers I've ever met were women. But it was the men the censors tied anchors to and sank to the sea floor." Still he watched Manon, unblinking. "Or, if they had an affinity for water, well, those they pressed beneath stones. Suffocation, either way."

"No need to threaten me, Commendatore. I have no desire to be suffocated." It was the most unruffled Manon had managed to sound all morning and she found she could meet his gaze fully and without hesitation. She took the spark of pride this gave her and let it warm the fire in her ribs—ever so slightly, not to be used, no, for that would mean certain death, but to bear up her spine.

"I don't threaten people, my dear, I kill them."

The spark fled. "Is that why I am here?"

The Archduke studied her for a long moment. "I see the question you won't ask and, as I am enjoying an exquisite wine on a fine summer's day, I'm of the mind to put you out of your misery." He paused just long enough for sweat to bead on the back of Manon's neck. "Your brother has been given his freedom."

Her face gave her away, she knew, showed far too much relief. But that was a price she was willing to pay for the certainty that Perrin was safe. She bowed her head into her glass.

"Do you love your father?"

His ability to turn the conversation, to throw her off balance, was truly remarkable.

"I do not know." She had no more defenses, no more ability to tell half-truths.

He nodded. "A complicated thing, when a parent, who ought to be the source of safety, certainty, and love, chooses instead to bring ruin to it all. Should you love him for who he was? The great treasure-hunter who brought fame to his family and wealth—however fleeting? The father who brought home shells from the seashore and told you stories at night? Or should you hate him for leaving you here in this lonely, punishing world? For tearing the seams of your family into shreds bound for oblivion?" The Archduke watched Manon, no doubt hearing her pounding heart as he gave voice to the two sides of her soul and the endless, silent battle they waged. "You don't need to answer that. Perhaps ever. But I do require an answer for my next question. A prompt answer, if you please."

The silence that followed seemed to demand something of Manon, so she nodded.

"I wish to acquire your services for a series of tasks. The only recompense I am willing to offer you is a reduction of your father's sentence—if, upon completion, you should wish it. The first task I'll ask of you is that you pay your father a visit at the Hibarium. There's a question I'd like you to put to him. Do you accept?"

Interlude 9

The Court Beneath the Sun
Case No. 476001

Presiding Justice: Sarmide de Evonnesque, Ninth Celestial Rank

In the matter of Julian Barca against the City, the Court rules on the following charges:

One (1) count of impersonating a government official ----- GUILTY

One (1) count of sedition ----- GUILTY

One (1) count of inciting violence ----- GUILTY

Three (3) counts of theft ----- GUILTY

Nine (9) counts of bribery ----- GUILTY

Sixteen (16) counts of tax violations ----- GUILTY

Seventy-two (72) counts of harbor quarantine violations ----- GUILTY

One hundred and seven (107) counts of trade law violations ----- GUILTY

One (1) count of murder ----- NOT GUILTY

Sentencing:

Justice de Helore, Second Celestial Rank ----- Life imprisonment

Justice Sici, Third Celestial Rank ----- Life imprisonment

Justice Carvaille, Third Celestial Rank ----- Death by hanging

Justice Davincinni, Fifth Celestial Rank ----- Death by hanging

Justice de Arane, Fifth Celestial Rank ----- Life imprisonment

Justice Theono, Seventh Celestial Rank ----- Death by hanging

Justice de Evonnesque, Ninth Celestial Rank ----- Life imprisonment

Julian Barca is sentenced to life in prison, to be undertaken at the Hibarium.

18

"Blind batriks, what a polished turd of an idea."

"Just like the Pialla Gorge, right?"

Eska watched her engineer as Gabriel stared down at the waters of Lake Delo. Across the lake, the city of Cancalo shone in the storm-crossed sun, vast rays of light streaming onto the rooftops as the retreating thunder rumbled its way into the green hills and rocky, snow-capped mountains behind, taking the darker clouds with it.

The storm had formed and lashed out with devastating speed, forked lightning splitting the sky over the choppy waters of Lake Delo, winds making any attempt of setting up camp impossible, forcing them to wait out the downpour huddled near the wagons. Though they were soaked and it would take a good deal of time to dry everything out, they had arrived, completing the journey to Cancalo faster than Eska had predicted, and the storm had done them the favor of cooling the air.

"Deeper, I'm afraid." Eska squeezed water from her hair, then twisted it up off her neck once more. She followed Gabriel's gaze to the lake. "But unlike Pialla Gorge, where we didn't know where to look, the sunken vault of Lake Delo is so famous, we know exactly where it sits."

"I suppose that's something." Gabriel frowned. "Still, neither of us is one of the famous Taracini free divers. I think we need another plan."

Eska sighed. "Agreed."

"Is it true what they say about the creature in Lake Delo?" Perrin came to stand beside Gabriel. The droplets of water forming on his earlobes glittered like gems.

"Why do you think no one has gone after the vault?" Gabriel grinned. "Only the stories seem to differ as to whether the creature has fifty eyes or fifty tentacles."

Eska laughed. "There are other reasons. For instance, the depth of the lake, the temperature of the water. Delo is always cold, thanks to the elevation. Not to mention the fact that while the stories about the vault differ a great deal, they nearly universally accept the fact that the vault was emptied before it sank, thanks to the heroics of a few swimmers who braved the flaming wreckage of Talarian's ship. Besides, just because we don't know some intrepid diver made it down to the vault doesn't mean it hasn't happened."

"Still," Perrin grinned, "I'd like to see this creature."

"Not up close and personal when you're down there in the dark depths of its domain." Gabriel had the uncanny ability to convey both a great deal of skepticism about such tales and a deep-seated superstition. Eska laughed again.

"Before we go conjuring up creatures, we need to figure out how we're getting down there and how we'll open the vault without a key. There's someone I need to see in the city."

Eska had told Gabriel and Perrin enough—but not all—of what had occurred in her final hours in Toridium for the looks of concern to be immediate.

"Are you sure you ought to be seen, my lady?" Gabriel asked.

"I'll be discreet. Besides, whoever they send to look for me won't immediately know where we've gone. They'll likely assume I fled back to Arconia, where I might expect to find some kind of safety. With any luck, that will buy us some time." Still Gabriel looked unsure. "No one is looking for me in Cancalo."

"I could go in your stead," Perrin said. "Tell me what I need to do."

"I appreciate the offer, Perrin, but the person I need to see is very secretive, very suspicious. If I don't go myself, we won't get another chance at finding him." Eska touched her engineer's arm. "Look after the equipment." She pointed to a village a short distance away on the curving shore of the lake. "If we need supplies, send Bastien to get what you can from the village. Then find a suitable place to make camp. I'll be back soon."

Eska took the horse Bastien had ridden to catch them after his successful errand into Toridium, slung her satchel over her head, and, with a boost from Gabriel, climbed onto the horse's bare back. She grimaced as she settled onto the bony spine. It had been years since she'd ridden a horse bare back. They hadn't forgotten much during their hasty departure, certainly nothing crucial, but she would have paid a great deal for a saddle.

Gabriel saw the look on her face and laughed. "Surely you can buy a saddle in the city."

It was something Eska had considered and already discarded. "I want to save our coin for more important things," she said. "And paying a visit to the de Caraval bankers in Cancalo would be rather like waving a flag and announcing my presence here. I will endure." With a smile, Eska touched her heels to the horse and rode off, turning away from the lake and heading back through the trees to the road that would carry her along the shore to the gates of Cancalo.

———◆—————

She found the right alley by chance more than anything.

In her defense, despite visiting Cancalo a great many times, only once had her uncle taken her to see the man he called the Tortoise.

Eska had laughed, the name enormously amusing to her twelve-year-old mind, and said she expected a thief to name himself after something more menacing and, well, faster. She remembered her uncle reminding her that tortoises were long-lived creatures, creatures who survived despite the world changing around them—and that some tortoises had teeth.

This particular tortoise had a burrow in an alley in Cancalo, and

Cancalo, a city that had grown up instead of out due to its placement between Lake Delo and the mountains that dominated the landscape to the south, was a maze of alleys and narrow places—rabbit warrens and badger burrows, Valentin liked to say, a fond smile on his face.

This particular alley was lined by rickety buildings stacked on top of each other, ladders and rope pulleys and some things that could possibly be called stairs providing a means of reaching otherwise inaccessible doorways. It was a dim place, lit only when the sun was directly overhead, and there wasn't much to distinguish it from any other alley in that particular quarter of Cancalo. Except Eska's roving eye caught sight of a garland of rats lining a doorway some distance above her head as she glanced down the alley. She remembered those rats and the rat catcher behind the door, a memory that raised the hair on her arms. Nevertheless, unless the Tortoise had taken his nest elsewhere, this was the right alley.

She did not remember her uncle knocking on the door with the peeling white paint on a platform three down from the rats, but she was fairly certain her uncle knew the man by the name his parents' had given him at birth and therefore might be allowed to come and go as he pleased. Eska, on the other hand, knew better than to enter a thief's den without permission, but her knock sent the door swinging open and Eska decided that was invitation enough.

The place was dark and Eska let her eyes adjust for a moment. As they did, she saw a table on its side, a lantern smashed on the ground, the oil spilling out to darken the floorboards, papers scattered as though by wind—a violent and angry wind. Eska hesitated, wondering what she had stumbled into, and then her gaze fell onto another substance staining the wood. Blood.

Eska knelt by the droplets, then followed them along the floor to a larger smear. They ended abruptly in the middle of the floor. Frowning, she dipped her finger in the blood and brought it to her nose. And then she smiled.

"Maridell and grove tuber?" Eska said, calling out to the empty room. "It's good, but grove tuber has a very distinct scent, you know.

And the placement of this stain would suggest your body evaporated into thin air, which I find quite unlikely."

For a moment she thought she might have it wrong. Either that or the man whose bluff she was calling might be contemplating spilling some actual blood. But then there was a click and a noise like a door opening, and Eska stood as a bookcase swung open and a man stepped out from a hiding place in the wall.

He held a knife and his large, red-rimmed eyes, set in a pale face, gleamed with distrust. "Who are you?"

Eska folded her arms across her chest. "I'll tell you when you put that blade away."

The man snorted out a sound that was half bitter laugh, half gulping fear and Eska realized he was truly afraid. "So now they're sending pretty women to do their dirty work. Bane's bagged balls, I should have known." His fingers tightened around the knife and he shifted his weight as though to spring.

"They? I work for no one." Eska lifted her hands, palms facing out, and held the man's gaze. "We've met before, you and I. I was a child, with my uncle. Valentin de Caraval."

Her uncle's name brought a flicker of something to the man's eyes, but he didn't lower the knife. "Are you armed?" he asked. And then, with more fierceness and more fear: "Or are you a thrice-damned Carrier?"

"Neither. My name is Eska de Caraval. You are called the Tortoise. We met in this very room when I was twelve years old."

Still he held the knife at arm's length and Eska began to wonder if she'd made a mistake.

"I've come to you about the vault."

The man lowered the blade at last but said nothing, and his eyes did not leave her face.

"Why did you fake an attack on your home? On yourself?"

That seemed to stir him a bit and he glanced at the door, still ajar, behind Eska.

"Not here. They'll be coming." He turned and walked into the next room. "You want to talk, you follow me now. Or you'll never see me again. You stay here, they'll kill you before they ask questions," he called over his shoulder. Eska hurried after him, slipping through one narrow, odd-angled room, catching glimpses of a cobbled-together home—was that a ship's porthole?—then a second room, as piecemeal as the first, and into a third, just in time to see him disappear through a trapdoor in the floor.

They emerged into a tunnel, dirt-bottomed but dry. The man called the Tortoise was already fifteen paces ahead of her. He had grabbed a canvas bag and a lantern somewhere along his dash to the trapdoor, but his hands shook too much to light the lantern. Eska caught up.

"Let me." With a steady hand, she struck a match and held it to the wick. It flared to life, bringing light to the way ahead.

"Smuggler's route," he said in response to the question she hadn't asked. And that was it. Not another word passed his lips as they traversed a maze of passages. Eska wondered if her uncle had ever been below the city, for this was the true rabbit's warren.

It also occurred to Eska that it was a very bad place to lose one's way, especially if one's guide was a nervous, untrusting sort, who had been brandishing a knife not very long before. She soon lost all sense of how much distance they might have covered, and she certainly could not have guessed the general direction they were going. She made certain to walk three paces behind the man, no closer, and kept an eye on his free hand.

They came to the end of their journey abruptly at another trap door, this one smaller than the first and held shut by a latch that looked like it had been recently replaced. After inserting an old key and turning it—with some effort—in the lock, the man pried at the latch with his fingers to no avail, then took his small blade to it.

Eska watched him struggle for a moment, then swung her satchel around to her front and withdrew her own knife, larger, sharper, and stronger than his. Without a word, she reached up and, with a single try, freed the stubborn latch.

The man looked from the trap door to Eska's face and then to the knife in her hand. He glared.

"I thought you said you weren't armed."

Eska shrugged. "Seemed prudent at the time."

They emerged into a cellar that looked like it had been out of use for some time.

"Smuggler's hold," the man said.

Eska raised an eyebrow. "Business is good, I take it."

"Raid last year scared the upstairs neighbor. Keeping things quiet for a time."

"Is that code for the owner of this cellar threatened to expose your business?"

The man grumbled. "Owner is the sort worth keeping happy."

He wasn't, as it turned out, wrong.

———— ◆ ————

"You might have mentioned you had a business relationship with the Regatta Master of Lake Delo."

"I might have," the man called the Tortoise said, "but that would imply we're friends, and we aren't friends."

They stood in a sumptuous courtyard that was, fittingly, given the owner of the courtyard, more fountain than anything else. A pool shaped like a ring encircled them, but for the narrow opening they had passed through to reach that spot. Jets of water arced gracefully above them, propelled by enough force that Eska was rained on only a little. Above them and climbing the walls and balconies surrounding the courtyard, was an intricate network of tiny water chutes and Eska could just make out, if she craned her neck to look, the sails of miniature boats riding the course.

The Tortoise had assured Eska no one was at home, that he did, in fact, have permission to come and go at will, and that the courtyard was the safest place to speak, due to the noise of the fountains.

Eska pointed up at the little boats and their endless circuit. "No one at home?"

"Don't mind the boats, they're always racing. He insists. Now, why don't you tell me how you knew I was hiding and not dead." Now that they were out in the light, Eska realized the man was older than she had thought. His eyes were crinkled at the corners with deep creases and his hair was greyer than the dim light of his home and the tunnels had revealed. But more than that, he had a tired look about him.

"A tortoise likes to withdraw into its shell when threatened, right?" Eska cocked her head. "Play dead?" Her answer earned her a glowering look. "But that performance wasn't for me. Who were you expecting?"

The glower intensified. "Didn't your uncle teach you not to stick your nose where it doesn't belong?"

"Actually, he didn't. Rather the opposite, I'm afraid."

"I thought I was the one asking the questions."

Eska rolled her eyes. "Are you always this miserable?" She threw up her hands. "I'm here because I need to know everything you know about the vault at the bottom of the lake. How's that?"

He laughed then, his face breaking from its normal grim expression for the first time. "You're as mad as a drakspur in mating season. The vault? At the bottom of the lake? Blind batriks, what a polished turd of an idea."

"You can keep your opinion to yourself. My uncle told me you were the best thief in all of Cancalo, maybe in all the Seven Cities. Surely you know something about the locks on a vault that once belonged to the Alescuan kings and queens. And if you say you don't know anything, I won't believe you, because the best," Eska leaned close and jabbed a finger at the man's lapel, "the best always want to know everything about the one thing that might be better."

The Tortoise backed away and shook his head. "Oh, I know a thing or two about that vault all right. I know there's a reason why it's been sitting there untouched for more than three hundred years."

"Please don't say the creature."

"You're thrice-damned right the creature! That thing has got fangs as long as my arm and a mouth the size of the gates to this city."

Eska turned away and began to pace around the interior of the ringed fountain.

"I'm not asking you to go anywhere near the lake, just tell me about the vault, the locks."

The man had apparently found some kind of backbone he was lacking at the moment of their first meeting. His head wagged adamantly back and forth. "Never. I won't help Valentin de Caraval's niece get herself killed because of some fool-brained scheme. He's been too good to me to repay him that way. Besides, I don't do that kind of work anymore." He was muttering by now. "Just small stuff, easy stuff. The kinds of things that aren't likely to get me killed."

Eska came to a stop and stared across at the man she had pinned a great deal of her hope on. "Please," she said, taking care to lower her voice, to take the edge off it. "This is more important than I can possibly even begin to say. Please help me. Tell me what you know."

She got the answer she wanted, but not from the person she was asking.

"I'll do it."

The voice came from above and Eska turned sharply and looked up at the balcony behind her. A man stood there, wrapped in a thin, nearly sheer dressing gown. It was belted lazily, leaving the intricate silver tattoos on his chest exposed down to his navel.

"I happen to know a thing or two about how to open a lock when one has," he paused and showed his teeth, "misplaced the key."

Eska tore her gaze away and looked back at the old thief across from her, who had the grace to look embarrassed. "You might have also mentioned that the Regatta Master of Lake Delo, who is not at home," Eska hissed, "is also a thief."

It was the Tortoise's turn to shrug.

19

"Tell Victor I know everything."

"I'M AFRAID THE PRISONER IS AT REST."

The warden did not so much as look up, not when Manon approached the desk he was enthroned behind, not when the guard escorting her whispered her request into the folds of his massive neck and the ear that rested upon them. His pudgy fingers flicked in Manon's direction as he spoke, in what might have been a gesture of dismissal.

"At rest," Manon repeated.

Silence. Then the warden deigned to raise his chin from his chest and his gaze from the papers he was pretending to bother with. He began to fix Manon with a stare that was surely meant to frighten unfortunate petitioners, but stopped short, leaving his lip unnaturally curled and his brow caught somewhere between furrowed and surprised. Suppressing a grunt, the warden attempted a smile.

"You are far too beautiful a creature to bother with any of my residents, surely." The warden smoothed back the scant hair that remained on his head, passing a greasy palm over greasier strands.

"At rest," Manon said again.

The hand gave an apologetic wave. "Medicinal rest. That's all."

"Medicinal." Manon worked to unclench her teeth.

"The latest standard," the warden went on, far too occupied with attempting to suck in his bulging gut behind straining buttons to notice Manon's rising anger. "It keeps my residents calm. You can come back in a week."

"A week." Manon was getting tired of repeating the warden and she plucked at the spark in her ribs. "I can't wait a week." It was true, and not just because the Archduke had impressed upon her the notion that she ought to work swiftly. Her desperate need to get this done and get it done immediately stemmed from the realization that if she didn't, she might never work up the courage to try again, to face her father at last.

The warden heaved himself up from his chair and ventured around the desk. "You are clearly a woman of good taste. May I offer you a glass of wine? I have a very fine vintage I've been waiting for the right occasion to open."

The spark flared and Manon forced herself to snuff it out. "I don't think you understand. I will see Julian Barca now."

The warden's wide face showed a hint of annoyance. "You could see him, but he won't be coherent."

"What do you mean?"

"He'll be up to his eyeballs in the dread, is what I mean," the warden spat out, the mask of chivalry slipping. "Won't know your face or name."

Manon nearly let the spark out, but the guard who had taken her to see the warden cleared his throat. "Sir, prisoner Barca isn't scheduled for dosing for another hour."

The warden turned his glare onto the guard, who, to his credit, seemed as unaffected by his superior's ire as Manon—and any other woman, she imagined—had been by his attempts at being charming.

"Visitors for all high-level prisoners must be approved in advance," he growled. "And none have been cleared for prisoner Barca." He turned away from Manon and made to return to his berth behind the desk. "But," he said, swinging his ample girth back around, "you might be able to," he paused to look Manon up and down, "convince me."

The Archduke could have chosen to make her visit easier. He could have given notice of her impending arrival. He could have made all the arrangements. But that would necessitate connecting himself to this visit, which he certainly would not do. And besides, Manon was quite sure he wanted to make this as difficult as possible. Without blinking, Manon reached into the leather bag hanging from her shoulder and withdrew a velvet pouch, pulled out a dozen large gold coins, and tossed them at the warden. The Archduke *had* furnished her with funds to use as she needed. This was needed.

He caught one—barely—the rest clinking loudly against their brothers and sisters as he fumbled them against his chest and they dropped to the floor. The guard looked away. A familiar habit, Manon guessed.

A discreet man would have understood the value of the coins on sight. A subtle man would have let them remain where they fell, perhaps even offer a slight bow. The warden, neither discreet nor subtle, proceeded to scramble under his desk and collect every last coin with all the grace of a pig rooting for scraps in the mud. But in the end his lust for gold proved greater than his lust for flesh and he graced Manon with a final leer before directing the guard to lead her away.

The guard took Manon from the dim chamber and escorted her back to the main entrance and the central shaft that stretched to the top of the vast tower. A network of staircases, cages on winches, and platforms with simple rope pulleys crisscrossed the shaft and climbed its sheer walls, providing access to all levels of the tower. The guard led Manon up a particularly treacherous stairway that leaned at an odd angle away from the stone wall, then on to a platform hardly large enough for the two of them. It wobbled reassuringly as Manon boarded.

"Might want to hold on to something, my lady," the guard said. After removing a locking device, he began to haul them skyward, hand over hand on a well-worn rope. As he worked, sweat forming on his hairline, he glanced at Manon with an apologetic smile. "It's not very elegant, my lady, all these ladders and pulleys. But it serves a purpose. There's a reason why this tower is still in use."

"Yes," Manon murmured, having quickly discerned why the patchwork infrastructure in the Hibarium would never be replaced with more efficient methods. "Hard to escape when your chosen route is as likely to send you to your death as deliver you to freedom."

The guard nodded. "And we move them," he said, pride burning away some of his sheepishness. "Just yesterday, this platform led to an entirely different level." He paused in his work long enough to tap the side of his skull with a finger. "Memorizing them does you no good." The platform shuddered beneath Manon's feet, the rope creaking with a certain degree of weariness, and the guard returned to hauling with both hands, this time with a new sense of urgency, Manon saw. She peered over the edge of the platform. The shaft opened up beneath her, darkness upon still more darkness. She wondered how many bodies lay at the bottom and if her father had ever considered becoming one of them.

They reached their destination, coming to a shaky halt at one of the highest levels of the tower. Manon looked down at the gap between the platform and the safety of the solid rock landing beyond.

"Faulty rigging, my lady," the guard said, pointing up. "Doesn't always align properly. Let me go first, then I'll help you." He made to step across the gap, but Manon stopped him with a forceful hand on his shoulder.

"You probably ought to set the lock, don't you think?"

Flushing crimson, the guard replaced the mechanism that would prevent the platform from plunging down the moment he let go. Manon hardly had to stretch her long legs to bridge the gap, and she was sure to set the platform swinging—just enough to make the guard clutch the rope with both hands.

"And I'm no lady," she said.

The guard hurried after her. "Just to your right, my lady. His cell is at the end of the row."

Manon's steps carried her the distance swiftly, but she paused before they could take her within the line of sight of the prisoner in the last cell.

"I see he has a window."

Light filtered between the bars of the cell, dust floating in shafts of hazy gold. It was not very different, Manon thought, from the way the light flooded across the terrace at the house on Isle de Gaustin, finding its way between the trunks of the peach trees as the sun rose. They had come for her father between those trees, breaking the morning glow. Manon had dropped her porcelain cup of tea as she rose up, heedless of the painted shards coming to rest at her feet. He had told her not to worry, told her that even as they struck him across the shoulders and sent him to his knees, even still as they lashed out at him once with a short whip, drawing blood through his white shirt, and dragged him from the garden. All before Manon could say a word. She had been left with tea steaming on the stones beneath her feet, the golden light of morning reforming in their wake.

"Manon."

———•—————

"You have grown."

Julian Barca studied Manon from behind the bars of his cell, his mane of dark hair made all the starker by the glowing light behind him. His silhouetted form made it difficult to make out his face, but the voice was just as she had heard it in her dreams for four years—that is, the voice was whatever Julian Barca wanted it to be.

That had always been his gift, the thing that set him apart from other men. He had an eager mind and a quick wit; he was bold, decisive, restless, eager to make his mark upon the world. And though he was skilled in many ways of achieving his ends, it was his voice that had carried him so far in life. Not his words. He was no great smith of language, no. But his voice alone could convince a steadfast soldier to sell himself to the enemy, a devoted priestess to turn her back on her god, or a loving father to abandon his children—if that was what Julian Barca wanted.

In that moment, Manon did not know what Julian Barca wanted.

"That is generally what happens, father, when four years see a girl become a woman." She hoped he would not recognize her dismissive response for what it really was—a defensive posture.

"Ah, but you were never truly a girl, were you Manon." Her father tilted his head, studying her. Still she could not make out his features clearly. "There was always something old within you."

Manon turned to the guard. He was hovering within earshot while attempting to appear deaf. "Leave us." For a moment she thought he might refuse, but then he shrugged and retreated around the bend of the curved hall leading to her father's cell. No doubt he would be straining to catch what he could, eager to report back to his comrades what was said between the prisoner and the daughter who had not visited once in four years—but he was out of sight and the other cells were empty and Manon could at least pretend what came next would be a private conversation.

"You've caused quite a stir, I'm sure," Julian said. "They'll still be talking about your visit in a month's time."

"You always did appreciate a good story, father, and a good show."

Julian Barca's silhouette shrugged. "People hear what they want to hear and see what they want to see. Give them what they expect and they will give you the world in return."

"Grand words for a man who tried to take the world and ended up here for his troubles," Manon said.

"No reward without risk."

The cool response set Manon's spark blazing.

"Is there no repentance in you? Do you feel no remorse for what you have done?"

Silence. Her father was still a shadow haloed by blazing sun. He would have liked that image, if only he could see it. Then again, he probably knew exactly how he appeared in that moment.

"You left your wife and children penniless. Does this not shame you? You roamed in search of treasure you could not find, forsaking all investment for the future, spending money you never had. Had you no thought for anyone but yourself?"

More silence.

"Once I thought you the greatest of men, but I learned you are nothing more than a selfish coward. You deserve to rot in here."

Julian Barca said not a word.

Manon clenched her fists, all too aware that he had the upper hand. He had always had the upper hand. She stared into his shadowed face, desperately in search of traction, willing him to break.

He spoke. But he did not break.

"Such a tirade deserves a final flourish. A grand exit. You should be striding away from me, your shoulders straight as stone, your head held high, the resolute tread of your footsteps telling me I'll never see you again. And yet here you are." Her father stepped closer to the bars in the very same moment a cloud passed between the sun and his window, dispelling the golden light. He could not have timed it better if he had been setting the stage to reveal an ancient treasure to the Archduke himself. Manon could not look away from the blue-eyed gaze that suddenly pierced her. "You had better tell me what you want, daughter."

There were so many questions she could choose to ask, so many things that needed telling. For a long moment, Manon longed to find the words that would bring her father back to her, the father who had made her laugh, who had shared his secrets, who had commanded every room he ever walked in to—most of all, the father who had told her not to worry and made her believe it.

"Come, tell me your dreams, Manon."

He waited. Oh, he was good at waiting. And even though he was the next to speak, the words seemed another kind of waiting.

"Very well, I'll tell you my dream for you first, and then you can tell me what brings you here." He shifted slightly and leaned one shoulder against the bars of his cell. "I dream of you, raising up our family name so that it is spoken in the Varadome once more, so that the people of Arconia thrill to hear it." His voice was deadly earnest, all fierce growl and smooth persuasion. "Manon Barca, she who discovered the lost city of Dumoduo, she who found the fabled lighthouse of Bellonis or brought home the golden pillars from the temple of the nine gods of Hasheptsyl. Those are dreams worthy of a Barca, worthy of you, and you could take that future for yourself."

Manon wanted to laugh. "With what funds, father? You speak absurdities. Or did you forget that you left Barca Company nearly bankrupt? Our coffers are empty. Our last ship is seized. I won't have the coin to pay the next rent on the home I grew up in. And you want me to waste away on your hollow, unreachable dreams of glory. Just as it was before they put you in here. Nothing has changed." Manon stepped close to the bars that separated them but found she did not have the fury to speak more.

"Why are you here?"

Julian Barca sounded tired, but there was something in his face that did not match his voice.

She ought to have disguised the question. Folded it into another conversation, covered it with a cloak of deceit, poked and prodded and found out what she needed to know without having to ask for it outright. Eska de Caraval could have done it. The Archduke was the master of such methods.

But not Manon. She had only one method.

"Your medicinal rest is nearly upon you, father. Do you enjoy that? Being drugged with the dread until you don't know your own name? Until you hallucinate all manner of horrors? How long will it take you to find yourself again? A day? A week?"

The cords and muscles in Julian Barca's neck tightened and there was something that might have been fear in his eyes. No, not fear, Manon realized. A revulsion for the weakness he knew she could see.

"Tell me what I want to know, father, and I will see that you are spared." Manon gave a small shrug. "This time at least. I won't be here when they come with your next dose." She took a deep breath. "You know where two of the six celestial reliquaries of the Alescu dynasty are. Tell me where to find them."

"Perhaps you have the will to run my company after all," Julian murmured. "I had thought that little pet project of mine to be a fairly well-kept secret." He straightened and released the bars. The sun was emerging behind him once more, the gold armor returning to envelope him. "Well, you said it yourself, Manon. I'm a selfish coward." He smiled at her. "Unfortunately, your information is incorrect. I only know where one of the Alescuan reliquaries is. You might enjoy a visit to the Onyx Coast. The Ulgorian era stone circle at Pontevellio is quite awe-inspiring."

Relief coursed through Manon and she felt the knot in her stomach loosen. She managed a nod, not trusting herself to speak, then turned and retreated from the cell and the golden light, her legs heavy and ungainly beneath her.

"And Manon?" Her father's voice was not that of a man who feared the dread or the isolation that would follow. It was the voice of a man who held the world in his grasp. And it was terrifying.

Manon fought the urge to look back and forced herself to continue walking, her gaze fixed on the empty hall in front of her.

"Tell Victor I know everything."

She nearly stumbled, but somehow she kept her feet, kept walking. Behind her there was only silence.

20

"Knowledge is my greatest treasure."

THE REGATTA MASTER OF LAKE DELO HADN'T BOTHERED TO CHANGE from his dressing gown.

As a result, Eska spent a good deal of their initial conversation trying not to look too closely at the tattoos on his chest. They were words mostly, but reading them would have required staring.

The Tortoise had scampered away when the Regatta Master had announced he'd be joining them in the courtyard, leaving Eska alone amid the jets of water.

"I apologize for the intrusion," she began when the Regatta Master appeared from an arched doorway fitted with a shutter-like door.

"No apologies necessary. I returned home unexpectedly only shortly before sunrise. The Tortoise can be forgiven for assuming my absence." He stood just inside the arc of the fountain, framed by mist turned to rainbows by the sun. Diamond studs, sparkling jealously alongside the water, lined the rim of his left ear.

He made no attempt to conceal his assessment of Eska, his gaze sliding the length of her.

"And I had thought my companion from the night before last beautiful."

Eska laughed. "You would flatter me before knowing who I am or what I am doing here?"

The Regatta Master shrugged. "You may think I merely flatter if you like, but you yourself announced your purpose here, so we're halfway to quite the intimate relationship, I should think."

"Ah, then you think to shock me. I assure you, that is not as easy as you might imagine." Eska let her own gaze drift to his chest and then down to where the sash tying the sheer gown in place was barely doing its job.

"Oh, I can imagine a great deal." He smiled then, a dazzling smile to match the diamonds in his ear. But it was also unexpectedly genuine, and it was for that reason Eska felt herself smiling in return.

She began to speak, but, as though sensing that her mind was turning to other matters, the Regatta Master cut her off.

"I'm famished. And I never do business on an empty stomach. Can I offer you some refreshment?"

Some refreshment turned out to be an elaborate spread of cheeses, olives, spiced nuts, fruit, pickled things, cold meat and a very fine bottle of wine. All of which he gathered himself, disappearing briefly behind a different shuttered door, then reappearing some moments later on a large balcony opposite the one onto which he had first emerged. After setting a laden tray down on a small table, he called down to Eska.

"Well? Better find your way up here."

Amused and marginally perplexed, Eska entered the house via the second door he had used and, after only two wrong turnings, found a set of stairs. These she climbed to a beautifully decorated chamber, part library, part office, part garden. Warmed by the sun streaming through windows and the three sets of doors to the terrace, now all flung open, Eska walked on earth-toned tiles past tall ferns and between gauzy white curtains billowing gently in the breeze and out onto the terrace.

Eska waited while he poured the wine into blue crystal glasses. After handing her one, he made as though to touch his glass to hers, but then pulled back.

"I never drink with anyone whose name I don't know," he said.

"Eska." That was enough for the time being.

He raised an eyebrow. "Just Eska?" But he wasn't really prying, she could see. The dazzling smile flashed once more. "Very mysterious."

"And yours?"

"Should I be insulted you don't know it?"

"If you must."

The man laughed and leaned back against the railing. "Eden."

"Very informal."

"You started it."

They both smiled then, recognizing something in the other, and the crystal clinked between them.

"I'm not a thief, you know," the Regatta Master said as he slipped into one of two chairs and plucked up a grape. He rolled it between his fingers and then popped it in his mouth.

"Neither am I." Eska took the other chair and sipped her wine.

"And yet here we are discussing how to open a vault that hasn't been opened in more than three hundred years." He spooned out a slice of soft cheese with a minuscule knife. "I'm a consultant of sorts. When I'm not organizing the annual regatta, of course. Which keeps me very, very, very," he drew each repetition out longer and longer, "busy."

"Of course. And what sort of things, may I ask, do you consult on?"

"Security sorts of things. The extraordinarily wealthy tend to be quite paranoid, if you haven't noticed, Eska. They like to keep the things that make them wealthy safe. I assist them. I also assist those who have," he paused and looked Eska in the eye, "an interest in ac-quiring those things."

"You play both sides."

Eden cast his head back in exaggerated horror. "You wound me. Such a vulgar way of saying it." And then he winked.

Eska laughed. "I give you permission to phrase it however you like. I myself am the owner of a fine set of lock picks, though I've never quite gotten the hang of them. But why trust me with this?"

Eden studied her for a moment. "You came here with a man I most-ly trust."

"Mostly."

"More importantly, I trust my own judgment. It's a great deal more reliable than trusting anyone else."

Eska, who also happened to trust her own judgment, could appreciate this. She chose an olive and then speared a piece of meat with a tiny silver trident. "What makes you think you can get to the vault and open it?"

"Tell me why you want it open and then I'll give you my answer."

"Tell me about your tattoos first."

If Eden was surprised, he didn't show it. The grin that curled his lips was exceedingly sensual. He pushed back his chair and stood, then, without taking his eyes from her, undid the sash holding his robe closed. He let it fall from his shoulders to the ground.

The silver ink covered nearly every part of him, forming words across his chest and abdomen, patterns that ran down his thighs, symbols on his arms. He turned slowly so that she might see his back, his sun-bronzed skin moving over lean but strong muscles. From his shoulder blades down to his pelvis, the silver ink caressed his skin in the shape of a phoenix in the moment of immolation, wings spread wide, flames consuming all.

"Well, you do make a good canvas."

Eden roared with laughter and turned back to face her. He retrieved his robe from the terrace tiles, draped it over his shoulders, and returned to his chair.

"Do you put on such a show for all your visitors?"

"I see no reason to find shame in the beauty of the human body. Modesty is a crutch for those who seek to control others. But, no," Eden grinned, "I am not always so inspired."

"What does it all mean?" Eska selected an apricot from the tray and took a bite, the skin over the ripe fruit peeling back under teeth.

A more serious expression settled over the Regatta Master's face. "My family has been in Cancalo for many generations. But once we had roots in a small country called Venadascar. It no longer exists. Swallowed up by the might of Irabor at the end of its years of conquest.

My people chose that moment to leave, rather than face the undoing of everything they understood and held dear. They took little in the way of possessions, but they carried with them their memories and among those memories was a poem, the kind of poem that tells the story of a people." Eden gestured to his torso. "This is but a glimpse of the words they passed down through the generations of my family, a verse that I chose for myself."

Somehow Eska knew not to ask about that verse. "And the phoenix?"

"A symbol of Venadascar. Not of its dead war lords, but of the very land itself."

"It's beautiful. As is the body that carries it." It was not said with a smile or a knowing glance or a gleam in her eye, not in the wake of the sincerity he had shown her. "Thank you for sharing it with me."

"I usually tell people it was copied from an ancient erotic manual." The grin returned to Eden's face.

Eska laughed. "With the intent of getting them into your bed or chasing them away?"

"Both. And with a very high rate of success, I might add. It's all a matter of knowing your audience."

"And to which audience do I belong?"

Eden smiled again, that strangely dazzling, genuine, warm smile. If she weren't already warmed from the sun over the terrace, Eska knew he would have seen a flush on her cheeks.

"The one that gets the truth, apparently." Eden emptied the wine from his glass. "Now, I've told you about my ink. It's time you told me why you want the vault in the lake open."

"Because I want to see inside." Eska ate a grape and smiled at the Regatta Master's raised eyebrow. She ate another grape and then settled back in her chair. "I don't believe the stories, the ones that say it's empty. I'm an archaeologist. An academic. My research indicates there's something in that vault. Something I would like to see raised from its watery grave."

The eyebrow stayed up. "You'll have to do a bit better than that."

Eska raised her hands in defeat. "It was worth a shot." She waited while Eden poured them both more wine, using the moment to choose how candid she wished to be. She watched the light play off the silver letters on his chest He watched her expectantly.

"Have you ever heard of the Godforged? The Hands of Fate?"

Eden shook his head, the diamonds in his ear glittering.

"Not many have. It's an old story, one of the oldest, as far as those who have studied it can tell. There were twelve, once, or so the story goes. Plucked from the moon or a fallen star, or fashioned from the hearts of twelve griffins, or forged in an island volcano by inhuman hands. Immortal hands, or at least close enough. There were probably as many stories about their origin as there were discs. They were given to twelve rulers, kings and queens of lands whose names we've long forgotten. Six disappeared soon after. How and why, we do not know. But six remained. The Hands of Fate they were named. Or Godforged, depending on which stories you might be inclined to trust. By whatever name, their stories are woven into the making and breaking of power for years uncounted. Until they vanished. Stolen, lost, reclaimed by their creator." Eska shrugged. "They became legends and then myths and then they were forgotten. Mostly. Few believe they ever existed, that they were created by mortal minds to explain the unexplained. Just as we create heroes when we need them most."

"And you believe?"

Eska sighed, trying to put words to the very thing she had grappled with since childhood. "It's not so much a matter of believing to me. I don't follow any gods. I hold the human mind as the most powerful thing in the world—after the chaos of nature, of course. Everything I have read and studied points to the existence of something, not just an idea or a story, something physical. Whether that something is capable of controlling the winds or tearing down walls or speaking to the dead…" she trailed off. "I reserve the right to doubt. But I also know that there are people who walk this earth who can conjure and control water and fire, and all the librarians and scholars in the world couldn't convince me there are not stranger things still that I will never lay eyes on." Eska looked at Eden, aware that she was, in some way, laying bare her soul not unlike he had. "And while I work within a domain of logic and common sense and evidence, I do not deny that I am also drawn to the idea of things I cannot imagine or comprehend."

Eden had not taken his eyes off her as she spoke. "And if one of these Godforged is in that vault. And if it can do the things the stories say it can. What then? What happens when you bring it out of the darkness of myth and into the light of this age?" There was no accusation in his voice, no judgment.

It was a question that had lurked on the edge of Eska's mind since fleeing Toridium in the night, Albus's letter freshly imprinted on her mind, but not one she had truly put words to, as Eden did in that moment, or allowed herself to think on.

"Then I have to think that the human mind, that second most powerful force in the world, will be able to think of a means of containing it." Eska stood, not sure how well she was bearing up under the weight of his gaze. She went to the balcony's railing and spread her hands down the length of the warm iron. She could see a slice of the blue waters of Lake Delo. "Knowledge is my greatest treasure. But it is also my greatest weakness. And now that I am here, now that I have been led to the vault out there," she went on, gesturing to the lake, "I cannot let it go." Her blood was rushing in her ears by the time she finished and she didn't hear Eden get up from his seat, didn't hear his footsteps.

But she did feel his hand on hers.

"Do you know, I think that perhaps for the first time in my life, I am persuaded that the beauty of the human mind is perhaps greater than that of the human form." His voice was low, earnest, slightly surprised. Eska dared to lift her gaze from where his fingers brushed hers. And somewhere in his dark eyes she forgot he was nearly naked, forgot they had just met, forgot what, precisely, she was doing there. "And to find both together," he went on, "combined to the highest degree of perfection. It seems I am in rare company."

Eska tried to laugh. "Now you do flatter me."

Eden gave a small smile. "Ah, Eska," he said, sadness interlacing with the humor in his voice, "now you do wound me. You and I, strangers who have given each other a piece of ourselves. I would not be foolish enough to throw that away with careless, empty words."

He kissed her then. Or she kissed him, she wasn't really sure. Either way, it was the kind of kiss she had not had in a very long time.

There could have been more. Eska opened her eyes at the end of the kiss and saw the same desire she felt looking back at her. But they both drew back. Not entirely. Eden's hand remained on her waist, hers on his warm, silver-inked arm, and she could practically count his eyelashes. But it was as if they both knew there was business yet to conduct, and that if they didn't immediately return to the matter that had brought Eska to his door, well, it might be a rather long time before they managed it.

"I can get you into that vault," Eden said.

———•———

The warehouse on the shore of Lake Delo smelled faintly of resin and alcohol. Wood varnish, Eska realized, as she followed Eden through doors wide enough to allow a ship's hull to pass through.

The interior was dim and cool—and vast. That was the second thing Eska noticed. She was aware of Eden watching her take it in, just as she had been aware of his—now fully clothed—presence beside her on the bench seat of the small, open carriage they had taken to the warehouse district. Just as he had prepared the meal himself, he had driven the carriage himself, and the guards at the warehouse were the first sign of anything resembling a servant. They greeted the Regatta Master with respect, one murmuring a "Good morning, Master San-Germain"—giving Eska his full name at last.

"My workshop," Eden San-Germain said. "It serves also as a boat-building school, a ship-designer's paradise, and a test facility. Master ship-builders come from all over the world to learn and share techniques and tools."

"Test facility?" Eska asked.

Eden grinned. "Below-ground pool, not to mention the slipway to the lake when our tests require more space."

They stood between the bones of two ships, one, a swift, slender racer nearing completion, the other a much larger beast, a pleasure barge only beginning to take shape. In the shadows beyond, Eska could see more hulls under construction.

"How does one get to be the Regatta Master of Lake Delo? And how does anyone work in such poorly lit conditions? And where is everyone?"

"Ah, I believe you'll have an answer to the second in a moment." As Eden finished speaking, a loud metallic clang in the rafters had Eska looking up. The sound of wood grinding against wood followed, and then a crack appeared in the roof, widening gradually as a large section of the roof slid open. Three men, Eska saw, worked a system of ropes and pulleys from the ground. When they finished, they moved deeper into the warehouse and began to repeat the process, gradually spilling light into the depths of the building.

"As for your third question, I give a day of rest for every four days of work. And to answer your first," Eden said, "it helps if one wins the champions race twice before one is technically old enough to enter."

"That's very enterprising of you."

Eden dismissed this with a shrug. "I spent far too much time on the water as a child." He took Eska's hand, an entirely natural gesture, and began to lead her to a narrow staircase that led to a loft at the back of the warehouse. "Come. I want to show you something."

They ascended the stairs and emerged onto a platform that covered nearly a third of the space under the roof. The loft was full, brimming with tools, model ships, oars of different designs, stacks of lumber in all hues, sheets of sails hanging from the eaves, and pieces of equipment Eska could not name. But there was order to it, and an epicenter.

Three large easels stood there, each holding drafting paper and carefully drawn designs and blueprints. A worktable four times as long as Eska was tall was covered in more paper. Despite the quantity of things, Eska understood that everything was exactly where it needed to be, not unlike her own excavation sites. No gauzy curtains and intricate mosaics here.

"My private studio," Eden said.

Eska wandered here and there in silence and he, standing quietly near his easels, let her. "Is everything up here of your own creation?" she asked at last.

The Regatta Master nodded.

"Then I wonder why you have not yet recognized the beauty of the human mind. Clearly yours is capable of a great deal of wonder."

He shrugged, uncomfortable under her gaze for the first time, and went to the worktable. "Here." Reaching under it, he opened a small trunk and lifted a swath of dark fabric.

She brushed a hand against it. Silk. "What is it?"

"Diving silks." Extending his arms above his head, he let the fabric unfurl. "Unexpectedly warm."

Eska took her hand away and held it close to her nose. "What do I smell?"

Eden smiled. "Something not unlike the resin mixtures we make to seal wood. But you won't find its like on a hull anywhere on this lake. Far too precious. The sap comes from a pine that doesn't grow anywhere within one hundred leagues of this city. It protects the silk, keeps the elements at bay. These particular silks have been passed down in my family for four generations, but you wouldn't know it."

"They're beautiful." Eska frowned. "But Lake Delo is far too deep to dive to the bottom."

Eden smiled. "Let me show you something else." He led her to a corner of the loft to where a heavy piece of canvas was draped over something bulky. "Take a look."

Eska reached up and seized the canvas, then, with a yank, pulled it away to reveal a strange contraption of leather, copper, and glass set upon the head and shoulders of what looked very much like a tailor's mannequin. Straps and buckles dangled from the apparatus.

"What on earth is it?"

"I call it a diving helmet." Eden reached around the back of the mannequin and produced a coiled leather hose that, Eska now saw, was attached to the back of the copper helmet. "Surface-supplied air." Eden dropped the heavy coil into Eska's arms and turned back to the helmet. "Exhaled air exits here," he said, pointing to a small copper tube that projected off the side of the helmet, "while a valve keeps water from entering." He rapped on the glass, an oval that seemed to stare at Eska. "The strongest glass man can make." Eden took the coiled hose back from Eska. "In theory, it would allow a diver to stay below indefinitely."

Eska allowed herself a moment to take in the design, to understand what the man beside her was saying. She then fixed him with her most skeptical expression, the one she usually reserved for Albus when he was being particularly difficult. "In theory."

Eden San-Germain sighed. "It hasn't been tested. I made the mistake of sharing the early stages of my design with the eminently wise Tribune of our fair city." A scowl crossed his face for the first time. "Unnatural was the word he had for it. I was forbidden from finishing it, a directive I, of course, ignored. But experimentation is all together a more public venture. And so it sits, gathering dust."

"You know," Eska said, feeling a smile forming, "I'm not a citizen of Cancalo. I don't have to do what your Tribune says."

Eden remained serious and shook his head. "I don't even know if it works. You could drown. I won't allow you to be the one to risk it."

They were standing very close, Eska realized. The acuteness of his gaze was nearly as heated as the warmth that emanated from him.

"Then how quickly can you make a second one?"

Interlude 10

Excerpt from Corin and Bravi's Genuine & Noble Bulletin

A DISCOVERY FOR THE AGES!

Deep in the Heart of the wild lands of far off Omin Dara, Firenzia Company, under the Masterful guidance of Valentin de Caraval, has uncovered the Cavern of Sorrows, a place out of Myth and Legend. The Expedition endured every Setback imaginable and faced, with Brave spirits, the infamous Storms and Wrath of that dangerous land. This Bulletin has it on good Authority that they fought three Warlords who wished to bring Pain and Death to our good People, and that Valentin de Caraval himself brought down the third with a Sword once wielded by the Celestial Knight Myrmidon. How Remarkable that one so Young should make his Mark upon the World! How bold! How valiant! His noble Countenance shines with the very Light of the Sun!

Firenzia Company's return to Arconia is imminent. Let us welcome these Heroes with Celebration and every Reward. Do not give Credence to those Reports that suggest the Cavern of Sorrows was empty and Void of any Prize. Those who speak so are an Insult to the very Spirit of our Fair city. Instead: Rejoice!

21

"Trust the Barcas to leave behind the tools to rob their own tombs."

"Hello, Victor."

Manon adjusted the high collar of her coat, pulling it up until it brushed her ears, but there was no use trying to ward off the persistent drizzle that had dogged her steps since morning. Her hair was matted down, stray strands plastered to her cheeks, the inelegant bundle at the crown of her head nothing more than a damp nest.

Her boots, too, were wet, perhaps beyond repair, for they were already worn, the leather weary of being endlessly subjected to rain and sun. The soles were leaking, the kind of leak undetectable to the eye but easily detected by the stockings within. Manon scrunched her toes against the damp and tried to loosen her shoulders after walking miles hunched into her collar.

The walk had not been necessary given the spending money the Archduke had given her—not necessary for her purse perhaps, but her mind was another matter.

Marble. It loomed all around Manon, monuments to the dead, columns and arches and cold-faced statues. White and grey and veiny.

The Barca mausoleum, its marble entry built into a grassy rise, stood before Manon, the leaf-strewn steps leading down into the ground. An iron door waited at the bottom of those steps. Manon could still hear the sound of that iron grinding shut against the marble foundation two years earlier.

She had not been certain she would find the key to that door. That it resided somewhere in the dark Barca house, Manon had not doubted. But she had never used the key since the day she shut Victor's remains underground, not even when Perrin had asked to visit the mausoleum, and she had no memory of where she had left it.

And yet she need not have worried it was lost. Because the key was in the only place she could have put it, the place Victor would have thought to look first.

The loose floorboard in the attic had been Victor's discovery, a secret he had shared with Manon after she had given her hushed, reverent word that she would never tell of it. She could not have been more than five or six years old, and the thrill of being trusted by her older brother was one of the brightest memories of her childhood. They had left gifts for each there at first, simple things, a string of pretty shells, half an agate, the striped feathers from a hawk's tail—until one day Manon had snuck up to the attic to leave a polished turtle shell for her brother only to find the hiding space occupied by a knife.

After that, things of value began to appear beneath the floorboard. A carved jade figurine, a ruby-studded brooch, the handle of a cane— solid gold and shaped into a leaping wolf. Manon never asked her brother about the items, seeking instead to match them, though she knew there was no mystery behind the origin of the pearl earrings or the fine-toothed bone comb she placed there.

But the game ended not long after Manon found a rolled up piece of paper scribbled with writing she could not decipher. She had peered at it in confusion, angling the paper toward the small attic window as though the sunlight might grant her understanding, so intent she had not heard her brother climb the attic steps.

Victor had snatched the paper from her hand, leaving behind a slice in the pad of her thumb, and told her he had not meant for her to see it. Crying, she had run to her room, and the next day it was as though that moment had never existed, but never again did Manon put something beneath the floorboard.

Until Victor's death, that is.

The key was heavy in her pocket as Manon contemplated the door at the bottom of the stairs and not for the first time did she wonder if she should turn her back on the mausoleum. After all, the Onyx Coast was a journey of several days, and she had the Archduke looking over her shoulder. She was delaying, and she had no convincing reason why.

And yet…though Julian Barca had said he only knew the location of one Alescuan reliquary, the stone circle at Pontevellio was not all her father had spoken of. Hence why Manon Barca was standing in the rain amid the relentless silence of the Marble Field with a key in her pocket.

Taking a deep breath that did nothing to relieve the knots in her upper back, Manon descended the steps and withdrew the iron key. Her hand shook as she fitted it into the keyhole, though whether from the chill of being over-wet over-long or due to the writhing of her stomach, she did not wish to contemplate. The lock slid easily, clean and cold and with the certainty Manon lacked. She pushed the heavy door open, meeting with faint resistance as iron scraped marble once more.

The interior had a chill of its own making, a child borne out of darkness and damp and the absence of all life. Manon let her eyes adjust to the gloom as the dim daylight fought valiantly—and failed—to reach the farthest corners, then stepped across the threshold.

Third on the right. That was Victor. Manon did not need to read the name carved into the marble sarcophagus to know. Her feet carried her there with ease, passing the empty space, the second on the right, the one reserved for her. Halting before the cold box that housed Victor's remains, Manon stretched out a gloved hand and rested her fingers on the lid.

"Well, brother."

The silence that answered Manon seeped into her bones more swiftly than the cold. She removed her fingers and tucked her hands back into her pockets.

"Perhaps I should have visited sooner. But I think you would have told me not to. You never wasted your time on anything that couldn't give you something you wanted—and the dead have nothing to give." Manon walked around to the head of the sarcophagus, her coat brushing the marble. "Then you should know that I am only here because of father." She shook her head, hardly daring to speak what was in her mind, even to the bones of her dead brother. "I saw him. I went to the Hibarium and I saw him." She pulled the glove from her right hand and let her fingertips rest against the cold marble once more. "And do you know what the last words he spoke to me were? He said to tell you he knew everything. A curious thing to say, don't you think? One might almost imagine he didn't know you were dead." Manon slid her hand across the marble as she continued her circuit.

"But he did know. I sent word to the Hibarium of your death. The last act of a daughter for her father." Manon's fingers traced the shapes of the letters carved into the marble. V. I. "He knew," she whispered. C. T. "He knew." O. R. She hesitated over the B. "Father breathed his last free air two years before I put you to rest in here. And yet somehow he has left a message for me beside your bones. Somehow." Manon leaned over the lid of the sarcophagus, her warm breath condensing on the marble. "And so I must ask your forgiveness, Victor, for what I must do."

Manon stepped away from the sarcophagus and looked to the shadows lurking near the entrance to the mausoleum. She knew what she would find there.

"Trust the Barcas to leave behind the tools to rob their own tombs."

Even through the leather of her glove, the crowbar was ice in her palm as she hefted it. Placing it in the fine groove between the lid and the base of Victor's sarcophagus, Manon adjusted her stance and brought as much weight and leverage as she could muster to bear on the crowbar, the sound of metal grinding on stone reverberating through the stillness and shadows. Four attempts before the lid relented, shifting slightly, reluctantly, as though it did not like being disturbed.

Manon moved the crowbar, bringing it closer to the head of the sarcophagus, and repeated her efforts until the marble yielded once more. She worked the lid, the damp of the rain beneath her collar mingling with sweat, until a gap began to appear. Manon set the crowbar on the lid and took a deep breath.

"For being nearly destitute, we managed to seal you up well enough."

Manon eyed the second crowbar where it lay near the entrance.

"Apparently you did not expect me to come alone, father, but I can't wield two crowbars at once."

And then something caught her eye. Manon crossed the distance in two strides and crouched on the floor. The bead tucked behind the second crowbar was no larger than Manon's thumbnail.

"Of course. You would never have left it to chance."

With shaking fingers, Manon seized the bead and turned back to the sarcophagus. She placed it on the lid, the dreary daylight illuminating the clear glass-like substance shot through with a familiar, hazy, smoky swirl. Manon stepped back.

"Perhaps one day I'll be able to afford to buy you a new tomb, brother. But I wouldn't count on it."

Manon closed her eyes, but the spark within her ribs was already flaring, demanding to be set free. The release was clumsy and violent, sending Manon stumbling back a step as the bead burst into smoke and the marble shattered into shards and dust with a symphony of cracks that jarred Manon's bones so forcefully she bit her tongue. As the white marble dust settled on Manon's damp hair and shoulders and she regained her footing, she saw the lid was gone, obliterated, and large fissures ran down the sides of the sarcophagus.

Manon ran her tongue across the back of her teeth, tasting blood, and wondered what the dead ancestors surrounding her would say if they could speak. Surely Aunt Leandra would approve.

"If you have lied to me, father," she said, "if I have done this for nothing, I'll see that you are pumped so full of the dread you'll never know a moment of sanity or peace again."

She had not, during her long walk to the Marble Field or in the sleepless hours of the night, dared to imagine what she might find inside. She had not given herself that luxury. To imagine was to hope and Manon had learned that hope was a restless, inconstant friend, as quick to disappear as to be conjured. The last time Manon had felt hope was the day she had knelt before the Archduke of Arconia and pleaded for mercy for her father. The Archduke had smiled at her, had said kind words about Julian Barca. And then he had sworn that her father would never leave the Hibarium—until he left as a pile of ash. Four days later, when Manon's mother had promised to return after seeking friends and finances in the other cities of Bellara, Manon had known better than to hope. And when Victor had stumbled home in the dark of night, pale, eyes wide and wild, blood streaming between the fingers pressed to his abdomen, Manon had turned hope away even as she admitted the finest physician her last sapphire could buy.

And so it was with a resolute blankness of mind that Manon stepped forward through the still settling marble dust and took her first look inside Victor's sarcophagus.

He was in there. Or, a thing that might have once been him was in there.

Sealed away in darkness and deprived of air, Victor was still a creature of skin. It had settled against his bones as the flesh beneath melted away, shrinking him. He was a thing made of collarbones and cheekbones and brow bones. No doubt his ribs and his pelvis, hidden beneath fine velvet gone slightly foul, were like sharp mountains rising up above sunken valleys that had once been filled with muscle.

His features were recognizable, if no longer handsome. His hair, once full and thick, had settled about his skull in limp strands. And he smelled. Sweet and rank. The odor took a moment to make its presence known, but then it sent Manon reeling backward, retching, eyes watering. Her hands on her knees, Manon waited for her lungs to clear, then spit excess saliva onto the marble floor. Straightening, she steeled herself, took a deep breath she knew she could not hold long enough, and returned to examine the contents of her brother's sarcophagus.

The first thing she noticed was the ring on her brother's hand. It certainly wasn't Victor's, nor had Manon ever seen that particular ruby before. Even in death, the knuckle was too large for the ring, though the gold filigree band sat loosely on the desiccated finger. Manon placed one gloved hand over Victor's and lifted the brittle joints until she could slide the ring free. In the dim mausoleum, the ruby was a dull red, but the quality was unmistakable.

"A pretty thing, father, but surely not why you sent me here," Manon murmured. She slipped the ruby onto her hand—the fit was perfect over her glove—and turned back to the corpse. "Now, Victor, what have you got in your pockets?" Easing open the velvet jacket to reveal the stained waistcoat and white shirt beneath, Manon slipped her fingers into the interior breast pocket and withdrew two items, the pocket watch she had stopped at the time of Victor's death and buried with him, and, so smooth it fled from the touch of her gloves, a small metal disc. She held it in her palm and eyed the unfamiliar markings for a moment, then tucked it into a small pocket of her coat, not yet impressed with her father's hidden treasures. A quick search of Victor's remaining pockets yielded nothing.

At last Manon, gingerly at first, then with greater nerve as the body proved resistant, placed her hands on what was left of Victor's shoulder and hip and rolled him onto his side. Roll was a generous term for it, Manon decided. Bones and partially decomposed flesh shifted beneath her touch, giving way, and as a result, Victor compressed more than rolled. Grimacing, Manon tried not to look at the newly misshapen figure that had been her brother.

This wasn't difficult to do because a rather large quantity of square gold ingots was staring back up at her—quite literally. The eye stamped into each ingot was unmistakable and synonymous with the former owner. She knew this gold.

What she did not know was how Julian Barca had gotten his hands on gold from the Principe of Licenza's personal treasury and stashed it in her dead brother's sarcophagus—all from the confines of a locked cell he would never step foot outside of again.

Interlude 11

Note to an unknown recipient, from Leandra Barca, dated just prior to Julian Barca's imprisonment

You're a disgrace. Don't be ridiculous. I will not permit you to leave your post. You've only endured three months in that house—a true friend to this family would never countenance such an idea. If you wish to marry my nephew, you will need to discover the whereabouts of your spine—if you have one. You will serve that family for as long as I say. You will report everything to me, unfiltered. You will make no attempt to decide what is important information and what is not. I do not trust your meager mind to decipher the difference. And above all, you will make the de Caraval family love you and trust you. Smile at them. I'm told that is effective on such people. By all my dead ancestors, I know it worked on my nephew.

Do not make me remind you what befalls you if you speak of this to anyone. Julian will know of your placement when the time is right, but not from your lips.

22

"These bones are too young."

The Regatta Master of Lake Delo had asked for three days.

First he had scowled, protested, tried to insist he alone would try the depths of the lake in the diving helmet. Eska had let him run the course of his objections, arms crossed, staring him down, until at last he had relented, succumbing, she thought, as much to the rush of anticipation she knew was running through his veins as to her silent insistence.

And so Eden San-Germain had banished her from his workshop and Eska was left to make her way back to her small band of Firenzia crewmembers with the promise that he would find her there when he had finished the second helmet.

Her story had been met with a great deal of skepticism, mainly from Bastien who did not have the authority to express such opinions, but made them known nonetheless by stomping about the camp for the next day. The young man was, she realized, quite protective of her, an appreciated but unnecessary quality that she hoped he could grow out of.

Eska passed the first day training with Perrin in the morning—footwork, footwork, and more footwork at the edge of Lake Delo—and then working on the skeleton through the afternoon and evening. Sequestered within her tent, she hardly looked up from the linen sheets the bones were occupying, her neck aching as she knelt and leaned over them for extended periods of time. They had recovered nearly every bone—save for those of the left arm, of which only the better part of a broken humerus had been found.

She slept in fits and starts that first night, her mind plumbing the depths of Lake Delo, and bent to her task of cleaning the bones first thing in the morning despite insisting the rest of the crew take a day for relaxation—there was little to do, after all. She could hear them splashing and laughing in the lake.

It was Perrin who came to stand behind her, his shadow stretching over her, who watched in silence until Eska could no longer suppress a very large yawn.

"So this is what you call not working. You're obviously exhausted. You should rest."

"My mind doesn't often rest. Especially when it has a puzzle in its grasp." Eska gestured to the skeleton. "I must know why this individual was buried in a refuse pit. In my line of work, I can't afford to ignore an anomaly." She bent her head to her task once more. "Isn't it time you had another lesson in proper brush technique?" Eska asked without looking up. "I'm afraid you're the worst apprentice I've ever seen."

The shadow didn't move for a moment, but then at last it shrunk as Perrin squatted down beside her. Eska turned her head to look at him, glad to see a smile gracing his lips.

"The worst? Am I to feel ashamed?"

"Exceedingly. I've taught children with more success."

"Then I suppose I had better behave and take copious notes."

"No notes," Eska said. "Notes won't teach you the feel of your brush." She took Perrin's hand and placed her brush in his palm. "Hold it like this," she said, bending his fingers around the slender handle. Her hand atop his, Eska guided Perrin toward the tibia she was working on. "Use long strokes here," she said, showing him the movement. "And then as we come to the joint, a bit more speed, more wrist motion, a bit more pressure. But always be gentle."

"You know, another woman once told me something very similar," Perrin said, not pausing to look at Eska.

"Oh? And did you follow her instructions closely?"

"Intimately."

"I imagine she was pleased."

"Decidedly."

"Ah, look," Eska said, halting the movement of her hand. "Take care here, it's splintered."

"Are we talking about bones again?"

Eska bit the inside of her cheek to keep from laughing and twisted to give Perrin a very severe stare, one eyebrow raised. "Were we ever not talking about bones, Barca?"

Perrin's eyes twinkled with amusement. "Apparently not." His hand twisted in hers as he tried to return the brush to Eska. "Here, you ought to do the tricky part."

"Nonsense. Learn by doing, Perrin, learn by doing." Eska removed her hand from his. "Go slowly."

His brow furrowing, Perrin dipped his head and began to work the soil from the splintered crack in the tibia, tentatively at first until he found a rhythm. After a short while, though, he paused, and Eska could see his forehead wrinkle into a deeper frown. "I think I need a smaller brush."

Eska produced the tiny bristled object before he even finished his statement, extending it with a flourish.

"Were you going to let me blunder on with this one?" Perrin asked, trading brushes.

"And miss the opportunity to watch you struggle? Not a chance."

"What if I had...," Perrin fished for a mock objection, "broken it? Made the crack worse?"

Eska held up the brush he had previously been using and poked at the hairs with one finger. "Adolescent capybara hair." She pointed at the tibia. "Bone." She waggled the brush. "Hair. Bone." Perrin rolled his eyes. "Now tell me how exactly you think a bundle of twenty hairs is going to break it?"

He bent his head once more, brush flicking in tiny strokes. "I'd like to lodge a formal complaint. You're a very poor instructor."

"How very unfortunate for you, then, that you are not an employee and therefore have no legal standing here." Eska stifled another yawn and lay back on the ground. "Tell me, Perrin," she went on, pursuing the question that had bothered her since learning the Barca ship had sailed from Arconia, "what did your sister know of the Toridium site? I'd had my eye on that stretch of riverbank for some time, but no one seemed to know who held the rights. It was a secret last understood by a long-buried Fortinesc baron."

Perrin ceased working on the shin and leaned back on his palms, confusion crinkling his nose. "The Fortinesc estate? That land belonged to it?"

"That and half of the plains east of the Alencio, thanks to treaties over two hundred years old, a series of entailed inheritances, and a family trust sealed up tighter than the fabled doors of Eilloncia. It's taken half a dozen of the brightest barristers in Arconia to decipher that trove of paperwork—and they're still at it." Eska sighed and rubbed at a smudge of dirt on her wrist.

"My father would have plundered it without the rights," Perrin murmured.

"On the contrary, your father wouldn't have bothered." Eska glanced at Perrin and shrugged. "No treasure. It was an academic's paradise, but not much more than that." She shifted onto one elbow the better to see his face. "Hence my question. What did your sister want with it?"

"In truth, Eska, I do not know. She didn't even want me to join her on this journey. Her contacts at the Court Beneath the Sun told her you were arguing a case for a piece of land near Toridium. She was convinced you had made a valuable discovery. All we had to do was get there first. But beyond that, I did not speculate and she said little." Perrin went quiet for a moment, his countenance darkening. "She said enough in the end. Words I never thought to hear from her. But then," and now the bitterness pierced his voice, "she is a Barca and we seem to have a habit of turning our backs on our family members."

Eska rested a hand on Perrin's forearm, knowing there were no words she could speak that might soothe his pain. She let him wear his anger and his grief, let him feel it, and at last he raised his gaze to her face once more.

"Perhaps you have refrained from saying anything for my benefit, out of some desire to keep my sister's image untarnished for me." Perrin shook his head. "You need not tread with such care. I have come to learn that none of my family members are what I once thought them to be. Not my father, who lived for himself and wasted away a fortune. Not my mother, who could not bear to suffer the blow of my father's imprisonment, not even for the sake of her children. Not Victor, who was the first to show me his true heart, his black heart. And now Manon," Perrin finished, his voice shaking, his gaze focused on something distant, something only he could see, though his green gaze burrowed into Eska with fierce intensity.

Eska was quiet, letting some of the heat burn out of Perrin's face before she spoke. "I am sorry, Perrin. I am sorry for what you have to bear. And I am sorry for any part my family might have played in your burdens."

Perrin shook his head, a sad smile on his lips. "I would have done anything for Manon. We were all we had left. I would have sold myself into servitude if she asked. I would have forsaken any dreams I had for myself if they conflicted with hers. Anything. Steal from the Archduke himself. Cut off a limb. Anything."

"I hardly think cutting off a limb would have helped her," Eska said, smiling, "not unless she could turn blood into coin."

Perrin smiled again, wryly this time. "My aunt Leandra probably could have. Uncanny woman. More schemes in her brain than ants in a sack of sweets. And strangely ageless." The smile vanished. "Eska? What is it?"

Eska blinked, her mind racing, unaware she had risen to her feet until Perrin loomed upward, his figure oddly out of focus.

"Ageless," she repeated, her voice a rough whisper. At once Perrin's face solidified in front of her as her thoughts became clear. "Perrin. I need the caterpillars."

"Caterpillars?" Gabriel asked, earning a quizzical glance from Perrin.

"Caterpillars," Eska said, nodding.

"Caterpillars?" Perrin repeated.

Rising to her feet, Eska smiled at him. "Trade secret."

"Now, this is cruel. You can't possibly leave me with that."

"What's this, a latent interest in bones surfacing after a long period of dormancy?"

Perrin laughed. "Bones, no, but I'll admit I am enormously curious what caterpillars and bones have to do with each other."

With mock seriousness, Eska turned to Bastien. "What do you think, Bastien, should we let the Barca watch?" The young man's sullenness had disappeared in the wake of Eska's evident excitement.

"Crueler and crueler," Perrin said.

Bastien, to his credit, held a straight face. "Only if he has a strong stomach." He looked to Perrin, who was frowning now. "Bit gruesome."

"I am not unfamiliar with gruesome," Perrin said.

"Very well," Eska said. "Bastien, fetch the jar, if you would."

The young man hurried off and began rummaging in back of one of the wagons. Eska set one of the finger bones from the skeleton's right hand on a separate, smaller piece of linen, far from the rest of the bones.

Bastien returned with a large glass jar cradled under one arm. Within, a mass of leaves, grasses, and twigs obscured the inhabitants. Eska shook the jar slightly until she revealed the fuzzy form of a caterpillar twisted around a stick.

"Aren't you a big one?" she murmured. After removing the cork stopper, Eska extracted the caterpillar, twig and all, and held it out for Perrin to admire. "Handsome, isn't he?"

Perrin examined the caterpillar. "He?"

Eska indicated the pair of curved black horns protruding from the caterpillar's head. "See those?"

"I suppose the females have none?"

Eska grinned. "On the contrary, my dear, the females have three."

Perrin laughed. "Of course they do. He's a very dull sort of brown.

Let me guess, he makes a gorgeous butterfly."

"Actually, he won't. He will never be a butterfly. This particular species doesn't appear to have learned how to do so."

Perrin cocked an eyebrow. "You're joking."

"Not in the slightest," Eska said, grinning wider still, enjoying the faint scowl on Perrin's face as he tried to decide whether to believe her.

"He's waking up," Bastien said, leaning close to the twig in Eska's hand. The caterpillar was uncurling, stretching its many limbs, horned head raised to the air. Eska handed the twig to Bastien and then took up a tiny chisel and hammer. Bending over the finger bone, she, with swift, precise movements, chipped off a small flake and placed it in the middle of the canvas, then returned the rest of the bone to its comrades.

"You may do the honors, Bastien."

The young man lowered the caterpillar, now suspended up-side-down from the twig, head stretched toward the table as though it could sense what was waiting. Upon reaching the linen, Bastien set the twig down gently and stepped back.

The caterpillar, hunched now in the shape of a horseshoe on the stick, did nothing.

"So terribly gruesome," Perrin whispered dramatically. "I think I shall never recover from seeing a caterpillar ignore a fragment of bone."

Eska laughed. "It's a good story for new recruits."

"In other words, I shouldn't trust another word out of your mouth."

The four of them watched the caterpillar intently for a moment—three of them, really, as Perrin's expression was decidedly skeptical.

"I think he's gone back to sleep," Bastien said.

"Must be the heat," Gabriel put in. "Making him lethargic."

Only Eska waited with any patience, her gaze never leaving the fuzzy brown caterpillar as she squatted on the ground, chin in her palm. At last the caterpillar stirred, releasing the twig, then making its way across the linen. It hesitated as it came close to the fragment of bone, head lifted, horns directed first in one direction and then the other. It approached, eliciting a slight narrowing of Eska's gaze, but its methodical progress came to an abrupt halt when it was half a body length away. Rearing back, legs waggling—looking as disgusted as Eska supposed a caterpillar could look—it retreated at top speed, taking refuge on the twig once more. Eska looked at Gabriel and Bastien with a smile.

"What does it mean?" Perrin asked, breaking the silent understanding shared by Eska and her crewmember.

Eska studied the caterpillar for a moment before straightening and addressing Perrin. "It means I was right to wonder why there were bones in the refuse pit. These caterpillars eat a plant-based diet, but they have a special taste for bone. And yet they will not touch a bone that is less than five hundred years old—give or take."

Eska watched as Perrin's gaze dropped to the flake of bone and then shifted to the skeleton and back to the caterpillar, watched him work out the significance of what the insect was telling them. "So, the skeleton is less than five hundred years old."

"Yes. But given the history and nature of the site along the Alencio river, any bones discovered there, at the depth we found these, should be more than two thousand years old. This skeleton should be that caterpillar's dream." Eska looked over her shoulder at the rest of the skeleton. "Something isn't right. These bones are too young. This isn't an Onandya skeleton."

23

"I didn't say I had a fear of drowning."

"How does it feel?"

Eden San-Germain stood looking at Eska, arms crossed, his forehead bearing the slightest furrow. His features were distorted behind the thick glass of the diving helmet, and the sound of his voice was muffled by the copper and the steady rhythm of Eska's own breathing.

"Heavy." It was the truth, but one Eska admitted reluctantly for fear that Eden might find reason to insist she not make the dive. This admission, however, did not seem to bother him. He was looking intently at the straps and buckles that held the contraption in place on her shoulders and torso.

Stepping forward, Eden tugged at the leather in a few places, the furrow deepening for a moment. When he stood back, his gaze shifted to Eska's face.

"It's secure. But I've already expressed my misgivings."

"And I've already reminded you that you yourself will be wearing this device for the first time. Logically, your misgivings need to apply to us both," Eska said.

"They do," he said, his voice even quieter. It was the first time he had suggested as much. They helped each other out of the helmets and then he leaned over, withdrew a parcel from his satchel, and handed it to Eska. "I had these made for you as well."

Eska undid the string, revealing a set of diving silks as black as

Eden's and smoother than the finest silk she had ever worn to the Varadome. She looked up to express her thanks, but Eden was already carrying on.

"We'll make the dive at noon, when the sun is highest and giving us the most light down there. In addition, I have secured two additional sources of light." Eden reached into the satchel once more and produced a small box. He lifted the lid to show Eska the contents.

Two small orbs lay nestled in straw. At first Eska thought they were merely dark glass, but as she lifted one out of the box, a thick, inky substance inside swirled to life.

"They react to your body heat," Eden said, as the substance inside the orb began to glow and emit a soft, golden light. Eska watched as it grew brighter. "Their lifespan is limited," the Regatta Master went on. He plucked it from Eska's fingers and replaced it in the box. It began to dim immediately. "So we don't want to waste any." He must have seen the tightness Eska could feel in her jaw. "What is it?"

"Carrier-made?"

Eden's gaze lay heavy on her for a moment before he answered. "Yes."

She swallowed, knowing she had to forget her personal aversion for the sake of what lay at the bottom of the lake, and said nothing more. But Eden wasn't done with the conversation. He strode to the edge of Lake Delo and stepped out onto a large, nearly submerged rock.

Eska knew what was coming. She wanted to look away.

Eden closed his eyes and held his hand out, palm down, over the water lapping gently against his rock. A single droplet lifted from the surface, clean and glistening in the morning sun. A second followed, and then a third and fourth. Each rose higher and higher, until they hung, suspended, just below his palm. He rotated his wrist and the water drops followed, then merged. With a sudden flick of his fingers, the water leaped into the air. Eden, his eyes still closed, tilted his head back and opened his mouth, his movement perfectly timed to catch the water on his tongue. He opened his eyes and looked at Eska, a challenge in his expression despite the child-like grin prompted by his own cleverness.

He remained on the rock and waited.

There were many things Eska might have said. She chose the one that would get her what she wanted most.

"I think I begin to understand why you won those sailing races at such an early age."

She had chosen well. Eden laughed and rejoined her on the shore. "I would never," he said, the very picture of solemnity. But then he grew still and looked down into Eska's eyes. One hand came up and tucked a lock of hair behind her ear. The hand lingered, then traced the line of her jaw down to her mouth. His thumb brushed her lower lip. "I am what I am, Eska," he said. The words, the exact words Alexandre had spoken to her just days before, sent a shiver down Eska's spine, a shiver that turned to warmth as he leaned in and kissed her. Gently. Briefly. "The water is a part of me and I am a part of it. Can you live with that?" Another kiss.

"I don't think I have a choice, not if I want to open that vault," Eska whispered.

"You always have a choice." A third kiss, so light she barely felt it.

Eska put a hand on his chest and applied a hint of pressure, making enough space between them so that he could know her answer was not because she was lost in his eyes.

"Yes," she said. "I can live with that."

The fourth kiss was long and deep and Eska emerged with a smile on her face.

———◆——

"I don't trust him."

"Hmm?" Hardly hearing Gabriel, Eska examined the diving silks in the relative privacy of her tent.

"San-Germain." Gabriel stood at the entrance, clearly uncomfortable voicing his opinion so strongly, but unwilling to stay silent. He fidgeted with the edge of the canvas as Eska turned to face him.

"There's a reason I asked you to accompany me here, Gabriel, and not Cedric. But he seems to have loaned you some of his nervous tendencies."

"What do we really know about him, my lady?" Gabriel was warming to his task.

Eska set aside the silks. "We know he took three days of his time to make me a custom diving helmet. We know he understands the lake, the water. And I happen to know he's been desperate for an opportunity to test his invention—though he won't say so much out loud." The engineer's frown only deepened. Eska closed the distance between them, uncrossed his arms, and took one of Gabriel's hands between hers. "I understand your concerns, Gabriel. But I do not see another means of getting to the bottom of the lake. And I don't know about you, but I would rather not have made my midnight escape from Toridium for nothing. We have to try."

Gabriel clasped his other hand to Eska's, his gaze unrelenting. "I can only imagine what your uncle would say if he knew a Barca had wormed his way into our work. And now another stranger."

Eska could feel her patience thinning. "Are you questioning my judgment?" Something in Gabriel's eyes retreated and Eska softened her voice, not wanting to drive him away. "I understand the reason for your concern, and I can appreciate it. But Perrin has given no cause for such suspicion. Indeed, he saved my life. And if you do not believe I watch Eden San-Germain carefully, then perhaps I was wrong to bring you here."

Gabriel's gaze dropped and he breathed out a sigh of defeat.

"Gabriel, I don't know what I would do without you. Cedric may be the right hand of Firenzia Company, but you are our spine. Please. Let's not argue."

"I trust you, my lady."

"And you believe I take your concern into account?"

"Yes."

Eska squeezed his hands. "We can do this." Gabriel gave a nod, and then left Eska in the privacy of her tent to change into the diving silks.

She undressed, then, taking a deep breath, she turned to the small table that held the string-wrapped parcel from Eden, her gaze searching out of habit for the familiar figure of the fox sculpture of Nehar. Its absence seemed a weight on her lungs and she understood then that she was afraid. The day was warm, but as Eska lifted the silks and they brushed over her bare skin, she shivered.

She was still standing there, the silks draped over her arms, her back to the tent flap and the lake, when his voice, made distant by the canvas between them, reached her.

"Eska. It's time."

Eden's words prickled her skin. Afterwards, she could not have said how long she stood there, how long he waited, how long the silence lasted. She knew only the sound of her heart pounding between her ribs and a deep desire for sunlight, made all the more fierce by the knowledge that it was the cold waters of Lake Delo that awaited her outside the tent.

She heard him push aside the tent flap, heard him hesitate, then step inside, heard his feet cover the ground between them, heard the quiet inhale that came a moment before he touched her.

His hand was warm and firm on her back and she felt the chill begin to ebb from her skin. Neither of them spoke as his fingers brushed up her spine and settled at the base of her neck. He applied a hint of pressure and Eska found herself leaning into his touch.

"You don't have to do this."

Eska smiled a little. "You still don't know me very well." A sudden shiver betrayed her.

Both of Eden's hands came to rest on her shoulders. "What are you afraid of?"

Eska hesitated, trying to organize her thoughts. "I have done free dives, but always in clear ocean waters and not very deep. I do not have the lung strength or training to truly be a diver."

"That doesn't quite answer the question." He began to massage her shoulders.

"I try not to succumb to irrational fears."

Silence. Then, "I don't think a fear of drowning is irrational."

"I didn't say I had a fear of drowning," Eska said. And yet her voice was very small.

"Eska, look at me."

She turned slowly, his hands drifting across her skin as she did so, until they were face to face. His palms settled on her shoulders once more.

"I will not deny that this thing we mean to do is dangerous. You already know that. But I promise to keep you safe."

Eska's gaze lingered on his for a moment and then she stepped fully into his arms.

"I could say something about how promises like that are futile," Eska murmured into his collarbone, "how we can never truly protect another person."

"You could." Eden's fingers moved up the back of her neck and into her hair. His other arm wrapped around her torso, his hand coming to rest at her waist. "And then I could say something about how we move through life like solitary icebergs, that we are nothing more than shells containing muscle and bone and sinew, that loneliness is our natural state. But that would be rather bleak, don't you think?"

Eska released him and looked up at his face once more. She smiled. "And then I'd say that such pontificating must surely be an excuse to keep me naked for longer."

Eden laughed. "This is probably not incorrect." He cupped her chin. "Are you ready?"

Eska nodded and began to slip into the silks. Eden helped her do the closures at the front and back of the neck opening, then stood back to assess the fit. A short nod told Eska it was acceptable. She turned to her small chest of belongings and dug down to the bottom to retrieve a dagger in a holster. This she buckled around her calf, then turned to Eden and presented him with the modified belt she had asked Gabriel to alter to carry a crowbar, a hammer, and a chisel.

"I would wear it, but the fit will be more secure on you, if you don't mind," she said.

He accepted the belt and fastened it around his hips. Their gazes met and then, with a shared nod, they emerged from the tent.

Eska's small crew was waiting at the edge of Lake Delo. Bastien, his trousers rolled to his knees, held the wide prow of the rowboat she had procured the day before. Inevra held two bags of fishing net each containing half a dozen flat stones larger than one of Eska's hands. Gabriel, Eska noted, was eyeing the stones dubiously. At Eden's word, Inevra waded out into the lake and placed the weighted nets in the bottom of the rowboat, among the seemingly endless coils of hose that would carry air to their lungs at the bottom of the lake. The diving helmets were just visible between the bench seats, their copper crowns gleaming in the sun.

Eska stepped into the water and wiggled her toes inside the silks, trying not to think about how little time would pass before she would no longer be able to consider the water temperature refreshing. Bastien held the rowboat steady while Eska and Eden climbed in. The Regatta Master took up the oars as Bastien, charged with monitoring the air hoses from the surface, joined them.

"Be safe, my lady," Gabriel called out. Eska acknowledged him with a wave and a smile as the other crewmembers chimed in.

Eden rowed in silence, though his gaze never strayed far from Eska. For her part, Eska found herself watching the water slide by. Bastien, tucked in between the diving helmets, could not stop touching the hoses, she noted, and casting nervous glances at her.

The Regatta Master's smooth strokes carried them southwest across the lake until he abruptly ceased rowing roughly a third of the distance to the far shore. For a moment, there was only the sound of water dripping from the oars.

"We're here," he said.

Without hesitating, Eska knelt in the bottom of the boat and lifted her diving helmet over her head. With Bastien's help, she pulled the straps tight and fastened the buckles, then secured the weighted net to a hook in the leather. She waited as Eden did the same and reminded Bastien to keep the hoses from tangling. He then knelt in front of her and took her silk-covered hands in his.

"Let the stones do the work. Just breathe deeply. We'll be down there before you know it," he said, pressing one of the glass orbs into Eska's palm. It flickered sleepily and then began to glow with growing intensity. Eden squeezed her other hand, prompting Eska to look up and meet his gaze. The panes of thick glass between them did nothing to diminish the intensity in his expression. "Keep sight of me at all times."

There was nothing left to say, nothing to keep her from the water. Eden released her hand.

Eska grasped the bag of stones by its cord and perched on the rowboat's rail. Eden mirrored her movement. Bastien took up the rower's seat, but Eska's vision tunneled and all she could see was Eden's diving helmet and face. For a moment, her breath caught in her lungs as though the lake were already swallowing her, but then the Regatta Master of Lake Delo smiled and Eska's heart beat once more and the fear filling her chest warmed to something that might have been joy.

She let herself fall back into Lake Delo's cold embrace.

———— • ————

The speed with which the stones carried Eska below the surface might have been terrifying were it not for the mesmerizing color of the water as it rushed by—shades of blue and green caught between the shafts of sunlight above warring with the black shadows below. Whether she forgot to breathe because of the sheer beauty around her or because of the cold, Eska wasn't sure, but at last she forced a breath into her lungs, both relieved to find the hose functional and hesitant to rely on it. She closed her eyes for a moment, remembering Eden's advice, and breathed as deeply and slowly as she could.

When she opened them, the water was a shade darker, the orb in her hand a more brilliant gold. She caught sight of Eden a short distance away and just below her, his heavier frame carrying him to the bottom at a slight faster pace.

The bottom came abruptly, looming up from the depths, and Eden unhooked the net of stones from his torso, letting them fall away, and signaled to Eska to do the same. The sudden decrease in weight caused her descent to slow significantly, and for a moment she felt as though her body were suspended in a substance far more viscous than water. Then Eden pointed along the lake bottom to Eska's right and they began to swim ensconced within the golden halo of the orbs.

They swam side by side, the vast darkness around them disturbed only by tall weeds rippling silently as they brushed past.

Eska saw the vault before Eden, her hand involuntarily reaching out to grab his arm. A nebulous shape, but one undoubtedly not natural to the lakebed, the bronze gleaming in the soft illumination of the orbs. As they drew closer, she saw it stood at an angle, one corner propped up by a rocky protrusion, the opposite corner embedded in the mud.

Eska swam slowly around it, taking in the level of decay caused by the unyielding force of time and water. To her dismay, the vault's door was on the side tilted toward the lakebed, making access more difficult. Worse, the door could only be opened a short distance before the corner would lodge in the mud, but she felt her heart beat a little faster as she caught sight of the unmistakable design stamped into the corroded bronze door: the tri-horned griffin, the symbol of the Alescu dynasty, raging at Eska there in the depths of Lake Delo, just as the Alescuan kings and queens had raged across so much of the known world.

Eska put her hand against the bronze, thrilled by the knowledge that she was touching something only fish had laid eyes on for nearly four hundred years. Eden swam next to her, careful to keep his breathing hose from crossing with Eska's, and held his orb close to the vault's handle and lock mechanism. The light revealed the corrosion to be far less significant. Everyone knew, of course, that the Alescuan kings and queens had delved deep into the study of their Carrier gifts, creating wonders and terrors alike. Strengthening metal to withstand the elements would have been a minor accomplishment, a child's trick, and yet the waters of Lake Delo seemed to grow darker and colder around Eska as she understood what she was seeing. There was no telling what other deterrents had been worked into the door to stand against assault—by Carrier or other means.

Eska freed the knife from the holster around her calf and began to clean around the lock, removing a layer of sediment and detritus. Eden held both orbs within one palm, the other resting steadily on Eska's back to help keep her still in the water. When she was finished, she put one hand on the handle of the vault, glanced at Eden with a shrug and a grin, and pushed down.

Nothing happened, precisely as she expected, but the knowledge that the vault was well and truly locked made her all the more certain there was something inside. She wiggled the tip of the knife into the keyhole and tried turning it. The mechanism moved slightly, but she hit firm resistance in both directions after no more than a few degrees of rotation. Replacing the knife in her holster, she took up the chisel from Eden's belt and inserted the tip between the vault door and the sidewall, then, with a short, sharp motion, rapped once with the hammer.

The sound, muffled and eerie, reverberated in Eska's helmet. She set to work building a rhythm, but the bronze gave no indication of weakness. Using gestures, Eden offered to try, and Eska let him, the hammering dissipating into the water like the ringing of strangely deadened, mournful bells.

As Eden worked the lock, Eska tried to pry at the corner of the door with the crowbar, iron scraping against bronze, both metals protesting, her frustration growing as her exertion increasingly appeared to be futile. Below her, Eden returned the chisel and hammer to his belt, then held up a hand. Eska frowned, uncertain why he would want her to stop, but watched as he leaned as close to the door as he could, one hand braced against the edge of the vault, the other suspended a forearm's length away from the lock, his fingers crooked unnaturally.

It took Eska a moment longer than it ought to have for her to realize what he was doing—after all, using water to crack a lock was not a method that would have occurred to her.

She held her breath. Eden's fingers moved slightly and the water between his palm and the lock shifted as though under heavy pressure from an invisible force. Tiny bubbles surged between his fingers as he began to turn his wrist. Eska put a hand against the door, sensed nothing. For the first time she could remember, she was aware of the faintest desire to feel what a Carrier felt.

A prick of pain stung her elbow just as Eden shuddered below her. Paying it no attention, she brushed at the back of her arm impatiently, bobbling the two orbs of golden light. She caught them, her focus entirely still on Eden, whose hand flexed and strained.

The vault groaned. The water around Eden frothed. And then the Regatta Master's faint and muffled cry of triumph came to Eska. He beamed up at her, grabbing her wrist to pull her down to the lock's level. Her breath coming hard and fast in her helmet, Eska took up both orbs in one hand, then placed her other on the handle of the vault. Hardly daring to hope, she pushed down. It gave way.

The vault yawned open, the edge of the door coming to rest in the lakebed. Silt and muck bloomed up, obscuring her view of the interior. When the cloud settled, Eska extended her arm through the opening, willing the orbs to illuminate the furthest corners. Her breath caught—there, somewhere deep in the gloom, a faint glimmer of gold, spied by the light of her orbs.

The second sting of pain struck her, followed quickly by a third. Tearing her eyes from her prize, she put her hand to her waist, feeling something small and sharp protruding from her flesh and silks. She brought her fingers to her face and saw a tiny smear of blood drift away into the water. Eden watched her movement, his face creasing with worry and then pain as a fourth stinger embedded itself in his forearm. Eska twisted in the water, her heart racing ahead of her lungs as she fought to control her breathing, aware that panic could likely lead to death.

Eden's hand grabbed her and spun her back to face him. His attention was fixed on a point above their heads and Eska, dread filling her stomach, raised her gaze.

The gills were the first thing she comprehended. Great heaving slits along a massive underbelly, six of them, pulsing to reveal a red interior that glowed far brighter than the orbs in Eska's hand.

The creature curled and uncurled its long body but made no other move, waiting, no doubt, to see what the strange things invading its territory would do next. It looked down at them with flat black eyes set in a scaled, bird-like face, the snout tapering to a point that would easily skewer the soft flank of an unsuspecting otter or the belly of a plump podfish—or human, for that matter.

Eden's fingers pressed harder on her arm and Eska would have glanced at him to see what he wanted to communicate—would have if not for the fact that the creature chose that moment to open its mouth.

The lower jaw unhinged, held to the upper by thin membranes, until it gaped at them. It appeared to be toothless—but then, it didn't need teeth when it had the ability to spit needles.

Which is precisely what it did. Not a lone stinger. A hailstorm.

Eden lunged for the shelter offered by the nearest corner of the vault, Eska scrambling after him, pressing herself between the bronze door and the lakebed. Darts stung her leg, more than she could count, her eyes filling with tears at the pain, her chest heaving inside the heavy contraption. Eden caught up the copper of her helmet in his hands and made her look him in the eye. He gave her a nod, then glanced down at the faint cloud of blood around Eska's lower body. The left leg of the diving silks was in shreds, a few of the needle-like stingers embedded in her calf muscle. Eden poked his head around the corner of the vault and indicated to Eska that the creature was still hovering above. They both glanced down at the orbs Eska carried and she knew they weighed the same choice in their minds: if they broke the orbs, which were already dimming under the influence of the cold water, they might have a chance to steal away in the dark—but she could see even the Regatta Master of Lake Delo was not overeager to forego the comfort of the golden glow, and there was no telling how keen the creature's eyesight was.

Eden took another quick glance around the vault and gestured that the creature was slowly swimming closer. Eska risked a look for herself and saw the thing coiling its way through the water, the gills opening and closing, the red glow spreading an eerie light through the deep blue.

Eska thrust the orbs close to the glass of Eden's helmet, causing him to lean back. She nodded furiously, trying to convey her thoughts, and he returned the nod and raised the crowbar and the chisel, indicating he understood his role. Eden placed his free hand on her shoulder, his touch faint through the heavy leather, and then without another moment's hesitation, swam around the opposite side of the vault, disappearing into the dark.

Eska held one of the orbs around the near corner and waved her hand, hoping to draw the creature's attention long enough for Eden to circle around and approach from the rear undetected. She took a quick look, just in time to see the creature—so close she could see the water rippling over its gills—open its jaws once more. Flinching inside her silks, Eska dove for safety again, curling herself under the tilted side of the vault. The stingers, pale as bone, rushed through the water like a storm of arrows and vanished in the muddy bottom.

Judging that she had little time before the creature finished its slow descent and pinned her to the lakebed, Eska took a deep breath, then burst out from her hiding place, kicking furiously, flashing the orbs in front of her in a manner she could only hope was threatening.

The creature halted, reared back its head ever so slightly, its black eyes staring down at her, the sharp snout no more than two rowboat lengths away.

They stared at each other for a moment, Eska's breathing coming in shallow gasps, the creatures' tail undulating in the water, its eyes betraying nothing. Eska's arms slowed, her muscles tiring, the orbs fading to nothing more than embers. She thought she caught a glimpse of Eden, but the creature unhinged its lower jaw and she could not look away from the faint red glow emanating deep in its throat.

Desperate, Eska threw first one orb and then the other. They floated for a moment, then sank, and she felt her breath catch as their light faded. But just before they winked out, Eden was there, stabbing the chisel into the closest glowing gill. At once the creature began to writhe, its silent pain eerie in the emptiness of the water, and the crowbar joined the chisel, ripping through scale-covered flesh.

It was too late. The stingers enveloped Eska, piercing the length of her body, pinging off the copper helmet, two even striking the glass of her mask. But it was the hiss of air above Eska that nearly blackened her vision and knotted her stomach with dread.

The hand that rose to her helmet's glass portal was studded with stingers. Her skin burned. Water surged through the breach in her air hose, rushing down into her helmet. Eska glanced up, saw bubbles of air escaping, saw Eden hacking furiously at the creature, saw it angle itself to strike her with its snout.

Reaching down, Eska ripped her knife from the holster around her calf. The water had reached her chin. She willed herself to take a final breath, found she could not hold it against the panic rising in her chest, swallowed water. Half-choking, Eska swam up, the knife aimed for the smooth plane between the creature's eyes.

Their bodies met, her legs entangling with its lower jaw, her arm wrapped around the snout, the knife descending, water flooding her helmet. She managed a gasp, felt the water rush into her ears and nose. Out of air, lungs screaming, Eska sank away through a cloud of blood that wasn't hers. Before the lake took her, she knew the satisfaction of seeing her knife buried deep in the creature's head.

24

"A wolf has no master."

IT WAS, MANON DECIDED, NOT IDEAL TO BE INTRODUCED TO THE PRINcipe of Licenza while carrying two mysteriously acquired ingots of the Principe of Licenza's gold in one's satchel.

To her immense relief, as the ingots seemed to burn a hole in her back, the Principe was far too intent on watching his hounds bay and strain at their chains to pay much attention to the herald introducing Manon, much less Manon herself. Still, she began to think that traveling with two of the stolen ingots, despite the security they offered her—especially if the Archduke choose to suddenly retract his dubious patronage—was perhaps not the best decision.

The Principe held up a hand, cutting the herald off mid-word, and proceeded to walk down the corridor between the baying hounds and stop to contemplate the object of the dogs' attention.

The wolf was a sorry, skinny thing with matted fur and patches of dried blood in more than one place. It panted at the end of its own chain, head down, but yellow eyes unmistakably fixed on the new threat approaching. It lunged, testing the chain, testing the man, but the Principe had gauged the distance well and the wolf came up just short, its teeth snapping a hand's width from the Principe's kneecap.

Slowly, the man lowered himself until he was squatting at eye level with the wolf. A rumbling growl grew in the wolf's throat, but it seemed to know it would have no better luck with the man's nose and it made no other move.

The Principe stood suddenly, causing the wolf to flinch away, and walked back through the dogs. He looked at Manon, a casual, cursory examination, and then turned his attention to the herald. A single snap of his fingers silenced the dogs.

"If she doesn't know how to teach a wolf to hunt like a dog, to obey, then I don't care to speak to her." The Principe's voice was deep and strangely melodious.

The abrupt dismissal set Manon's jaw and though the weight of the ingots on her back suggested she ought to take the opportunity to disappear, she found herself once more in possession of the backbone that had deserted her when she faced the Archduke—and said backbone seemed determined to make up for its absence, consequences be damned.

"A wolf has no place among dogs. A wolf has no master."

The Principe's gaze slid back to Manon with such weight that she felt the need to step back. He had a handsome face, but it was the kind of handsome etched by cruelty and viciousness, and he wasn't so young that he could be said to be aspiring to cruelty. He wore it without artifice and with an appalling frankness.

Frankness, though, Manon could understand. Better that than the Archduke's slippery deception.

The Principe's gaze did not leave Manon as he addressed his herald. "Who is she?"

The herald just barely managed not to clear his throat. "Manon Barca, a representative of our fair sister city, Arconia."

"And what does she want?" Still his heavy gaze lingered on Manon.

Manon spoke before the herald. "I seek permission to visit the stone circle at Pontevellio. I'm studying the inscriptions." It was a story of her own concoction and one Manon was quite pleased with. Innocuous but respectable—and far better than admitting she needed to visit the Principe's private estate because the Archduke wanted her to. The Principe was notoriously protective of Pontevellio. Manon wondered how her father had gotten permission—or if Julian Barca had forgone such niceties entirely.

The Principe's gaze narrowed. "I suppose you think you'll learn something new that the countless useless scholars before you somehow missed."

Manon put on as cheerful a smile as she could muster and hoped the anger biting away at the edges of it wasn't too obvious. "My employer is optimistic."

The Principe of Licenza's mouth curled into a scathing, contemptuous smile—in other words exactly what Manon wanted to see. The sooner he forgot her existence, the better. He turned back to the herald. "Tell Rinalto to write her a four day pass." He contemplated the hounds once more and sighed when the herald spoke.

"Shall the pass include use of a guest room?"

"No, that would imply I wanted her there. But a hunting lodge should do. There's one close to the stone circle. Rinalto will know it." The Principe glanced at Manon once more. "I won't be furnishing you with supplies or assistance. Anything you bring in with you must come back out with you. The lodge is," he paused, his eyes gleaming at the anticipation of Manon's discomfort, "rustic." The Principe began to walk away but then stopped and faced Manon again. The gleam grew brighter as he smiled a vicious smile. "And beware of the wolves, madam. They run rampant on that part of the coast and are bold enough to attack people—and not just the careless ones."

⸺◆⸺

Wolves or no, Pontevellio was quite possibly the most beautiful place Manon had ever been.

She did not, however, appreciate this while arriving on horseback, soaked through by unrelenting rain, each step of her horse's hooves squelching into the muddy track. The second horse, the one weighed down by a bundle of supplies strapped into a frame on its back, had planted its feet after the rain went horizontal, refusing to take another step until finally the lead horse must have bribed it, or so Manon imagined, to continue. Though what one horse might bribe another with was beyond her.

It was in that semi-delirious state that she nearly missed the hunting lodge. The track she was following rambled along the coast in a vaguely southwesterly direction, taking her along cliff tops and through pine forests—the sparse kind with plenty of space between the trees, providing precisely no shelter from the rain—and it was after a particularly terrifying, muddy descent into a cleft between hills that had Manon convinced she and the horses were about to attain the bottom on their, well, bottoms, that she found herself in a dense thicket of pines. So dense, in fact, that she could barely see the pebbly beach and the sea to her right and almost rode past the timber hunting lodge sheltered back in the trees to her left.

The horses were only too glad to stop and for a moment, Manon and the beasts of burden were both content to savor the fact that they were no longer being pelted with fat drops of rain. When she began to shiver, Manon slid from her saddle and led the horses through the trees toward the lodge, her mind focused solely on the question of whether she would find dry firewood inside.

A small stable stood just across the clearing the lodge was hunkered in and Manon led the horses inside, glad to find it solidly built and leak-free. She got the horses settled, being sure to put out some of the grain she had purchased before leaving Licenza, then made her way to the lodge.

Rustic the Principe had called it, but small it was not, and Manon found herself in a cavernous great room filled with antlers and more than a few skulls of various beasts that had been unfortunate enough to cross paths with the Principe of Licenza and his predecessors. Manon saw, with relief, an ample stack of firewood next to the massive stone hearth at the far end of the hall. After depositing her supplies on a long table, Manon laid some logs and kindling in the hearth and, though her shivering was so violent she could hardly feel her gift, called upon the spark in her ribs to light them.

The fire crackled to life and Manon forced herself to step away from the kernel of warmth and strip out of her wet clothes. She dragged a rough timber chair close to the fire and spread her trousers, shirts, and cloak across it, then pawed through the rest of what she had brought with her. Nothing had escaped the rain entirely, but she found a second tunic nestled deeply enough that it was more dry than wet. Manon slid it over her head, set out everything else to dry on the long table, and then crouched as close to the fire as she could get, knees tucked up into her shirt and arms wrapped around her legs.

She woke later curled on her side, warm enough to tell she'd slept for some time, but damp enough still to grimace at the way her hair clung to her. She stretched and straightened and came to her feet, and only then did she notice the woman seated at the far end of the lodge, back to the door, feet up on the table, bow resting across her thighs.

Manon backed up to the hearth and cupped a ball of flame behind her back. "Who are you?"

The woman pushed back from the table and stood, rain sliding down her thick, oiled hood and cloak to drip at her feet.

"You first." She had a long dark braid that fell over one shoulder and she watched Manon with sharp eyes, but it was her feet that caught Manon's attention. Her right leg ended just above her ankle and where her foot should have been, a metal contraption supported her weight.

"I don't make a habit of exchanging pleasantries with bandits."

The woman laughed. "If I were a bandit, you'd be lying in a pool of your own blood after I cut your throat while you slept, and I'd be far gone from here already." Her gaze shifted minutely to take in Manon's pack of supplies and the belongings spread out to dry. "Along with your valuables."

"Valuables? You'd be disappointed." Manon curled her fingers around the flames in her palm.

"Isn't that precisely what someone with something to hide would say?" The woman's fingers made no move for the quiver at her hip, but Manon had the distinct impression she could nock and loose an arrow with deadly speed if she chose. Her bow was strung, after all, and experienced archers didn't tend to walk around with their strings exposed to the elements, leaving Manon to deduce it had been strung after the woman entered the lodge and for the strict purpose of intimidation. "Fortunately for you, your valuables don't interest me. But your purpose here does. Because my valuables are out there." She pointed her thumb back over her shoulder toward the door.

Manon waited for her to continue, waited for an explanation or any indication of who she might be, but the woman seemed content to stand in silence, her thumb brushing back and forth against the taut bowstring.

"I have a pass," Manon ventured at last.

"Let's see it."

"Not until you set that bow out of reach."

The woman grinned. "I assure you, I have more than one way to kill you. But if you insist." She stepped close to the table and unstrung the bow, then set the slender piece of curved wood on the table's broad planks. She then removed her rain cloak, revealing a leather strap running diagonally across her chest and holding sheathes for four—no, five—knives of varying size.

The gesture was not lost on Manon and she, suddenly out of patience, brought her arm out from behind her back, revealing the fireball cradled in her hand.

"Enough of this. I don't take well to being threatened." Manon gestured at the door. "Leave."

The woman was watching the fire with a certain amount of healthy respect, but she did not seem overly concerned. "Unexpected," she said, her mouth curving into a smile. "I can appreciate that. I don't take well to being threatened either." One hand reached for a knife and the blade flashed in the firelight as she drew it. The other hand released a buckle on her quiver, which fell to the floor at her feet, where it might no longer hamper her movement.

It was in that moment, as Manon was deciding whether to dodge first—in anticipation of a knife streaking toward her—and then launch her fire, or the reverse, that the door to the lodge flew open with a bang and a cursing, bedraggled figure stepped across the threshold.

"Gods, woman, do you want my cock to wash away in this rain? You've left me to shrivel up like an old man's balls."

The woman's face twisted in annoyance. Without looking at the new arrival, she spoke. "I told you to wait outside."

The man at the far end of the lodge pushed back his hood and shook his shoulders like a dog. He seemed unaware of Manon's presence. "And I waited. But I'm done waiting. Last time you told me to wait outside, you forgot to tell me when I could come inside."

Something told Manon the woman hadn't forgotten at all.

"I'm a little occupied, Luca. If you didn't notice."

The man was pulling a heavy woolen overshirt over his head. "Not sure why I should care." He seemed to get stuck somewhere in the armpits and it took several yanks to free his broad shoulders. "You don't even want a partner."

"Then we agree on something."

At last the man, now that he had littered the ground around him with two swords, a bow made from a dark wood, a holster of knives, three drawstring leather bags, and a pair of toothy steel traps—not to mention his wet cloak and sodden wool shirt—looked up long enough to take note of Manon standing in front of the hearth. A wide smile spread to his wind-pinked cheeks.

"Hello. Nasty storm, isn't it. Haven't seen rain like this all season. Those horses both yours? Traveling alone?"

From another mouth, the questions might have been ominous, but the man's soggy appearance and the woman's exasperated expression told Manon quite the opposite.

The man strode the length of the hall and rested his elbow on the woman's shoulder, either oblivious to the knife in her hand—and the fire in Manon's—or entirely unsurprised by such behavior.

"Ah, I see my partner is threatening you. She's delightful, isn't she."

"She threatened me," the woman said, her annoyance descending into petulance.

"And now you both appear to be threatening each other. Seems like good fun. Just your sort of rainy day activity, eh, Justina?"

Her frustration mounting, the woman shrugged out from under the man's elbow and flung her knife into the floorboards at his feet. It quivered there for a moment. "Have you no concern for who this woman might be? On the Principe's private lands?"

The man smiled cheerfully again. "I'm sure a civilized line of questioning would be acceptable to the lady."

"You're forgetting this," Manon said, interrupting and taking a step forward. She allowed the ball of flames to blaze brighter for a moment. "I'd like you both to leave."

Justina bristled. "You have no authority here. I'll give the orders."

Manon felt her spark surge with anger. She let the flames grow to encase her arm. "And I'll burn you where you stand."

Justina lunged at Manon, surprising her enough to cause the flames to wink out. Manon stumbled back to avoid the collision, desperately kicking a stool into the woman's path as she called the fire back to her hand. Justina leaped—awkwardly, her metal foot catching on the stool, and crashed to her hands and knees at Manon's feet.

Manon went to one knee and grasped the woman's collar, her flames bright in Justina's eyes. The hunter flinched away from the heat.

"No!"

Luca's shout drew Manon's attention. She braced herself, but he made no move to attack her. Instead, he thumped his chest once, as though he needed to cough, inhaled deeply, and exhaled with sudden force.

The lodge went dark.

———— •— ————

Someone was screaming.

Manon dropped to her knees, the darkness suffocating her, her fingers reaching across the flagstones of the hearth for something, anything. She wished for the agonized, desperate screaming to stop, wished for someone to put the poor creature out of its misery.

It was when she reached for the spark between her ribs that Manon recoiled violently in horror and her mind realized what her body had already felt.

The spark was gone, sucked away, a yawning void in its place, its absence a thing Manon could not comprehend.

She was the wounded, broken creature. The screams were hers.

Voices, words Manon's shattered mind couldn't understand. Then the woman's voice cut through, clearer, but no longer ringing with certainty. "Holy sister, what did you do?"

No answer. Hands reached for her. Her limbs went limp, the will to fight forgotten, though her body shuddered and spasmed against the floorboards. The hands held her fast, but not unkindly.

"Make it stop." The woman again.

"I can't."

The voices seemed to echo around Manon, coming from all directions at once.

"She'll be all right. I've seen it before. Just give it time. Don't let her hurt herself."

"Some light would be nice." The acerbic tone was creeping back into the woman's voice as the shock slipped away.

"Right. I forgot."

"What, don't tell me you can see in the dark, too?" Silence. "Fucking gods, Luca. What are you?"

The man gave no answer.

Manon felt her body still, saw a match catch, saw the hearth flare with fire once more from the corner of her vision. Her screams had turned to whimpers and she had never before wished so completely to die.

As the light from the fire grew, two faces looming over Manon came into existence. The woman was frowning, whatever concern she felt tinged with impatience. The man was smiling pleasantly and leaned closer to peer into Manon's eyes. She tried to twist away, moaning, tears spilling from her eyes unbidden, but their hands kept her from moving.

"She's coming out of it," the man said. "Her pupils are returning to normal size."

"Just kill me," Manon mumbled, exhausted from endlessly reaching for the fire that wasn't there.

The man grimaced. "Why would we do that?"

"Please." A final spasm shook her body. "Please," she tried again. "I can't live without it."

"Oh. Your gift. I understand. It'll be back." He smiled again. The void inside Manon pulsed, as though taunting her, and she shivered from fear and doubt.

The woman, Manon realized, had vanished from sight, and her voice called over to the man.

"She wasn't lying. There's a pass here. Looks to be in order." A pause. "She has four days to study the stone circle."

"I hope you'll forgive me," the man was saying, apparently unconcerned with his partner's rummaging. "I don't like doing that to people. But you seemed unwilling to compromise."

Manon's eyes rolled up in her head and she felt sick. She coughed, choking on the bile rising in her throat, and the man turned her on her side.

"Don't worry. That happens," he said, as pleasant as ever.

Manon heaved out the contents of her stomach and when she had finished, the man lifted her into a sitting position. She swayed in his grip. She tried to speak, wet her lips with saliva she didn't have.

"What did you do to me?" she croaked.

"Let's get some water down you first." The man stood and caught the water flask his partner threw, then knelt quickly to prevent Manon from pitching over. "Ah, now you're dizzy," he said. "Everything is progressing as it should." He held the flask to her lips and, though a great deal of it dribbled down her chin, she managed to swallow some. The dizziness didn't abate, but Manon focused her concentration and grabbed the man's wrist before he could move away.

"What did you do to me?" she repeated, wishing she sounded less desperate and more forceful. Still she grasped for what wasn't there, her hysteria rising.

"I hate to say it, but I'm with her, Luca." The woman stood near the hearth, hands planted on her hips. "I think you need to start talking."

The man's face, a melted, blurry version of it, swam before Manon. "Have you heard of Carrier fever?"

Manon shook her head and was rewarded with a fresh wave of dizziness.

"The blood curse?" The man lifted her as he spoke and deposited her in a chair. "Espahdiza's Haunting? I think that's all the names for it. All the names I know at least."

Manon shook her head again. "I don't care what it's called," she rasped. "Tell me."

"I can take away a Carrier's gift. Temporarily, of course." The man shrugged. "I don't know why or how or what exactly it is I'm doing."

"When?" Manon asked.

"When will your gift return? It's different for everyone, I think." He looked at Manon closely, hesitating for the first time. "I'm told it's nearly unbearable."

Manon wanted to scream, wanted to hurt him the way he had hurt her, but there was nothing she could do to him to make him feel what she felt, nothing she could do to rip away his very existence and leave a shell of himself to understand what was lost. She seemed to convey some of this in her glare, for the man reddened slightly and turned away.

Manon closed her eyes. She couldn't stop searching for the spark, to do so was as natural to her as breathing, but she could feel her balance and strength returning.

"I can't believe you kept this from me, Luca. We're supposed to be partners," Justina said.

Luca stood up from where he had crouched next to Manon's chair. "You made it abundantly clear you weren't interested in a partner, Justina. I think that gives me grounds for keeping secrets. Especially secrets that could get me killed."

"What's Espahdiza's Haunting? Who's Espahdiza?" Manon said,

interrupting the tension between the two.

"Espahdiza? No idea. Some long dead woman, I'd wager," Luca said. "It's just one of the names I've managed to discover for the loss of a Carrier's gift. Carrier fever is the more common name, I think, but it's a rare thing, and I've found that asking too many questions about it puts more interest on my head than I care for." He crouched next to Manon once more. "How are you feeling?"

Manon glared again. "If I had my gift, you'd be ash already. Does that answer your question?"

To her annoyance, Luca smiled. "Well enough to threaten me. I'll take that as a good sign."

"Who are you?" Manon asked. "And what do you want with me?"

"We're hunters, guardians of the Principe's estate. We keep an eye on the animals, herd health, pack numbers, that sort of thing," Luca said. "Oh, and we track down poachers."

It took Manon a moment to realize the implication. "If I were a poacher, why would I take shelter in the Principe's own lodge?"

"You might be surprised at what they think they can get away with," Justina said, crossing her arms in front of her as she stared down at Manon. It was enough to recall the earlier standoff, knife against fire, and Manon shivered with anger—no, helplessness, she realized. She held Justina's gaze, though, determined not to let her weakness show, willing herself not to be the first to look away.

"Did you know the old stories say the stone circle is a doorway that drags malicious spirits of the dead to the afterlife?" Luca was studying Manon's pass, oblivious to the silent standoff between the two women. "Folk have been passing down those stories in this region for generations. Seems like nonsense, if you ask me."

Justina rolled her eyes. "A fine thing for the man who can steal Carrier power to say."

Luca frowned. "I don't steal it. That implies I keep it for myself," he said. He turned back to Manon. "I'd give it back if I could."

His apologetic expression was genuine—indeed, his face didn't seem capable of subterfuge or shadowing his thoughts—but Manon could not forgive what he had done. She looked back at the fire.

"Still raining," Justina said. "Harder, if my ears aren't lying and if that's even possible. Think you can stop fussing over her long enough to help me fry up a meal?"

"You're staying?" Despite herself, Manon turned in her chair.

"I'm certainly not going back out in the storm."

Luca seemed to notice the tension this time and he stepped between them. "Plenty of rabbits to go around. Apples, too. And bread, fresh from the oven this morning. Might be a bit soggy, though," he said, trailing off.

It was that moment Manon's gift chose to return, surging through her with such ferocity, such wildness, that flames blazed from her hands unbidden, a deluge of fire to rival the storm outside. Manon twisted in her chair, falling to her knees, dizziness overcoming her once more as she wrestled with her gift—wrestled and lost as the lodge began to burn.

25

"I don't recall there being skill involved."

ESKA COUGHED.

Her lungs burned. Water spewed from her mouth. Another cough. More water dribbling down her cheek.

Her eyes flew open but she could see nothing other than bright light. Another cough wracked her chest.

A voice. Faint. Disembodied.

A hand on her back, keeping her on her side, another hand on her waist.

At last her eyes processed the shape of a head leaning over her. Warm eyes. Dark hair. Silver ink curling up his neck. Eden.

She became aware of something digging into her hip and tried to shift away. Eden helped her sit up, his hands seeming to hold her ribcage together as a fit of coughing surged through her chest.

"Breathe. Just breathe," he whispered in her ear. "You're safe." Using his foot, he shoved away the diving helmet and the metal buckles on which Eska had been lying. The rowboat rocked gently. As her coughing subsided, Eska assessed her body. The diving silks were nearly in tatters, stingers protruded from her skin, and here and there blood oozed from her many tiny wounds.

"Is it dead?" she heard herself ask.

Eden let out a hoarse, strained bark of laughter. "Quite dead. Somehow I'm not surprised you know how to use a knife."

"I don't recall there being skill involved." Eska tried to laugh, but the sound her throat emitted sounded rather more like a sob. Eden's arms wrapped around her and for the first time Eska was aware of the warm sunlight shining down from a clear sky. She also became aware of the third person in the rowboat.

Bastien was staring at the water, tear marks visible on his pale cheeks, hands clenched in his lap as he knelt in the bottom of the boat.

"My lady," he said, fresh tears spilling from his eyes. "Forgive me. Forgive me."

Eska stirred from Eden's embrace, reaching out weakly towards the younger man. Their fingers met and tangled together. "Bastien, you are not to blame." His hand trembled in hers and he didn't meet her gaze. "Look at me," she said. After a moment, he did as she asked. "There was nothing you could have done." Eska tried a smile. "And don't even think of saying you should have been the one to make the dive. That would be nonsense and you know it."

He nodded and wiped at his tears, but then his gaze dropped once more, this time landing on the diving helmets.

The glass masks stared up at Eska. The leather of her suit was studded with spiny needles and rent through in multiple places.

"We seem to have ruined your invention," Eska said, glancing over her shoulder. The Regatta Master sat on the rowboat's stern, his gaze fixed somewhere over Eska's head. He drew in a long breath, but rather than speak, he dropped backward over the edge.

"No!" Eska shouted—or tried, but it came out as a weak gasp. She made to scramble across the rowboat, but dropped to the bottom, her lungs burning, hands grasping her chest. "No, no," she repeated. Stricken, she looked back at Bastien. "What is he doing?"

She knew the answer of course. He was going back for the reliquary. Her mind raced, trying to calculate the depth of the lake and how long a diver could hope to hold a breath, trying to fathom how he could find the vault in time, with no stones to speed his descent and no light to see by. But every scenario she could imagine ended with him thrashing somewhere in the depths of Lake Delo, the last of his air escaping from his lungs as his body sank down to rest in the mud. A Carrier gifted in the ways of water could control it, conjure it—but not breathe it.

The horror she felt was written across Bastien's face. Eska wanted to cry out, wanted to dive in and follow Eden, but she was helpless and could only grip the sides of the rowboat and stare into the deep blue of the lake.

They waited in silence, the moments dragging on, each beat of Eska's own heart a cruel reminder of the air she could breathe but Eden could not. She scanned the surface of the lake continuously, her mind tricking her into thinking she saw a shape rising from the depths. But there was only the quiet lapping of waves against the wooden hull of the rowboat.

She was crying, she realized, tears coursing silently down her cheeks, marring her vision. Too much time had passed. No one could survive that long. Eden San-Germain had died for her.

The lake heaved under the rowboat, nearly capsizing it and sending Bastien overboard. They reached for each other, Eska fearing a second creature come to seek its final revenge.

But no scaly body emerged from the lake, no stingers pierced the bottom of the rowboat. Instead, as though riding an invisible wave, the Regatta Master surged above the surface of Lake Delo, his black silks gleaming in the sunlight as water streamed off him, and—Eska's breath caught—an ivory and gold reliquary box in his hands.

— ◆ —

"Impossible."

It was not an especially erudite statement, and as observations go, the evidence in Eska's hands proved it to be utterly false, and yet when she had regained the use of her tongue some moments after Eden San-Germain had returned to the rowboat and deposited the precious reliquary in her hands, that was all she could manage to say.

Eden ran a hand through his wet hair, a smile that Eska could only describe as apologetic on his face.

"Can you," Bastien spoke up, then hesitated, his gaze dropping quickly when Eden looked at him.

"No, I can't breathe water like a fish," Eden said, the smile broadening.

They drifted on the lake, none of them yet thinking of taking up the oars and returning to shore. Bastien could not take his eyes from the box and Eska, well, she was hardly better off. As for Eden, the smile aside, he seemed to be utterly at ease, lounging against the side of the rowboat, soaking up the sun.

"I take it you know how to open it?" Eden asked.

Eska turned the box over in her hands—as she had done more than a dozen times already. "It's different from the other," she murmured. "But yes. Eventually."

"The other?"

Now it was Eska's turn to smile, though her lungs still ached. "It seems I have made a habit of coming across these. But I got lucky with the first one. Somehow I don't think I was meant to be able to open it while traversing rooftops in Arconia."

Eden raised an eyebrow. "Rooftops. A second box. You are a very interesting woman, Eska."

Eska looked him in the eye. "De Caraval." He waited. "That's my name. Eska de Caraval. I'm not sure why I kept it from you."

Eden shrugged, his face tilted to the sun. "We do what we have to do. You had me at a disadvantage when we first me, thanks to our mutual friend." He stirred at last and motioned for Bastien to give up the rower's bench. "Come. Your friends will begin to wonder."

Eska laughed. "If they haven't already assumed the worst."

Their return to shore was greeted with excitement, followed quickly by consternation when the state of Eska's diving silks was noticed. It was Gabriel who first caught sight of the nearly severed air hose and stingers in the leather suits, but to Eska's relief, the engineer kept his lips firmly pressed together. The others exclaimed over the ruined equipment and it was Bastien who began to tell the story, the bits and pieces spilling forth in a jumbled confusion until at last the oldest member of the small crew, Ilius, begged him to slow down and tell the thing properly.

Eska smiled and drifted away to her tent, eager for a moment of peace and desperate to tend to her irritated skin and lie down and rest. She had removed the stingers and felt she could, by that time, safely assume there was no toxin coursing through her bloodstream, but the red bumps the darts had left behind burned sharply. She didn't notice Eden had followed her until she, kneeling in front of her small trunk and unable to find the salve she was looking for, kicked at the trunk in frustration and then promptly cursed her toes for having the gall to hurt. Eden's laugh drew her attention to the tent entrance.

"You may have just done something rather heroic and splendid," Eska said, "but unless you can rip my skin off in one piece like a shedding snake, I'll thank you for not laughing." She stood with her hands on her hips, aware the shredded silks and her half-dried hair made for a wholly disheveled picture.

He was still grinning. "I don't think such extremes will be necessary. But I do think the best place for you right now is a hot bath followed by a liberal application of indicca oil."

"That's a fine suggestion, but I have neither of those things."

"But I do." Eden, seeing her gaze shift, stepped between Eska and the table bearing the reliquary box, breaking her line of sight. "The box can wait."

And so Eska, after riding to Cancalo and entering the Regatta Master's home for the second time—by the front door this time, found herself soaking in a tub in a beautifully tiled bath chamber, steaming water up to her chin, the pleasant smell of eucalyptus and mint wafting around her head, suspended in that delicious place between wakefulness and sleep.

After drawing the bath—the man still appeared to have no serving staff—Eden had left her in peace, and when Eska felt refreshed and clean and as steamed as a clam, she ventured out of the tiled room, pulling on a silk painted robe he had thoughtfully left for her as she went. There were two doors to the chamber and Eska chose the one she had not entered through, opening it to reveal a room that was the twin of the one on the opposite side of the courtyard—green and lush and full of billowing white curtains and dark wood screens—except for the addition of a large bed sunk into the floor with a small, burbling reflecting pool at its foot.

Eden stepped from the balcony. He was once again wearing nothing but the sheer robe she had first seen him in. Without a word, Eska untied the belt on her robe and let it fall to the floor, then she closed the distance between them until she could feel the faint flutter of his breathing.

"Did you know?"

Eska's question hung for a moment between them.

"Did I know what?"

"That you could swim to the bottom of Lake Delo without air. That you could bend the entire lake to your will as easily as the wind does a sapling." She held his gaze. "Did you know you would survive?"

"No," he said at last. "I would never have put you in a diving helmet if I had known that."

"Then why did you do it? Why risk it?"

Eden stood quietly, gaze boring into her, then took up her hand and placed her fingers on his chest. "You know what is written here." He sighed. "There are some who believe Venadascar is gone. Vanished. A thing of memory only. A thing that belongs to the dead. But I am not dead. I am alive. And as long as I am alive, Venadascar survives. Her story lives on my skin and my very existence is part of that story. But what is existence without risk?"

The heart under Eska's hand beat with a steady, strong rhythm as Eden touched his forehead to hers. Still, they held each other's gaze. At last she brought her hands to the sides of his neck, his hair curling through her fingers.

"Thank you," she whispered. "It is not enough, but I thank you. Now about that liberal application of indicca oil."

He took her by the hand and led her to the bed, then, as she settled on her stomach on the soft linens, fetched a small blue pot from the bath chamber. Sitting on the bed next to her, Eden pushed the hair off the back of her neck, then poured the amber-colored oil into one palm and rubbed his hands together. Eska closed her eyes. His touch was gentle but firm. Experienced, she decided, as he worked his hands up the back of one leg.

"You haven't said anything about my name," she said as he massaged one of the raised, irritated areas with his thumbs. The oil was instantly soothing.

"What name? The one you happen to share with two of the most senior officials in the Arconian government?"

Eska smiled into the bed. "That name."

"You felt the need for secrecy when you arrived, who am I to demand otherwise?"

"You mean for me to believe that you didn't ask around? Didn't try to find out who this strange woman was?"

Eden's hands paused for a moment and Eska expected a confession. What she got was entirely different. "I respect the boundaries people put up. Is that so unbelievable?"

It was Eska's turn to hesitate and she lifted her head from the pillow to look over her shoulder at him, her hair falling over one eye. "I suppose I have come to expect differently from the world. And the people in it."

"That sounds like a very difficult world to live in."

"Everyone wants something. Needs information. Seeks acclaim. Wants to cut down the competition. You mean to tell me you don't see it? You don't feel it?"

The hands on her lower back went still. "Oh, I see it. Which is precisely why I try not to live it."

Eska sat up, twisting so she could better look him in the eye. But it wasn't words that spoke for her, not in that moment. She reached over and placed one palm on his cheek, then leaned in to kiss him. His hands slid down her back and his eyes seemed to ask for permission to go further, but it was Eska who pulled him down to the bed and demanded a great deal more from him.

———— ◆ ————

"Why do you dislike Carriers?"

The question came after, with sunlight streaming through the filigreed balcony doors and a platter of juicy grapes and figs between them on the bed. Eden had poured a crisp, refreshing wine and the light pierced Eska's glass, shattering it into countless pieces over Eden's bare skin. He lay with one arm behind his head, the other hand trailing up and down Eska's stomach.

"Do you mean other than because the most infamous family of Carriers our world has ever seen were so powerful they destroyed everything that stood between them and their quest for dominance and immortality?"

Eden smiled. "Let's leave the Alescu dynasty out of the equation."

"What makes you think I dislike Carriers?" It was an evasive tactic—and a poor one, Eska knew, but instinctual.

The smile grew. "I seem to recall a moment on the shore of Lake Delo in which your face became exceptionally severe and, dare I say, terrifying. It was, if you can imagine, the precise moment you understood that you held an object flowing with Carrier-gift."

"Why not ask me about it in that moment?" If they were capable, Eska's eyeballs would have been rolling themselves at her continued avoidance.

Eden propped himself up on one elbow and his other hand came to rest on her hip. "Boundaries."

"And now?"

He wrapped his arm around her waist and pulled her to him in one swift movement, then removed the wine glass from between her fingers and set it aside as he kissed her. "I would hope that risking our lives at the bottom of a lake, facing a deadly creature that definitely wanted to eat us, and emerging triumphantly from the depths with a priceless artifact might have caused some of those boundaries to vanish. Coincidentally, of course."

"Not to mention the events of the past two hours," Eska said, smiling.

"Now you're catching on," he murmured, leaning close to kiss her neck.

Eden had kissed his way down to her navel before Eska was able to summon the words.

"My prejudice against those who Carry was built first on my early lessons about the Alescuan kings and queens. Like any child, I learned about that malevolent, vicious family, men and women who did not hesitate to kill for power, who used their unmatched Carrier skills to bend the will of the world to their whims. But you're right, that's not all." Eska sighed and lay back on the closest pillow, casting her gaze up at the painted ceiling.

"It's two stories, really. Though in my mind and heart they quickly coalesced into one, branding me. I cannot think of one without the other. I was young, impetuous, and already fiercely proud. Of my family name, my parents, my uncle, myself," Eska added in response to Eden's unspoken question. "The first took place twelve years ago. I was at the Varadome, brought there by my uncle. I was sent to wait in a garden while he met with the Archduke. I had brought with me a manuscript, a gift from my uncle, who had recently unearthed a trove of scrolls, the personal correspondence of Leonato de Scipicus. The astronomer," Eska added, "the one who first theorized about the rotation of our earth around the sun."

"Oh, that Scipicus," Eden said with mock seriousness. "And here I was thinking of the one who told the first rude joke."

"Do you want to hear the story or not?"

Eden brought her palm to his lips. "Go on."

"It wasn't Leonato's papers that entranced me. It was his wife's. Geneveira. Letters between them revealed she was an equal partner in his discoveries, that her contributions helped him through thorny problems. I could hardly believe what I was reading. I tore through the letters, perhaps the only person since Geneveira herself to know just how valuable her mind was to the scientific understanding of her era. It was remarkable." Eska sighed. "I brought one of the letters with me to the Varadome that day. My favorite. And I met a girl in the garden. We were about the same age. She asked what I was reading. And so I shared it with her. She listened to me for a few moments as I prattled on and then asked my name. I gave it to her. To this day, I don't know who she was, but she knew me. Her face twisted into a sneer as she insulted my family, calling my parents corrupt." Eska looked at Eden. "And then she plucked the priceless letter from my hand, summoned water from the fountain and drowned Geneveira's words right in front of me. I could have, if not forgiven, forgotten the insults. I could have gone home in an ill temper but woken up the next day determined to move on. If not for the letter. That she could, without a care, for nothing more than spite, destroy such a thing." Eska shook her head. "Some might call it childish, but I had never truly known anger until that day."

"Generally speaking, Eska, and correct me if I'm mistaken, it might be considered childish to pout over the absence of a sweet before bed, or to make up stories about how the dog got covered in green paint. Not, shall we say, distress over the loss of a priceless object that would have affected the work of countless—or at least six—scholars."

Eska laughed but then grew quiet. "I still think about that letter."

The humor vanished from Eden's face and he leaned close to kiss her. "Of course you do." For a moment they were lost in each other once again, hands exploring, lips tasting. And just when Eska began to forget the conversation that had brought them to that point, Eden paused, his fingers hovering teasingly, his breath hot against her skin.

"And the other story?"

Eska groaned and shoved a pillow in his face. "Is of absolutely no importance, I assure you."

Laughing, Eden poured more wine and settled back on the bed, but Eska got to her feet and began to pace, driven on by the words that followed.

"Do you know anything of the Cult of Mercuria?"

"A harmless rabble?" Eden said. Eska was quite sure he was guessing. "Intent on seeing a horse made supreme ruler of the Seven Cities?"

Eska's smile was short-lived. "Something more than harmless, I'm afraid. The Cult of Mercuria is young and full of young fanatics. It only came into existence shortly before I was born. They believe they are called by a dead prophet to honor a dead woman who supposedly sacrificed her life to save the city when Arconia was in its infancy, generations before the Alescus, before the league of the Seven Cities of Bellara was even conceived of."

"And how would they honor this dead woman?"

"By killing my mother." The words burst from Eska, bitter and sharp.

"Why?"

"They never managed to explain themselves with any clarity," Eska said, her jaw tight, glad for the sarcasm to take some of the anger from her voice. "Something about her blood and how the spilling of it would save the city again, or some such nonsense."

"And they Carried?"

"Not all. Just the ones who broke the legs of the horses pulling the carriage transporting my mother home from Vienisi, who opened a chasm beneath the poor beasts, who set the carriage on fire as it plunged into the would-be tomb."

She had expected a muttered oath, an expression of outrage. But Eden's silence was a far better echo to the rage that shook her voice and shivered her skin.

"I'm sorry," Eden said at last. "I am sorry that was done to your family. How did she survive?"

"By her own quick thinking and that of two men charged with protecting her." Eska met Eden's gaze. "She carries scars from the fire. The men died." She took a deep breath. "This was mere days after I met that girl at the Varadome. And in the aftermath of that day, the actions of those Carriers fused with her petty spite. So now you see the making of my prejudice."

"Were they punished? These cultists?"

Eska nodded. "My mother was and still is a diplomat of the highest order—the law demands death for such an assault, after a fair trial, of course. The trial was swift, for they offered no defense and asked for no mercy. My father did not wish me to witness their execution. My uncle said it was my duty as the daughter of the Vice-Chancelier and the Ambassador-Superior of Arconia. My mother insisted the choice was mine to make."

"What did you choose?"

Eska closed her eyes as a breeze ruffled the thin curtains and lifted the hairs on her bare arms. "I watched. One of the usual methods." She opened her eyes and looked at Eden. "Did you know Carriers can stem the flow of their own blood? Some, I should say. I don't imagine it's a skill many possess. Something about controlling the water in the blood, I understand. One of these would-be assassins could. I watched as they cut open his belly, watched as the blood flowed out and then back in, by the sheer force of his own will. They made a second cut and began to draw out his intestines. Still the blood welled but did not spill. I wonder how long he could have continued on before his strength and abilities failed him. I'll never forget the silence as we watched him defy death, his skin fading to ash grey, his eyes rolling in their sockets with the effort. But then the executioner pierced his heart with a small blade and that, well that was apparently too much." As she finished speaking, Eska came to stand at the balcony doors, her arms crossed in front of her. She heard Eden rise from the bed and approach. A hand settled on her waist but nothing more, as though he understood the difference between supporting and smothering. When he spoke, his voice was soft in her ear.

"I am what I am."

And this time, the words were his alone, the echo of Alexandre de Minos forgotten.

"Can you live with that?"

Eska answered him without words.

Interlude 12

Excerpt from the Songs of Mercuria, the definitive text of the Cult of Mercuria comprised of the teachings of their prophet, Malo

For she is the shield against the dark and her light is the very light of the Bright One. She will shine it upon the worthy and wield it against the ruined and the fallen and those who deny the Bright One—sharper than any blade, stronger than any armor, her light shall be the scourge of the world and her death will bring both end and beginning, a new age.

Three times will she do this. Three lives will she live. Three deaths and three purifications. The first has come and gone. The second is near. The third will be revealed by a prophet yet to come. Watch for him, and heed him, for he will be the last and greatest, the true herald of the Bright One.

26

"At least I shall never do anything half so tedious again."

IT MIGHT BE POSSIBLE, WERE ONE TO UNDERTAKE A SEA VOYAGE OF SOME considerable length, even if one were a reluctant passenger harboring a great deal of trepidation for ships and sails and seas and things of that nature, it just might be possible for one to develop, if not a passion for the open water, at least a tolerance and, dare it be said, an appreciation.

This was not the case for Albus.

By the time the Seycherran pirates deposited Albus—rather like a sack of root vegetables gone limp—in a rowboat and put to shore, he would have been willing to wager a great deal that the crew was regretting their captain's decision to bring him aboard.

Not that Keleut, daughter of Nestor, seemed to care or share in their regret. No, she watched Albus pitch his insides over the side of her ship each morning—and usually again in the evening—with faint amusement. It was, he decided, her natural state, though it could be at turns tinged with intimidation, skepticism, and scathing dismissal. Indeed, when Albus's appreciation for the sea had not developed, the pirate captain had appeared to develop a condescending sort of affection for the librarian, offering a handkerchief—his own, complete with embroidery—and making comments about the pallor of his complexion, only to playfully insult his constitution, or lack thereof, within his hearing a moment later.

Though his insides ached and he was thoroughly tired of burning his throat each day with his stomach acid, it was their direction of travel that had most concerned Albus. It did not take long for even his landlocked mind to realize they were not headed for Seycherran waters, not directly, at least. The ship's course was far too northerly for that.

He had tried asking Keleut on the third day of the voyage, and then, when she rebuffed him with a laugh, put the question to various crew-members who didn't glower and grimace at his very existence. They either pantomimed that they could not understand his Seycherran—a ridiculous notion—or developed selective hearing in his presence.

And so Albus was left to ponder the Anerrean Sea in his head, ticking off possible destinations but coming no closer to an educated guess no matter how many arguments he held in the confines of his head. By the sixth day, he wanted to give up thinking about it. He wanted to crawl into the cramped bunk he had been allotted, curl up clutching his bottle of ink and crumpled pages of a book—all that was left of the Conqueror of Calviza's heroic accomplishments—and imagine he was back in his beloved Lordican. In fact, he did all three of these things, but he could not forget he was on a ship and his brain, no matter how he implored it, would not stop thinking.

As such, when the crew tucked Albus into the rowboat to go ashore, he was a pitiful excuse for a librarian and a scholar. His robes were wrinkled and stained, his normally clean shaven face was sporting an unsightly amount of reddish-brown hair, and his stomach tried to climb up his throat once more for good measure, earning him the annoyed glances of those in the rowboat with him.

But it was Keleut Albus was looking at, despite his poorly state. The pirate captain sat at the bow, her hands grasping the sides, leaning forward as though she could propel the small boat to shore through sheer desire. As it was, the rowers clearly went about their business far too slowly for her tastes, and she barked at them in Seycherran more than once, her anticipation undiminished, her gaze remaining fixed on the shore.

And what a shore it was.

The sea wall of Onaxos rose up to an astonishing height, blocking out all sight of the city within. Indeed, the nature of the headland the city was built on was such that the sea wall was very nearly all Albus could see, rearing up out of the waves like something left behind when some ancient gods fled the world.

Solid iron it was, and crowned with ten towers. A horn called down to them and Keleut looked back at her ship, nodding as she spotted the flag waving in response. Whatever the signal was, it appeared to be acceptable, and Albus watched in astonishment as a door slid up from the water, revealing a passage large enough to accept a ship many times the size of Keleut's pirate vessel. Albus supposed the fact that they were taking a mere rowboat through had something to do with the nature of Keleut's relationship with whoever was expecting her. Were he less ill, he might have taken some satisfaction in suspecting that his kidnapper was less than thrilled by this. As it was, he merely clutched at the rower closest to him—earning himself yet another grimace—as the rowboat pitched over a wave.

It was said in the Seven Cities of Bellara that everyone who saw what was behind the sea wall of Onaxos was dead. Naturally Albus didn't go in for that sort of generalization. Onaxos had stood on that headland for longer than most cities on the Anerrean Sea, and most of the cousins of its time had been turned to ruins in an era when recorded history was in its infancy. Therefore, logic—and a large quantity of sarcasm—would dictate that, indeed, most of the eyes that had seen beyond the sea wall belonged to dead men and women. But Albus was equally aware that he had not met an individual, not in Arconia, not in Licenza or Cancalo or Vienisi or anywhere on the roads between those four cities, who could say what lay behind the great wall. Onaxos was, in short, something of a mystery, an insular city, notorious for shunning foreigners.

As such, when the rowboat passed through the iron wall, so thick they rowed through twilight, the sounds of the waves pinging off the iron around them, that Albus took in everything he saw with the weight of the Lordican and his fellow scholars on his shoulders.

Or so he intended. In reality, when he caught sight of the colossal statue straddling the harbor inside the sea wall, Albus's jaw dropped open and he could not have been sure of the color of his own eyes in that moment.

"Gets your attention, doesn't it," Keleut said, that expression of amusement curling her mouth as she watched Albus gape.

"It's remarkable," Albus managed. His gaze roamed up the statue's legs, taking in the image of a being split in two, the right half clothed in the thick folds of a heavy robe, the left half in armor. A raven perched on the right shoulder, while the left hand grasped a trident taller than the statue. Albus craned his neck to catch a glimpse of the statue's head, noting the tiny forms of birds flitting and soaring over its mane of curly hair. Just like the body, the head, too, was divided down the middle, the right half that of a man, the left a woman. From that distance, though he could make out faint differences in their countenances, the overarching impression Albus had was of equal and shared sternness.

"Taalo and Toora," Albus breathed. "The twin gods of Onaxos."

"I'm glad your scholarly learning hasn't failed you," Keleut said with a snort. "But I didn't bring you here to tell me about this lump of stone, as big and impressive as it might be."

Albus tore his gaze from the face of the gods. "Why did you bring me here?"

Keleut smiled, giving Albus a decidedly unpleasant sensation, and a persistent rumor about Onaxos he had first heard as a child came back to him in a rush that sent a fresh wave of nausea roiling through his belly: the twin gods had a taste for blood. Specifically the blood of naughty children who had pilfered one too many sweets, but Albus, as they passed beneath the Twins' legs, could not quite shake the distinct notion that Keleut intended to make some sort of sacrifice out of him.

With the twin deities behind them, Albus could properly study the city of Onaxos for the first time. Built predominantly out of grey stone, it rose out of the headland in neat layers, each slightly smaller than the one below. But the dominant feature was a spire that rose from the highest level, jutting up from the city like a needle, grey and imposing and wrapped in white smoke.

The rowboat put in at a pier and Keleut jumped ashore to speak quickly with a uniformed man waiting for them. He nodded at her words, asked a single question, and then beckoned for a subordinate, a bare-chested man wearing a trident across his back. More words were exchanged, and then Keleut's pirates and Albus were waved onward and allowed to disembark. The trident-wielder led the way—as three other identically armed men fell in behind them—but he did not take them to a road or a wagon or even horses. Instead, Albus found himself, where he would have expected a wide thoroughfare adjacent to the port in any number of cities, confronting an exceptionally large trough of water. He might have said pool, except it was not decorative, that much was certain, and the water level was far below where he stood. The word canal came to mind, a word only, as Albus had not seen the distant city of Eresii which was said to be built on water and have canals instead of roads. But even with that kernel of knowledge, Albus was uncertain, for the trough before him was hemmed in on all sides by sturdy iron walls. It seemed incapable of transporting anyone or anything.

One by one Keleut and her crew were ushered over the side of the trough and down a ladder. Albus peered over the side to see them climb into a slender craft with a brightly colored awning spread over it to block the sun. Albus clambered after them, nearly tripping on his hem not just once, on the ladder, but a second time as well as he made his way over the side of the boat as ungracefully as a fish flopping on dry land. One of the trident-wielding men steadied him, and Albus was very grateful that the soldiers of Onaxos were either selected for their stoicism or had it trained into them.

As Albus squeezed into a seat near the rear, machinery trundled to life, the iron walls on his left and right rose even higher to match the height of the wall in front of them, and a sudden rush of water from behind the boat caused him to turn in alarm. The wave proved harmless and Albus studied the trough for a sense of where the water was coming from—as such it took him a moment to realize the water level was rising at a considerable speed, raising the small vessel higher and higher until it drew even with the top of the starboard and port walls.

They drifted there for a moment and then the wall at the front of the trough began to drop and disappear into the water—and at last Albus understood what was happening.

Propelled forward by two sets of oars, the vessel moved into the second trough and Albus watched in fascination as the process was repeated—water flowing in, the boat rising to the water level of the third trough, and so on.

And so on. And on.

It turned out that while imminently fascinating, traversing to the top of a very tall city by such a method lost its charm after two or three repetitions, even for one so curious as Albus.

Albus decided Keleut had not made the journey to the top on her previous visit, evidenced by the drumming of her fingers on the bench she occupied and the increasing ferocity with which she turned her attention to the bare-chested man shouting orders and directing their progress.

There was one further—fleeting—moment of interest when the next trough, Albus had lost count, curved, demonstrating that they would, in fact, curl their way around each level of the city, but beyond that it became a tremendously dull experience and Albus could not imagine making the journey again or, the horror, on a daily basis.

When at last they emerged in the final trough, high above the rest of the city with only the spire reaching higher, Albus sighed.

"At least I shall never do anything half so tedious again."

Onaxos had other ideas.

—◆—

"How many stages?"

The words hissed out through Keleut's clenched teeth and she took a step toward the young woman in the hooded robe who stood before the pirate captain, hands folded neatly in front of her stomach. The young woman smiled, creasing the blue paint that covered her left cheek, and Albus was left to translate the Seycherran to Bellaran, the language of the Seven Cities, conveniently spoken and understood by this acolyte of Taalo and Toora. For reasons she had yet to explain but he could guess at, Keleut had told Albus she wanted him to act as translator despite the fact she was perfectly capable in Bellaran.

"Eighteen. The same as the number of labors performed by our beloved deities."

"And this," Keleut gestured to the still figure seated cross-legged in the middle of the circular room, "is which stage?"

"The third," the woman said after Albus translated the question. She smiled again. "Meditation."

Albus glanced down the short, narrow hall that opened up into the round, domed chamber. A latticed silver door obscured little. A single shaft of light spilled down from the ceiling, coming to rest on the seated figure's knee. There was a faint odor of burned incense.

"And how long will it last?"

The woman's pleasant smile faltered for the first time since being given charge of the visitors. "The meditation? Or the entire cleansing process?"

Keleut seemed to debate whether she wanted to clarify the question or strangle the woman. Albus stepped in.

"My employer is not accustomed to waiting and has important business with the Wisdom. Can the cleanse not be resumed another time?"

Clearly the suggestion was horrifying. The young woman put a hand to her mouth and then made a hasty sign against her chest with the fingers of her other hand. "And defy and defile the commands of Taalo? Unthinkable."

Albus looked at Keleut, aware of the woman's growing impatience. "Then perhaps there is another Wisdom who is not spiritually engaged at the moment."

The young acolyte had regained her composure, but a tinge of prejudice had crept into her expression. "I'm afraid that's impossible. All five Wisdoms are undertaking the cleanse. They do it communally once each season."

Albus frowned. "You mean to say the rulers of Onaxos withdraw at the same time and are fully unavailable? What an utterly asinine way to run a city." The words were out before he could think about them. "What if the city fell under attack? What if half the lower levels were on fire? You mean to tell me the Wisdoms would remain locked away in their meditation chambers and do nothing?"

To his disbelief, the woman smiled, as though Albus were the asinine one. "Not rulers," she said. "The Wisdoms are representatives of Taalo and Toora, their guides here in the mortal world. Only the divine Twins rule in Onaxos." The smile grew and her cheeks flushed with something Albus recognized as fervor. "And in the event of any catastrophe, Taalo and Toora will provide for us."

A snort from Keleut, hastily disguised as a cough, nearly gave her away. To preserve the lie, Albus quickly turned to mumble a translation she didn't need.

"What do you want me to do?" he asked in Seycherran. Keleut wasn't even looking at him. Her attention was fixed on the acolyte, derision radiating from her gaze.

"You have an agreement with this person, correct?" Albus asked, gesturing to the figure behind the latticed door. Keleut didn't answer. "You were expected. There must be some prior arrangement we can call on." He shifted his weight from one foot to the other, wondering how likely she was to turn on him for his next words. "Would it be so difficult to wait?"

The pirate captain did not turn to Albus. Instead, she grinned wolfishly at the acolyte. "Let's see your Wisdom meditate through this," she said in Seycherran. While her words might not have been understood, her actions were all too clear.

Turning away, Keleut marched down the tunnel, reared back, and stomped her foot against the dully gleaming door. The sound shattered the stillness around them and reverberated down the tunnel. The acolyte gasped, clearly unprepared for such profane behavior. Albus, torn between laughing and cringing, produced a strangled sound and wondered if the Twins would provide a cell—they had not provided an armed guard, demonstrating a trust in strangers Albus thought rather foolish.

Keleut brought her boot down on the door a second time, and then a third, until at last the figure within stirred.

Albus nearly choked on air. Blinking furiously, he peered down the tunnel, his mind telling him he had not seen what his eyes insisted manifested in the moment the figure rose from its seated position, telling him it was impossible. Impossible, because a human being could not be transparent, not even for so brief a moment.

If Keleut noticed, she gave no indication, a fact that only added to Albus's discomfort. Logically it would suggest he had imagined it. But his mind was not the sort to imagine things outside the realm of possibility. Perhaps the seasickness had altered his brain. Perhaps the salt spray endured for so many days had affected his vision. He had no time to dwell on it further. The Wisdom was speaking.

"Who disturbs my communion with the gods?" The voice was calm and cool and wholly unidentifiable as either male or female. And yet there was a sharpness to it that suggested this dignified response to Keleut's interruption was tightly controlled.

For a moment, there was silence, and then Albus came back to life, suddenly recalling his purpose there. He rushed down the tunnel to stand at Keleut's side and keep up the charade of her ignorance.

Keleut spoke in Seycherran, keeping her voice low. "Tell," she hesitated, "them, tell them we had an agreement. Tell it my name."

Albus straightened and drew a deep breath. "Wisdom, may I introduce Keleut, daughter of Nestor, of Seycherra. She has come by your invitation and demands the audience you promised her."

The Wisdom looked back at Albus from the other side of the latticed door, pale unblinking eyes and smooth skin just visible beneath a deep white hood. Albus had never before seen a person so easily defy both male and female physical characteristics. He swallowed and wished for Eska. She had no more experience dealing with Onaxians than he did, but she had a talent for reading people he did not.

"Seycherra." The Wisdom moved the word around their mouth like a particularly delectable morsel of food—delectable and foreign, Albus realized. He wondered if the delay was due to the deep meditative state the Wisdom had so recently withdrawn from or if there was a true ignorance. "Yes." Though spoken with a sudden brisk authority, this was hardly convincing either way. "But you are mistaken, I have made no such invitation and I have never heard the name Keleut, daughter of Nestor or no." It was not a threat, not yet anyway, but Albus understood the situation was becoming increasingly delicate. He resisted the urge to glance at Keleut, aware still of his need to impress her. Though they were allies in this moment, and on strange footing, he would not presume to imagine the pirate captain would not abandon him if it meant saving her own skin.

"You are Wisdom Isopho, yes?" he ventured.

"I am." The serene answers continued, but the Wisdom's eyes were far from kind.

"Tell them I have a letter," Keleut said.

Albus pressed on. "She can produce evidence of your correspondence."

"That won't be necessary," the Wisdom said.

For a moment Albus dared to breathe easily.

"You are strangers here and cannot be expected to know our customs and laws," the Wisdom went on, the face and voice as blank as ever. "Even so, to disturb a Wisdom who has entered into a cleanse and communion with the Twins is to ask for a swift and harsh justice." The gaze shifted over Albus's shoulder. "Applicable equally to all who are guilty."

With mounting horror, Albus turned to catch the young acolyte's expression crumple. Her hands went to her throat and she gasped as though in physical pain. Perhaps she was. Tears began to course down her cheeks and she fell to her knees. But there was no protestation, no argument, only blind, willing acceptance.

The Wisdom reached a hand up to the wall beside the latticed door and Albus, feeling Keleut coil beside him like a snake about to strike, tried to maintain his composure.

"You yourself said we cannot be expected to know the law," Albus cried out. "We have trespassed, yes, but surely your Twins are merciful to those who do not know the wonders of their divinity."

The Wisdom said nothing and pulled a lever installed inside the round chamber. With a clang, a gate slammed shut behind them, blocking the entrance to the tunnel. Keleut's hands clutched at the latticed door and she seethed with fury—and yet somehow managed not to burst out in Bellaran. Then again, her feelings were perfectly clear, especially after she uttered a few choice insults in Seycherran. The Wisdom merely turned their back and settled once more into meditation pose, no longer concerned with the trifles of the physical world, and moments later Albus heard the slapping of sandaled feet on stone as guards rushed in, tridents drawn.

They were handled gently, all things considered, and Albus made a mental note to read up on the doctrine of the Twins if he ever passed outside the confines of the sea wall again. Toora was, without a doubt, a martial being and Onaxos had a bloody past, but Albus knew the Twins held equal sway and Taalo was said to be a compassionate sort—as compassionate as a celestial being could be when it came to the foolishness of mortals. Their hands were not even bound, though Albus rather thought this had to do more with the fact that the guards were quite convinced, rightly so, by the superiority of their tridents than any spiritual kindness.

Albus, Keleut, and the acolyte were led down the spire's central staircase and out the door they had come in. But instead of descending through the city via the water troughs, they were gestured into a litter— were there no horses in this city?—borne by four men with blind white eyes. A ritual blinding, Albus realized as he noted the identical scars splitting each eye socket down the middle. He grimaced and boarded the litter without complaint. The acolyte wailed, but then, she'd been wailing every step of the way. Predictably, Keleut spat at the nearest guard and tried to disarm him. She got one hand on the trident and the other around his neck before the guards descended on her, bringing her to her knees without shedding blood. She screamed her frustration and swore Seycherra would bring fire and vengeance to Onaxos, and it was in that moment that Albus, perched in the litter, realized what the pirate captain seemed to have known for some time: they were not being taken to trial, they were not being brought to a cell to await judgment. Their fate had been decided the moment the Wisdom pulled the lever.

His heart racing, Albus made room for Keleut as she was bundled, kicking and screaming, into the litter.

"What do we do?" he whispered to the woman, sure the fierce pirate would have a way out. Pirates always had a way out. The litter lurched to life and the wailing had stopped. The acolyte, blue paint marred by tear tracks, nose sniffling, cast a look of disdain on Albus.

"Do not speak," she hissed. "You offend the Twins."

He ignored her. "Keleut," he tried again, shaking the Seycherran woman by the shoulder this time. "What do you want me to do?"

There was no answer—not from Keleut anyway. The acolyte, infused with holy fury, it would seem, had plenty to say.

When she had finished, running out of breath more than words, Albus, who had sat straight-backed and stiff throughout the tirade, watching the city go by as they were carried around the cliff edge toward the sea wall, turned his gaze on her.

"I don't suppose it matters now, seeing as how we appear to be moments away from dying, but you should try reading Erona. Maybe Aristivicus. Even Dephonides would do, though he does tend to use twice as many words as necessary to make his points," Albus said, quite giddy with the mildness in his voice.

The acolyte looked at him blankly.

"Philosophers. You might learn a thing or two about the yoke of religion. How it can corrupt the human spirit."

The young woman didn't speak for the rest of the journey.

Albus closed his eyes, a strange calm falling over him. He had, after all, thought quite a lot about death. Not in any morbid way, of course, but of the nature of death and its relationship with life, of the temporal state of men and women, of their need to be more than dust lost to time.

He was, in short, prepared to be dust. Oh, there were things he had intended to do, of course, opportunities these strange Twins would rob him of, contributions he wanted to make to the study of linguistics, for instance, translations of great works of philosophy or literature. He even, he could admit, felt a deep pull to study the god discs, those infamous Hands of Fate—which he attributed to spending too much time with Eska. He thought of the strange bronze disc she had left in his possession and wondered if she would ever discover where he had hidden it during his hasty departure from Arconia—or why he had left.

The sensation that he would never know settled over him. But that was the nature of life. Things were left undone, unknown. Albus could live—die, he supposed—with that. By the time the litter reached the middle of the sea wall, Albus was ready to die.

He was not prepared for the method, as it turned out.

━━━━━━◂•▸━━━━━

It was the reverence in the acolyte's expression that turned his stomach.

The young woman, her face still streaked with tears, her eyes still puffy from crying, stared at the tool of her destruction with such fervor, such adoration, Albus wanted to strike the jar of oil from her hands and let it shatter upon the iron walkway that lined the top of the sea wall. Even Keleut, for all her fierceness, was subdued by this show of docility and acceptance.

Except it wasn't a show, Albus realized. It wasn't a performance on a stage. He felt certain the young woman would have gone to her death in this manner with or without an audience.

Albus leaned over the short parapet of the iron wall, risking a glance at the sea below. He was startled to see more than just white-tipped waves slashing against the sea wall.

"Are those sharks?" The question was out—loudly, too—before he quite realized he was speaking. Albus glanced at Keleut and then at the stoic guards surrounding them. When no one answered—he did detect a twitch in the pirate captain's jaw—Albus looked again. "Have you," he began, then hesitated, sure he was imagining it. It was a great height, after all. "Have you put offal in the water to summon them?" The horror squeezing his throat pitched his voice high. "Surely not." But the sharks below swarmed, frenzied, their dorsal fins darting here and there, and the sea around them was stained a darker color and dotted with bits of matter. Albus swallowed, feeling his inner peace quiver and diminish.

The acolyte raised the jar above her head, her eyelids fluttering madly as she worked herself into a state to match the predators below. As she poured the oil over herself, there was a rush of heat behind Albus and he quickly leaned aside to let the two men bearing the flaming wreath through, their arms protected by thick leather gloves. It was taller than a man and smelled of laurel and the sight made Albus shudder.

The men walked the wreath to the edge of the wall and settled it into a pair of prongs where it burned with a satisfying crackle. As the flames weakened its structure, boughs of laurel collapsed into the center of the wreath, creating a fiery web. For a moment, Albus thought this a mistake, that the wreath would surely be replaced with a new one.

He realized his error when the acolyte, with a horrifying cry of joy, sprinted across the width of the wall, leaped—

—and burst into flames when she passed through the burning laurel.

She fell to the sea, a tumbling ball of fire and limbs, the smell of burned hair lingering behind her.

Albus wanted to retch. For all his sickness at sea, he had not felt so desperate a need to empty his stomach as he did in that moment. Keleut's hand clutching at his elbow was enough to keep him from doubling over, though his chest heaved with fear. A glance at Keleut showed the same fear in the pirate's face. Fear and something he supposed was resolve.

In the silence that followed, the trident-bearing guards stared calmly at the place in the air where the acolyte had been. And Albus, throwing caution to the winds, found his voice.

"This is how you treat your faithful? This is how the Twins reward devotion? Your gods are barbaric," he shouted, waving his arms. "And someday your gods will fall to mine, for my gods are the only gods: truth, knowledge, logic, and free will." He thought he was finished, thought that was all he needed to say. "And compassion," he burst out. "Mercy, not destruction."

It was, he thought, with that hazy sort of clarity that accompanies death, his finest moment. It was a pity there was only a Seycherran pirate to hear him.

Two guards grabbed him away from Keleut and shuffled him along the wall. Two more replaced the spent wreath with a fresh one. The oil came in a sudden flood, poured over him by an unseen hand. He tried to blink it away, tried to spit it out of his mouth, but it coated everything. He sought Keleut's face, though it was not the face he would have chosen to look upon at the moment of his death, and was relieved to find sorrow and solidarity in its strong lines.

Hands pushed Albus forward. He stumbled, was righted. The heat of the wreath seemed to beckon to the oil covering him. Albus tried to lean back. Hands propelled him again. The flames waited.

And then the fight left Albus, replaced by the resolve he had seen in Keleut's face. He would not allow them to take his free will. He would die with that.

Albus stepped forward and prepared to leap.

Shouting. Frantic voices.

A figure tackled Albus to the ground.

As he lay sprawled on his back atop the sea wall of Onaxos, trying to understand that he wasn't falling to the sea in a ball of flames, Albus saw black smoke rising from the spire, black smoke and the wings of white birds.

27

"If you're lucky, your neck snaps quickly."

SOMEHOW MANON DOUBTED HER FOUR-DAY PASS GRANTED HER PERmission to burn the Principe's hunting lodge to the ground.

She had made it out alive, Justina a step ahead of her and Luca a step behind, each of them clutching as many things as they could carry, Luca going back to the stable for all four horses, and from the safety of the pebbled beach, they watched the grand timbers and high rafters of the lodge transform into a smoldering frame of charred wood. The horses danced nervously, the whites of their eyes showing.

The rain, for all its earlier ferocity, had only managed to enhance the smoke rising from the ruins—though it made quick work of the witnesses. Even Justina hadn't repressed a shiver, though, Manon reflected, that could have been at the sight of the roof collapsing.

"I imagine that's the rope for us," the huntress mused, the first to break the silence.

"The Principe will hang you for this?" Manon asked.

"I never said anything about hanging," Justina muttered. Manon waited for an explanation and then, when one failed to materialize, turned her gaze to Luca's melancholy face.

He sighed. "The Principe prefers a different method. Stretching." Manon flinched. The big man saw it. "If you're lucky, your neck snaps quickly."

"Most aren't lucky," Justina said, her gaze still fixed on the ruined lodge. "And you forget, Luca, he also likes a good hunt."

"Our Principe isn't fond of mercy." Luca said it as though he were apologizing. He glanced down at the clothing and packs and supplies strewn at their feet and then at a piece of paper crumpled in his fist. He spread out the wet parchment in his palm and squinted at it. "Manon Barca?"

Manon nodded blankly, then stooped down to shove what remained of her belongings into her pack. She drew her cloak back over her shoulders, its damp weight settling on her, and gathered her saddle in her arms.

"You should go," Luca was saying. "Take your things. Disappear."

"What are you talking about?" Justina cut in, taking a step toward her partner. "She is responsible for this. We turn her in, we might get away with our lives."

Luca shook his head. "We are responsible for this, Justina. She had a pass. Your inability to trust that led to everything that followed."

Manon set the saddle on her horse and looked from one to the next, trying not to feel like a piece of prey waiting to see which hawk would swoop in for the kill first. But she wasn't prey. She pulled her shoulders back and straightened to her full height.

"I'm not running."

Luca frowned. "Manon, I believe you would never have set fire to the lodge if I hadn't done what I did to you, so I'm trying to help you now. Do you want to die?"

"Your Principe doesn't frighten me." This wasn't exactly true, but there was someone else who frightened Manon more, and she was carrying his seal of power in her pocket. "I have work to do at the stone circle and I will complete that work. If you want to help me, take me there and get me back to Arconia alive—after I've found what I came for."

Justina shook her head, her exasperation clear, and turned her back on her partner. She paced away from the beach, her metal-wrought foot clacking on the stones. Manon kept her gaze fixed on Luca.

"I can protect you in Arconia, Luca. The Principe won't be able to touch you there." She didn't add that this would all depend on the Archduke's willingness to extend his protection to a disgraced hunter whose life another ruler of the Seven Cities might very well demand. That could come later.

Luca looked out at the grey sea and pushed rain-plastered hair from his forehead. "Both of us," he said at last. "Or neither of us."

"Something tells me she'd rather see me stretched even knowing the ropes would bind her next."

"We're partners, whatever she might say about that," Luca said. He nudged at the pebbles with the toe of his boot. "She'll come." Manon had the distinct impression he was trying to convince himself.

"I'm riding away," Manon said, reaching for her mount again. She cinched the saddle and adjusted the reins, then checked to see the second horse was secured before climbing onto the first's back. "Just," she shook her head, "just stay away from me. I think we've caused each other enough damage to last a lifetime."

She turned the mare and set it to a trot, eager to put as much distance between her and that fateful place as she could. The sounds of pursuit came a moment later. Boots scuffing on slippery pebbles. A hasty plea directed at a skittish horse. And then hooves hastening to catch up.

Manon didn't look back. When she cleared the beach and the track she had been following began to angle up and away from the coast, she urged the horse to greater speed, but Luca's mount, a true hunter's steed, agile and sure-footed and swift, caught her lesser creature with ease. The hunter settled behind Manon like a shadow.

"You can hate me for what I did," Luca said. "I wish only to make it right." He hesitated and Manon resisted the urge to look over her shoulder. "Though I doubt I can."

Manon rode on. "You know," she said at last, "I begin to sympathize with Justina."

A moment of silence. Then: "What do you mean?"

Manon smiled to herself. "You have a talent for being irritating."

Another moment of silence. "Yes, she has mentioned that."

Despite the rain, despite the looming shadow of the Principe's wrath, despite the weight of the Archduke's seal in her pocket, despite even the memory of the void Luca had opened up inside her, a memory that ached and twisted and tore at her still, Manon's smile grew.

"Come on. Don't follow after me like a dog."

———◆——

"Makes you think," Luca said.

Manon looked away from the stone circle and frowned at the hunter. "Think about what?"

"Who put them here, of course," he said, gesturing at the tall stones. They glistened with the remnants of the rain, illuminated by the rays of sun slipping through the bruised clouds on the western horizon. The sky had turned a mottled purple and pink in the wake of the storm. "And why."

"Speculation," Manon said. "I put my trust in facts. And the facts are that something is buried here and I intend to get it out of the ground." The words were very like something her father would have said, Manon realized. She wasn't sure whether to laugh or curse him. She swung down from her saddle and strode into the stone circle. It was large, the stones imposing, the interior dotted with wildflowers.

Luca jumped to the ground and grabbed her horse's trailing reins. He led both animals after her but stopped just short of passing through the stones.

"I thought you were here to study the inscriptions. Surely you know something about who built this place."

Manon turned and put one hand on her hip. "I lied," she said, appreciating the look of consternation that spread over his face. "Don't look so surprised. I think we're past all that, Luca. After all, collectively we've burned down a piece of property that belongs to a very powerful man and could lose our lives for it."

Luca frowned and looked down at his feet. Manon sighed and continued her traversal of the circle. When she reached the other side, she turned back and noted the hunter hadn't moved.

"Didn't you say something about the stories folk tell? Nonsense, I think was the word you used. Don't tell me you harbor some sort of superstition about this place. Don't cross through after twilight? Toss a stone over your shoulder and spin in a circle three times while hopping on one foot?"

Luca tried to laugh. "Nothing so specific. Respect is all. Something my gran taught me."

Manon ran a finger over the indecipherable inscription on the nearest stone. The letters were worn away in parts, nothing but smooth stone left. For the briefest of moments, Manon felt a flicker of something she was astonished to name as loss, a feeling to which she was not accustomed, especially in relation to ancient objects that held no meaning for her. But the thought was quickly washed away by a glance toward the setting sun. She looked back at Luca.

"Are you going to help me or not?"

"Now? It's getting dark."

Manon smiled. "Of little consequence." She breathed in, breathed out, and summoned fire to her palm once more. She grew it between her hands, then lofted it over her head. It floated above the stone circle. The spark in Manon's ribs purred, content in the wake of her fear, settling the last edges of her nerves.

Still the hunter looked unsure. "How do we begin?"

"Begin?" Manon walked back towards her reluctant companion. "That would imply a method. I intend to dig until I have found what I came for. I'm assuming you can use a shovel." She unstrapped the pair of shovels from the packhorse and held one out to the big man. "Something tells me your partner isn't going to wait around pondering her options. We don't have much time."

Luca took the shovel but didn't move. "She'll be here," he insisted.

"I don't doubt that. The question is whether she'll come alone." Manon scanned the stones, looking for, but not expecting to find, an indication of where to start digging. "Which would you choose, father?" she murmured. The stones all looked the same. The sunset was nearly swallowed up by the dark clouds over the sea, but Manon's ball of fire cast the stones in a faint light. Blowing out a long exhale, Manon marched to the western most stone and thrust her shovel into the dirt near its base. A moment later, she was rewarded with the sound of the second shovel doing the same.

After she'd pried some large chunks of earth from the ground, Manon looked over her shoulder. Luca was making impressive progress—but then, he was built like a small bull.

"How did she lose her foot?" Manon called out, bending to her task once more.

Luca tossed three more shovelfuls over his shoulder before answering. "Justina?"

"Do you know another woman missing a foot?" Manon nearly laughed at herself, wondering what had prompted this strange good humor. Delirium, most likely. The thought wasn't comforting.

"Bear trap," Luca said, his face grim. "She was trying to save a young wolf caught in a second trap. Poacher's trap. Her partner was less fortunate." He stood up straight and, wiping sweat from his forehead, glanced at Manon. "Bear got him. That's why she says she doesn't need another partner."

"What do you mean?"

"Justina had to watch the bear maul him." Luca held Manon's gaze. "And the only reason she's alive, at least as far as she can figure, is the bear's stomach was too full of Beloque to need her, too."

Manon's mood faded. "I'm sorry."

Luca turned back to his work. "That was a year ago. After she began to recover, she insisted on being fitted for the metal foot. We've been together for just a season. Some who knew her before the accident say that metal foot took something from her, that she changed the moment she put it on. They're wrong. She changed the moment Beloque's face was bitten off."

They worked in silence until the ball of light above them began to fade. Manon snuffed it out and called a new spark to her fingertips to survey their progress. The grass within the stones was a ruined patchwork, holes scattered here and there, some deep enough Manon could have stepped in up to her knee, others much shallower. It looked like a wild animal had gone on a rampage.

Manon laughed. "Now if this is not the handiwork of a Barca, I don't know what is."

Luca raised an eyebrow in her direction but said nothing. He began to rummage through his pack, pulling out a bedroll and a small parcel tied with string. He checked the horses, who were grazing outside the circle, then settled on his back on his bedroll, hands behind his head, the parcel resting on his chest.

"Out with it, Luca," Manon said. She sat against one of the stones, her back aching, her hands raw from the shovel.

Silence from the big man. The parcel moved up and down on his chest as he breathed. Then, "Before I was a hunter at Pontevellio, I was a member of a wealthy merchant's private militia. We protected convoys, stood guard on his estate, that sort of thing. There was an old soldier, trying to put together enough coin to buy himself a few peaceful years and a quiet death. Only every time we got into a skirmish, he'd come out of it with this smile on his face. And this laughter." Luca paused. "He liked the killing, you see. Liked the blood." Another pause, this one longer, as the hunter stared up at the emerging stars. "One day the merchant brought in some new fellows, young and strong, and the old soldier's time was up. He knew it. He went away quietly enough. But that night, he strapped on every bit of armor and every weapon he owned and walked into the middle of the largest, most vicious bandit camp I've ever heard of." A third pause, so long Manon wondered if Luca had fallen asleep. "They carved him up before he could touch any of them. And his corpse was smiling that smile."

Manon frowned to herself, trying to work out the story's relevance. She laughed again, unable to repress the giddiness that had bubbled within her since riding away from the charred remains of the hunting lodge. "If you're trying to convey something to me, I'm afraid you're being far too subtle."

"That's just it," he said, his voice quieter. "You nearly died today and you've been laughing to yourself ever since."

"Ah." Manon shifted her weight against the stone and lifted her face to the night sky. "And you think I'm mad. Looking for a reason to die." Manon sighed, preparing to refute it. But then she hesitated, the words falling to pieces in her mouth. "Perhaps I am," she said, her voice shrinking to a whisper. "But if I'm the old soldier in your story, you can be damn sure I'm taking some of those bandits with me." She meant it, and for a moment, she thought she knew who those bandits were. The Archduke. Eska de Caraval. Her father. But then she saw Julian Barca's face behind the bars of his cell at the Hibarium and she could not have said if she wanted to laugh or cry.

"Cheese?" Luca's voice came to her out of the dark. Manon had never shed a tear over cheese before. But she did that night.

———— ◆ ————

In the morning, Manon's eyes were dry as she watched Luca bend down and pick up his shovel. They had shared a small meal in silence as the sun spilled across the stones, sending their long shadows westward.

"Luca."

The hunter looked up.

"You should go. Go home. Go back to your forest, your wolf packs and your herds," Manon said. He opened his mouth to respond, but she hurried on. "I know you feel responsible. I know you feel a need to make amends. But you're not wrong about me." She took a deep breath. "I am drowning. Surrounded on all sides by forces I can't control, can't even make out with any clarity. I can barely keep my head above it all and even if I find what I'm looking for and take it back to Arconia, the city is a web and I am caught in too many places. You don't want to be a part of that."

Luca sighed and looked out over the sea, his hair ruffling in the morning breeze that blew off the water. "Justina will have reached Pontevellio some time in the night. She'd have insisted on waking

Marveaux, the estate's master hunter. And she'd have told him enough to get him and half a dozen other hunters on horseback before dawn. I misjudged her and it's too late for me to turn back."

"I expect no mercy for myself, but would she betray even you?"

Luca shrugged. "The way I see it, she told Marveaux one of three things." He held up one finger. "You burned down the lodge and I helped you escape." A second finger. "You burned down the lodge because I took away your Carrier gift and then I chose to follow you, which you and I know to be the truth." A slight hesitation, a heavy inhale and exhale, and then a third finger. "Or, you burned down the lodge, I tried to stop you by taking away your gift, and then you escaped and I chased after you." He dropped his hand to his side. "If it's one of the first two, I'm as guilty as you are. And if it's the third, she might be trying to spare me, but I'll never be a free man again. If the Principe learns what I can do, even if he doesn't lock me in a cell as a danger to others, I'll be a creature for him to control, like one of his hunting dogs." Luca looked across the circle at Manon. "I'm not wise. I haven't traveled the Seven Cities, much less the world. I can write enough to get by, but nothing more." His gaze dropped a little, as if in shame. "I'm just a man who knows his forest," he said quietly. But then he looked up again and Manon could see the determination in his eyes even from that distance. "But there is one thing I know without a doubt. Twice now I have taken a Carrier's gift—intentionally. I will never let anyone use me because of this thing I can do."

Manon looked down at her hands. Tender blisters had formed overnight. "How long do we have?"

"Not long."

Manon picked up her shovel and, stifling a gasp against the pain, began to dig.

The shadows of the stones had grown considerably shorter and the holes within the circle considerably deeper by the time Justina came into view across the wind-buffeted moor. Luca saw her first, as though his hunter's instinct had sensed a change in the air. Manon saw him stand and squint into the distance.

"She's alone," he said, surprise making his voice quiet. Manon lifted a trembling, bloody hand to brush a strand of hair from her face. Justina approached slowly, letting the horse amble toward its fellows without any apparent desire to hurry. When she reached the circle, her horse bent its neck to sample the grass and Justina watched Manon and Luca from the saddle in silence.

"I rode ahead," she said at last, then dismounted, her metal foot clanking slightly as she hit the ground. She had eyes only for Luca as she entered the circle, making a point not to acknowledge Manon. "A horse came up lame. They won't be long, though."

For once Luca didn't appear to have anything to say. Manon turned away and resumed her digging.

"I don't want to see another partner destroyed in front of me."

"Then why did you do it?" The words came out of Luca's mouth in a rush and the pain in his voice nearly made Manon flinch. She dug faster, her palms screaming in agony.

"Because I owe everything to the Principe. For whatever fucked up reason, he let me keep this position after I lost my foot. Probably thought it'd be fun to watch me limp around and fall getting into a saddle and run as slow as a wounded animal. But I won't turn my back on that." For all the hardness in her words, Manon could hear the quaver in Justina's voice. "Besides," the huntress went on, "you're a shit partner. Half the hunter Beloque was." Manon knew the manner in which Justina was forcing the brusqueness into her voice—knew it because she had done it countless times.

Manon flung her shovel to the earth, sending a clod of dirt flying. She rounded on the pair across the circle and fixed Justina with a hard stare. The spark beckoned to her, begged to be released, but Manon pushed it away. She closed the distance to Justina and didn't stop, forcing the huntress to take several hurried steps backward until she bumped up against one of the tall stones.

"He doesn't deserve your insults." Manon leaned in close, her nose nearly touching Justina's.

"What do you care?" The huntress breathed back the reply with ferocity, but Manon could see the hurried pulse at her throat. "You're just using him to get what you want."

"Better that from a stranger than cruelty from someone who ought to be looking out for him."

"Are you going to burn me for it?"

"I won't waste my gift on the likes of you," Manon snarled. Some quiet part of her realized it was true, realized she didn't feel the need to let her anger win. She held that thought for a moment, unsure where it stemmed from, unsure what corner of her to stash it in. In the end it fell away as softly as it had come.

The two women stared hard at each other, neither blinking, neither backing down.

"Stop this," Luca said. His voice was strangely distant. "Manon. Look."

Manon tore her gaze away and turned. Luca was kneeling in the overturned earth, one hand on the shovel Manon had discarded, the other hovering over the ground.

And there, gleaming through a dusting of black earth, as bright and brilliant to Manon as her father's stolen ingots, was a piece of pale, dirty linen.

Manon was on her knees next to Luca before she could take another breath. She thrust her bleeding hands into the dirt, raking it away with her fingers, trying to uncover the rest of the object, then cried out in pain, her torn hands protesting.

"Let me." Luca lifted Manon's hands by her wrists and set them in her lap, then began to use his own to scoop the dirt away. It wasn't long before the rectangular shape of the object could be seen and Luca reached in and lifted a linen bag cinched with rope from the ground. He set it in front of Manon with reverence and looked up at her. "Is this what you came for?"

Manon took a deep breath and loosened the opening, revealing a plain wooden box. She pushed back the linen and ran a hand across the pale grain of the wood, leaving behind a streak of blood. It wasn't locked. Just a simple clasp of dull, hammered bronze. Manon hesitated.

"If I open this and it's what I think it is, there's no escaping him," Manon heard herself say, not caring that Luca heard it too. "There's no release from his yoke." The truth of it was like a weight settling on her shoulders. For a moment she was back in the Archduke's garden sipping rosé, and she realized that she had held out hope that there was no reliquary in the stone circle at Pontevellio, that she would fail at the task the Archduke had given her, and by failing she could find Perrin and disappear, like her mother four years before.

Manon lifted the clasp and the lid of the wooden box. Within, nestled in a bed of straw, lay a box of ivory and gold, and Manon knew there would be no disappearing.

Interlude 13

A letter from Celestine de Remaux, Tribune of Cancalo during the Great Rising, to Godefroy Elmina, Tribune of Toridium, dated three months after the death of Varin II

My brother-in-rule,

This must not continue. Varin is dead, Elysium is shattered. We have earned our freedom at great cost—and now that cost ought to come to an end. And yet I hear of death after death, executions carried out in all manner of hideous methods, methods learned from the very tyrants we sought to destroy.

You must cease purging your city of those who Carry. I beg you to hear me, for the love we both bear for our Seven Cities, for the honor of those who died for this cause. Do not punish the innocent for the crimes of dead kings and queens. Have we not lived through enough bloodshed? Enough hatred and fear? Enough cruelty and oppression? Do not become what we fought so hard to eradicate. Do not let Varin and his ancestors rule us from beyond life. Those who Carry do not choose the gift and many fought with us. They must be given a place in this new world we said we would forge, not be feared and persecuted.

Do you remember the day we stood beneath the Sungate? We knelt and joined hands, we Tribunes, speaking a vow that made us the enemy of our king, a vow that pledged our lives to the people of our cities. Do you remember what that moment felt like? Sometimes I forget. It was so long ago, and the endless dark days that followed crushed the spirit of what we shared that day. But when I catch moments of silence and peace, I can still feel the sunlight on my skin, hear the bird-song and the voices of my fellow Tribunes. And my heart soars at that sound, Godefroy, as I remember what hope we carried within us. I pray that you, too, can remember that hope and find it within yourself once again.

Hear me, Godefroy. But if you cannot, I will be forced to invoke the ancient summons of the Tribunes, a law far older than the Alescus. And let this be a warning to you, my brother-in-rule, I will not hesitate to see you expelled and exiled. I will do what I must to preserve this new world. Do not doubt me.

For the Seven Cities and for freedom,
Celestine, Tribune of Cancalo

28

"We hardly know each other."

THE KNOCKING WOKE ESKA FROM A DREAMLESS SLEEP. SHE STIRRED, EX-
tricated herself from Eden's arms, pushed hair from her face, yawned.

The knocking came again, louder, reminding her why she had awoken. Eska leaned over Eden's sleeping face and kissed him lightly on
the cheek. His eyes opened and he smiled.

"You have visitors," she murmured.

"I heard. I was rather hoping they would go away."

A fist fell on the door again, heavy and forceful. Eden frowned.

"Stay here." He rose from the bed and pulled his robe over his shoulders, tying the belt as he left the bedchamber. Eska waited a moment,
then, draping herself in another robe, stepped out onto the balcony. It
was from that vantage point that she saw Eden traverse the courtyard,
his bare feet padding silently, then saw him stop abruptly. Eska's gaze
narrowed as she tried to gauge what had caught his eye in the opposite
portico. She drew in a breath, her heart suddenly racing. The pounding continued and now she could hear faint shouting.

"I don't suppose you know what I'll find when I open that door,"
Eden said.

"Seven or eight soldiers, give or take," came a voice from within the
portico's shadows.

"Why?" Eden's terse question bit through the gentle sound of the
fountain. A tiny boat on its course whizzed by Eska's feet.

The figure that stepped into the courtyard was as disheveled as the last time Eska had seen him.

"You know how it goes," the Tortoise said. "Found something they wanted more than they wanted me."

Eska ducked and crawled off the balcony, hoping the thief hadn't seen her. Moving as silently as she could, she rummaged through Eden's wardrobe and a chest of clothes, searching for anything she could use as a weapon.

"And what is it you told them I've done?" Eden's voice drifted up from the courtyard.

"Well, to begin with, there's the Delucca, of course. You've got it hidden away behind one of these other canvases. But we're talking bigger. The deed you stole from Magistrate Umbero, for instance."

"I won that," Eden cut in.

"In an illegal game." The Tortoise's voice was unwavering, far more convincing than Eska had heard at any point during their previous encounter. "And I didn't even need to provide the Tribune with the rumors about your forbidden activities in the lake yesterday. He'd already heard. And he wasn't pleased." The thief paused. "But it's not just you they want, as it happens."

Eska froze just as her hands came into contact with a piece of leather. She pulled it free from the bottom of the chest, finding herself in possession of a coiled whip. It looked old, the handle fraying, but it was better than nothing.

"I begin to think I might get a straighter answer from whoever is trying to break down my door," Eden was saying. "I don't know what you're talking about, but I'm willing to ask what you want."

Eska moved across the bedroom and through the bath chamber, then crept down the stairs as the Tortoise began to answer.

"You can't do better than what they've promised me."

"Ah, a full pardon, then. But you can't really think they'll be willing to overlook your entire career."

"It's a chance I'm willing to take."

Eska moved through the house, choosing a door to the courtyard that kept her out of the Tortoise's sight. She slipped through, hoping the steady noise of the fountain would muffle any sound she might make, and emerged in the portico the thief had vacated a moment before. The knocking had ceased. A reprieve only, Eska knew. Eden's gaze remained fixed on the Tortoise, but Eska knew he could see her.

"The woman," the Tortoise said. "They want her, too."

"What woman?"

"Don't play the fool with me. We both know you're not. The de Caraval woman."

Eska's breath caught at the sound of her name.

Eden sighed and spread his hands. "Fine. But you truly have me at a loss. Eska de Caraval is a guest."

"Regardless of what you two were doing in the lake, she's also wanted for murder in Toridium. But I gather she didn't mention that. Her uncle has been good to me, but I can't refuse what they've offered me, not for a murderer."

Eska stepped out from behind a slender pillar and let the whip uncoil. It whispered against the slate tiles beneath her feet. The Tortoise began to turn. Eska snapped the whip, cracking it through the air.

And missed—whips were apparently more difficult to wield than she had imagined. She grazed him, though, as he ducked away, and it was opportunity enough for Eden to hit him with a wave of water from the fountain.

Cursing, spluttering, falling off balance, the Tortoise stumbled over his own feet and fell backwards against a bench, hitting his head with a sickening thud. He landed on the ground, limp, legs bent awkwardly beneath him. Eska raced to his side and crouched, feeling for a pulse. She exhaled with relief when her fingertips found a faint but steady beat at his throat. Without moving him, Eska felt the back of his head where it had struck the stone. Blood, but only a small amount. She looked up as Eden approached.

"Alive," she said. But before either of them could speak further, a resounding boom reverberated through the house.

Eden cursed. "Ram," he said. "It won't hold for long." He looked at

Eska and she knew he was seeing her for the first time through someone else's eyes. She held his gaze, willing him to believe in her. The ram hit again.

"I didn't kill anyone."

He seemed to reach a decision. Turning, the Regatta Master strode to the other side of the fountain, the water arcing gracefully above him, and reached down to lift a piece of slate disguising a hatch. He beckoned to Eska.

"The tunnels. Go."

She approached, trying to read what was behind his eyes. "They'll take you."

"I'll be fine. Go."

Eska wanted to say more, wanted him to say more, wanted to make him follow his own advice, but the cracking of the ram against the door a third time propelled her down the hatch. Eden shut it most of the way, then he knelt and whispered through the crack, "Back the way you came. Two lefts, a right, and another left. The hatch with a white circle drawn in chalk will take you to a friend. She'll help you get to your people."

And then he was gone and Eska was alone in a dark tunnel wearing nothing but a loose robe.

Her eyes strained to take in something other than pitch-blackness, but Eska did not dare wait for her vision to adjust, knowing it would only be a small improvement. Feeling for the wall to her left, she worked her way along the tunnel, her fingers trailing against cool dirt, her bare feet quiet against the packed earth. Reason told her she would see anyone approaching, for surely no one else would be traveling the tunnels without a torch or lantern to light the way—but darkness has a way of convincing even the most reasonable minds that any number of unlikely things could happen.

She found the first left without incident, her progress slow but steady, her vision improving minutely—just enough, it turned out, to make her question every step, sure she was seeing the outline of an obstacle that would send her sprawling, making her lose her sense of direction or, worse, incapacitate her and leave her at the mercy of whoever happened upon her first.

Eska paused and forced herself to take several deep, slow breaths, suddenly aware that her heart was doing its best to emulate a galloping horse. When she had calmed it to a steadier lope—the best, it seemed, she could do—she continued on, making her second left soon after, and then switching to the right side of the tunnel.

The right turn was so long coming, she began to be certain she had missed it. But that was not her only point of concern.

"Even if I don't get lost," she muttered, "how do you expect me to be able to see the chalk mark on the door? And now I'm talking to you, and you're not here, so this is perfect."

She had known, of course, that word of her supposed culpability for the death of Chancellor Fiorlieu would reach Cancalo eventually. When the daughter of a high-ranking diplomat is accused of murder, well, these things tend to get out rather quickly. She supposed, as she felt her way for that elusive right turn, that the Tortoise had heard the story from Toridium and, as one of only two people in the city on the shores of Lake Delo who knew her full name, decided to make a play for his own skin. Which all left Eska with only herself to blame. She had, after all, decided to approach the Tortoise and reveal herself.

"Some risks are worth taking," she said, smiling as at last her fingers met empty air on the right side of the tunnel. She made the turn, then immediately tucked herself back around the corner, blinking away the traces of the light she had seen bobbing through the darkness.

Eska's mind raced. The approaching light gave her some notion of what lay around her—in short, an empty tunnel, a far cry from the obstacle-riddled place her dark-addled mind had conjured. But there, back in the direction she had come, the remains of an abandoned, rotten crate. Eska ran to it, found it smaller than expected, but one side had clearly been smashed open by violent means. Avoiding the splintered shards of the planks as best she could, Eska wedged herself through the opening, pulling the hem of her robe out of sight just as the torch came into view around the corner.

Eska peered through the slats and counted three, no four, figures. They moved without speaking and their strides were those of men trained to move efficiently. And they were all armed, Eska realized as they drew closer. Sword hilts glinted on their belts. One carried a spiked club. All wore deep hoods concealing their faces. Eska crouched as low as she could and held her breath.

"Tell me again how we know the old git wasn't lying?" one said.

The man leading the group answered. "You ever see an animal cower in fear, Andros? That's how I know. Never seen him look more like a turtle. All we need to know is that whatever was recovered from that vault in the lake is sitting there, ripe for the taking."

It wasn't, of course. The ivory reliquary was safe with Gabriel and if she wasn't so afraid of being discovered, Eska would very much have liked to have scoffed at the notion that she would have risked bringing her prize into Cancalo. As it was, she was beginning to feel grateful for the city watch's timely arrival at the Regatta Master's home. If not for that, she and Eden might have been moments away from having their throats slit by men unhampered by duty or conscience.

Eska waited until the last light of the torch faded from view, then waited longer, letting herself readjust to the dark. She wormed free from the crate, brushing away spider webs and dust as she went, and resumed her blind navigation of the tunnel system.

The final left came quickly, the tunnel dropping away from her touch. Eska followed it and began to strain her eyes for any sign of a trapdoor above her, a ladder, a rope, anything that might indicate her destination.

In the end, she found the door because of the beetles.

She heard them first, clicking away, their armored shells making music. She came to a halt, her mind processing the sound until she was able to place it. Eska had spent enough time underground to know that some beetles traveled in packs, and, if she had a light, she knew she would see a herd of shiny shells marching single-file along the wall of the tunnel.

She followed the sound, tracing it along the wall until it arced over her head. And then vanished as the last of the beetles trickled away—perhaps, perhaps passing through an unseen crevasse, a crack in a door leading to, say, a cellar with a puddle of water or a tasty crop of spiders. Perhaps.

Eska raised a hand above her head, feeling for a change in the surface of the tunnel. Her knuckle grazed against wood and she exhaled in relief. Standing on her tiptoes, she thought she could see a chalk circle—either that or she imagined it, but Eska didn't much care. She felt along the wood, searching out its size and shape, then ran her hands across it, at last making contact with the iron pull ring. Grasping it, Eska pulled.

It didn't budge.

She tried again, leveraging as much of her weight as she could, but the trapdoor remained steadfast. As it should, Eska reminded herself. After all, leaving it unlocked invited all manner of trouble.

And so she knocked.

Once. Twice. Three times. All the while weighing in her mind, like a goddess of fate balancing her scales, the likelihood that someone above would hear her before any of the aforementioned trouble came along the tunnel.

The answering knock came so abruptly, it startled Eska off her aching tiptoes and she stepped back. Hesitating a moment, she repeated the pattern and was rewarded with silence for her efforts. She tried again, and after what felt like an eternity, the trapdoor creaked open.

There was no face to greet her, no words of suspicion, no drawn weapon to intimidate this stranger who had clearly failed the knocking test.

Just a fist-sized object dropping down the hatch to land at Eska's feet. The impact compressed it and it burst open, releasing a pale vapor.

Had Eska been able to examine it, she would have understood it to be the stomach of an animal—goat or sheep or some such—and she would have smelled a strange blend of herbs and ale, or more precisely, the yeast used to ferment grain.

But Eska was doing none of these things because she had collapsed to the tunnel floor.

—◦—

She awoke to the sound of wind chimes.

Eska opened her eyes and saw a brilliant array of colors dancing over her head, sunset oranges and pinks, shades of blue both sharp and gentle, a green that seemed to whisper to Eska, and drops of crimson as bright as freshly shed blood. She blinked and tried to sit up but her muscles didn't respond. She tried again, her mind thrashing when her body could not.

"It will pass," came a voice from somewhere outside of Eska's field of vision. The knowledge that she could not even twist her neck set Eska's heart racing. Above her, the wind chimes, forged from colored glass, played their melancholy song with no melody. And above them, the sun pierced a glass ceiling, sending the colors dancing.

Though she could not move to see it, she could feel that she lay in a bed. There were soft linens beneath her, a thin woven blanket over her legs, and a plush pillow beneath her head. She swallowed, but the muscles of her throat seemed incapable of anything so dexterous as speech.

A face emerged from above, a woman's face, hard and angular, the sides of her head shaved, leaving a thick knot of dark hair at the crown of her skull.

"Once, I would have used a harsher substance on any stranger who came knocking on my cellar door," she said. "Fortunately for you, I've begun to find it more useful to extract information first. But make no mistake, I'm not one to forgive lies." The woman leaned a bit farther over Eska, revealing a flash of silver ink at her collarbone. If she had been able, Eska would have sighed in relief. As it was, she was left to withstand the woman's examination with no means to deflect the attention.

The woman withdrew from Eska's sight. The wind chimes continued their song. Eska watched the colors dance, merging, separating, spinning.

Her body came back to her in a rush, her muscles twitching violently, nearly jolting her out of the bed. The convulsions ceased as abruptly as they had begun, leaving Eska panting.

"I wouldn't suggest moving. But I will allow you to speak."

Eska turned her head. The woman sat, stiff and straight-backed, on a divan, the sort of thing meant for elegant lounging and being used for precisely the opposite. She did not look like she had lounged a day of her life. She wore a black tunic belted at the waist with braided leather, but her legs and feet were bare, as though her morning had been interrupted—no doubt by a very unexpected knocking at her cellar door. Three concentric circles of silver ink lay across her collarbone and around her neck like a wide necklace. And she held a crossbow in her lap.

Eska waited for her to ask a question, to begin the interrogation, but the woman stared silently across the room, her body impressively still, and so Eska ventured to begin.

"You have ancestors from Venadascar." Might as well launch a bolt of her own. It was a shot into, if not the dark, certainly a thick fog, for Eska was not certain the silver ink was a hallmark of Venadascar heritage. One piece of evidence does not make for a convincing theory, as Albus was consistently reminding her, but then, she didn't have much choice. The woman's eyes narrowed slightly before returning to their impassive state, suggesting her shot had found a mark. "I know this because of your tattoo and I know that because Eden San-Germain sent me here." Eska paused. "I need your help."

The woman's jaw worked a little as though she were chewing Eska's words. "Is he all right?" she asked at length.

"I don't know," Eska said. "The city watch came. He sent me through the tunnels." She left out the part about the thugs below the city. And the Tortoise, the Tribune's prejudice against Eden's invention, the vault, the item inside—no need to mention all that. "I don't know this city, but I have friends camped on the eastern shore of the lake. Eden said you could get me there." Eska studied the woman. Friend, lover, family, simply a soul who shared a homeland, however distant—whatever she was, she kept the emotions she was feeling, if any, below the surface. "I can pay," Eska added, "if that's what it will take."

"Does it look like I need your money?" The words were the first the woman had spoken with something more than indifference.

"It doesn't," Eska said mildly. It was true. The room was at odds with the woman occupying it. Beneath the glass ceiling and the wind chimes, the furnishings were rich, the windows large, the woven rug enormous and soft and obviously expensive. There was an elegance to the room—which is not to say there wasn't an elegance to the woman. Her cheekbones, posture, and voice all possessed a sharp kind of luxury. But that was just it—the room was comfortable and delicate and she was not. "But I suppose it all depends if you're in a mercenary mood," Eska said.

The subtle goad hit its mark. The woman stood abruptly, the crossbow hanging limply from her hand. She paced close to the bed, then turned back, her face writhing. "Is that what he said about me?"

In fact, Eden San-Germain had said exactly nothing about the woman, but Eska wasn't about to ruin the moment by admitting that, not when she had finally spurred her host to action.

"I told him this day would come. Told him he'd eventually play the game against someone who couldn't lose." The woman rounded on Eska, who had propped herself up on one elbow. "Get up," she snarled. She turned and pawed through a wardrobe, producing a tunic and trousers that billowed out before tapering sharply into a band below the knee. "Put these on," she said, tossing the clothes toward the bed. Eska caught them and slipped out of Eden's robe quickly, not about to give the woman any reason to slow down and think. It was only when she stood and cinched the tunic around her waist that the woman took note of her bare feet. Sighing with exasperation, she pointed to a pair of leather shoes designed to slip on. The shape felt strange to Eska, whose footwear usually consisted of tall and short boots fastened with laces. These were soft and flexible and the soles had little support to offer. But they were roughly the right size and Eska didn't dare ask for something else. When she was ready, the woman, whose focused energy was still running high, charged out of the room, leading Eska out into a courtyard.

Lacking a fountain or any greenery, it was in stark contrast to Eden's. Indeed, it was little more than a dry, dusty patch of ground, and they crossed it quickly to enter a stone kitchen. From there, they descended to the cellar and the woman pulled a pair of torches from a barrel. These she lit from a lantern burning in the corner of the cellar and she handed one to Eska, then, first setting down her crossbow, she retrieved a large leather belt fashioned with several pouches and holsters—but not, Eska saw, for traditional weapons. She recognized two of the goat stomach devices dangling from the back of the belt, and there were vials and jars and countless other things—was that a bunch of feathers?—secured and stashed all around the belt. The woman fastened the buckle, reclaimed the crossbow, and pulled open the hatch to the tunnel below, then she looked up at Eska, a strange glint in her eye.

"When you see him again, tell him I'm done with him."

And with that, she dropped into the tunnel, the flames of her torch nearly winking out at the sudden rush of air. Eska followed, landing lightly and hurrying after the woman, who, it appeared, had no intention of waiting.

She soon lost track of their turns, but the increasing dampness of the ground beneath her told her they were surely headed toward Lake Delo. They encountered three other parties on their route, but whether due to the furious glare on the woman's face or to a shared desire for anonymity, not a word was exchanged—at least not the first two times.

Against her better judgment, Eska attempted conversation after the second encounter. "This seems like a terrible liability. Why doesn't the city watch blockade the tunnels?"

The woman stopped moving for the first time since springing off the chaise. "Who do you think dug them in the first place?"

Of all the possibilities, that one had not occurred to Eska, and she made a mental note to do some light reading on the history of Cancalo when she had the chance. At the moment, though, she was rather more occupied with the fact that another torch was bobbing toward them, this one at a much faster speed.

Shouting soon followed, and then a man was sprinting toward Eska and her escort, his lantern swinging dangerously, the shadows bouncing off his face to reveal bruises and a blood-streaked cheek. Another light was in pursuit.

Eska flattened herself against the tunnel and the woman did the same, but the man knew an opportunity when he saw one. Before she could react, he dropped his lantern and grabbed Eska, knocking her torch away and pulling her to him so she stood between him and whatever was chasing him. She struggled, but went quiet when the knife appeared in front of her. To Eska's horror, her guide had vanished, slipping back in the direction they had come, her torch snuffed out. The only light remaining was the lantern's feeble glow at Eska's feet.

"I'll cut her!" the man screamed, his voice hoarse and hysterical. The approaching light slowed, then stopped for a moment before starting up again, cautiously this time. Eska's wild gaze flitted around the tunnel, searching for anything she might be able to use against her attacker.

"Got yourself a kitten to play with, I see." The new voice was deep and full of smiles. "How convenient. Saves me the trouble of finding a woman tonight." The speaker came to a halt twenty paces from Eska and her captor, close enough for her to see the long butcher's knife, already wet with blood, in his hand. Eska squirmed and tried to kick the man in the knee with her heel, but her leather slipper slid off his leg harmlessly and the arm around her neck cinched tighter.

"She's all yours if you let me go," the first man said.

The second man shook his head and clicked his tongue behind his front teeth. "That's where you're wrong, my friend. She's mine no matter what. But first I'm going to hang your guts out to dry." The man paced forward.

"Don't come a step closer," the first man shouted. He took three hurried steps backward, dragging Eska with him. "Or I'll slit her throat."

The pursuer held his hands, as though one was not holding a knife, out to the side. "Which is it? Do you want to fuck her or do you want to kill her? Make up your mind." He kept walking.

"I mean it," Eska's captor shrieked.

"So do I," the second man said softly. And then he leaped.

Three things happened in that moment. Eska bit down hard on her captor's hand. Then she elbowed him in the kidney. And then a flash of light blinded all three of them. Of the three, the third was infinitely more impressive, but it was the first and second that freed Eska from the man's grip. Acting on instinct, her eyes bursting with white light, Eska slipped out of his loosened hold as he clutched at his side. She turned and ran, feeling more than seeing the form of the woman next to her. A hand slipped into hers and together they raced through the dark, Eska relying on the women's sense and knowledge of the tunnels to lead her to safety.

Eska was out of breath long before they stopped and she continued running on will alone, heart pumping, lungs burning, until at last the woman slowed and then came to a halt at a dead end lit by a single stubby candle placed on a small wooden crate. A rotten trapdoor hung askew from the ceiling. Eska closed her eyes and leaned against the tunnel wall, fighting to catch her breath.

"I thought you had left," she managed at last. "Thank you."

The woman let out a deep exhale, her own breathing returning to normal unnervingly quickly. "I would have if I hadn't thought you would fight back." Eska glanced over at the woman and would have sworn she saw the hint of a smile on her face.

"What caused the light?"

"Trade secret," the woman said, and there was no mistaking the smile then. It vanished quickly. "You're bleeding," she said, gesturing to Eska's face.

Eska felt her cheek. "Not mine." She hesitated. "My name is Eska."

The woman studied her for a moment. "Isaure," she said, then nodded and looked up at the trapdoor. "Come on. We're nearly there." Eska boosted her up through the hole, and then Isaure reached down to help her.

Eska emerged inside a hollow tree wide enough to contain three or four crouching people. Following Isaure's lead, Eska crawled over a bed of mushrooms and out through a vine-covered hole. Standing up straight, she saw Lake Delo spreading out in front of her, calm and blue, through a fringe of branches smothered with pink blossoms. The water lapped against the rocky shore and Eska closed her eyes and drew in a deep breath. The air was layered with the subtle sweetness of the lady slippers at Eska's feet and the deeper scents of pinesap and cedar. Eska walked through the flowering branches to the water. To her left lay Cancalo, tucked between the lake and the steep hills behind the city. Snow-capped, forbidding mountain peaks loomed above.

"Where are your people?" Isaure asked from over Eska's shoulder.

"I can find my way from here." Eska turned to face her. "Better perhaps that you don't know exactly where I've gone. That way if anyone asks, you can tell the truth."

The woman gave a slow nod. "Very well."

Eska glanced back at the city.

"He's clever," Isaure said quietly, reading the direction of Eska's thoughts. "And not without friends." The words were meant to reassure, but it was what she didn't say that Eska heard loudest—she didn't say Eden San-Germain would be all right. She looked back at the other woman and tried to smile. "He must care for you."

It was simply stated, but it set Eska's mind tumbling. Eden's smile. The silver ink on his bronze skin. The way his fingers curled in her hair. The way he seemed to know what her body wanted before she did. It was care of a sort, she decided. But that wasn't fair. She remembered the way he listened as she spoke of the attack on her mother, how he accepted her ire toward Carriers without feeling a need to defend himself, how he dove back into the waters of Lake Delo and risked his life for her dream. That suggested care of a different sort.

"We hardly know each other," she heard herself say. Eska looked down at her borrowed clothes. One set of bare toes looked back up at her. "I lost a shoe," Eska said, "but I will send these back to the city."

Isaure shook her head. "Don't bother." She turned to step back behind the curtain of pink flowers.

"Thank you," Eska called after her. And then she was alone on the shore of Lake Delo.

———◆●▸———

"So we are now fugitives in two of the Seven Cities."

The Firenzia Company crewmembers and Perrin stood in a circle around Eska. Gabriel's statement hung in the air as Eska looked at their faces. They had given her no cause to question their loyalty, but Eska could not help but wonder if any had reached a breaking point.

She smiled. "While I appreciate your willingness to share in this, I'm afraid I alone am the fugitive."

Gabriel brushed this away and asked the crucial question. "Where are we going?"

Eska looked across the lake at the city and sighed. She had been wrestling with the question since parting ways with Isaure. And if she were honest with herself, she would admit her mind kept slipping away to Cancalo and a man with silver tattoos. Not knowing Eden's fate was gnawing a hole inside her.

"Surely Arconia," Perrin said. "Your family is there. They will protect you."

He had a point, the exact point Eska had been making to herself. And Albus was in Arconia. She needed to know what else he had learned about the god discs. She looked down at the ivory and gold reliquary in her hands.

"I can't risk my father and mother's positions. Or the Company's reputation. There is more at stake here than my future," Eska said, voicing the other side of the argument. "If I return to Arconia, I will be too visible, too close, and my parents and my uncle will be dragged through the mud with me. If I don't," she trailed off. "If I don't, there's a chance they come out of this unscathed. Relatively."

"Then where?" Gabriel asked.

"The de Caraval estate in the Vachon Valley. It's secluded and re-mote. From there, I can marshal my case against the accusations from Toridium." She looked around the circle once more. "Any of you who wish to go home, you are free to do so without any fear of losing your place with the Company. I have already asked more of you than I have any right to do."

Bastien bristled. "Anyone who abandons my lady now is a coward."

"Bastien," Gabriel began, his voice stern, but Eska broke in.

"There is no cowardice in choosing a simpler path, Bastien," she said. "I can make no guarantees of safety from this point on, no prom-ises of when you will see our city again. It is no small thing to follow a woman wanted for murder, even an innocent woman. Your loyalty will make you complicit even though you knew nothing of my actions in Toridium. Those who wish to bring me down, to bring my family down, will not feel guilty over any collateral damage."

Bastien's gaze had dropped to his feet as she spoke, but he raised his head again. "That may be, my lady," he said, his voice less fierce but perhaps all the more meaningful for that, "but who am I if I stand aside now? I am with you."

Eska smiled sadly. The young man, barely more than a boy, who had raced up to her bath chamber to tell her the Barca ship had sailed was gone, replaced by a harder man who was beginning to understand something of the whims of the world. "Thank you, Bastien," she said.

In the end, not a single crewmember chose to leave her. Some ex-pressed their choice boisterously, others quietly, but none gave Eska reason to doubt them.

The decision made, the crew dismantled the small camp quickly, loading the two wagons efficiently. Perrin helped Eska pack up her tent, wrapping the skeleton bone by bone in linen and then securing the reliquary, which Eska had not even had a chance to examine, in a small chest. Perrin paused with his hand on the ornate ivory before they closed the lid of the chest, a distant expression on his face.

"What do you think is inside?"

If he felt her hesitation, he did not reveal it and he removed his hand for Eska to shut and lock the chest.

"I don't know," she said, tucking the key in her leather satchel. It was the truth—she didn't know with any certainty the reliquary contained another god disc. But Perrin had asked her to speculate and she was choosing not to, not in his hearing at least, though she could not have said exactly why. Habit, perhaps. She was accustomed to dissecting every one of her theories with Albus, and Perrin, despite his attentiveness to the skeleton and his eagerness to learn, was no Albus. Perrin did not seem bothered by her answer. His expression was still that of a man who wasn't truly present, but Eska could not fathom where his mind had wandered.

Eska turned away and shoved the last of her belongings into a large oiled leather bag, then bent to trade Isaure's remaining leather slipper for a sturdy pair of boots. When she finished lacing them up, she straightened and saw that Perrin was still standing motionless in the middle of the tent, staring at nothing. He looked pale.

"Perrin?"

He seemed not to hear, but when Eska walked over to stand in front of him, he stirred the moment she entered his vision. Frowning, he put a hand up to the back of his neck.

"Are you all right?"

The nod came slowly, haltingly. "Yes, I think so. Just tired." He ventured a smile. "I haven't been sleeping well."

Eska put a hand on his forearm. "Manon?"

He nodded again, his gaze on Eska's hand. "I can't put her out of my mind, though I would like nothing more than to forget." He sighed and closed his eyes. "Just for a moment." When he opened his eyes, Eska was reminded of how young he was. "You are very kind," Perrin said. "I don't know why. I am a Barca. Barcas do not have friends, not any more."

Eska smiled a little. "Are we not friends?"

She had hoped for a lighthearted reply, a quick quip. Instead the question seemed to confuse him and he looked at her, lips parted slightly, a crease between his eyebrows.

"I do not know," he managed at last. He bowed his head, the formality of the gesture surprising Eska. Without thinking, she stepped closer to him and put a hand on his cheek.

"Perrin. We are friends. I did not expect to say such words, but whatever is between my family and yours, believe that. Trust that. You do not need to be alone in this world. You are not alone."

He seemed to lean into her words, as though he needed their strength—and then his knees buckled and he collapsed to the ground at Eska's feet.

———— ♦ ————

Perrin was sweating profusely by the time they got him loaded into one of the wagons. When Nahia examined him—after Eska had run from her tent shouting for help—and pronounced him not to be in immediate danger, the rapid decision was made to continue their departure from Cancalo. She sat in the back of the wagon as Bastien encouraged the horses into motion, Perrin's head in her lap, his long legs stretched out next to her. They had wrapped him in two thick blankets, though the evening was warm.

Nahia had given her verdict to Eska with a wrinkled brow, concerned because, though he presented some of the physical symptoms of a fever, his forehead and armpits were not hot to the touch. In the end, they had agreed to treat it as a fever, assuming the heat would come later.

They took the northwestern route away from Lake Delo, following the shore road until it began to curve back around to the southwest. Night had fallen by the time they left the dark lake waters behind and turned onto a smaller track, this one bumpier and made dangerous by ankle-deep holes. As such, their progress was slower than Eska would have liked, both for Perrin's sake and to put as much distance between them and whatever authorities might be searching for her in Cancalo.

Perrin had passed in and out of consciousness in the moments before he was lifted into the wagon, and now he dwelled in a fitful sleep, made all the worse by the condition of the road. He cried out after one particularly rough jolt, his fingers scrabbling at the blankets at his throat. Eska tried to keep him comfortable, but there was little she could do other than wipe the sweat from his face.

He became lucid once in the night, shortly after Gabriel had called a halt to water the horses at a stream before turning from their cart road and crossing a stone arch bridge. Across the bridge, they would join up with another narrow track, this one leading up into far-reaching, heather-rich moors. Eska and Gabriel had conferred on the best route to take to the remote Vachon Valley, and chosen the moors for the isolation. The route would grant them little in the way of civilization, which would necessitate hunting and foraging and perhaps a little fishing if they were lucky, but it would keep them from unwanted eyes.

As the horses drank and the crew stretched their legs and argued good-naturedly over who would have to drive next and who would get to sleep, Perrin stirred.

"Manon?" he asked, his voice a mere whisper. He opened his eyes as Eska looked down at him.

"Are you comfortable?"

"Eska," he said, recognizing her. "I'm sorry."

"Don't be sorry. How are you feeling?"

Perrin shut his eyes, as though keeping them open was too difficult. "Tired. Is there water? Where are we?"

Eska reached for the flask tucked in the corner of the wagon at her hip and helped Perrin lift his head enough to drink from it. When he had enough, his head sank back to her lap and Eska was quite certain he looked paler than before.

"We've left Lake Delo. We'll be passing into Revellion moor soon."

"I'm sorry to be a burden," Perrin murmured. "The last thing you need is an invalid."

"I'd hardly call you an invalid," Eska said, making sure he could hear the smile in her voice. "You just need to rest."

Perrin's lips formed a ghost of a smile. Gabriel gave the order to continue on and the wagon lurched forward once again. Perrin dropped into a more restful sleep shortly after, but Eska did not sleep that night. Her mind roamed across thoughts of the Hands of Fate, of the ivory reliquary that lay in a chest at her feet, of the Regatta Master of Lake Delo, of Alexandre de Minos, of the dead man in Toridium, of her family and the uncertainty that lay before her. Even had she not wished to remain awake should Perrin need anything, she could not have found enough stillness within her mind to succumb to sleep.

When they halted again in the darkest hours before dawn, she extracted herself from beneath Perrin, walked a bit to get the blood flowing in her legs, then dug into her satchel for a small packet. The raw harrow root powder burned her tongue, but Eska welcomed the sensation, welcomed the taste, unmarred by water or tea or herbs, and she felt, when she returned to the wagon and took up a perch next to Cosimo on the driver's bench, that she could forgo sleep for one hundred nights, that she could, even, climb among the stars in the night sky and rattle the dreams of the gods who slumbered there.

Interlude 14

Excerpt from the confiscated journals of disgraced scholar Dionus Barrachio

Day 62

Subject 7 appears to be developing muscle spasms, concentrated in, but not exclusive to, his left arm and leg, as well as the left side of his torso. His heart rate slows tremendously, dangerously, one might say, in the aftershock of these spasms, though not if orally dosed with the harrow just prior to the event. In those cases, the subject's heart rate accelerates beyond a state of moderate exertion and maintains this state, and yet the subject shows no signs of exhaustion or other ill effects during this time. Two components of this must be further examined: the window of time in which an oral dose can produce this effect after a spasm, and how, and for how long, the state of exertion might be maintained.

Day 64

Subject 3 has died of self-inflicted wounds. Dissection reveals blackened liver and inflamed intestines, as well as a curious sticky substance in the lungs.

Day 67

Subject 6 can no longer tolerate ingestion of the harrow due to the breakdown of the muscles that allow her to swallow. Further doses will be administered topically. See diagram.

Day 71

Subject 7 entered state of extreme violence, made all the more destructive by enhanced strength. Three assistants harmed. Subject tortured the third until she provided him with the purest harrow currently in the laboratory's possession. Subject ingested dose five times greater than any yet administered. Subject currently appears to have entered a wakeful sleep: eyes remain open, but he shows no response to stimuli.

Day 94

Subject 7 escaped.

Day 103

Subject 7 found. The subject was hunted down after rampaging through the City, killing at random. Subject demonstrated enhanced strength and endurance, and retained intelligence and presence of mind, unlike Subject 1. I tried to lure him back to the safety of the laboratory, but the Celestial Knight Armira, who led a contingent of elite soldiers at the express order of Archduke Nimicus, thwarted my efforts. Subject 7 was cut down in the middle of the Decadronum. I will redouble my efforts with the last of my charges, Subject 6, though I do not expect her to live long.

Day 112

I have been betrayed. They are coming. My work is lost.

Part
III

29

"Well, I couldn't allow my guests to be eaten by sharks."

"I'm not sure how they've managed it," Albus said, "but Onaxos is even more tedious now that I'm supposed to be dead."

Keleut suppressed a laugh, which was precisely the reaction the librarian had been hoping for given that the pirate captain had, after pacing endlessly, begun to try to drag what was clearly a sacred altar across the floor. Her end destination was, Albus reasoned, the large ceremonial, sickle-shaped staff that rested—reverently, if any inanimate object could be said to possess such abilities—in a golden cradle on the wall behind the altar. What she intended, precisely, to do with said staff, well, Albus could not imagine given that he was the only other occupant of the space.

"We've only just won a reprieve. Do you think perhaps we could attempt not to destroy their sacred space?"

Keleut's smile turned to a pained grimace. "I'd much rather hit something with that staff."

"Not me, I hope."

"Unfortunately, no. It turns out you're even more useful than I hoped."

"Nearly setting myself on fire and falling from a horrible height into the waiting jaws of sharks is useful?"

"Well, when you consider the fact that you were before me in the order of dying, had the smoke and the birds come a moment later, at least I would have been spared. Very useful." Keleut laughed when she saw Albus's expression, which he imagined was very similar to the face he might make when confronted with a particularly awful smell on a particularly hot day.

"Glad to help," he said. And yet he was glad, oddly enough. Not because he had nearly died and not because he had been spared at the last moment—well, yes, because of that—but because there was a new tone between him and the Seycherran. Where once she had disdained him but for the information in his brain, he had begun to feel, since being whisked off the sea wall and back to the spire—to wait, again— that she had a burgeoning respect for him and the manner in which he had comported himself. Certainly they had reached some sort of silent agreement that being at odds with each other—though she *had* kidnapped him—was not to their mutual benefit.

And so they waited in what Albus assumed was a hall of worship. It was six-sided and blindingly white. The walls rose up to an astonishing height while tall, narrow windows angled slightly against the plane of the walls, sent sword-like shafts of light spilling in all directions. The altar, draped in a lacy cloth, dominated one of the six sides but the floor was empty—no chairs, no benches—and, but for the staff and a chalice on the altar, the hall was free from adornment.

"I've had a rather bad thought," Albus heard himself say as he sat cross-legged on the floor and gazed up at the ceiling. He glanced down in time to see Keleut roll her eyes slightly, but she gave no indication he shouldn't continue. "What if sparing us on the sea wall was all part of the plan? And now they're preparing the true manner of execution."

"Fortunately for you, creativity is not the strongest quality of the Wisdoms of Onaxos."

The voice came from the only door to the hall and Albus shot up, trying to stand and turn at the same time. As a result, he went lurching sideways, his balance only restored by Keleut's firm hand on his shoulder.

The new arrival stood just inside the door. She was dressed in white robes with a lace hood through which peeked a thin circlet of silver.

It wasn't until she approached, her feet silent on the floor, and pushed the hood off her head to reveal long, white-blonde hair, that Albus realized how young she was. Poised, confident—but young. Hardly more than a child. And she spoke perfect Bellaran.

"Are you here to bring us to them? Or whatever comes next in this farce?" There was steel in Keleut's voice and Albus was very glad she hadn't succeeded in removing the staff from the wall.

The girl smiled as she tucked her hands into her sleeves. "I am what's next." She walked in a tight circle around Albus and Keleut, eying them both.

"I don't have time for this," Keleut said. "If we are not meant to be executed, then I will be leaving. I never should have come here. Onaxos is full of liars and empty promises."

Albus debated whether to attempt to discreetly reach out and touch the pirate's forearm, a restraining gesture she would no doubt fail to appreciate. But the girl did not seem offended. The smile returned—polite, pleasant, and wholly unnerving, Albus decided, though he could not have said why.

"You are not wrong, I'm afraid. But my promises are not empty."

"Speak plainly, girl," Keleut demanded.

And she did. "You wrote to Wisdom Isopho one hundred and forty-eight days ago. You received an answer thirty-two days ago." These were not, Albus realized, questions. "In that response, you were invited to Onaxos, to meet with the Wisdoms, and to discuss a matter of great importance to you. Unfortunately, I'm afraid a bit of deception was necessary. You see, I invited you to Onaxos, though I had to use the name and authority of a Wisdom to do so."

Albus very nearly expected Keleut to walk out of the hall, but, though she radiated tension and frustration as tangibly as a flame does heat, she held her ground—and her tongue, which was most certainly the more remarkable of the two.

"Would you like me to explain myself?" the girl asked.

When there was no answer from Keleut, Albus decided he had earned the right to speak for her. "Tell us about the black smoke and the white birds."

The girl laughed, a beautiful sound that filled the hall of worship more completely than the shards of light passing through the windows.

"The smoke is a conduit between the Wisdoms and the Twins. A fire burns eternally at the top of the spire and the smoke is always white," she said. "Except when the Twins speak. If a Wisdom receives a divine message, the smoke turns black." The girl was smiling as though she were party to a great secret she wasn't quite ready to share. "At least, this is how the city of Onaxos understands it." She didn't elaborate.

"And the birds?"

"Ah, that was the crucial touch, you see. Black smoke, while it signals celestial communication, can mean any number of things. But a flock of white ravens means something else entirely." The smile grew wider. "White ravens are most precious to Taalo, who is our beacon of justice. Seeing the sky above the city, above the sea wall, fill with the white wings of ravens would be the equivalent of," she paused, searching for a comparison, and fixed her gaze sharply on Keleut, "of seeing the mother spider descend from the stars of her web."

Though Seycherran in origin, the meaning and enormity of the comparison was not lost on Albus. He studied the girl in front of him. She seemed to welcome the examination. "You manufactured a divine intervention on our behalf."

"Well, I couldn't allow my guests to be eaten by sharks."

Albus stole a moment to digest this revelation by glancing at Keleut, who returned the look. He could see no course plotted in the pirate's eyes. They were both treading water in the wide open sea of this girl's scheme. He turned his attention back to the girl.

"And the acolyte? Could not the ravens have flown a moment earlier?" Albus asked.

"Her death was a shame," the girl said, her tone implying it was anything but, "but surely letting one of the faithful die and interceding only on behalf of the strangers is far more convincing."

The coolness of the reply chilled Albus's skin. Whoever she was, no matter her age, he began to understand this girl was not to be underestimated.

The girl continued, her smile as sweet as ever. "If it's acceptable to you, I'd like to introduce you to my brother."

———— ◆▸ ————

Logically, he should have been anticipating a boy a short span of years either younger or older than the girl. And yet Albus, as he and Keleut followed the girl from the hall of worship and further up into the spire, was so shaken by the initial encounter, he was entertaining the notion that the brother would certainly be much older, a fully grown man, surely, who had charged his much younger sister with conducting the first part of his plan.

He was entirely wrong, as it turned out, both in terms of his logic and his speculation. The brother was neither younger nor older, but an exact copy of the girl.

Twins.

Not an exact copy. His hair was shorter. Albus looked again, searching for further differentiation in size or lip shape or eye color and finding none.

The girl had led them to a set of chambers. They were richly furnished and comfortable, but the lack of windows was so unlike the rest of the spire Albus had seen, he found it remarkable. The brother, dressed in a short tunic and leggings, had been removing a set of greaves from his shins when the sister had opened the door and ushered Keleut and Albus inside. He wore a plain leather cuirass, made dull by the brightness of his hair and his fine features. The smile with which he greeted them was identical to his sister's.

"I think introductions are in order," the girl said. "I am Aurelia nox Macedonos. This is my brother Aurelian." She looked at Keleut. "You are Keleut of Seycherra, daughter of Nestor." Her gaze shifted to Albus. "But you I don't know."

"Tristan," Albus blurted. He could feel the heat of the lie in his cheeks and he was quite certain Keleut, visible in the corner of his vision, was desperately trying to restrain a sigh of exasperation. "Tristan Tarvonos, her interpreter."

"We apologize," Aurelian said from behind his sister, "for the reception you endured. This is not how we would have visitors treated."

Keleut looked to Albus. For all her prowess at sea and ferocity when faced with intimidation, she seemed uncertain how to proceed.

"We welcome your courtesy," Albus said. "But there is a great deal we do not understand. What is your position here? How is it that the Wisdoms are allowing this?"

The twins exchanged a glance, and then Aurelian spoke again. "The Wisdoms are unaware of this conversation, just as they are unaware of the fact that you did not fall from the sea wall a short time ago."

"What do you mean?" Albus asked. "Surely they know."

"All six of the Wisdoms are in communion with the Twins," Aurelia said. "They will not emerge until sunset tomorrow. I changed the color of the smoke. I loosed the ravens from the top of the spire. My brother, in the name of the Wisdoms, saw that you were escorted to the Chamber of Dying. I met you there under the pretense of taking you to see Wisdom Isopho, who had received a message from the Twins reversing the order of execution—and with strict orders that under no circumstances should your meeting with Wisdom Isopho be disturbed."

Albus looked from one face to the other. Their composure was frightening. "And you are allowed to speak for the Wisdoms?"

"It is a privilege we have cultivated with care," Aurelian said. "And our name has some meaning here in the spire and in the city."

If Albus were ensconced in the safety of the Lordican, perhaps with a cup of tea at his elbow and a familiar book on his lap, he would have eagerly delved into the meaning behind the boy's words. But he was not in the Lordican and there was no familiarity or comfort to be had here. He sensed that despite the twins' equanimity, they had limited time at their disposal before the careful deception the twins had built suffered a fatal crack.

Keleut seemed to sense the same. She stirred next to Albus. "What do you want? Why did you answer my letter when clearly the Wisdoms had no intention of doing so? You know what I asked, what it means." Albus was left in the dark, but the pirate's last words were heavy with meaning.

"That is a long story," Aurelia said. "We do not have the time to share it with you now."

"But know this," her brother said. "We can bring Onaxos to stand at your side."

Keleut let out a harsh laugh of disbelief. "Preposterous." She threw up her hands and began to pace back and forth behind Albus, muttering a few words in Seycherran before coming to stand directly in front of the twins. "This is no game. This is no place for children playing at power."

"We do not play." Aurelian offered no further explanation, no reason to trust his word, but Albus could feel the conviction in him. It was terrifying.

"You have seen something of what we can do," his sister said. "We can show you more. If you wish to see."

Albus answered for them, feeling a deep need to understand the unsettling, precocious pair. "Then show us."

The twins smiled.

———•——

Albus tugged at the white robe, its unfamiliar seams sitting in all the wrong places. He felt quite certain it made him look short.

Keleut snorted, her own robe resting easily on her shoulders and draping just so. "I never thought you were one for appearances. Tristan." She threw out the false name acerbically. Albus had already apologized for that slip up the moment they were left in private, but then, he had not truly expected Keleut to let it go.

"I panicked," he said again, feeling his face grow hot with embarrassment once more.

"Come on," Keleut said. "The sooner we do this, the sooner we can leave."

She walked to the door of the chamber, but Albus hesitated to follow.

"Keleut," he said, then faltered. She turned to look back at him, one hand on the door. There was an unexpected softness in her features. "What brought you to Onaxos? What did you write in that letter one hundred and forty-eight days ago?"

The last time he had asked a question about her plans and purpose, they had been in the middle of the Anerrean Sea and the most difficult part of Albus's day was deciding how many spoonfuls of broth his stomach could tolerate. The last time had become the last time because she had rebuffed every question and Albus had decided to put his breath to more useful tasks—like breathing. It seemed an age ago.

"You will hate me if I tell you," she said at last. "But I suppose you have earned the right to know." She sighed and retraced her steps toward Albus. "The day we met. Do you remember the final question I asked you?"

"I will remember that question and that moment until the day I die." Albus tried to laugh. "Maybe even beyond and you know now I don't believe in a beyond."

Keleut nodded, his attempt at humor lost. He had seen the pirate captain look fierce and determined. He had seen her look confused and even show the faintest hint of uncertainty. He had seen her laugh uproariously and he had seen her kill with ease. But Albus understood, as her deep brown eyes stared at him, that he had not, until that moment, seen the true Keleut of Seycherra. The words she was about to speak lay at the very heart of her.

"Your Alescuan kings and queens seized my country. They raped it, land and people. They stripped it of treasure, yes, but of dignity and its sense of self, too. And then they left it, like a predator, having gorged itself, leaves a carcass to rot in the sun. They moved on to the next prize, and my country has never been the same since." Keleut hesitated, but not for a lack of conviction. For his sake, Albus realized. But there was no subtlety to the blow that followed. "I mean to make your Seven Cities bleed the way they made my country and my people bleed. I mean to have vengeance."

It was with those words in his head that Albus followed the twins out of the spire. He walked in a daze, hardly noting the movement of his own feet. Destroy the Seven Cities. The pirate had gone on to say that she knew it was unlikely she could truly achieve her goal. The Seven Cities were wealthy and powerful and not without friends—and she would likely have only one chance to strike a devastating blow, one chance before retaliation came for her. But, she had said, if she could bring just one of the Seven to its knees before she went to join her ancestors in the stars, she could rest well.

Albus had not had the will to ask which of the Seven she was aiming for first.

The twins took them down through the city—not using the water route, but by simply walking the streets, Keleut and Albus in tow and dressed as attendants.

As soon as they left the uppermost level, an old man spotted the twins and rushed forward to bow before them. His action attracted more eyes and soon they had drawn a crowd. Some citizens reached out to touch their robes, others simply knelt as they walked by. Some shouted out praise and prayers to Taalo and Toora, others invoked the Wisdoms, and still others looked at the twins' young, beautiful faces in adoring silence.

By the time they had reached the third level below the spire, curving around to face the sea wall once more, their progress was impeded by the number of Onaxians following them, joining them, offering them flowers and prayers and well wishes, and Albus, jostled from the stupor of Keleut's words, had to work to keep up.

Aurelia and Aurelian came to a halt on the fourth terrace of the city. They waved to the assembled crowd, spoke a few words of thanks, and then asked to be allowed to pray to the Twins in peace. The crowd melted away slowly and at last brother and sister entered a small garden at the edge of the terrace. The garden was walled off from the street but open to the sea view, and two small, neat shrines to the Twins flanked the path that led to the white stone balustrade that separated the garden from empty air. Aurelian and Aurelia, hand in hand, walked to the balustrade and turned to face Albus and Keleut. Their white robes and pale blonde hair glowed in the bright sunlight, and their youthful features seemed to radiate with the light of something that wasn't mortal.

The prayer garden was no chance stopping point. For in that moment, as no doubt they intended, Albus saw behind them, like a shadow, the colossal statue of the divine Twins in the harbor, the right half, Toora with her spear and her armor, matching up behind Aurelian, the left half, Taalo and his raven, behind Aurelia.

It was a breathtaking image and Albus could understand how a person who wanted to believe in such things could succumb to it. But for him, the hair on his arms stood on edge not because he saw living gods before him, but because he saw the destruction of his home in their shadow.

30

"Because I had brothers."

It was the wolves that brought Manon to her feet.

The long, undulating howl raised the hairs on the back of her neck and the answering cry had Luca reaching for the knife at his hip as they both searched for the origin of the sound.

But it was the sound of far off hooves that had Manon rushing to her horse and heaving the saddle up onto its back, her movement made awkward by the reliquary tucked in the crook of her elbow and pressed hard against her ribs. With the saddle secured, Manon shoved the reliquary in the saddlebag and made to mount, but a sharp tug on her cloak sent her sprawling to the ground, the breath fleeing from her lungs.

Justina stood over her, her intent written in the fierceness in her eyes and the tautness of the cords in her neck. With one swift movement, she freed her bow and nocked an arrow on the string.

"You're not going anywhere," the huntress said.

Manon never had the chance to decide if she thought her fire could beat the woman's arrow. A lean grey shape charged into the stone circle and leaped—not at Justina, not a Manon, but at Luca, who stood between it and the other horse.

The hunter tried to dodge, catching the wolf on his shoulder instead of full on in the chest. Three more wolves, teeth bared in silent snarls, stalked into the circle, watching their pack mate crouch in front of

Luca, who had regained his balance, and Manon caught a glimpse from the corner of her eye of more grey shadows.

Taking advantage of the stand off, Manon got to her feet and flung herself at her horse once more. Justina got there at the same time and they wrestled each other to the ground. Manon fell hard on her elbow and cried out in pain, a cry Justina echoed a moment later when Manon caught her with a forearm to the throat.

Voices shouted in the distance, men urging their horses to greater speed, and as Justina pushed Manon's face into the dirt, she saw the rest of the hunting party arrive, a blur of hooves and horse tails, barely seen through the blades of grass masking Manon's sight. The horses shied from the wolves, but stood their ground, and the wolves, driven to a frenzy at the sight of the men, circled together, forming a tight group behind Manon. Flinging out an arm, Manon summoned the spark in her ribs with a desperation she had rarely felt. Without the aid of the powdered white Carrier substance, her range and strength was limited, but with a cry, she sent a burst of flames across the circle toward the group of mounted men. The horses reared back as the grass blazed to life. The flames, hot and hungry, licked their way to the sky, forming a temporary barrier. Another burst of flame at the wolves sent the stone circle into chaos.

Justina, caught with a shower of sparks, rolled away from Manon, who scrambled to her feet and vaulted into her saddle. The mare, eyes rolling wildly, half-reared, forcing Manon to cling precariously until she could find the second stirrup and take a grip on the loose reins. The wolves snarled and barked and one leaped through the flames at Justina. The horse settled beneath Manon—and then bolted.

The windswept plateau was a blur beneath the horse's hooves as its instinct drove it away from danger. Manon bent low over the horse's neck, as much for her own preservation as to keep out of the wind. Still, the wind whipped tears from her eyes and she had little sense of direction or distance until at last the horse slowed enough for Manon to regain control. She turned it, trying to catch a glimpse of the stone circle, but other than a faint tendril of smoke from the burning grass, she could make out nothing. The horse had raced inland, taking her away from the pounding sea, and the sudden silence was startling—and all the more crushing because it allowed Manon a moment to think.

And she had only one thought: Luca.

She had left him—well, the horse had left him and not given Manon much choice in the matter—and he would certainly be arrested, once the wolves were chased away or killed and order was restored within the stones. What followed only the Principe could have said with any certainty, but that alone was enough to knot Manon's stomach.

And yet...she was free. There was no time to ponder the fate of a near stranger. She had far too many troublesome things weighing her down to take on that burden.

Manon turned the mare once more, angling her in a northeasterly direction. To Arconia.

———————— ◆ ————————

Or she tried to head to Arconia.

But come nightfall, for reasons she couldn't quite fathom, much less put words to, Manon was wading through a boggy pond, crouching among tall reeds and cottontails and breathing in the occasional insect. Beyond the muddy shore ahead of her flickered the light of a campfire. And somewhere within that firelight, hopefully conscious, almost certainly with his hands bound, was a moderately irritating hunter.

She could not have said, as she rode the mare far from the stone circle, which of the many thoughts roiling through her mind was the one that ultimately prompted her to turn the horse around. But of one thing she was sure—the moment she did so, her mind went quiet and stayed that way.

She had traced her route back toward the stone circle, but short of reaching the stones, she had turned more sharply south, trying to cut off some of the distance and assuming the master hunter and his band had followed the same track she had taken from the lodge. If she could catch them by the time they reached the ruins, she would be on territory she had passed through after taking the coastal road from Licenza. If she did not, she would be forced to try to find their tracks, for she did not know where the Principe's residence lay within the massive estate of Pontevellio.

She did not catch them.

Cursing as she dismounted within sight—diminishing sight, given how low the sun hung in the sky—of the burned lodge, Manon had paced back and forth, the mare watching her nervously as she tried to determine how to proceed. The band of hunters had not remained on the path, that much even Manon, who had never tracked an animal in her life, could ascertain. The soft earth of the coastal path was marred by only one set of hoof prints—her own from the previous day.

The trodden-down grass of the clearing was a quagmire of mud and distorted tracks, but as she had increased the range of her search behind the ruined lodge, she stumbled upon a fallen branch hidden in the underbrush. Righting herself before she plunged face-first to the earth, she noticed the first clear hoof print—and then a second and a third. Beyond that, the prints were a tangled mess and were quickly swallowed up by the thick layer of growth on the forest floor, but it was enough. Returning to her horse, Manon had mounted once more, her legs, unaccustomed to riding such distances, protesting every move. She guided the horse along the edge of the burned timbers of the lodge, the scent of smoke and ash still strong in her nose, and then—slowly, carefully, lest she lose the way—continued in pursuit of the hunters.

Pursuit which ended with Manon up to her thighs in a swamp.

She paused, watching, waiting, trying to discern movement. Though the faint sound of voices reached her, she could see nothing. She crept closer, then felt the treacherous ground beneath her boots begin to slope downward. Manon grimaced, having hoped to avoid a true swim. But the pond provided more cover for her approach than trees, and so she lowered herself to her chin and began to glide through the water.

When she reached the shallows on the shore closest to the camp, she waded in a crouched position, flinching at every wave her movements made in the water around her. The voices ahead of her went quiet and Manon froze, waiting for one of the hunters to appear in the reeds above her, a torch in hand to illuminate—and terminate—her rescue attempt. But after a moment, the low voices resumed and Manon let herself breathe again. She waited, aware that she had not thought past the point of reaching the opposite side of the pond. The spark in her ribs itched for some of the pale powder she had used in her attempt to blow up the Firenzia ship. But the safety of a ranged attack was a luxury she did not have, and so Manon forced her limbs to extract her from the pond and she crawled through a thicket of cottontails until she emerged into a precarious middle ground—outside the firelight but equally removed from the sanctuary of the reeds.

From that vantage point, her stomach plastered to the earth, her hands black with mud, Manon could make out the shapes of three men sitting around the campfire. A fourth stood a short distance away, his hands cupped around a pipe he was trying to coax to life. Another figure was stretched out on the ground, and for a moment Manon thought it to be Luca, but a flicker of light on metal told her it was Justina's iron foot. Beyond Justina, the horses, six in all, were staked in the darkness. Manon continued to let her gaze rove over the camp, and at last she picked out Luca.

The broad-shouldered hunter sat slumped against a tree trunk at the farthest reaches of the firelight, hardly more than an outline in the darkness. His head hung toward his chest, though whether due to sleep or distress, Manon could not tell.

A cold fear snaked into Manon's belly, but it was the uncertainty, the lack of control over the situation, that nearly made her turn around and swim back across the pond and disappear into the night. No one would ever know. Luca would never know she had come for him and her courage had failed. She could return to Arconia, hand over the reliquary to the Archduke, and pretend she had never waded through a swamp on the private estate of the Principe of Licenza.

But then a strange thing happened to Manon. As she lay with her cheek pressed to the earth, her heart thudding in her chest, she saw Perrin's face—just as she had last seen him. Confused, scared. Forsaken by the one person who should have been willing to sacrifice everything for him.

And so Manon stayed, with the thought of Perrin like a spirit over her shoulder, though whether he was admonishing her or encouraging her, Manon could not decide.

The camp grew quiet as one by one the hunters went to sleep—all but one, the pipe smoker. But they were on familiar land, safer than most other stretches of dark forest thanks to the name of the Principe of Licenza, and the pipe smoker sat down close to the dying fire. He stretched his legs out and rested against a fallen log. Manon watched the bowl of his pipe glow and fade, glow and fade with every breath, and then it went dark as it slipped from between his teeth.

Manon waited until she knew her chances were as likely to decline as improve, then stood, having chosen to forgo stealth for speed. If one of the hunters woke up, there was nothing to hide behind. Better to be ready to run than caught in a crouch like a frightened rabbit.

She strode around the edge of the camp, trying to quell the trembling beneath her skin. Luca didn't stir at her approach, forcing Manon to wake him and hope he didn't startle and alert the sleepers. He didn't appear to be injured, though his clothes were dirty and there was a long tear in one of his sleeves. His wrists and ankles were bound with slender cord.

Manon knelt and cautiously placed a hand on his shoulder. When her touch had no effect, she moved her palm to his cheek, his stubble rough against her skin, and he came awake surprisingly gently, to Manon's intense relief.

His head came up slowly, turning toward the touch, his gaze taking Manon in with sleep-induced confusion, which faded quickly when his eyes focused on her face. She pulled her hand away from his cheek and reached down to where his hands rested in his lap. The knots were too intricate, her fingers too unsteady. Luca lifted his hands and gestured toward the horses, then mouthed the word knife. Nodding, Manon darted between the trees, her feet whispering over pine needles. The horses shifted at her approach, and she came to a halt, hoping their unease would pass quickly. The sixth horse was hers, the pack horse she had hired in Licenza, and after a moment, the gelding dropped his head, his eyes half closing, and the other horses followed his lead. Manon slipped among them, freeing her pack horse and the tall mare Luca had been riding. The gelding shoved his nose into her back as she began to lead them back to Luca, his soft whicker stopping her in her tracks. She dared a glance toward the glowing remains of the camp-fire, just in time to see the pipe smoker move—but he merely slumped lower against the log.

Manon returned to Luca, who managed to take the reins between his palms while Manon fished in his belongings for a blade. She found two, a large hunting knife with a smaller blade tucked into the sheath. Luca nodded and pointed to the smaller knife, and though Manon might have chosen to trust the brute force offered by the larger one, she discovered the hunter kept his blades in fine condition. Despite its small size, the blade cut through the ropes around Luca's wrists with minimal effort. She let him take care of the bonds around his ankles, and then they were leading the horses into the dark and Manon, as though a piece of her had remained pressed to the mud on the shore of the pond, realized it was done.

Not a word was exchanged between them until after they collected Manon's mare from where she had secured it to a tree some distance from the camp. Only after they mounted and rode north did Luca venture to speak.

"Why did you come back?"

It was a long time before Manon answered. The horses trotted on-ward. A shooting star streaked to the horizon.

"Because I have," she stopped, cutting herself off. "Because I had brothers."

31

*"You are brave and bold and probably more clever
than you should be."*

The de Caraval family estate in the Vachon Valley was exactly
as Eska remembered it.

The stately home lay in the embrace of a narrow valley that ran east
to west. The hills that rose above it were thick with pines and oaks and
birches, lush and green, and a swift stream snaked its way along the
valley floor through forest and meadow.

As the party approached, the sound of water grew louder, though
the waterfall was buried deep within the cool shade of the trees and
out of sight. Eska urged her horse ahead toward the home in which she
had spent so many summers.

The valley had taught Eska the silence of an owl's wings, the cheery
call of a wood warbler, and the grace of the speckled trout in its watery kingdom. And patience. Stillness. Quiet. Things the governesses—
three in all—in Arconia could not impress upon her. But there, among
the pale birch bark and the faces of the wildflowers tilted to the sun
and the ceaseless turning of the stars overhead, Eska had learned of
peace.

She also hollered from the hilltops and listened to her voice fade
into the sunlight, laughed wildly when she splashed through the stream
to chase after lightning bugs, and sang songs of her own creation at
the top of her lungs—very poorly—while traipsing through the pines.

As she got older, she and her family had begun to spend less time away from Arconia, both as her education became more demanding, her future more promising, and as her mother and father rose in prominence in the governance of the city. As Eska rode into view of the house, it was the first time she had done so in nearly two years.

She had come alone that time, riding through a valley clinging to the last façade of summer. But no amount of peace could shake the image of Alexandre de Minos's face as it had looked when she rejected his offer of marriage just days before—or the feeling of her own hot tears, shed in private the moment she closed the door with Alexandre standing on the other side. She had thrown herself into the refuge the estate offered, intent on letting the late summer sun and the sound of the stream erode the persistent ache in her chest. She had even climbed to the highest peak the valley had to offer and shouted her confusion and anguish to the sky, but all she managed to do was startle a den of rabbits.

In the end, after a miserable ten days in the place that should have made her happiest, Eska discovered it was only the distractions of Arconia that could mend her. She had immersed herself into her studies and her work, producing an extensive treatise on the ceremonies and rituals of the tribes who had once occupied the mountains between Cancalo and Vienisi and leading two Firenzia expeditions into warmer climes during the winter months—she had, in short, worked herself to what should have been exhaustion. But rather than wear her down, the constant use of her mind had built her up, made her whole again.

To her relief, Eska's first sight of the two-level house fashioned from blocks of grey-blue stone dredged from the very stream that ran through the valley made her smile.

Smoke rose from behind the caretaker's house, situated across the meadow and down a narrow dirt path from the main house. Eska turned in her saddle and signaled to Gabriel to have the wagons halt and wait, then she guided her horse through the meadow and around the back of the smaller stone house.

As she expected, the source of the smoke was a rack of fish set above a gently smoldering fire in a stone pit. Eska smiled, thinking of fishing with Master Pietro and learning the unpleasant task of cleaning the fish from Mistress Rosina. A vegetable garden, fenced in against scavenging rabbits and deer, lay beyond the fire pit.

Dismounting, Eska looped her reins over a fence post and walked to the rear door. She made it as far as the stairs before the door swung open and a woman, her cheeks bursting with a smile, stepped out.

"My lady!" she exclaimed.

"Rosina," Eska said, her own smile widening. "Forgive my unexpected appearance."

Rosina shook her head. "Nonsense, my lady. This is your home." She rubbed her hands on her apron, leaving behind a smear of flour. "Let me just fetch the keys."

The woman disappeared inside, then emerged with a ring of iron keys. "Pietro is looking after his traps," Rosina said as she and Eska walked around the house, "but he just pruned the hedges the other day and," she broke off when she saw the wagons and crewmembers waiting at the far end of the meadow. "Oh. You haven't come with your family?"

"Sadly Mama and Papa are far too busy to enjoy the valley this year," Eska said. It was the truth, but it had been the truth for nearly a decade and Eska knew Rosina was saddened by the rarity of their visits. "These are men and women of Firenzia Company." Eska grew serious as they traversed the meadow. "Rosina, one among my party is ill. We'll put him in my parents' chamber. I'll take my own. The others can share the guest rooms."

Rosina's gaze roamed over the small party, taking in the wagons and equipment. "No servants?"

Eska laughed. "No such luxuries when we're working, I'm afraid. We've come directly from an excavation." Close enough to the truth to suffice. "We are very capable of fending for ourselves," she added, seeing Rosina's brow crease with concern.

The woman nodded as they joined the crewmembers. After Bastien and Cosimo lifted Perrin from the bed of the first wagon, Eska directed

Gabriel, Gael, and Nahia to the stable with the wagons and horses. Rosina unlocked the main entrance, a double door made of dark wood and reinforced with iron, and the rest of the party was ushered inside. Eska led the way up the stairs and down the corridor to her parents' bedchamber. Bastien and Cosimo laid Perrin gently on the stripped bed, then Eska sent them downstairs with instructions for Bastien to return with hot water and broth.

As the door closed behind them, Eska untied Perrin's boots and pulled them free, then tucked the blankets tighter around him. He had not grown worse in the four days it had taken to travel to the Vachon Valley—at least not in any manner Eska could detect—but neither had he improved. He would sweat without growing hot and toss and turn in a waking sleep, then he would rest so soundly he hardly appeared to be breathing. When he was conscious, he made attempts at humor and insisted he had improved, but always the sweating returned and Eska could see how difficult it was for him to even grasp a flask of water and raise it to his lips. As for Eska, a second dose of the harrow root halfway through the journey was still deep at work inside her veins.

She felt Perrin's forehead, as she had done countless times in the previous four days, but he was still cool to the touch. Lifting his head, she settled a feather-stuffed pillow beneath it. He moaned at the touch, his hands reaching up through the blankets to claw at his collar. This, too, she had seen before, on the road to the valley. Taking first one hand, then the other, she held them until he grew still.

"Perrin," she whispered. "It's all right."

He went ridged and his eyelids fluttered open. As his back arched away from the bed, his eyes rolled back into his skull. And then he went limp.

Eska let out a sharp exhale, her heart racing. "Perrin?" The weight of his hands in hers suddenly frightened her and she jumped up from the bed. Her hands shook as she took a small mirror from her mother's dressing table and held it under Perrin's nose. The glass fogged over ever so slightly.

Still shaken, Eska returned the mirror but it was a long moment before she willed herself to touch him again. This time, as her fingers brushed away a lock of hair that had fallen across his forehead, he remained unmoving. Eska took a deep breath and stood just as Bastien slipped into the room with a tray.

"The broth, my lady, and hot water," the young man said.

"Thank you. Bastien, will you stay with him? I need to ask Rosina what herbs she has readily available that might help him." The harrow root spoke the words more than Eska did, imbuing her with steadiness. Its heavy influence, made stronger by the fact that she had ingested it raw, was insisting she could renew Perrin's health, and she walked slowly down the corridor, trying to piece together the puzzle of his ailment, trying to will herself to greater understanding of healing and what could be done for him. She came to a halt at the top of the stairs, her hand on the balustrade, her mind elsewhere, and so intent was she on her thoughts that she did not notice the figure with one foot on the bottom step.

"Eska?"

The familiar voice broke through and Eska looked down at the face of her uncle.

Valentin de Caraval was still dressed in his traveling clothes, his hair wind-ruffled, dirt on the toes of his boots. It was, Eska realized faintly, not unlike many scenes that had played out in her childhood: him just returned from a far off place, her at the top of the stairs, rushing eagerly into the laughing embrace of the man who had been as much a parent to her as her mother or father. Eska knew he was thinking of the same moments—and his hesitation, which matched hers, told her he was also thinking of the last time they had seen each other.

They met in the middle, Valentin looking her over with concern, Eska smiling a smile given to her by the harrow root. He kissed her cheek, his hand on her elbow.

"I didn't know you were coming to the valley," Valentin said quietly.

"I didn't know myself."

"I saw Gabriel." The statement disguised the question. "Rosina said you just arrived."

"There are nine of us," Eska said. There were ten, in fact, but Eska was trying to maneuver her way around mentioning that a Barca was sleeping in her parents' bed. "We needed a place to rest." The ambiguity of that was laughable.

Valentin's gaze narrowed. "Are you all right? I would not have expected you to finish at the Bourdillon-Leveque site so quickly."

"We came from Cancalo, actually," Eska said, evading once more. Not because she didn't trust her uncle—she did, with her life if need be. But how to begin when one needs to explain that one is wanted for murder in one of the Seven Cities and been chased out of a second for, well, what her crimes in Cancalo were, she supposed she wasn't certain. But she suspected she wouldn't be welcome in the city in the near future.

To her relief, her uncle shifted the subject, taking a slender wooden box from a leather bag slung over one shoulder. It was still tied with a white ribbon, just as it had been that morning in the kitchen in Arconia, though the ribbon was decidedly crumpled.

"I've," Valentin began, his gaze fixed on the object in his hands, "I've been carrying this around."

Afterward, Eska could not have said what words might have come from her lips in that moment. Equal parts of her wished to push the gift away and take comfort in it, in that piece of her childhood. But the decision was taken from her when a scream carved open the silence.

Her chest constricting, Eska whirled and bolted back up the stairs. At the landing, she took the corner and raced back to her parents' chamber. She flung the door open and was aware of her uncle a few steps behind her, but she had eyes only for the figure on the bed.

Perrin's body was contorted in a horrible manner, his back arching as before but all his limbs splayed at uncomfortable angles. One hand had caught hold of Bastien's collar, and the young man was being pulled down onto the bed. Eska rushed forward and tried to disengage Perrin's hand without hurting him, but his fingers were locked in a claw-like grip. From behind Eska, Valentin hurled himself at Bastien and his weight knocked the younger man free. Both men went crashing to the floorboards.

Perrin panted, his eyes pushing back into his skull once more, but gradually his arms and legs loosened and the hand that had latched onto Bastien dropped to his chest.

"What was that?"

The question came from Valentin, who got to his feet and offered Bastien a hand.

"I don't know," Eska said. She looked to Bastien. "Was it violent? His movement, I mean."

Bastien was already shaking his head. "No. He woke, tried to speak. I leaned over to hear him. And then he screamed and the rest you saw."

Eska shifted her gaze to Valentin. "He's been ill since we departed from Cancalo. Sweating without fever. Muscle weakness. Losing consciousness. I was hoping Rosina could help him."

Valentin was looking at Eska with questions burning behind his eyes, but as he glanced at Bastien and then back to her, she understood he would wait for privacy to ask them. What she could not see in his face was whether he recognized Perrin as the son of his greatest rival.

Only after Rosina had brewed a tea that would help Perrin sleep more soundly, after Eska and Gabriel had settled the Firenzia crewmembers into the guest rooms and the small servant quarters, after Master Pietro had returned from his traps and tramped through the house with his customary cheer and laughter, after Gael and Inevra prepared a root vegetable soup, after Eska refused Pietro's offer of a fresh-caught doe—which somehow ended up roasting on a spit in the back garden regardless of the refusal, after the small group had gathered around the enormous rough-hewn oak table under a linen canopy and eaten the soup and venison in the burgeoning twilight, after Eska had helped wash and dry dishes in the kitchen—only after all of that did Eska and her uncle find themselves alone.

Drying her hands on an apron she had found hanging on a nail in the kitchen's closet, Eska went to stand at the rear door of the house. She looked out over the garden and the dying fire, at the swallows darting from branch to branch, and as she turned her gaze to the path to the stream, she saw him, a tall dark shape standing on the bank of the small river.

It took a moment for Eska to realize Valentin was not watching the water rush by. He was watching her, as though he had known she would appear in the doorframe.

Her hands were steady as she untied the apron and returned it to the closet, and her steps were sure and unhurried as she walked the path to the stream. After all, she did not intend to lie to her uncle. There was, however, one question she hoped he wouldn't ask.

The effects of the harrow root had faded to nothing over the course of the day. Her mind told her that was for the best. But part of her wondered if she would not rather have the coming conversation with it supporting her, despite knowing that consuming it so close on the heels of her last use was dangerous. She pushed thoughts of the powder away.

They stood shoulder to shoulder for a long moment, the stream gurgling through the rocky bed at their feet. Eska was content to wait.

"What's going on? Why were you in Cancalo?" Valentin asked at last. Once he would have begun by reassuring her that whatever her troubles were, they could be righted. But the shared memory of their last conversation in Arconia lay like a shadow between them.

"Would you like my version of events or the story no doubt circulating the Seven Cities?" Eska asked. "I'm surprised you haven't heard it already, actually."

"I've been across the Anerrean Sea," Valentin said by way of answer. "Making preparations in Anderra for an expedition to Sandalese," he continued, surprising Eska. The republic of Sandalese lay far to the north and was yet uncharted ground for Firenzia Company. "Part exploratory for Firenzia, of course, but also for the prince of Anderra, who is generously contributing funds and a security escort." He went silent. "There's a place for you, of course." It was a peace offering of sorts and normally Eska would have jumped at the chance to travel to new lands, even if it meant swallowing her differences with her uncle for a time.

"Perhaps I will take it." She heard herself laugh. A bitter sound. "After all, I'm not likely to be hunted all the way to Sandalese."

"Hunted?" Valentin's voice dropped low and he stepped close to Eska.

Eska took a deep breath. "A Chancellor of Toridium is dead and I am accused of poisoning him," she said. She glanced away from the stream, black now as night gathered, and up at her uncle's face. The disbelief she saw there would have been comical if the subject was anything other than murder. "That's the story spreading from Toridium. I didn't kill anyone."

She had spoken those exact words five days before to Eden San-Germain. This time she had the chance to explain herself. Eska looked back at the river, wondering if she would ever have that opportunity with the Regatta Master of Lake Delo.

And so she told her uncle of the diplomatic delegation to Toridium, of the negotiations with Chancellors Fiorlieu and Pelle, of Chancellor Fiorlieu's illness and her attempt to influence the negotiations by suggesting a remedy, of the sudden news of his death and her subsequent detainment in her chambers—and of course of her midnight escape from Toridium.

Valentin de Caraval took in her words in silence, not once interrupting to ask a question or to clarify a point. When she finished, he folded his arms behind his back, one hand clasping the other wrist, and looked out at the pines and the rising hills on the other side of the stream.

"Why Cancalo?" he asked. "Why flee? Or if you felt you had no choice, why not home to Arconia and your father?"

Eska took a breath, trying to order her thoughts. "Amidst all the events in Toridium, I received a letter from Albus Courtenay. You remember Albus, from the Lordican. Untidy librarian. Fluent in sixteen languages."

Valentin nodded.

"Before I left Arconia, Albus and I were studying an unusual object. He continued to do so after Mama and I departed for Toridium," Eska continued, speaking as vaguely as she could. "In my absence, he identified the object—or at least he appears to have—and his letter spoke of a second one. In Cancalo."

Again her uncle was quiet. When he spoke again, his gaze came to rest on Eska's face. "So you absconded from Toridium, no doubt confirming your guilt in the Vismarch's eyes, all for something buried in the earth." His voice was not quite scathing, but closer to it than Eska would have liked—certainly he had never used that tone with her in all her life. It did not seem the time to correct the details of what she had sought in Cancalo.

"I know what you're thinking," Eska said, determined to remain calm. "That it was a foolish decision. That I have risked myself and my family's name without reflecting on the consequences. I would hope, uncle, that you know me well enough and respect me enough to know that if my actions have been rash, I have had a good reason for them."

Though the night had overtaken them completely, the light emanating from the stone house allowed Eska to see Valentin's stern expression loosen enough to permit a hint of begrudging acceptance of her argument.

"If I ask what you were looking for, will you tell me?"

"I think that counts as asking," Eska said, smiling slightly. But she sobered quickly. "But I," she hesitated, unsure of her answer, "I don't think I should. Not now anyway." That the Alescuan reliquary was at that very moment sitting inside her bedchamber, begging to be opened, was a thing not to be thought of. "I don't mean to be rude or possessive," she hurried on, not wanting to close up the gap that had opened in the wall between them. "But things happened in Cancalo. And until I know the situation there, the fewer people who know, the better. I intend to stay here, where few might know to look, until I know how things stand in both cities." She attempted a laugh. "I expect I'll be writing letters from dawn to dusk tomorrow."

"Things happened," Valentin repeated. "First a poisoning and now mysterious events you won't explain." To Eska's relief, the harsh tone did not return to his voice. Her uncle turned away, raised his face to the stars, and sighed deeply. When he turned back to her, he placed a hand on her shoulder. "I won't demand more explanation. You are brave and bold and probably more clever than you should be. And I trust you to take care of yourself." He ducked his chin slightly to look her more squarely in the eye. "Just promise me that if you need my help, you will ask for it."

Eska reached up and took his hand, then threw her other arm around him. "I promise," she said, though the secrets she was keeping, secrets under the very roof they would both sleep beneath that night, made the words sour in her mouth. Still, it felt good to have him hold her as he had so often done when she was a girl. They both leaned into the embrace for a long moment.

When Valentin straightened, he asked the question, or very near to it, Eska had hoped he had forgotten. "And the man who is ill? Surely he needs more assistance than Rosina or Nahia can give him. He could be a danger to someone." But before Eska had to answer, her uncle went on. "Then again, I suppose further travel might make his condition worse." A pause, the darkness keeping his expression from her. "This was his first job with the company?"

Eska made a noncommittal noise that could have passed for confirmation.

"That's a shame." And then his mind seemed to shift once more. "Wait here a moment." Valentin retreated into the house, emerging a moment later with something in hand. As he approached, a silhouette against the windows of the stone house, Eska saw he once again held the wooden box tied with a ribbon. He held it out. "I had it made after my visit to the island of Lanore last year."

Eska took the gift and pulled away the ribbon. Lifting the lid of the box, she could just make out the gleam of black pearls amid tiny diamonds, all fastened to an intricate silver hairpin. She touched a pearl with one fingertip.

"I hope you like it," Valentin said quietly. "Black pearls are a Lanorish specialty."

Eska smiled. "It's beautiful," she said. And her uncle smiled, too.

But all Eska could think about as she closed the box was what ancient artifact he had dismantled to create the pin and what had been discarded, regardless of the story it might tell—if only someone would listen. All for the sake of a pretty thing Eska could wear in her hair.

Eska checked on Perrin before retiring to her chamber. He was sleeping soundly, thanks to Rosina's tea. Tomorrow, she would have to see that he ate something of greater sustenance. But sleep did not come for Eska that night and in the morning, after waking before the rest of the house, she went out to the stable in an old pair of her father's slippers and returned to the house with a large canvas feedbag.

This she filled, one by one, with every gift her uncle had given her over the years that had ended up in the house in the Vachon Valley. The cracked, rudimentary spyglass that had belonged to a warrior empress of old Kyoria. A carved amber bear from Novere. A necklace of sapphires and obsidian once worn by a princess of Altidor. Other gifts, great and small, all taken from their place of origin for the sake of the gold and silver they were worth at auction or could conjure from a private buyer's purse. When she finished, Eska cinched the feedbag shut, aware of a curious sensation filling her chest: relief.

———◆◆———

"I don't suppose you know what's wrong with me."

Perrin sat propped up on pillows in the massive bed. He had dark circles under his eyes and Eska thought his cheeks looked thinner, his cheekbones more prominent, but he had awoken in the late hours of the morning and, for the first time in three days, declared he was hungry.

Eska lifted the tray from his lap, the only remnants of the meal a smattering of breadcrumbs and residue in the bottom of the soup bowl. She set it aside and returned to her perch on the velvet-cushioned bench at the end of the bed.

She shook her head in response to his question. "It could be any number of things. Perhaps a bad reaction to an insect bite or something you ate. With any luck," she said, smiling, "it's behind you now."

Perrin nodded but did not look convinced. "I dreamt of," he hesitated. "Strange things. Troubling things." He took a deep breath, as though doing so could banish his discomfort. It was Eska's turn to not be convinced. "Do you think you could help me outside? I would like to feel the sun on my face."

Eska nodded her agreement. "I think fresh air sounds like a splendid idea." With her arm supporting him, Perrin swung his legs off the bed and got to his feet. His face went pale with even that little effort, but Eska kept that to herself, not wanting to worry him. Together, they made a slow trek to the top of the stairs, where Perrin had to halt and steady himself in preparation for the descent. Gabriel, passing by the bottom of the staircase, hurried up to assist, but Perrin bravely waved him away, insisting he could manage. He leaned heavily on the bannister, though, and Eska could feel his arm tremble in her grasp.

At last they emerged onto the back terrace and Gabriel arranged a chair out of the sun, then fetched a footstool from the kitchen while Eska settled Perrin in the chair and tucked a blanket over his lap. She herself sat at the table the crew had broken bread at the night before, prepared to keep Perrin company should he wish to talk, but the journey from the bedchamber had evidently sapped him of whatever small ember of energy he had. He closed his eyes and Eska took the opportunity to ask Gabriel to bring her writing case.

Eska wrote two letters.

She had hardly finished the second before she crumpled the paper in her fist, smearing ink on her palm. Letting the ruined sheet fall to the table, she leaned over the oak table, elbows supporting her upper body, and rubbed the back of her neck with heavy hands, her fingers sliding over the bones at the top of her spine. The ache that had built up in her neck as she wrote did not dispel, nor did the ache in her chest, the one that was both empty and overwhelmingly full of swirling emotions—the one that had prompted her to write a letter to Alexandre de Minos.

She couldn't send that letter. She wouldn't. The words had tumbled onto the page, falling from her mind with such a desperate need to be released that she had nearly spilled her ink in her haste. In the end, the words formed a confused tangle, hardly coherent, slightly hysterical—not to mention barely legible—and Eska could no longer see herself on the page.

He would come to the Vachon Valley in an instant if she were to ask it of him, she knew. Her pen had hovered over the page in that instant of realization, the one moment of hesitation as she wrote. But she hadn't asked the question, instead she had signed her name and then promptly mauled the offending piece of paper into submission.

Sighing, Eska sat upright and read over the letter to her father. That one had been easy. The fears, the concerns, were not present in those pages. It was a simple recitation of facts, of what had transpired in Toridium—though no doubt Maximilian de Caraval had learned the full story from Sorina by then. She had glazed over the decision that had sent her to Cancalo and bolstered up the role Albus's letter had played, overstating the evidence he had discovered in order to make her choice more justifiable. Her father would, of course, stop to consider why there were so few details about her days in Cancalo, but she did not intend to commit to paper the story of the sunken vault, the creature that had nearly taken her life, or her ambiguous departure from the city. She certainly made no mention of Eden San-Germain. Better to keep the focus of the letter on the Toridium predicament. No need to delve into the revolving carousel of thoughts about the god discs and the strange skeleton or—by no means—the fears she had about being named a murderer. No, those thoughts and fears were not for her father.

"They aren't for you, either, Sascha," Eska murmured to herself. "They are mine alone."

Abandoning the ruined letter, Eska folded the one for her father and applied a small amount of the tree sap she used to seal documents while on expeditions. Waving the folded pages gently to dry the sap, Eska thought about her next letter—not a letter, really, but a full account of what had happened in Toridium, a more thorough version of what she had relayed to her father.

It was a tedious task and Eska had to take several short respites to ease the cramping of her hand. She would stroll down to the river, flex the muscles of her writing hand, idly speculate about the number of seeds in the cheerful faces of the sunflowers growing by the water, and then reluctantly make her way back to the table and her paper—all while Perrin rested silently. Whether he slept through it all, she did not know, but his face looked less pale and he seemed comfortable.

Once, as Eska looked up from her ink and paper, she caught sight of her uncle through the glass of one of the windows on the upper level and for a moment her mind fled, like a guilty child's, to the bag of treasures she had stuffed under her bed with only the grey morning light and the rather gloomy face of a small clock shaped like a sunburst to witness. Her conviction had not diminished, but she was honest enough with herself to know she would gladly avoid the coming confrontation with Valentin over her actions.

When at last she finished her account, she wrote it out again—four times in all—and marked the various copies for the intended recipients: her father, the Vismarch of Toridium, the Firenzia Company lawyer, and the fourth to Albus at the Lordican for safe keeping.

The last letter folded, sealed, and set aside, Eska put her forearms on the table and rested her head on them, her right hand aching terribly. The late afternoon sun was warm on her back, but clouds rolling in from the north told of a storm to come under cover of darkness.

"I don't think I've ever written so many words in one day in all my life." Perrin's quiet voice brought Eska's head up from the table. He was looking at her through half-closed eyes, his mouth attempting a smile.

Eska groaned. "If I don't see a bottle of ink and quill for a year, it won't be long enough."

"That's a lie," he murmured, still smiling. "I've learned things, you see, and not just how to hold a brush made of adolescent capybara hair. Words are like an exotic perfume to you, intoxicating, a symbol of the known and unknown, of what is possible." Perrin closed his eyes as he finished speaking, leaving Eska to appreciate the idea on her own. "Eska," he said, so quietly she wasn't sure he'd spoken. Frowning, she got to her feet and moved around the table to his chair. His face, peaceful throughout the day, was marred with tension, though his eyes were still closed. Pain, she realized.

"What is it? What do you need?"

He took several ragged breaths as his hand searched blindly for hers. She took it and crouched at his side. When at last he managed to speak, his voice was merely a whisper. "If the worst should happen," he said, the words sending a chill across Eska's skin despite the warmth of the day, "please find Manon." Another difficult breath. "Tell her I forgive her."

"Don't say such things, Perrin. You're going to be all right."

He squeezed her hand faintly and a smile curved across his lips, but vanished quickly, chased away by pain.

Eska shouted for Gabriel, Bastien, anyone who could hear. It was her uncle who came first, and together they carried Perrin inside. Nahia hurried up the stairs after them, listening intently as Eska relayed the extent of his weakness and her suspicion that he was experiencing more pain than he previously had. Eska and Valentin returned Perrin to the bed as Nahia felt Perrin's pulse and forehead, then prodded his abdomen gently, frowning all the while. The woman rushed off to confer with Rosina, leaving Eska and her uncle to exchange glances.

"If it spreads?" Valentin asked, his voice low.

Eska shook her head. "One of us would have shown symptoms by now. Whatever it is, I don't think anyone else is going to get it." Eska watched her uncle watch Perrin. "Uncle." He looked up at her. "You asked me to rely on you if I needed it. I need to ask something of you, though it will cut short your time here."

"Your letters?"

Eska nodded. "I can trust any member of Firenzia Company, I know, but," she shrugged helplessly, "they aren't family, and it's time I sent them home, to be free of this mess I've made for myself."

"Of course. I will leave at once."

Eska's heart ached at the words, at his easy willingness to do what she asked, all while a Barca, the son of a man who had caused him endless grief, lay under the same roof and his priceless gifts lay under a bed, shoved there in shame.

True to his word, Valentin de Caraval rode away from the stone house in the valley mere moments later, a packet of letters tucked in the pocket of his riding coat. Eska watched him go, and for the first time since returning to the valley, she felt the isolation of the place. And where normally it would bring her peace, now it made her feel alone and powerless.

Interlude 15

"You can do that?"

The girl looks up from the notebook in her lap, her brow furrowing against both the bright sun turning her uncle into a silhouette and the words he has just spoken.

"Do what, my dear?" Valentin de Caraval is gazing over her head, his mind no doubt already fixated on the logistics of how one should disassemble and transport a temple the size of a not insignificant hill. But then, he's done this before. She knows that.

Eska closes her notebook and stands, maneuvering herself so she can see her uncle's face. "Just take it all? Doesn't the temple belong to the people of Fiera?"

Her uncle considers her for a moment. Or perhaps he's considering her words, as though he has not done so before. "I suppose it does. But Eska, you must understand, Fiera doesn't have the wealth or infrastructure to support this temple. They struggle to feed themselves. They hardly have the time, inclination, or means to maintain such an ancient site." He shrugs. "Besides, worship of the horse gods faded away in Fiera long ago, just as it did elsewhere across Bellara. We will be offending no one." He smiles down at her and pats her shoulder.

"That's not what the woman said."

The smile falters. "What do you mean?"

Eska feels her cheeks growing warm. "There was a woman here yesterday. Watching just before dusk. From over there." She points to a copse of trees opposite the dilapidated stone temple's western door.

"And you spoke to her?" It is Valentin's turn to frown.

"I offered her water. It's hot, Uncle."

"What did she say?"

"That we are stealing." Eska is surprised by how calm she is as she speaks the words that the day before set her heart racing. The woman's voice had been quiet, free from malice, and yet imbued with fierce certainty. And Eska, perhaps a third the woman's age, had done as she had witnessed her mother do countless times: listen with a carefully diplomatic expression, hands tucked behind her back.

Valentin's frown has darkened with irritation and he glances up as though he expects to see the woman. "You need not concern yourself with the angry opinions of a peasant woman from Fiera, Eska."

"But she wasn't angry, Uncle. She was sad."

Valentin waves his hand aimlessly. "If they are sad now, they should have done more to keep the temple in good condition. As it is, the mosaics are nearly unsalvageable and the friezes hardly identifiable. Not to mention the state of the statues. Don't worry, Eska, the temple will be in good hands. The finest scholars and craftsmen will restore it to its former glory. The Archduke will pay for it all."

"So it's his now?"

Valentin smiles again. "Well, my dear, he did fund this little expedition."

Eska looks down at the notebook in her hands. She smooths the cover and picks at a nonexistent flaw in the leather.

"Just think, Eska," Valentin continues, "the temple will be reconstructed at his palace at Almiraal and it will be open for the public to enjoy and appreciate, as it should be. Not here in a forgotten valley surrounded by dust and neglect." He leans down and catches his niece's gaze. "It will be beautiful. Just imagine it."

And Eska smiles a little, because she can imagine it. She knows enough about the horse gods of old to know their temples were home to colorful mosaics and murals, stallions and mares charging the length of the walls, tails streaming, hooves pounding in silent honor of the horse gods who rode the night winds and the sun's rays.

Her uncle leans close, pushes strands of Eska's dark hair behind her ear, and kisses her cheek, his blonde beard tickling her skin. "Your mother and father would be proud. Always considering every angle, always asking questions."

He grins. "Never content with the easy answer." He stands up straight. "Never change, my dear."

Eska returns the smile and watches as her uncle walks away, his voice carrying as he shouts directions to the crew. She opens her notebook to the page her thumb has been holding. She does not draw well, despite the best efforts of a tutor, but there on the page are two shapes, a horse and a woman. The horse is clumsy, the woman inelegant. The spirit and strength Eska had hoped to capture went missing somewhere between her mind's eye and the page—as usual. And so Eska speaks—quietly, heard only by the grass at her feet and the breeze in her hair—for the nameless woman she will never see again:

"Why not rebuild it here, where some trace of the horse gods might linger in the earth? Why not give the people of Fiera the tools and means to care for it?"

32

"Fine, but we're not smashing it."

"You're going to open that, right? Or just admire it?"

Luca looked down at Manon, a bundle of kindling in his arms. The reliquary sat at Manon's feet, looking far more innocuous than it had any right to look. She had taken to removing it from the wooden box her father had buried it in each night when they stopped riding. But she never did more than look at it.

"Don't tell me you're going to hand it over without knowing what's inside."

Luca squatted in front of Manon and set down the kindling, one eyebrow raised as he looked at her.

Manon met his gaze with as much nonchalance as she could muster, nonchalance she did not feel. Luca continued to look at her, a smile quirking his mouth, and Manon had the distinct impression he knew exactly what she was feeling. "I don't know how to open it," she admitted at last, wondering when she had begun to admit such things to anyone.

Luca's brow furrowed as he looked down at the box. "May I?"

Manon waved a hand in his direction. "By all means."

The hunter picked up the reliquary in his large hands, the delicate ivory and lustrous gold a far contrast to the callouses on his palms. He turned it this way and that, peering at all sides—but Manon already knew what he was seeing. The box had no locking mechanism, no hinges, no latch, and worst of all, no visible seams, which Manon would have argued to be impossible before examining it.

"I don't suppose you have a hammer in that pack of yours."

Manon shook her head. "I'm not sure what good that would do."

Luca grinned. "I'm sure it's not the recommended method, but I'd be willing to wager I could break it open."

Manon laughed. "That's a very generous offer, but I was tasked with collecting the box. Nothing was said about what might be inside. I can't imagine the man seeking this would be pleased if I presented it to him in pieces."

Luca looked at her as though she were a small child. "Boxes are meant for putting things in. Whoever he is, he wants whatever is inside."

Manon rolled her eyes at him. "I know that," she muttered, but the testiness she expected to hear in her voice did not make an appearance. She and Luca looked at each other for a long moment. "Fine, but we're not smashing it," Manon said. "Let me see it."

Luca handed the box to her and began splitting some of the kindling in two over his knee, then arranging it in a tent shape over the bare ground he had scraped free of pine needles and dead leaves. Manon examined the reliquary once more, feeling for changes in texture that might indicate a hidden latch.

"This man, why not come for the box himself? Why did he have to send you?" Luca asked.

"Because he likes to demonstrate his power over people," Manon said, before she had truly formed the thought. Luca looked up at her, his blue eyes expectant. "Not in an overt way, but subtly, so you don't see the ties he is binding you with until it's too late. Besides, he's the sort of man who is accustomed to having people do things for him. "

Luca stood and brushed dirt from his palms. "Sounds like a bully. Someone ought to teach him respect."

Manon let out a harsh laugh. "When you meet him, if you meet him, I wouldn't advise leading with that. I don't imagine the Archduke of Arconia would tolerate such a lesson."

It was not a slip of the tongue. She could have stopped herself. But she was ashamed to admit to feeling some satisfaction at the look on Luca's face—and perhaps some relief at obliterating one of the many secrets she carried.

"You're serious," Luca said after a moment of silence in which he appeared to be waiting for Manon to laugh and admit to a joke.

"Very. I said I could protect you in Arconia. He's the reason I can say that."

"You would trust him to keep his word? A moment ago I would have sworn you despised him."

Manon thought for a moment. "I would trust him to protect you if I asked it of him. Because that would tighten the hold he has over me. Yet another thread binding me to his will."

Luca hung his head.

"Don't feel guilty. I have accepted this. And he would have done it by other means, if not through you. He's very resourceful. And very well informed." Not well informed enough to know of a horde of stolen Licenzan gold in the Barca family mausoleum, Manon reminded herself. But well enough to know her father had been trying to collect the Alescuan reliquaries, a secret he had admitted having shared with no one.

"What does he have over you?"

Manon looked at Luca, her fingers idle on the reliquary, unsure how to answer that question—or if she should or wanted to. The answer was mired in her conflicting feelings about her father and the Archduke's promise to reduce his sentence.

In the end, she chose a truth that revealed nothing.

"I don't really know."

To her relief, Luca didn't probe further. The hunter simply nodded and resumed building the fire, as though he had asked a question about the weather in Arconia or whether she thought the sea was blue or green—and as if she had given a perfectly reasonable, logical answer. Manon couldn't remember the last time her words—her feelings—had been accepted without argument, silent judgment, or willful misunderstanding.

As she watched Luca's fire spark and grow, the small flames eating at the wood hungrily, Manon's finger ran aimlessly along the curls of carved ivory on the underside of the reliquary. She brushed over the aberration in the ivory three times before she realized she was feeling an irregularity. Sitting up straight, she leaned close to the light of the fire, holding the box on edge so she could see the bottom better. Luca said nothing, but she heard him go still and knew his attention was fixed on her.

The flaw was small but, now that Manon had the feel for it, unmistakable—and it was growing softer under the warmth of her skin. Manon looked up at Luca.

"Wax."

Wordlessly, Luca extended the smaller of his two blades to her, hilt first. She accepted it, but first held the box closer to the heat of the fire, as close as she dared without risking scorching and charring the ivory. As it softened, the tiny wax plug began to reflect the firelight, and Manon judged it ready. Tucking the box between her knees, she applied the tip of the knife gently to the edge of the wax. It resisted for a moment, then gave in, and Manon lifted it free. Carefully, she removed the plug from the knife blade and set it aside to be reinserted later, then she returned the knife to Luca. At last she examined what the wax had concealed—a small round hole no deeper than the length of the fingernail on Manon's littlest finger and a narrow slit in the ivory at the bottom of the hole, unable to accommodate, Manon judged, anything thicker than a heavy piece of parchment or a piece of metal thinner than the point of Luca's small knife blade.

Manon glanced up to find Luca's face close to hers, his eyes intently focused on the reliquary and her discovery.

"I suppose it was foolish to hope it might be that simple," she said. "Unless you happen to have whatever key this requires." To her surprise, Luca didn't laugh or smile at her attempt to lighten her disappointment.

"Not a key, no." He straightened abruptly and paced away to where their packs rested against a log. One of the horses grazing nearby greeted him with a snort, but the hunter had no response for the mare or for Manon when she tried to ask what he was looking for after he crouched next to his pack and began to rummage through it.

When he returned to kneel next to Manon, he held out a small metal tool. "I don't know if it will work," he said, a strange sort of sheepishness in his voice and expression.

Manon smiled. "Considering I have nothing of use to offer in this situation, I'd say you're contributing a great deal more than I am." She took the tool, a narrow rod just slightly longer than Manon's fingers and with a small hook on the end, and turned it in her fingers. "If you weren't the most honest person I'd met in some time—honest to an irritating fault, mind you—I might be tempted to think this was meant to pick a lock." She gave Luca a sidelong glance and laughed when he blushed, the color rising to his cheeks made all the more fierce by the light of the fire.

"You're not far off," he said, shifting onto his other knee. "I had it modeled after a lock pick."

"You designed this?"

The hunter nodded. "Needed some additional tools to help fine tune traps. We target sick animals, you see, or overpopulated herds, to keep the Principe's forest healthy. But if you want to take down an old wolf, left behind by his pack, you don't need the force of a bear trap." Luca glanced down at the tool in Manon's hands. "To tell you the truth, I'd rather we didn't use traps at all. There are ways to hunt what we need to hunt without risking catching other animals, healthy animals. But the Principe insists."

Manon nodded. "Powerful men and women have a way of getting what they want. The Archduke would have twisted your words until you agreed with him—and on top of that made you feel it was all your idea in the first place. The Principe seems more blunt in his methods, but equally effective." After a moment's hesitation, Manon lifted the reliquary from her lap and handed it to Luca, along with the tool.

Luca looked at her, already shaking his head and leaning back on his heel.

"I want you to do it," Manon said. When he didn't take the reliquary, she turned one of his hands palm up, her eyes fixed on his, and set the ivory and gold box on it, then slid the tool across the ground between them. He broke eye contact with her and stared down at the small piece of metal for a long moment, then plucked it from the earth.

Manon watched him take a deep breath, watched his shoulders rise and fall, and then watched as he tested the narrow slit, probing for resistance and finding none. The tiny hook disappeared inside the ivory. It was, astonishingly, a near perfect fit. Manon felt a shiver of anticipation and covered her mouth with one hand.

Luca glanced up at her. "I think I could turn it to the left."

Manon had no words. She could only nod her permission.

There was no physical change in the box, no audible click of a mechanism sliding free after three hundred or more years—three hundred years! The magnitude of what Manon was witnessing was not lost on her and some piece of her, she realized, was expecting the box to burst open in a flash of dormant Carrier power. But the Alescuan box, despite its grand exterior, despite its former owners and their passion for spectacle, remained unchanged—that is, except for the fact that it was open.

Manon never quite saw it open. Her mind conceived of the lid—for suddenly there was a lid where before she had detected no seam—being closed and then, with no in between, open. The triumph and satisfaction she should have felt was diluted, muted, as though a great distance lay between them and Manon, and she, at the end of a rope, could just feel their vibrations. In their place was the unsettling certainty, descending on her like a heavy fog, that whatever was in the reliquary, indeed, the very thing itself, did not belong in the world of the light and the living.

That moment of strange understanding flashed through Manon at the same time she realized Luca was trying to hand the reliquary to her—and both were followed quickly by the desire not to touch it. And yet she reached for it. After all, it was just a box.

The interior of the reliquary was lined with red silk. A single item lay on that luxurious bed. A disc, sized just right to fit in Manon's palm. Bronze. Unremarkable. But for the curious pattern of black grooves and markings on its smooth, cool surface.

"You know this thing?" Luca was looking at Manon, not the disc, trying to comprehend her silence.

She shook her head slowly, and then her tongue caught up to her mind. "It is a nameless, meaningless thing to me," she said. "And yet I have seen one of these before."

Not just seen. Held. It was still in one of the pockets of her coat, the small interior one, worn close to her chest since that day at the Barca mausoleum, the day she destroyed her brother's tomb for the sake of mysterious words spoken by her father. Worn over her heart—but forgotten.

33

"Sounds like the most excitement I'll have all day."

"WITH ALL DUE RESPECT, MY LADY, MY ANSWER IS NO."

Gabriel stood before Eska, arms hanging from his sides as though he didn't quite know what to do with them. His stance suggested strength and determination, but his upper body appeared to be far less certain. All told, the engineer looked terribly uncomfortable.

"I know it could cost me my employment," he went on, "but I won't leave you here."

"Gabriel," Eska began, nearly taking a step toward him. She stopped herself and sighed. "I am sorry that you think I would cast you away from Firenzia over this. But I must urge you to reconsider. Go home. Let this madness I've created pass. You do not deserve to be caught up in this."

Gabriel's arms at last came across his chest and he seemed to settle in to his refusal. "Neither do you." It was laughable as counterpoints go, but Eska began to see that she would have to tie him to a horse to get him to leave the Vachon Valley, perhaps even render him unconscious, and this she would not do.

"All right," Eska said. Gabriel's furrowed brow smoothed over instantly. "But," she added, holding up a finger in admonishment, "no one else. I'm holding you personally responsible for that. No one else even mentions staying behind. Not even a whisper. Not Cosimo, not Bastien. Is that clear?"

Gabriel nodded—as though they both didn't know Bastien would do more than whisper.

Perrin would be staying, of course. He was too weak to travel and had been sleeping peacefully since Valentin departed the afternoon before. Eska had no desire to disturb the rest that had eluded him, but his low food intake was quickly becoming her primary concern. Already his cheeks were hollowing out and Eska was sure he weighed less than he had upon their arrival in the valley. If his appetite did not return with some vigor, and soon, he would not have the strength to fight off the illness attacking him.

Leaving Gabriel to relay Eska's decision to the rest of the crew, Eska fetched the Alescuan reliquary from her room and then returned to Perrin's bedside. She settled into a chair covered in embroidered fabric, positioned so she could catch the warm breeze through the tall window she had cracked open that morning, and began to examine the ivory box.

It was not identical to the box she had accidentally opened that night on a rooftop of Arconia. That much was clear. That one had a tri-horned griffin leaping off the lid, and swords lining the sides—a deadly reminder of the identity of its first owners. While running across rooftops and leaping over a narrow alley, the Iron Baron's thugs in pursuit, her mind on making it home in one piece rather than on the box that was too awkwardly sized to hold comfortably in one hand, Eska had shifted her grip on the reliquary to hold it by one of the ivory legs—which promptly clicked and twisted in her grasp. She had dropped the reliquary in surprise and skidded to a halt to collect it. Her heart pounding from exertion, Eska had taken a moment to examine the suspect leg and saw that it had twisted to point inward and was now shorter than the other three, having pushed up into the ivory belly of the box.

She had pushed in the other legs.

Of course she had—and with more enthusiasm than she ought.

The box had slipped from her hands once more, flying open as it nearly landed in a gutter. The small bronze disc within had skittered across the tiles of the roof, coming perilously close to disappearing over the edge and into a private courtyard below. Eska had collected it quickly, which resulted in her second unexpected discovery of the evening. As she had picked it up, the moment the pads of her thumb and fingers came into contact with the edge, she witnessed the bronze crumple into a ball—which, very decidedly, it should not be capable of doing.

The strange phenomenon had halted Eska in her tracks as she collected the reliquary, the thugs momentarily forgotten. Frowning, she tried to pry it apart and reshape it, but the bronze, naturally, resisted all such attempts. At last, as the shouts grew louder and she became aware of the sound of someone climbing a drainpipe, Eska resorted to shoving the bronze ball into her undergarments—the stomping that flattened it once more would come later, when she had a moment to breathe in the darkness of a temple garden before reaching the Decadronum and the Lordican. She had just enough forethought to close the reliquary, thereby removing evidence of tampering, and then she was running again, this time to the northern side of the roof, where a conveniently placed balcony, followed by an equally convenient garden wall, helped her descend into an alley.

An alley that happened to have a large man with a club waiting in the shadows.

The upshot of that rooftop chase and subsequent confrontation with Thibault de Venescu and his band of brutes was that Eska had never had a chance to properly look over the reliquary.

This one was astonishingly beautiful, as the other had been. The ivory was smooth and flawless beneath her fingertips, the gold inlaid in intricate curling vines and flowers. A solid gold stag with ornate antlers pranced in relief across the top. The box had four animal feet of solid gold, each one different from its neighbors—a wolf paw, an owl's talons, a boar hoof, and a bear paw.

The feet didn't move.

Eska frowned and set the box in her lap, then immediately picked it up and repeated the motion, trying to determine if it was just her imagination or if the reliquary was noticeably heavier than the first one she had held, and if it was, what that might signify.

Sighing, Eska's gaze drifted to the window and the gentle waving of the tree branches beyond. She could smell bread wafting up from the kitchen and the faint murmur of voices—Gabriel's and Bastien's, she realized—drifted into the room as well.

She turned her attention to Perrin, though she doubted he could hear her. "The Alescuan kings and queens were clever and brilliant," she mused, finding a familiar rhythm in speaking her thoughts out loud, "but imbuing six reliquaries with six different methods of opening seems far too subtle for their tastes." Albus would chide her for such speculation, of course. Eska had no means of knowing the other boxes were different from the two she had held in her possession. But it felt right when she said it. "Puzzles weren't their style. Destruction and chaos, yes. But irritating puzzles? I can't imagine the Princess Above the Sands engaging in such frivolity, not when she had empires to crush."

She wished for more information on the Alescuan reliquaries. They were legendary, relics of the dynasty that had brought fear and devastation to much of the known world, revered for their history but hardly more than children's stories in their detail. Eska had no sense of their origin or how they came to belong to the family.

But most of all, Eska wished for Albus. She missed the back and forth, the question and counter question. She missed his ability to challenge her thinking and propel her to greater insight.

Perrin stirred within the blankets and Eska, reliquary in hand, went to the bed, hoping to encourage him to take a drink of water. As she sat on the edge of the bed, his pale face twisted into a grimace. Eska reached out a hand to feel his forehead, but the moment her fingers made contact with his skin, his breathing increased drastically, his pulse an unnatural flutter in his throat, his chest rising and falling with each shallow gasp and hurried exhale. Eska drew back, fearing another attack of pain and muscle rigidity, but he quieted quickly.

Frowning, Eska retreated to the window and set the reliquary down, then returned to the bed and tried to wake Perrin. She doused a cloth in a bowl of water, wrung out the excess, and folded it against his forehead.

"Perrin," she said, her hand on his shoulder. "Perrin."

He woke slowly, emerging from sleep as though from a great distance, but Eska was glad to see him attempt a smile when at last his eyes focused on her.

"You need to eat something," Eska said. She helped him sit up, sliding tall pillows behind his back, and then held a glass of water to his lips. He drank greedily, which pleased her. The way he leaned back, heavily, and with a small sigh, after he had finished did not. And yet he made a valiant effort to chew and swallow a few bites of bread slathered with fresh butter, a slice of peeled apple, and half a piece of cold wild boar. The act seemed to exhaust him completely, but he surprised Eska by asking for a bath.

"I feel grimy," Perrin said. "And I don't imagine I smell like a bouquet of flowers."

Eska shrugged. "Noses can go blind to bad smells after enough exposure."

Perrin laughed, a weak laugh, but enough to make Eska smile.

"I don't think we should attempt the tub," Eska said, imagining the arduous process of getting him to the bath chamber and navigating the slippery porcelain tub and tiles. His last journey down the hall to relieve himself had been a lengthy affair. "But what if we bring in a small basin of hot water and wipe you down?"

Perrin made a face. "You make me sound like a horse." He sighed. "If you think that's best."

"I'll start heating the water." Eska pointed to the tray beside the bed. "There's more bread if you feel you can manage it."

Perrin stopped her before she reached the door. "Have you opened it yet?" He was looking at the tall chair by the window. Ensconced within the chair's embrace, the gold detail on the reliquary gleamed in the sunlight streaming through the glass.

Eska shook her head. "Perhaps you'd like to try?"

"I'm unlikely to succeed where you have failed, but even failure might take my mind off," he trailed off and gestured broadly at himself, at his pale skin and the shape of his legs beneath the blankets, "all of this."

Eska brought him the reliquary. "I expect you to have it open by the time I return," she said with a smile. Perrin laughed again, a touch louder and stronger than before, and waved her away.

While Rosina stoked the fire outside the back door, Eska hauled buckets of water up from the stream until she had filled a copper laundry basin. By the time the water had begun to steam, Gabriel appeared.

"They're ready," he said.

"And the skeleton?" Eska had asked Gabriel to leave the bones, along with her chest of tools. The mystery of their identity and how they had come to be buried among Onandyan refuse still captivated her, and while she waited for news from Arconia and Toridium, she had nothing but time. If nothing else, examining the skeleton might prove to be a welcome distraction should the reliquary's secret continue to elude her.

"In the library, as you asked."

Eska nodded and accompanied the engineer to the stable yard where her seven crewmembers waited alongside one of the wagons. Horses, saddled and loaded with packs, stamped their feet in the dirt, sensing the impending journey. Bastien, Eska noticed, stood near the back of the group, his gaze fixed on the ground and his hair falling across his forehead to hide his expression. Eska could guess it well enough.

She smiled at them all. "Thank you. Thank you for giving more than I have a right to ask of you. Thank you for your patience and loyalty. Thank you for seeing this equipment safely back to Arconia. In addition to the contracts you signed for the excavation at Toridium, compensation for which you will receive in full despite the work being cut short, you will receive bonus pay for the additional time and travel to Cancalo, as well as hazard pay for the risks to which Firenzia Company has exposed you." She saw Bastien's head come up, but it was Nahia who voiced words of protest first.

"My lady, I will accept no bonus pay. We all know what we signed up for, we all know the dangers we might encounter."

Eska shook her head. "I will not accept your refusal. My decisions and my conduct have not been in the best interests of the Company— and therefore not in the best interests of its employees."

"My lady," Bastien broke in, "you could not have known what would happen in Toridium or Cancalo. There is no blame at your door. "

"You may argue this point until we both die, Bastien, but I will not yield. The company is responsible for all of you. You signed contracts with us, but we also signed contracts with you, and those contracts state that we must compensate each of you in cases of excessive and unreasonable endangerment. While your stubbornness is appreciated, this is not an argument you can win. I'm afraid the law is on my side."

The silence that descended on the crew was edged with tension. Gabriel spoke up. "Lady de Caraval has asked this of you, and we dishonor her and ourselves if we undermine the very loyalty she has praised us for. This is our duty, as much as it is our duty to dig in the earth."

Eska glanced at Gabriel and knew he understood her expression of thanks.

"My lady." It was Inevra who spoke. "I beg to ask one thing of you."

"Ask, Inevra."

The young woman looked steadily at Eska, her deep brown eyes radiating confidence and wisdom greater than her years. "You speak to us of dangers. Do not forget, those dangers can touch you, too. You are not impervious to them."

Eska smiled. "I will try to remember."

And with that, Gabriel gave the order for the crew to depart. They mounted horses or clambered aboard the wagon. Cosimo lingered to squeeze Gabriel's hand, then climbed into the driver's seat. With a flick of the reins, the wagon lurched forward and lumbered through the stable yard, the riders falling into place behind and to the side. Several twisted in their saddles to look over their shoulders and wave farewell as they passed through the gate and onto the path that would take them west, through the valley until they could turn to the north, to Arconia. It was Bastien's face Eska saw last.

"Well, Gabriel," Eska said, as she turned back to the house, "those who stay behind are required to play nursemaid."

"I'll wager my tincture administering skills are better than yours, my lady. And I'm very talented with a bed pan."

Eska laughed. "Thank all the dead librarians we haven't had cause to employ one of those yet."

Together Eska and Gabriel lugged the heavy copper basin up the stairs and into the master chamber. Perrin had drifted to sleep, the reliquary—still shut—in his lap, but he woke as they sloshed their way into the room.

"Now, Perrin, it's the moment you've been waiting for," Eska said as she added several pinches of soothing salt to the steaming bath water. "Take off your clothes."

Perrin pretended to consider his options. "I don't know that you're ready to see this bag of skin and bones."

Eska winked. "Oh, I know a thing or two about bones, young man."

Perrin laughed, but Gabriel, to Eska's immense amusement, grew red in the face and busied himself shifting the copper basin minutely here and there until it was just so.

"Come now, nursemaid," Eska teased. "A little humor is good for the patient."

Gabriel straightened but still wouldn't look Eska in the eye.

"No gallows humor just yet, though," Perrin said. His voice remained light, but a tightness appeared around his mouth.

Gabriel and Eska stripped Perrin out of his clothes, keeping the blankets pulled over his lower half to prevent a chill, and Eska soaked a soft cloth in the hot water, twisted the excess out, and began to wipe down Perrin's torso, first one arm and then the other. Gabriel, after asking Eska if she needed anything else, moved quietly out of the room.

"I see you've made considerable headway on the reliquary," Eska murmured as she rinsed and wrung out the cloth again, then shifted her attention to Perrin's chest.

"Yes, I slept on it. Solved it entirely while snoring."

"Delightful," Eska said, laughing. "We'll examine it again after I've finished." She continued to smooth the cloth over his body, his skin prickling slightly as the water cooled in the air. With her help, Perrin shifted onto his left side, allowing her access to his back.

"I feel like a child," he said quietly, his face close to her lap. "My mother used to sit with me when I was sick."

"What was she like?"

Perrin was quiet for a long moment. "She wasn't a very good parent, it turns out," he said at last. "Of course I worshipped the ground she walked on when I was too young to know any better." Eska soaked the cloth again and continued down his back. "She was too tolerant of bad behavior. I think because she wanted us to love her more than my father. But in trying to earn our love, she became more like a child herself, letting us splash through pans of paint when work was being done on the house, encouraging us to hide our father's belongings, insisting we gorge ourselves on sweets before going to bed." He closed his eyes and went quiet again and Eska waited, not wanting to interrupt. "I used to love her laugh. Even once I began to understand what kind of person she was and the poor influence she had on her children, Victor most of all, I still clung to that idea of her laugh—because then I could pretend she was happy. A happy wife and mother." Perrin shivered—not, Eska thought, because of the air or the water. She drew the blanket up to his shoulder. "But her laugh was the last thing I heard from her, the last thing she did before she abandoned us. She told us she would be back—that she would return with money and powerful friends, that we'd have our life back." Eska rested her free hand on the back of Perrin's and his fingers sought hers, entwining them together, a subconscious, desperate grasp for human connection. "I think I knew before either Manon or Victor that she wasn't coming back. I think I knew before I could even put it into words." Perrin opened his eyes and looked at Eska. "Perhaps in some ways that made it easier."

Except there was no ease in his eyes, only long-subdued heartache.

And then even that was quickly replaced by something Eska recognized as shame. Perrin abruptly released Eska's hand and he rolled onto his back, his gaze anchored to the ceiling by his invisible burdens.

Wordlessly, Eska shifted the blanket up around his torso, exposing his lower body. She soaked the cloth and went to work.

"I wouldn't expect you to understand." Perrin broke the silence after Eska had finished cleaning his left leg and moved on to the right.

"I would never expect to understand another family's complexities," Eska said. "That doesn't mean I can't listen."

"You are a good listener," Perrin said, his earlier playfulness maneuvering its way back into his voice. "Probably because you have two parents who love you." His voice caught then, stumbling over those last words. He took a deep breath, steadying himself. "I don't begrudge you that."

"I know."

"Manon might," he said, something less than a laugh breaking free from his chest.

Eska smiled. "I think I know that, too." She patted his knee and rearranged the blanket so it covered him fully. "All done. I thought you might like to soak your feet in the basin."

"Sounds like the most excitement I'll have all day."

It took some effort—the talking had worn him out, Eska could see—but she was able to sit him up and swing his legs over the side of the bed. He sighed when his feet hit the water, and Eska settled behind him to serve as a backrest, her shoulder holding him upright.

Reaching across the bed linens, she pulled the discarded reliquary back toward her and then handed it to Perrin. "Go on. You'll have to earn your keep somehow." She explained how the legs had moved on the first reliquary—and her subsequent opening. "It stands to reason that each is a different sort of puzzle."

"Perhaps the stag is the key," Perrin mused. "The four feet belong to predators. The stag is their prey?"

"Imaginative. But I've never seen a boar eat venison. Have you?"

"True. Then maybe it's the flowers. This one looks like a bellflower.

And this one could be mistaken for a bleeding heart."

Eska smiled over his shoulder as Perrin continued to amble his way through theory after theory, each outlandish and ridiculously endearing. She helped him into fresh clothes, and then they made the slow journey to the second floor privy closet so Perrin could empty his bladder.

By the time they returned to the bedchamber, Perrin was exhausted and Eska moved quickly to help him back to the bed. But she froze before they reached it, her gaze fixed on the reliquary.

"Perrin," she said, her voice quiet and hesitant. "Does it look different to you?"

He shifted next to her. "The flowers," he whispered.

His words confirmed what Eska had not dared believe. Two of the bellflowers had grown, for lack of a better understanding of it, and now stood higher than the rest of the golden garden surrounding the stag.

Together, they hurried the final steps to the bed and Perrin sank down onto it as Eska reached for the reliquary. Her fingers brushed condensation on the telltale flowers, and she pulled back.

"The steam," she said, glancing at the bath water. Her mind whirred, setting the pieces of the puzzle in place—and then came to a sudden halt thanks to an obstacle the size of Lake Delo. "But it was already wet," she murmured. "Underwater."

"But not salt water," Perrin said. The wonder in his voice almost masked the weakness.

Eska shared a glance with him, then grabbed the box with both hands and submerged it in the copper basin.

For a moment nothing happened, and Eska had the sudden fear that her rash decision would result in the destruction of a priceless object—but then the reliquary began to change.

More golden flowers pushed their way out of the lid until they protruded significantly above the surface of the box, and then the stag began to do the same, emerging from its bed of ivory and twisting until it stood nearly upright, prancing just like its woodland cousin.

When the golden pieces ceased to move, Eska plunged her hands into the water and pulled the reliquary out. She turned to Perrin, rivulets of water streaming down the box and through her palms to pool at her feet. Perrin stared, apparently just as unable to form a coherent thought as Eska.

Eska's hand went to the stag's back, sure it served as a handle for the lid, but then she stopped and smiled. "You open it. It seems only right," she said. "I would never have thought to bathe it in salt water."

Perrin smiled sheepishly as she put the box in his lap. His fingers grazed the golden flowers, then tested the stag. Nothing happened as he tugged upward. Eska frowned, but Perrin seemed unconcerned. As though by instinct, he turned one of the flowers, the one underneath the stag's raised hoof, clockwise, and Eska thrilled to hear a hidden mechanism clicking quietly with each rotation until the flower would turn no more. Perrin hesitated, then put two fingers under the stag's belly and lifted.

Eska's heart skipped faster as she caught her first glimpse of the telltale bronze, the grooves stained with black. This god disc was larger than the first, she realized, larger than her palm, and its markings, its pattern of lines and dots, seemed more erratic, less deliberate.

Eska glanced at Perrin, who was staring at the disc as though looking at his own reflection in a mirror, his brow creased with thought, his lips slightly parted.

"Watch this," Eska said.

She picked the disc up by its edges. The reaction was instantaneous. The bronze folded into itself, crumpling as easily as discarded paper.

Perrin blinked, his jaw dropping slightly. He laughed softly, the sound infused with delight. "What is it?"

Without a word, Eska stood and completed the demonstration. She stepped back from the bed so Perrin could see, placed the ball of bronze on the floor, and, a childish grin of anticipation creeping onto her face, brought her heel down hard on top of it.

The bronze went flat under the pressure and weight of her boot, a disc once more.

"I begin to understand why you put up with the dirt and the dust and the pieces of broken pottery," Perrin said softly, his face suffused with wonder.

Eska smiled. "Believe me, there is a lot more dirt and dust and broken things than mysterious, ancient artifacts in my line of work." She glanced down at the disc. "But, yes, there is always something to discover, even if I'm the only one who finds it interesting." She looked around the chamber, her gaze lighting on a small iron figurine. As expected, when she held the little iron ship over the disc, it leapt into the air, the metals clinging to each other. Eska returned the disc to the reliquary. "You asked what it is. The truth is I don't really know. But I suspect it is one of six, just like the Alescuan reliquaries, only it comes from a time long before that dynasty was born, long before the Seven Cities were the Seven Cities, long before the first people to hunt and farm and raise children on these lands journeyed from the east and chose to call them home." Eska looked at Perrin and then back at the bronze disc set in red silk. "I mean to find them all, if I can, and study them. I could not begin to recite to you all the questions I have about them—but first and foremost in my mind is why the Alescuan kings and queens were collecting them. I can only imagine what purpose they were meant to serve."

Perrin, his face a study of concentration, raised his hand as though to touch the disc, then thought better of it. He closed the lid.

"The reliquary itself is just as fascinating. I'll have Gabriel look at it," Eska mused. "It seems the salt triggered some sort of valve that released the mechanism. But I can't imagine exactly how."

"I also begin to see that you are incapable of looking at a thing without demanding understanding of it," Perrin said. He leaned back into the pillows. "I, for one, would like to enjoy the mystery of both the box and its contents." He closed his eyes. "Some things are better when left unexplained."

"Then I promise I won't reveal all the secrets of the disc once I discover them," Eska said, laughing.

Perrin grinned, though his eyes remained closed, but as Eska left him to rest, she saw him looking over at the reliquary, at the golden stag standing proud over its treasure, saw his features grow serious with contemplation, and knew the enigma of the Godforged pulled at something within him just as it did her.

34

"Please."

As though their success had imbued him with hidden strength, Perrin's health improved steadily after he and Eska solved the riddle of the reliquary. Two days passed before he could join Eska in the library, but he made the journey there largely under his own power, halting twice on the stairs and a third time in the middle of the entry hall. He wavered then, the nearest object that might support his weight—a statue of a thoughtful-looking, long-dead philosopher—too far out of reach to be of use. Eska took his hand, steadying him more than supporting him, and he took several deep breaths, then nodded at her and continued on his own.

"I do hope this is worth it," Perrin said as he lowered himself into a plush chair near the empty fireplace. Eska had promised to share a discovery she had made about the skeleton—only if Perrin could make his way to the library. To her delight, curiosity had spurred him out of bed—though he had grumbled about it.

"I have a confession," Eska said. "I told you I made a discovery this morning about our friend here," she went on, gesturing to the array of bones scattered on a large sheet of linen on the floor. The library was decidedly out of sorts, furniture pushed haphazardly out of the way, tools lying in wait to trip up the unsuspecting traveler. "It wasn't this morning. It was yesterday. I didn't say anything because I wanted to make sure the news got you out of bed."

Perrin put a hand to his chest and adopted a wounded expression. "Your duplicity is truly unconscionable. Vengeance will be mine—by not listening to a word you say."

Eska smiled wickedly. "Then you don't want to know who this is?"

Perrin looked at her sharply, alert now. "You know who that is?" he asked, waving a hand at the bones on the floor.

"Cyprian II, the Fisher King, the Prince Beneath the Moon." The names rushed out of Eska on a wave of elation.

Perrin opened his mouth, shut it, then tried again. "You mean that's an Alescuan king."

"Yes." The single word hovered between them, caught somewhere between Eska's certainty and Perrin's skepticism.

"Everyone knows the Alescuan kings and queens lie in their tombs of gold beneath the Mountain of the Long Night. Well, all of them except the last, of course."

"Everyone knows," Eska said. "Exactly. Breaching the tombs in the mountain would be dangerous, difficult. Even if we had a precise map, which we don't. Don't think I've not contemplated it—not to steal anything," Eska added, rolling her eyes at Perrin as he began to interject. "From an academic standpoint. And out of curiosity," she admitted. "But if anyone were to attempt such a feat, what better way to keep the kings and queens and all their vast treasures safe than to bury them elsewhere?" Eska glanced down at the bones around her feet. "And what better way to hide them than among the dead of centuries past, in graves dug long ago, graves the existence of which we hardly even know." She returned her attention to Perrin. "Look, I'll show you." Taking up the left humerus bone in her gloved hands, Eska had to keep herself from shoving it in Perrin's face. "I should have seen it before, but I was distracted, we were all distracted. This bone, we thought it was broken, and it is, but that's not the whole story." She pointed at the shattered end. "See how blunt it is? And how smooth the edges are? Only time and healing does that. That's why we never found the lower bones of the left arm—not because we left the site before we could uncover them, but because there are none to be found. This individual lost part of his arm long before he died."

Perrin frowned. "I'm a bit foggy on my Alescuan dynasty, but it seems to me I recall a childhood rhyme in which a king was rather violently deprived of his left arm—lost it above the elbow."

"Cyprian II, seventh ruler in the Alescuan dynasty. A lion bit it off."

Perrin was quiet for a moment, his gaze roaming over the bones. "All right, I'm enjoying this. But surely there are any number of arm-less skeletons buried in the earth."

Eska grinned. "Surely. But I don't imagine there are very many skeletons missing their left arms *and* demonstrating signs of a debil-itating illness."

Perrin crossed his arms over his chest. Eska imagined the gesture was meant to keep his growing enthusiasm for her theory in check. "Go on."

"There's fracturing in his shin. The one you did such a fine job cleaning out." Eska returned the humerus to the linen and exchanged it for the bone in question. "I assumed upon first glance that the cracks were a natural occurrence due to age and time, but here," she knelt by Perrin's chair and pointed while pulling a small square of glass from her pocket, "you can see many of them are in various stages of heal-ing." Eska held the magnifier close to her eye and leaned down.

Perrin bent his head for a closer look at the tiny fissures, taking the magnifier when Eska offered it to him. "I concede that to my grossly untrained eye, it would appear some of these are mending. What does that mean?"

"The Prince Beneath the Moon had a disease of the bone. So schol-ars speculate now," Eska added. "In his lifetime, he was known to suf-fer extreme pain in his legs. His physicians had no diagnosis and the king kept the severity of his ailment secret from all but those closest to him. It wasn't until many decades after his death that a physician's documentation of his condition—the terrible extent of it—came to light."

Perrin examined the cracks once more. "And these are consistent with the disease he had?"

"As far as can be determined, I'd say they are."

Perrin leaned back in his chair, his gaze fixed on Eska's face. "How certain are you of this?" He gestured around them. "Of all of this?"

Eska took a deep breath. "I can't make the bones tell me who they are."

"I should hope not."

"And there are tests I'd like to carry out—in Arconia. But given the apparent age of the bones and the identifying markers," she trailed off and exhaled loudly. "It's a strong case, Perrin." The thrill of the words she was speaking raised the hairs on her arms.

Perrin gave a slow nod in response.

"Though," Eska said, "I would prefer if Albus were here to confer on the theory."

"Albus?"

"A deceptively infuriating, most beloved librarian," Eska said, smiling as she imagined her friend hunched over a book, a pose she knew all too well, a forlorn meal ignored at his elbow, his hair violently askew from being ruffled in concentration an untold number of times.

"You mean to say there is a person in existence who knows more than you?"

Eska laughed. "I am a rather well-versed encyclopedia, Perrin. Albus, however, he is a library unto himself."

"I'm assuming you've thought of the repercussions of this, of the knowledge that the kings and queens who once ruled over our Seven Cities are not buried where we have always thought them to be buried—or at least one of them isn't."

She had. In fact, she had thought of little else since forming the theory the day before. She nodded. "It would change what we understand about the end of the dynasty, about their unlikely overthrow, the loyal followers they left behind, and the rise of the Seven Cities as we know them." Somehow, as she spoke those words, her voice remained impassive and sober. Beneath it, she was a bundle of questions and nervous energy.

There was also a small part of her mind that was aware that a discovery of that magnitude might be exactly what she needed to wipe away the false accusations from Toridium. The Archduke would take an interest in protecting any citizen of Arconia with such an achievement to her name.

Perrin was looking down at the bone in his lap, looking but not touching, as though the enormity of its identity, of the man to whom the bone had belonged, was suddenly too much to take in.

Eska removed the bone from his lap and returned it to the rest. She began to organize the skeleton as it ought to be, joint by joint.

"You ruled by terror, Cyprian," she murmured as she worked. "Some might believe it the pain that drove you to such anger and violence." She placed his toes beside each other, one by one. "But pain, even such terrible pain as you suffered, could never be an excuse for the deaths of so many innocent Seycherrans."

"You would pass judgment on a long dead king?"

"Are we not allowed to judge our forebears?"

"Discuss, argue over, rant and rhapsodize and compose poetry, yes. But judgment? It's so very final." Perrin spoke the words easily, his gaze moving with Eska's hands, as though he did not put much stock in his own opinion.

"Cyprian ordered a forced march across the very plains which later became his burial place, sending hundreds of Seycherran laborers to certain death, all because he wanted to build a pleasure garden in the small corner of Toridium these immigrants had made into their home." Eska's hands were still and she waited until Perrin's gaze rose to meet hers. "Children, Perrin." He had the grace to look ashamed. "Some kind hearts followed the Seycherrans, trying to bring them forbidden aid. Water. Food. Blankets. Do you know what they found?"

Perrin shook his head.

"Mothers and fathers, dead, their own wrists gnawed open, their blood staining the dry ground. They tried to nourish their children with their own blood, Perrin. The little ones were curled around them, fingers tucked into the palms of their parents' lifeless hands, eyes staring at the cloudless sky and the killing sun." Eska took a deep breath, not bothering to mask the tremor of anger in her voice. "Do you really think Cyprian beyond judgment for such a crime?"

"I remember now," Perrin said, his voice quiet. "I learned that. Once."

Eska bent her head and continued placing the bones. "I could go on about the Alescuan kings and queens and the lives they ruined, but I'm afraid it's a long list."

"And yet the discovery of these bones delights you."

Eska looked up, ready to sharpen her tongue and her gaze, but the sight of the unfocused softness in Perrin's eyes, the wrinkle in his brow, brought her up short. She sighed. "They are a discovery to be proud of. How could they not be? And, yes, to have my name alongside a discovery of such historical significance, it is a thing to be proud of. But I will never forget these bones belonged to a malevolent, vicious dynasty, men and women who did not hesitate to kill for power, who used their unmatched Carrier skills to bend the will of the world to their whims. We must never forget that."

"I don't think the world could ever forget what they did," Perrin said.

"You'd be surprised what humans can forget given a combination of time and willful blindness."

———— ◄ ● ► ————

"Is this yours?"

Perrin held up a glazed clay jar, far too small to hold anything useful.

Eska looked up from the chest she was packing. The letter from Arconia had come that morning, clutched in the hand of an exhausted messenger who had come so close on the heels of the sun, Eska knew he had ridden through the night to complete his errand. But then, orders from the Archduke had that sort of effect on their messengers. It was from her father—but in his role as Vice-Chancelier, not as her father—and it required her return to Arconia. She would, it said, find a representative of Toridium there and it was the Archduke's chief hope that a resolution in the matter of the death of Chancellor Fiorlieu would be found.

Perrin had declared himself well enough to travel, and though it had only been two days since he had gotten out of bed and he still was weak and thin and unendingly tired, Eska had to admit he was improving—and besides, he had little choice.

And so they were packing their belongings with the intent of leaving at once. Eska was on her knees in the library, returning her tools to their home. Perrin turned the jar in his fingers, frowning at it.

Eska shook her head. "Where did you find it?"

"It fell out of here." Perrin lifted the reliquary in his other hand. "I was holding it upside down, not realizing the lid was unlatched."

"Strange." Eska got to her feet.

"I happen to agree," Perrin said.

Together they examined the reliquary and discovered the silk bedding beneath the disc did not extend to the bottom of the interior. A second clay jar lay tucked in a corner.

"Very odd," Eska said. She took the jars and shoved them in her satchel where she could look at them while on the road. Then she closed the reliquary, making certain the stag and the flowers were safely flat against the ivory, and wrapped it in a blanket and then placed it in the tool chest. "Perrin, please tell Gabriel we've nearly finished here. I'll bring these out and then we'll come back for the bones," she said as she locked the chest and slipped the key alongside the clay jars. She turned and saw Perrin standing motionless over the carefully wrapped bones of the Prince Beneath the Moon. She thought she saw him sway and rushed forward to support him—and protect the bones should he fall. Perrin looked at her with a start as her hand grasped his arm, confusion knitting his brow.

"Are you all right?" Eska asked, fearing a relapse. He looked pale, but Eska couldn't have said with any certainty whether he was any paler than he had been a moment before.

"Yes." The word was drawn out of Perrin slowly. He opened his mouth as though to continue, then, shaking his head slightly, seemed to change his mind. Finally he said, "Just a spell of dizziness." He tried to smile but it didn't reach his eyes and his neck muscles were tight with tension. "I'm fine."

Eska nodded, not because she believed him, but because she had no choice. Clearly he was still unwell, but she could only hope he could make the trip to Arconia without incident.

They loaded the remaining wagon quickly, Eska's chest taking pride of place behind the driver's bench, the bones wrapped in linen and canvas and tucked between the chest and Perrin. Gabriel led the horses out to the wagon and harnessed them, then took up the driver's seat as Eska thanked Rosina for taking their unexpected appearance in stride—thanks the woman brushed off. Eska mounted the one spare horse, her satchel strapped across her back, and, after exchanging a nod with her two companions, guided her mare through the gate and out into the meadow.

The day had dawned clear and cool, but heat and clouds overtook them soon after they passed out of the Vachon Valley and began to follow the shore of a narrow lake through a wider valley surrounded by gentle, rolling slopes. Sweat began to trickle down Eska's back, causing her shirt and vest to stick to her skin. She circled her horse back to check on Perrin, who lay with one arm flung over the side of the wagon, his forehead damp with sweat. His eyes were closed, but he opened them at the sound of her approach.

"I think I'm melting, Eska. Am I melting? Not even noon and I've liquefied like butter in a skillet."

"I'm more concerned with the sun. Much longer and you'll be a lobster. Which, by the way, goes exceptionally well with melted butter."

"So I'm delicious, is what you're saying."

Eska laughed, then sobered as she glanced up at the sun. "I wish I had thought to ask Rosina for a parasol. Gabriel," she said, "try to keep to the shade. We could all use it." The engineer nodded and steered the wagon as close to the sparse maples and birches lining the shore as the wheels would allow.

At last the lake fell away behind them and the rough path, little more than a faint hint of wagon tracks in the ground cover, turned to the north and the shade of towering oaks and wide-spreading beeches. As a breeze cooled Eska's skin, she caught the sound of Gabriel humming aimlessly and smiled.

"Eska." They had traveled to the sound of Gabriel's tune for some time before Perrin called out to catch her attention. She pulled her mare up and let the wagon pass her, then followed in its wake.

"What is it?"

"I've been thinking about this a great deal and I can no longer put off the question I have formed." Perrin looked out at the passing landscape for a moment. "Arconia is my home, and yet there is no longer anything there for me." Another pause, his eyes focused on something only he could see. "I know I have a lot to learn," he continued, meeting her gaze at last, "but I was wondering if you might consider taking me on, if Firenzia Company might consider hiring me." Perrin swallowed, clearly unsure of her response. "I will do whatever menial task you ask of me. Scrubbing pots and pans. Cleaning tools and brushes. I'm sure I could learn to cook." He was rambling now. "Fetching water. Hauling equipment."

"Perrin," Eska said, cutting him off. "I think we can do better than employing you as a pack horse." He smiled weakly. "I am glad you asked."

◆

They were a day out from Arconia when it happened.

They had begun to pass villages the day before, even stopped for ale and a fine meal at a small inn attached to a mill, and Eska's mind had shifted to what lay ahead. As such, she was startled when Perrin, as they shared a small morning meal around the ashes of their fire, asked her about the clay jars they had discovered in the reliquary, specifically if she had opened them.

Shaking her head, Eska laughed a little. "I'd forgotten all about them." Brushing crumbs from her fingers, she fished the jars out of her satchel. "I suppose we might as well see what's inside. After all, someone thought it important enough to hide them in the reliquary."

Later, she would fault herself for that choice and wonder if she would have made a different decision had she not been faced with answering the charges from Toridium the next day. The close proximity of the jars to the god disc should have been enough to keep her from opening them outside of the relative safety of the Lordican, where any number of experts could be on hand.

Or at least, that's what she told herself afterward.

As it was, when she unstoppered one of the jars, the deep amber substance inside seemed innocuous. It smelled faintly of cinnamon.

"Is that honey?" Gabriel asked while peering over Eska's shoulder.

"Unlikely," Eska said.

"Then what?" That from Perrin.

"I have no idea."

The substance was glossy and thick, the color indeed not unlike the rich honey Arconians drizzled on their sweets. Gabriel reached for the jar and Eska let him take it, then turned her attention back to her meal, eager to begin the final leg of the journey.

It was Perrin's face that made her freeze with a mouthful of soft cheese spread over cured meat. He was staring over her shoulder, a look of horror on his face.

Eska turned.

Gabriel was crumbling.

The engineer fell to his knees, upsetting the remainder of his meal and overturning the small clay jar he had dropped at his feet. From one finger dripped a viscous amber vine. And his forearm was disintegrating, his fingers falling away before Eska's eyes.

Eska lurched to her feet.

"My lady," Gabriel gasped. He stared up into Eska's eyes, desperation mixing with fear. "Please."

Stunned, Eska could only gape. Fingers, wrist bones, forearm, all crumbled away until the engineer's arm ended in a stump at his elbow.

For a moment, all was still. Eska drew in a shaky breath. Gabriel, in shock, could only stare.

And then the first vein turned orange. Like a snake, it crept up the remains of Gabriel's arm, soon joined by a second, then a third, a fourth. They crawled over his bicep, disappearing up his rolled sleeve before reappearing above his collar.

"Please," Gabriel repeated. "Please. Help."

Eska tore her gaze from his skin and met his eyes. She tried to speak. Tried to tell him it would be all right. Tried to lie. But her silence was the last thing Gabriel heard.

The academic in Eska would not have believed it possible for a body to crumble so completely, to fall to dust in empty clothes in an instant. The existence of organs and a great deal of fluid made the notion absurd. And yet her eyes witnessed exactly that. One moment Gabriel was kneeling on the ground, pleading for help she could not give, the next he was grey and cracking and gone.

"No, no, no, no," Eska repeated again and again, falling to her knees just as Gabriel had, her hands reaching toward the vacant air he had so recently occupied, as though she could somehow summon him back. She heard Perrin take in a ragged breath. Heard, somehow, the song of a bird overhead. Heard her own sobs rip out of her throat.

And then Perrin was at her side, his hands hovering over the dust, the grey, chalky remains of Gabriel, until at last their eyes met, each desperately hoping to see something in the other's face to reassure them what they had just witnessed was a lie.

It wasn't, of course.

They made no further progress that day. After Eska's tears dried, after she could no longer look at the pile of dust without her stomach heaving, she managed to lead the team of horses and the wagon a short distance away, into a copse of pines, though there was no distancing herself from the horror she had seen. Perrin followed, stronger on his feet than he had been since Cancalo, leading Eska's horse. He returned to the campsite and collected the remainder of their belongings and together they sat in silence, Eska too numb to move.

When she did stir, the sun had passed its highest point. She checked to be certain the second clay jar was secure in her satchel, refused when Perrin suggested she keep it off her person, then extracted a tin cup from the canvas pack of equipment in the wagon.

Walking slowly, a stiff wind whipping her loose hair across her face, Eska returned to the place where Gabriel had died. Had disappeared as though he had never existed. The clay jar he had dropped was empty. Eska prodded it with a stick and saw that the grass beneath it had turned black and grey and dry. Taking care to keep away from the stain of death on the ground, Eska turned her attention to the ashy substance that had been her engineer. The tears returned hot and fresh then, but silent this time, as she scooped what she could into the tin cup before the wind carried it away.

"It was my fault," she said when she returned to Perrin and the wagon. "I should have known better."

"It's not, and you know it. He wouldn't want you to think that way," Perrin said. "Your people love you, Eska, in a way my father's employees never loved him—certainly Manon has never earned that kind of loyalty. She is too aloof, too distant and unknowable. They respect her, but they don't love her."

"I do not want love if this is what it leads to." The harsh words burst forth unbidden and Eska frowned in their wake. She closed her eyes and inhaled deeply and slowly through her nose. When she opened her eyes, Perrin was watching her closely.

"You don't mean that."

He was right, but that didn't stop Eska from feeling it.

That night, Eska and Perrin slept—if they slept at all—close to each other, his arm tucked through hers, her back pressed up against his chest, each answering an unspoken plea from the other not to be left alone, each trying to banish fear and horror to the dark—if only until dawn.

Interlude 16

Fragment of a letter from Talarian, the Prince Among the Stars,
fourth ruler in the Alescuan dynasty—recipient unknown

Let me make this world new for you. Let me break time and give us forever. I will burn any who stand in our way. I will lay waste to cities, drain the waters of the world dry, summon spirits of dead gods, cure the very stars of their envy—all for you, my love.

Let me show you. Let me do this.

35

"Forsaking all other bonds."

IT WAS, WITHOUT A DOUBT, THE MOST RECKLESS THING MANON HAD ever done.

Oh, to be sure, attempting to blow up a ship in full view of Toridium's harbor authorities ranked high on that list and had the added factor of instigating immediate reprisal. And Manon had made any number of questionable choices while working alongside her father—jumping from the top of a monstrously tall waterfall, swimming the Borneau channel at night, and impersonating a priestess of Kela, to name a few.

But handing over the Alescuan reliquary—with the strange disc inside—to the Archduke of Arconia while keeping from him the fact that she had a second disc, that she was, in fact, carrying said disc in her pocket at that very moment—well, it defied sense, not to mention the laws of self-preservation.

Luca had tried to argue against the decision, or at least the decision to keep the second disc on her person rather than stashing it somewhere for safekeeping. The hunter had even begun to question whether it wouldn't be best to just give the Archduke both discs, but a stern look from Manon had silenced him.

"I don't trust him," Manon had said. "Think of the second disc as an insurance policy. Having something a powerful man wants grants its own kind of power."

And so they waited at the Varadome, ushered to a garden just as Manon had been on her previous visit, only instead of manicured hedges and citrus trees, this one was brimming with rose bushes in countless varieties and colors, the scent so strong it made Manon light-headed.

The Archduke did not make them wait long. He entered the garden from the opposite end, dressed simply in plain trousers and a loose shirt—as though their arrival had interrupted his dressing. Manon did not doubt for a second that the image was intentional.

Valexi Arcturos de Vauquelin-Preux smiled at Manon as he strode through the rose bushes, walking the straight stone path until he stood before her. He did not so much as glance at Luca, who lingered three steps behind Manon.

"Your journey seems to have agreed with you, Manon," he said. "You look quite beautiful."

Of all the things he might have said, Manon had not expected him to pay her a compliment. For a moment she had the sinking sensation that he might have expectations of her service to him beyond what they had agreed to, but she nearly laughed aloud at the thought. Somehow it seemed impossible to imagine the Archduke, handsome as he was, engaging in such activities. She returned his smile.

"It was quite pleasant," Manon said. She could practically feel Luca's discomfort.

"And the Principe? Hospitable, I hope?"

"He spoke to his hounds more than he spoke to me at our meeting."

To Manon's surprise, the Archduke laughed—a proper laugh, she felt, though she supposed she couldn't be sure.

"Corannos has always prized his hounds above humans. I wouldn't take it personally. I trust you recovered our elusive item?"

"I did," Manon said, her heart fluttering for the first time. "But I have a request to beg of you, Commendatore."

The Archduke removed one hand from behind his back and waved it, palm up, in Manon's direction, the very image of a generous ruler. "Ask."

Manon stepped to the side of the path. "I had assistance," she said, indicating Luca. "This is Luca D'Armand. He serves as a guardian of the estate at Pontevellio. He chose to assist me, defying his superior. I am afraid the Principe would not look kindly upon his actions."

The Archduke took Manon's words in stride—but then he was the definition of equanimity. Manon wondered how many layers would have to be peeled back before Valexi Arcturos de Vauquelin-Preux revealed a true reaction to anything.

"By all means," the Archduke said, "the young man is quite safe here, but I doubt my brother-in-rule will trouble himself with such small matters."

Manon hesitated under the Archduke's stare. She swallowed. "There was an incident, Commendatore. And the Principe will know by now that I was not at Pontevellio for the reasons I gave him and that I took something from his land. He will know that Master D'Armand helped me."

"Incident?"

"It was my fault," Luca broke in. Manon forced herself to continue looking at the Archduke, trying not to show any change in countenance off which he could feed.

The expression on the Archduke's face as he turned his attention to Luca at last sent a shiver across Manon's skin. There was no outward alteration, nothing so obvious as malevolence or even calculation. And yet she had hoped to earn Luca's safety in a manner that would allow him to fade from the Archduke's thoughts—if anyone the Archduke laid eyes on was ever truly forgotten. That hope was dashed the moment Luca opened his mouth. It was like watching a hunter discover prey that had been invisible.

The Archduke turned back to Manon. "Is this true?"

"The fault lies with us both, Commendatore. There was an accident and one of the Principe's hunting lodges at the estate burned down."

The Archduke smiled and Manon tried not to flinch. "Come now, Manon, fire is your specialty. Take pride in your talents." The smile disappeared. "However, this is troubling. I may not be able to protect your friend after all."

And so they had come to it, the moment Manon had been anticipating since passing through the gates of Arconia the day before, since, if she was honest, the instant the reliquary opened in Luca's hands. The second, smaller disc seemed to sit like a stone in her pocket, suddenly heavy with the weight of Manon's fears. She knew what she had to say—just as the Archduke did. Manon had the distinct impression he had been planning for this moment from the first time he welcomed her into the shade of his citrus grove and poured her a glass of rosé.

When she spoke, she surprised herself with the clearness of her voice. "In exchange for his safety, I pledge myself to you entirely. To whatever task you set before me, to whatever service I can provide. Forsaking all other bonds."

She had hoped to see a glimmer of satisfaction, of triumph, to know that her sacrifice meant something to him. All she got was that smile that flirted with benevolence.

"I will see what I can do."

Despite the vague nature of the statement, what he meant, of course, was that the deal was struck. Luca would be safe. The Archduke of Arconia needed permission from no one.

"And now, Manon, you have what you wanted from me. What about what I wanted?"

Manon tried to maintain a neutral expression as she slid her leather bag around from where it rested against her back. Her fingers shook slightly as she undid the buckles and extracted the linen bag containing the reliquary. She held it out.

Valexi Arcturos de Vauquelin-Preux took it in his hands just as he would anything else handed to him, no ceremony, no relief, just ownership. He slipped the reliquary free from the linen, which he let fall to the ground. The ivory and gold shone brilliantly in the sun.

"I think you know what comes next, Manon."

Six. There were six reliquaries—or so he had told her that day among the lemons. She nodded. "My father insisted he had knowledge of only one."

This did not seem particularly upsetting to the Archduke. "No matter," he said, smiling a little. "You will no doubt find other methods of tracking them down. And as it happens, I have a place for you to start." He turned the box over in his hands and Manon's breath caught in her throat. She had replaced the wax plug, warming it just enough to shape it back into place and smooth it over until it looked as it had before.

Manon ventured a question, one she had debated asking for days. "Do you know how to open it, Commendatore?"

The smile grew. "Each of the reliquaries offers a different puzzle. Did you know that?" He didn't wait for an answer. "I'm looking forward to solving this one."

Manon didn't dare exhale her relief for fear of indicating that she knew more than she was saying. The tension that had been building in her chest since walking into the rose garden felt like it would soon burst free, and Manon fought to control her racing heart.

The Archduke told Manon to return the next day to receive information on how to continue her hunt for the reliquaries, then dismissed Manon and Luca with impeccable courtesy, summoning a steward to see them out of the garden and back through the halls of the Varadome. They were released outside the main gate and back into the heat of the day, the dome behind them nearly too bright to look at.

Luca said nothing until they had walked most of the wide lane leading away from the Varadome and into the city.

"Thank you. For keeping my secret from him."

Manon felt little relief on that front. "He may yet find out, Luca."

"But not from you." The hunter flashed her a smile, sending Manon's insides twisting with the knowledge that he trusted her implicitly. The smile vanished quickly. "You were right. About how he manipulates people. The Principe relies on threats and anger and cruelty. But he," Luca shook his head, "he does it all with a smile on his face. I wonder which method would win out over the other."

The thought made Manon shudder. "Let's hope we never have to find out."

"I'm coming with you, you know," Luca said after a moment.

"Wherever he sends you next."

"I was afraid you would say that."

And yet Manon smiled as she said it.

36

"Welcome home."

ESKA TOLD COSIMO ABOUT GABRIEL'S DEATH FIRST. THAT MUCH AT least she could do.

She and Perrin arrived in Arconia in the dark of night, but the next morning, before speaking with her uncle or addressing the questioning glances of her servants, before answering the summons to the Varadome, before conferring with either her mother or father regarding the accusations against her and her actions since that fateful day in Toridium, before seeking out Pierro Gustini to check on his research into the Iron Baron, she went to Cosimo.

It went about as she had expected, which is to say, it left them both in tears and Eska knew the hollowness she felt in her own chest was no doubt infinitely magnified in the soul of the man receiving her news.

There was no anger from Cosimo. She had not expected there to be, but that hadn't stopped her from hoping, if only a little, that he might rail against her for letting it happen—that at least would match the guilt she felt in herself.

Eska offered him the dusty remains of Gabriel she had gathered from the grass, transferred from the tin cup to an urn made from blue-veined marble and purchased on her way to visit him. He accepted, though the act of taking the urn from Eska, of holding in his hands all that was left of the man he loved, brought on a fresh onslaught of tears. Eska left him after extracting a promise from him, a promise she did not think he would keep—that he would not be alone these next days, that he would go to family or friends. Eska knew her own heart and herself well enough to know she would want to be alone, so though she asked for the promise, she would not blame him if he ignored it.

As she returned home, she passed through the extensive park and gardens that backed up against the Lordican, reveling in the shade and the whispering branches of the trees and the sounds of children laughing as they played in the fountains. And yet Eska could see little other than Gabriel's face as he died—and Cosimo's grief. As such, she was not prepared to be accosted by a pair of riders—though accosted was far too harsh a term for the manner in which they sidled up on each side of Eska, just off her own mount's flanks.

She stiffened as her horse reacted to the newcomers, but it was too late. The rider on her left surged forward and reached out and grabbed Eska's bridle. From the edge of her vision, Eska caught sight of the telltale ring of daggers on the man's sleeve and inwardly cursed herself for dropping her guard. The assassin sent to the banks of the Alencio was never going to be the Iron Baron's last attempt on her life.

"What do you want?" She kept her voice calm for the sake of her horse. The mare danced under Eska. If she bolted, it would go badly for them both.

"Just keep riding," the man on her right said, matching her easy tone.

"And if I'd rather scream? We're hardly alone."

"Do you see that boy?" The man made a small gesture in the direction of a maze painted on a stone terrace. A young boy was walking the maze, his gaze intent on his feet. "And do you see that woman?" The man's fingers flicked again, indicating a woman standing at the center of the maze. She was smiling and Eska saw her say something. The boy looked up and smiled in return. "She befriended him moments ago using lemon candy. Unsupervised children are quite predictable." The man looked at Eska. "She's carrying a stiletto and is very adept at placing it here," he said, tapping the soft spot below his ear where his jawbone met his skull. "I think you know what happens if you scream or try to get away."

Eska's skin crawled at the thought, but she fixed the man on her right with a heavy stare. "Only cowards threaten children."

He shrugged. "I've been called worse things."

"Oh, I'm not speaking about you. I'm talking about your employer, Thibault de Venescu. You can tell him I said it, too."

The man raised an eyebrow but said nothing in return. Instead, he glanced across Eska at his partner and together they increased their pace, forcing her to do the same. Ahead of them, a large, dense grove of trees deep at the back of the Lordican's park blocked the city beyond from view—and separated them from the wide boulevards and grand houses of the eastern quarter.

It was, Eska realized, a good place to commit murder. The grove was a wild place, a far cry from the manicured hedges and carefully orchestrated trees of the rest of the park. Few people wandered into those shadows, preferring the sunshine and flowers offered by the open lawns. Even if her companions didn't kill her the moment they passed out of sight, there was every possibility she would be detained there until the Iron Baron arrived to do the job himself. She didn't doubt he had the stomach for it—and she had provoked him at their last meeting, not to mention foiled his previous attempt to have her killed. Either way, Eska knew she might not leave the shade of those oaks and beeches alive.

But the trees also provided an opportunity.

And Eska seized it the moment the gardens were obscured behind them.

With a quick slashing motion, Eska brought her riding crop down on the wrist of the man holding her horse's bridle, at the same time giving the mare a hard nudge with her knees. The man let go and Eska's horse surged forward. One stride, two, three, and then Eska heard a crack in the air and suddenly she was falling as her mare's momentum was arrested with bone-snapping intensity. Eska twisted free of the stirrups as she went down and landed just out of range of the mare's kicking legs, one of which, she saw, was caught in the tight coil of a long black whip held by the other man.

The first man, already dismounted, leaped toward her, landing on top of Eska hard enough to push the breath from her lungs. She fought, kicking her knees up into his abdomen and earning a reprieve that allowed her to scramble to her feet—just in time to dive out of the way of the oncoming whip.

She made it, mostly. The tip of the whip seared against her shoulder as she fell. Eska cried out, pressing her fingers to the place. They came away bloody, but she was already running. The first man hurled himself after her and Eska heard the whip crack a third time. A gurgled cry told her the whip-bearer had caught his partner instead. She didn't look back.

She couldn't outrun the man still on horseback. Her only hope was to weave her way into the thickest part of the grove where his pursuit would be hampered by low branches and heavy underbrush.

She didn't make it that far before the horse caught her. She braced for the crack of the whip and the pain that would follow, but to her surprise, the man pulled up his horse in front of her and vaulted to the ground instead. He dropped the whip, a smile spreading slowly across his face, and reached for the sword on his hip.

"I'll be sure to give him your message, my lady," he said. "I'll tell him you put up a good fight, too."

Eska reached down to her boot and withdrew the knife stashed there—Perrin's knife, preferred now to the glorified letter opener she had carried before the Iron Baron's attempt on the banks of the Alencio—just as he slid his blade from its scabbard. She tried not to see how her hand shook.

The man laughed and gave a lazy flick of his sword in her direction.

He likely expected her to lean back. That is, after all, what anyone trained in the ways of sword fighting would do.

But Eska wasn't trained. She had a mere two lessons with Perrin under her belt. She didn't even see his sword coming until it was too late—or it would have been had her momentum not sent her tripping over her own bootlace, narrowly avoiding his sword and stumbling directly into him, her dagger somehow finding its way into his chest.

Eska jerked back. The man's eyes went wide. He reached for her, his mouth working silently. And then he dropped to his knees. He stared up at her until he died and Eska could not have honestly said, as the dead man toppled over, who was more shocked at the turn of events.

She needed to alert the authorities. She needed to claim it was self-defense. She needed to see her lawyer and protect herself from further action by the Iron Baron. These thoughts came to her—and then vanished just as quickly.

Eska leaned over the body and pulled her dagger free. It came out with surprising ease and she watched the blood drip from its point for a moment before wiping it clean on a patch of moss. Her hand was no longer trembling as she returned it to her boot.

She went back for her horse. The other man lay face down on the ground, a deep gash carved into his neck by the whip, the grass under his head soaked with blood. She took a moment to peer through the trees, her gaze roaming the wide lane and the terrace maze. There— the boy, the woman no longer in sight. The woman was quite possibly searching for her—but with any luck she had assumed the men had finished their work. The boy, at any rate, seemed safe.

Eska collected her riding crop, checked that her mare was sound enough to ride, and then mounted and rode back through the trees.

She emerged on the far side of the grove onto a wide and sunny boulevard lined with food stands and fresh fruit and flower stalls. Vendors shouted about their flaky, cheese-filled pastries or rare varieties of roses, but Eska heard none of it. She guided the horse methodically back to the de Caraval complex, and the moment she was able, she shut herself in her chambers and closed the shutters and curtains.

She changed out of her bloodied shirt and dirty clothes, then washed her face and the small slash the whip had made in her shoulder. She dabbed a thin salve over it, gritting her teeth against the sting, and then dressed in fresh clothes.

Emerging from her bath chamber, Eska pulled the porcelain jar of harrow root powder from a cabinet with sharp, angry movements and added two spoonfuls to a cup of hot black tea a servant had delivered while she had washed. She hesitated before stirring, then dipped the spoon in the jar once more, adding a third and then a—heaping—fourth. Killing a man seemed to necessitate such things, and besides, she still had the Varadome ahead of her. She needed to be at her best, her strongest.

Sinking into a couch, Eska leaned back and propped her feet on the opposite armrest, the tea balanced on her stomach. She took a sip, relishing the lung-expanding first swallow, the sudden force imbued into her heartbeat, both telling her she could face down whatever mercenaries Thibault de Venescu would send for her next—and that if only she had taken the powder the day Gabriel died, she could have altered the outcome, changed his fate.

"No one can be fated for such a death," Eska heard herself say, as though speaking the words might push out the thoughts of how the dagger had felt in her hand, how the man had stared at her as he died. She focused all her attention on Gabriel. The sheer swiftness of that death was what had stayed with Eska, the way he had existed and then disappeared. "Who could create such a vile substance?"

She knew the answer. The Alescuan kings and queens had created horrors wherever they went. There were stories of war hounds bred to monstrous size and raised on the blood of humans, of torturous experiments conducted on disabled children to fix what could not be fixed, of poisons so foul they need only be breathed in. The worst of the stories, if any could be categorized as such over the rest, revolved around the dynasty's insatiable drive to achieve immortality. It was said they had been close, it was said Persea, the second-to-last Alescuan ruler, was murdered by her son, Varin II, for the sake of the secrets the mother had been stockpiling, secrets which were thought to include the path to immortal existence.

When the Seven Cities rose up under the Tribunes, when the shining palace Elysium was razed, and when Varin II was executed—drawn, quartered, and fed to a savage panther—the people had held their breath, waiting for Varin to defy the very meaning of life. But the last Alescuan king, though he ranted and raved his way to death and promised vengeance upon the rebellion that had deposed him, died as all women and men die, leaving behind nothing but a smear of blood on the panther's jaw.

The second clay jar, as small and seemingly innocuous as its sibling, sat on Eska's writing desk across the room. Whenever she opened her eyes to take another sip of tea, her gaze, without fail, fell on it. She would visit Albus at the Lordican the following day, provided her afternoon appointment at the Varadome went well enough to permit it. In the meantime, she didn't intend to let Thibault de Venescu continue to terrorize her or the rest of Arconia.

Eska scribbled off a quick note and summoned a servant to deliver the message to Firenzia Company lawyer Pierro Gustini, then returned to her couch to finish her harrow-infused tea.

A distant commotion on the first floor of the house—voices, one of them raised, the other nearly indistinct—made Eska sit up, frowning. She drained the rest of her tea, stood, and went to her door, putting her ear against it as the disturbance grew louder. Unable to make much out, Eska opened her door and stepped out into the hall. She glanced down the hall to her right, toward where Perrin slept in a guest chamber, then made her way to the balcony surrounding the first floor entry hall.

Valentin de Caraval was taking the wide marble stairs two at a time, his steps dogged by poor Nonetta, who was fruitlessly trying to collect his cane and hat. The maid was not the object of his anger, that much was obvious, but she was bearing the brunt of it.

Eska stepped away from the railing and into the middle of the hall just as her uncle rounded the top of the staircase and froze at the sight of her.

"Where is he?" Valentin growled. "Where is this thrice-damned Barca you've let into my company?"

So that was it.

Behind Valentin, Nonetta dipped a curtsey to precisely no one and disappeared. Eska resisted the urge to put her hands on her hips or cross them in front of her. Better not to look too defensive.

"Our company, Uncle. And don't forget it."

It was, perhaps, not the best thing to say, but Eska could not even blame the harrow root for it. It was long past time Valentin remembered they were equal partners in Firenzia, had been for three years.

"Not for much longer, niece, if you keep this behavior up." He started toward Eska, his long strides eating up the ground between them.

Eska held her ground and squared her shoulders. "I'm not a child to be threatened. I am your equal. You will not speak to me this way."

That stopped him in his tracks, his anger mingling with surprise to form an ugly shade of resentment.

"You chastise me for my actions, uncle, but I could do the same for you. Or have you forgotten that the Seven Cities recently instituted a strict policy regarding the exchange of goods and services with our neighbor across the sea? Somehow I don't believe your arrangement with the prince of Anderra has been approved by the necessary authorities." The steadiness of her barrage turned that resentment to shock. But then she went a bit too far. "I don't think providing aid to a sick man, no matter his name, is likely to be as detrimental to this company as violating the law—the law agreed upon by all seven of our esteemed rulers."

She had provided Valentin with a means to return to the topic at hand and he seized it with fervor. "He's a Barca, Eska! You know his father made it his personal agenda to sabotage this company—this family. How do we know he hasn't been planted here by his sister to learn our secrets? How do we know he isn't going to claim credit for something our company discovered?" Valentin began to approach once more and made to move past Eska—presumably to begin searching rooms—but she stepped sideways to block his way.

They stood face to face, his chest heaving with fury, Eska hardly daring to breathe.

"Uncle, do not bring yourself to Julian Barca's level. It demeans you."

Valentin's face went white and he made to speak, but Eska cut him off.

"Perrin is my guest. He has lost everything. His sister, his only remaining family, abandoned him in Toridium. He has done nothing but support my work in Cancalo, for which he was rewarded with a devastating illness that he has not yet recovered from." Eska took a breath. "And though it may be more than your limited prejudice can comprehend, Perrin is my friend. He saved my life. You will not touch him. You will not even see him."

Her uncle was not a violent man. And yet in that moment, though he would never have acted on it, she saw something in his eyes that longed to be set free. It did not frighten her—it broke her heart. There would be no going back from the words said that day. And she had not even had the chance to tell him of Gabriel's death. Another thing he would hold against her later.

Valentin turned on his heel and walked away without a word. Eska lingered long after the front door closed behind him, so long that she was still standing there when someone rapped on the door.

Eska stirred from her thoughts and walked down the stairs, waving away Nonetta, who appeared from the servants' wing.

"I'll get it," she said, looking over her shoulder as she hauled open the heavy door. Eska turned, prepared to send away the unexpected visitor—after all, she had an appointment to keep and making the Archduke wait was not advisable—and came face to face with Eden San-Germain.

Her surprise must have been evident—her lack of words certainly was—and yet there was no change in the Regatta Master of Lake Delo's expression.

"May I come in?" he asked.

"Eden," Eska said, taking in the armed men and women behind him.

Eden looked away from her face for the briefest of moments, then fixed his gaze on her and waited for her answer.

"Come in," she said, stepping to the side so he could pass. The escorts watched him enter, then turned their attention away from the door as she closed it. Eska stood a few paces from Eden. He held his hands behind his back and his expression was more sober than she had ever seen it. "I confess, I am surprised." The harrow root was swirling inside her, clamoring—but for what, Eska was not sure.

"I am here on behalf of the Tribune of Cancalo," he said, the picture of formality. "This is an official visit."

"Very well," Eska said in the pause that followed, because it seemed expected. She was quite unsure what would follow.

"Is there somewhere we may speak in private?"

Eska frowned and looked around. The entry hall was empty. Indeed, the house was empty. Any servants in the vicinity knew to make themselves scarce. But there was something—at last—in Eden's eyes that made Eska think twice before questioning him.

"Follow me," she said, trying to match his stiffness though she did not feel it.

Eska led him to the smaller of the two libraries, the one she liked best, and offered her visitor a chair while she closed the door. When she turned back to him, he was still standing, and he had dropped whatever mask he had been wearing, replacing it with a searching expression that seared into her.

Eden took a halting step toward her, pulled up, took another. "Eska," he said, his voice soft.

They moved at the same time, reaching for each other, her hands sliding up his arms as his went around her waist. The kiss that followed was long and necessary, rain after a drought. When Eden pulled away, he finally smiled that smile Eska had seen when she first met him.

"Are you all right? Your journey was untroubled?"

Despite the harrow root, Eska felt something inside her sag. She lowered her gaze, unbidden tears threatening. Lest she dissolve entirely, she stepped out of his embrace and paced away.

"Gabriel," she said at last, unable to look at Eden for fear she might reveal what had happened in the Lordican gardens that morning.

"He died." She told the story of opening the reliquary with Perrin, of discovering the small clay jars, of the way the honey-like substance turned Gabriel to dust. Eden let her talk without interruption and to Eska's relief she was able to keep her emotions in check. When she finished, he took her hand in his and simply stood by her side.

"I blame myself. I was responsible for him."

Eden squeezed her fingers. "The blame lies with those who created such a thing."

His words nearly penetrated the wall the harrow root had built up inside Eska. Nearly, but not quite. She wasn't ready to let go of the need to fault herself. Not yet. And she could not shake the memory of the way life had drained from a pair of blue eyes in a grove of beeches.

Eska took a deep breath and looked up at his brown eyes. "And what of you? The Tribune was lenient?"

"That remains to be seen. And that's why I'm here. Also why I needed to be sure the friends I'm traveling with couldn't listen to our conversation." It was Eden's turn to pace. "The Tribune and his councilors came to the consensus that whatever was in the sunken vault is the property of Cancalo, no matter its origin or that they have never cared to know what might be in the vault before now. As such, they want to see it returned. That is my task." He looked at Eska, a crease in his brow. "If I complete it, I am free to live my life, though no longer as Regatta Master. My companions are here to assist me in that endeavor." Eden stepped close to Eska. "Believe me, I have no intention of completing that task. But I must be seen to try."

"But if you were to succeed, what did they promise you?" The question belonged to the harrow root, Eska realized faintly, but echoed her own mind.

Eden blinked. "Things that I don't need or want or care for." He took a step backward. "You don't believe me."

"Eden, the last time we saw each other, you learned that I am accused of murder and I saw the confusion, the need to understand, in your eyes. And yet not a word about that has passed your lips." The thoughts were forming as quickly as she spoke them, but Eska felt strangely confident in them. "Instead you insist you are here as a friend and you speak to gain my trust. Forgive me if I find that odd."

It was only then that the hurt bloomed in Eden's eyes. "Would you rather I believe you to be a murderer?" he asked. "Would you rather I just accept someone else's word? I have chosen to believe the last thing you said to me." He shook his head in confusion. "Is that not what you would have wanted?"

Eska heard him, but she could not shake the image of him in the moment she opened the door, the indifference and distance etched into his features—and she could not reconcile the two.

Eden took half a step toward her. "I came here to warn you, to see if we might devise some means of foiling the Tribune and his efforts to claim what isn't his."

She looked away. "I must go. I am expected at the Varadome," she said, taking refuge in the summons to avoid answering Eden. "We can speak of this tomorrow—if," she added, bitterness creeping into her voice, "if I am a free woman tomorrow."

He accepted her dismissal with resignation and a hint of the steeliness she had first seen in his face returned. The harrow root whispered inside Eska, reassuring her she was doing the right thing. The truth was, she knew Eden San-Germain only a little. Perhaps it was time she replaced some of the boundaries he had spoken of in Cancalo.

They exchanged no further words as they returned to the entry hall and Eska opened the door—indeed, the only thing that passed between them under the watchful eye of the armed escort was a stiff nod from Eden, and even that seemed reluctantly given. Eska did not watch them leave.

She returned to her darkened rooms and began to prepare for her audience with the Archduke. She chose a gown of black silk with a sharply plunging neck that rose up to a high collar that caressed her jaw. Forgoing the usual ornamentation expected for a visit to the Varadome, Eska slid a single ring onto the middle finger of her right hand, the enormous sapphire glowing even in that dim light. She then summoned her maid and sat stiff and straight, unspeaking, while Alize wove intricate braids that pulled Eska's hair off her neck—a style that complimented the gown's severe lines and sharp edges.

"Have you given any thought, my lady," Alize said as she worked, "to how you would like me to dress your hair for the masquerade?"

"The masquerade?"

"Surely you hadn't forgotten. It's in three days."

She had forgotten. When one is faced with accusations of murder and attempts on one's life, not to mention killing a monstrous creature at the bottom of a lake, the horrifying death of a friend, and taking a life for the first time, one might be excused for forgetting about something as trivial as a masquerade.

"I won't be attending, Alize."

If the maid had an opinion on the matter, she knew better than to voice it.

When Alize finished, Eska was pleased with the reflection she saw in the tall, freestanding mirror. The woman looking back at her was a woman who would not beg for mercy for a crime she did not commit, a woman who could look the Archduke in the eye and know herself to be his equal—a force to be reckoned with.

———◆▸———

By the time Eska walked the length of the audience chamber, the Archduke watching her every step, the harrow root had forged her into something cold and unbreakable, stronger than iron, more brilliant than the stars in the night sky. The opulence of the painted silk wallpaper, the richness of the embroidered runner beneath her feet, the awe-inspiring beauty of the painted ceiling above—all was insignificant.

So, too, was the man seated at the Archduke's left. She did not grant him the courtesy of a glance and her deference to the Archduke was given in the form of the smallest nod.

"My Lady de Caraval." The Archduke stood when Eska came to a halt in front of the small dais occupied by two chairs—one of the finest black wood with ornately carved antlers spreading from the backrest to frame the occupant, the second plain and unremarkable.

Valexi Arcturos de Vauquelin-Preux descended from the dais and took Eska's hand. He bowed smartly over it. "Welcome home."

The visitor on the dais cleared his throat, no doubt intending to suggest that the Archduke ought to be more impartial, but Arcturos ignored the expression of displeasure. He gestured for Eska to take a seat on a bench at the base of the dais and seemed pleased when Eska said she would rather stand.

"Yes, of course, I don't imagine we'll be here very long," the Archduke said, earning a furious flush on the visitor's cheeks. "This is, after all, only a preliminary hearing." As appeasement goes, it was minimal. "My lady, may I introduce the Honorable Rodrigo Scarpia, recently appointed special ambassador to our fair city by my brother-in-rule, the Vismarch of Toridium." Arcturos gave a bright smile meant to diminish. "Because apparently one ambassador isn't enough."

"Commendatore, I beg you, please grant these proceedings the weight they deserve. My colleague is dead." Scarpia's voice was deep and suffused with gravity—but Eska heard unease there, too. As there should be.

"Ah, yes," Arcturos said as he released Eska's hand and returned to his antler throne. "Poor Chancellor Fiorlieu. I assure you, Ambassador, I grieve with you." Assuredly he did not, but Ambassador Scarpia accepted this falsehood meekly. The Archduke looked back at Eska. "Now, my dear, I imagine you would like to declare your innocence?"

This was hardly the standard procedure for this type of hearing and the Archduke's casual approach was clearly irritating the representative of Toridium. Eska smiled inwardly, appreciating the combination of the Archduke's deft touch and easy apathy.

"You imagine correctly, Commendatore. While tragic, the Chancellor's untimely death was an accident, as far as I know."

"Your account mentioned that you spoke with him not long before he died, indeed, you speculate you might have been one of the last people to do so." The Archduke sat his throne much like a mountain cat, lithe and athletic, his legs stretched lazily in front of him, one ankle crossed over the other, one arm draped over an armrest. Compared to the stiff posture of Ambassador Scarpia, they were a study in opposites.

"That is correct," Eska said. "The Chancellor had complained of stomach pains for some time, the result of which was a considerable delay in our negotiations. I merely sought to offer what relief I could."

"And to your knowledge, the Chancellor appears to have followed your advice? Eldergrass and finallian root was it?"

"I don't know the answer to that. Others said he did. I have no knowledge of his actions after we parted. As for my advice, yes, it was eldergrass and finallian root."

The Archduke smiled. "I have fond memories of imbibing the very same when I had an upset stomach as a child. And by fond, I mean excessively disagreeable."

"Indeed, Commendatore," Eska said, smiling just as easily. "It is a foul remedy and I told the Chancellor as much."

"Commendatore, if I may?" Ambassador Scarpia's deep voice broke through, disturbing the easy back and forth between Eska and Arcturos. She fought back the urge to scowl at him. The Archduke, under no such obligation, waved at him to continue, the gesture dripping with condescension. Scarpia ignored it and plowed onward. "My lady, a witness has come forward swearing to have seen you leave the Chancellor's private chambers." All amusement fled from Eska, replaced by icy fury. The ambassador consulted his notes. "According to our timeline of events, corroborated by other servants in the kitchen, this was after the servant made the tea and left it in the Chancellor's rooms, but before Chancellor Fiorlieu himself returned."

Eska had eyes only for the Archduke. "This is a lie, Commendatore. And the first I've heard of it, which means it was clearly fabricated after my departure from the city in order to suggest my culpability."

The Archduke's expression remained neutral.

"Thank you, my lady," Scarpia said, "for bringing up the matter of your departure. Even you must admit that escaping out a window and disappearing in the middle of the night are the actions of a guilty woman."

"On the contrary, Ambassador. They were the actions of a woman far too busy to waste time on lazy conspiracy theories.

"Why," Scarpia persisted, "did you have to leave under cover of darkness, my lady? What could not wait until the light of day?"

"Business matters that are none of your concern." Eska looked back at the Archduke. "Commendatore, you know my business. You have, in fact, frequently been the beneficiary of Firenzia Company's work. As you have benefited from the efforts and talents of both my mother and father, who have served Arconia and you faithfully their whole careers. If you believe me capable of such a cold-blooded act, then by all means, send me back to Toridium to face justice. But if you believe these accusations to be false, then I ask you to end this now."

The Archduke sighed—again like a cat. "I wish I could, Eska, but a man is dead. A man my dear brother-in-rule cherished for his counsel. And while an Arconian delegation was in residence at the Vismarch's palace. What kind of brother would I be if I did not do my due diligence in this matter?"

Afterward, Eska could not have said if she owed the sudden realization she had in that moment to the harrow root or to her own intuition. But in the end it didn't matter. It hooked into her mind and she could not rid herself of its barb.

It was her own mother's words that fed it, the words Sorina had spoken about the relationship between the Archduke and the Vismarch, the long-concealed chasm between them. Sorina herself had said the Archduke might see fit to use Fiorlieu's death as an opportunity to change the status quo. Would it be so difficult to imagine Valexi Arcturos de Vauquelin-Preux might go one step beyond that and manufacture that very opportunity?

It would not.

Whatever the harrow root's role in her new understanding, it was, without a doubt, responsible for Eska's ability to smile pleasantly at the Archduke, her face a smooth mask of innocence and dignity.

"Of course, Commendatore, I would expect nothing less."

"You are wise beyond your years, my lady." The Archduke straightened in his chair. "I believe that will be all for today," he began, but Eska, emboldened by her new knowledge, cut him off.

"If I may, Commendatore?" The harrow root was crowing in her veins, reveling in her recklessness. The Archduke's eyes narrowed slightly, but he indicated she should continue. "Not only will I prove my innocence to you, I pledge to discover the true culprit. Ambassador Fiorlieu deserves nothing less."

The narrowed gaze, nearly imperceptible, lingered a heartbeat too long, then smoothed over as the Archduke smiled and spread his arms expansively. "Your ambition is admirable, my dear. If only your mother could convince you to leave behind your archaeological work and join her staff full time—or your father's. You would rise quickly, you know. I like to reward talent and initiative."

Eska lowered her gaze, at last displaying the modesty that might have been expected from her the moment her name was announced at the door. "You are far too generous with your compliments, Commendatore."

The Archduke laughed and began to descend from the dais as though he would accompany Eska out.

"And how shall we proceed from here, Commendatore?" Ambassador Scarpia's voice recalled him.

"The usual way," Arcturos said dismissively. And with that, he took Eska's arm.

It was a curious thing, to walk arm in arm with a man who wanted to sacrifice her to his ambitions. Curious, but not frightening. He might have all the power, but now Eska knew the game.

37

"I hope it was worth the loss of your integrity and honor."

"Should I be worried?"

Maximilian de Caraval, a matter of moments removed from a meeting with several prominent bankers from Bartok Row and equally little time before his next engagement, had time to look sternly at Eska as they stood in an alcove somewhere within the labyrinth that was the Varadome. Two statues loomed over them, a naked, winged man wielding a spear and a fiendish half-man, half horse—the former in pursuit of the latter.

The look was stern but only because Maximilian de Caraval's features were so often arranged in that expression it had taken on a degree of permanency. Eska could see the kindness and warmth in his eyes and that was enough.

Another daughter with such a father might have taken that opportunity—really, opportunities didn't get much better than that—to share her theory that the Archduke was framing her for the murder of Chancellor Fiorlieu. The Vice-Chancelier of Arconia would make a formidable ally in the game she was now playing with the Archduke.

But Eska wasn't another daughter and she had no intention of drawing her father into an investigation that might result in his utter ruin—not until she had something more than a harrow root-infused theory.

"Not yet," she answered brightly. "He's hiding his true feelings on the matter, but that's better than condemning me outright, isn't it?" Maximilian acknowledged this with a nod. "At least I still have my freedom. I can go about my business, which now includes clearing my name."

Her father smiled, a hint of mischief creeping into his eyes. "I know my daughter well enough to know when she's discovered something interesting." Maximilian leaned in closer as though to keep the statues from listening in. "What did you dig up in Toridium and Cancalo?"

"Honestly, Papa, sometimes I think you should have gone into business with your younger brother. You have the soul of a man who wants to dig in the dirt."

Maximilian laughed. "Fine, keep your secrets."

Eska smiled. "I need to consult with Albus. There is a great deal to discuss. But soon I hope to be able to share what I have found."

Father and daughter said their goodbyes, then Eska began to work her way back through the many wings of the Varadome. So intent was she on reaching Albus at the Lordican, she nearly walked straight into another woman as they each rounded a corner.

Eska pulled herself up, pulled her thoughts together, and began to apologize—but the words never left her mouth. She was about to apologize to a woman she thought imprisoned, a woman who had tried to blow up her ship.

Manon Barca looked as startled as Eska felt. Her gaze searched over Eska's shoulder, as if hoping for an escape route. For Eska's part, she realized she was searching for armed guards rushing in pursuit of this person who had clearly escaped custody.

Fruitless searches, both.

"Lady de Caraval."

"Madam Barca."

Both women performed elegant expressions of courtesy they did not feel.

"I'm surprised to know there were sufficient funds in the Barca coffers to pay your way into the Archduke's good graces."

The woman's smile was devoid of warmth. "Money isn't the answer to everything. But I wouldn't expect you to understand that."

What Eska did understand was two-fold. First, the only thing Manon Barca might have to offer the Archduke were her Carrier skills. And second, Alexandre de Minos had broken his word.

They broke apart from each without another word and Eska continued her exit from the Varadome, her mind on an edge sharper than it had been that night she decided to escape from Toridium, boiling with thoughts of the Archduke and his schemes, of Eden San-Germain, of Manon Barca walking free and the implications of that, of Gabriel's death, of her uncle's stormy visit, of Alexandre de Minos, of a blade piercing a man's chest and ending his life—all swelling under the influence of the harrow root.

On one point Eska was clear, at least. She needed to see Albus.

And yet the Varadome was not through with her.

In an attempt to vacate the premises as quickly as possible, she slipped through a minor entrance in the government wing, passing through a courtyard and then into a garden so full of statues it looked like the place the stewards chose to stash all the statues they didn't know what to do with. And it was there, surrounded by dancing men and warrior women, by rearing horses and leaping lions, just as she decided she would be better off turning around and finding a proper exit, that Eska saw perhaps the most inexplicable thing she had seen that day—which was saying something.

Tucked behind a tall hedge to the right of the wide lane of statues, indeed, surrounded on all sides by hedges, was a large patch of burned ground. Blackened and charred and smelling still of smoke. Eska looked over her shoulder, saw no one, and poked her head through the narrow opening between the hedges.

The empty, burned ground stretched out before her. It was littered with remnants of things made of wood. Splinters and shards, some the length of Eska's arm, lay scattered across the charred earth.

Targets.

The word came to Eska suddenly.

This was a training ground. Not for swords or arrows or cavalry maneuvers. A training ground for people who could wield fire.

Manon Barca walking free suddenly made a great deal more sense.

————◆•▸————

"What do you mean he isn't here?"

It was not that Eska didn't understand the words the pale young woman had uttered, it was that they defied Albus's very existence.

"Albus Courtenay," Eska said. "You're sure you know who I mean? Slender, prominent nose, dark hair? Has an irritating habit of being right?"

The young woman stared at Eska as though she had two heads. "The only Albus Courtenay I know hasn't been here in weeks." She returned to her stack of books and left Eska standing in the middle of the reading room. Albus's favorite reading room.

Eska looked over at the statue of Lyndronicus. "If you'd seen him, would you tell me?"

Certainly not.

Eska hurried after the young woman, who was headed back toward the public stacks. "Are you quite certain? Is he ill? Did no one think to check his home? I should go myself. How could I be so thoughtless? He could be lying dead for all we know."

The librarian didn't slow. "What home? Albus gave up his place nearly a year ago. Preferred the dormitory, he said. Between you and me, he's a little odd."

"Oh, I am aware," Eska said as she tried to follow the librarian through a small doorway.

The librarian stopped. "You're not allowed back here." She wedged her shoulder into the doorway and Eska had to step back to avoid being stepped on.

"Yes, but this is important. Could I just speak with your superior, please? Or Master Diomede?"

The librarian took another step toward Eska, nearly shoving her stack of books into Eska's throat. Eska leaned back, and with unanticipated quickness, the woman stepped back through the door. It shut loudly, a final reprimand.

The knowledge that Albus had given up his small apartment—and so long ago!—without thinking of mentioning it to Eska sank in slowly as she stood in the empty corridor. She was about to curse Albus for his stubbornness, but was silenced by the thought that perhaps she might have known had she only asked him about something, anything, that couldn't be found in the ground or in a book.

For the first time since leaving Arconia weeks before, Eska was unmoored. Even through the turmoil of Toridium and the trials of Cancalo, through Perrin's illness and Gabriel's death, even that very day, in the wake of the death-shadowed moments in the park, the visits from her uncle and Eden San-Germain, her audience with the Archduke, and the unexpected confrontation with Manon Barca, she had carried with her the certainty that Albus would be waiting for her in the bowels of the Lordican. Bedraggled, brilliant, beloved Albus— whose mind could help her unpack everything cluttering her own. His absence was a physical blow.

Eska wandered back to the public stacks and sank into an aisle between shelves, her thoughts meandering through Albus's last letter. He had identified the Godforged, then told her about the possibility of finding a second disc in the sunken vault in Lake Delo, but he had said nothing about going on a journey or an absence from the Lordican. For Albus not to be in the one place he loved and to have given no advance notice or indication why—it was disturbing.

She could not have said how long she sat there, searching for clues in what she could remember of the letter, her mind constructing a scenario around his passing mention of the city of Parphea. He had fled there, she was nearly convinced—or at least the harrow root was— chased away by a vengeful lover. No, not Albus. More like in pursuit of a tome inadvertently removed from the Lordican.

An intrusion of voices, perhaps only an aisle or two removed from her own, penetrated her thoughts at last and Eska sat up straighter as she listened.

"What do you mean it's not available?" The speaker had a cultured voice made ugly by nastiness.

"One of our scholars has reserved the collection for study. As such, it is not available to the public." The second voice was also a man's, familiar, older, and hoarse from years of lecturing, but resolute.

"Do you know who I am?"

Eska rolled her eyes.

"Indeed," came the answer. Far too politely as far as Eska was concerned. "You are Lord Sylvain de Ulyssey."

Now that was interesting.

"And do you know the de Ulysseys have been funding this institution for generations?"

"Of course, my lord. Your illustrious family has been very generous." The librarian seemed to be making a pointed effort not to follow de Ulyssey's line of questioning toward its natural conclusion. Eska could appreciate that.

"Then do you not think it wise to keep your benefactors happy?"

"I wish I could oblige you, my lord, and I am truly sorry to have to disappoint you. The item is unavailable and has been taken from the building for further study. It is, quite literally, out of my hands."

De Ulyssey said nothing further, but the silence in the other aisle was as loud as if he had been shouting. Eska could picture his silver mane of hair and piercing blue eyes, perhaps a vein throbbing at his temple. Footsteps at last signaled the end of the encounter, but only one set. Eska fancied the steps fairly oozed with perceived superiority—which meant the librarian remained.

Eska waited until de Ulyssey was long gone and then stepped out of her aisle. She made sure to ruffle her dress and make enough noise to alert the poor librarian to her presence, and then she leaned around the stack.

"I bet you wish you'd gone home early today."

The librarian greeted her with a smile. "No need. I was thinking of the roast waiting for me. While he frothed at the mouth, I was imagining its juices dripping down my chin. Makes for good mental armor."

He patted his ample belly.

Eska laughed. "Master Diomede. It's good to see you."

"Indeed, Eska, I think you've been avoiding me. You owe me a game of stars, after all."

"I'll have to forgo the embarrassment. We both know it'd be a repeat of last time, a thorough demolition."

The elderly librarian acknowledged the likelihood of this with a chuckle, followed quickly by a sigh. "You're here about Albus, aren't you."

"Do you know where he is?" The question Eska couldn't ask burned inside her. It wasn't just Albus she needed to locate. He had a Hand of Fate. She needed to find that disc of bronze—before someone else did.

Master Diomede shook his head. "I wish I could say otherwise, but Albus left without giving word."

"And the authorities?"

The librarian spread his hands. "Asked the necessary questions. Performed the necessary searches. But there was little to go on. No home to search. No friends to question."

Eska nodded her understanding, then hesitated, unsure, despite her cordial relationship with the master librarian, if he would divulge anything further given his refusal to do so for de Ulyssey. She took a deep breath and plowed onward. "Was de Ulyssey here for Albus, too? Or something Albus was working on?"

The librarian's steady expression was answer enough.

"Whatever it was, Albus removed it from the Lordican?"

The slightest of nods and a slow blink.

"Master Diomede, I beg you," Eska said, stepping close, "please tell me anything you can. I'm afraid for Albus. You know as well as I do that he is not well-suited to taking care of himself in a dangerous situation."

"How dangerous?"

Eska shook her head. "I don't know."

Master Diomede heaved out another sigh. "I truly don't know where he is, Eska. But he removed a scroll before he left—a scroll from a collection that has, by unhappy chance, caught the attention of Lord de Ulyssey."

"What collection was that?"

Master Diomede studied Eska for a moment, his normally cheerful, immense presence reduced to a crease in his forehead and tight lines around his mouth, then spoke as he turned away. "Come, I'll show you to his workstation. Perhaps you will glean something from what you find there."

The worktable at the far end of a cavernous, utilitarian room looked much like it had the last time Eska had visited, though the added novelty of being escorted there—and pretending she didn't know the way herself—by one of the Lordican's twenty master librarians made her look at the space with new eyes.

The long table was a haven for a busy mind. Stacks of books on various subjects tottered on high, scrolls in various states of unrolling were scattered here and there, and several spindly-looking contraptions featuring gears and dials and crystal prisms occupied one end of the table, rather like a clan of creatures. Master Diomede followed Eska's gaze to the devices.

"I learned a long time ago not to attempt to follow the workings of Albus's mind. I do believe he said something about trying to measure the weight of time."

"That does sound like Albus." Eska scanned the rest of the table. There was no bronze disc with black markings to be seen. "These scrolls?"

Master Diomede shook his head and pointed to a crate lost in the shadows under the table. "Those. It's a collection accumulated by Ardemis the Deceiver. You know her?"

Eska nodded. Ardemis de Vail, a secret admirer of the dead Alescuans. A decade after the execution of Varin II, she had tried to lead a revolt in Vienisi to reestablish monarchical rule, nearly burning the city to the ground.

"She kept the ears of dead men in jars."

Master Diomede raised an eyebrow. "Not the most common

association with her."

Eska shrugged. "It's the first thing I remember learning about her. Something about it stuck."

Master Diomede chuckled and continued. "Each scroll deals with the legends of Ivonia. Given her predilection for power, I'm sure you can understand why she would have been fascinated with those myths."

Myths. Fabled Ivonia. It was common practice among the learned community to dismiss stories of history so ancient no one could say with certainty any of it was true. Indeed, Eska would once have done the same. But the strange bronze disc sitting in an ivory reliquary in a house across the city from the Lordican—a sibling to the one Albus had been studying before he disappeared—required her to do otherwise. Not that she could say as much to Master Diomede.

Eska pulled the crate out from under the table. "Do you mind if I look these over?"

"I don't know what the mind of a madwoman might tell you about Albus's disappearance, but you are welcome to stay."

The librarian turned to leave her. Eska bit her lip. "And when I've finished?"

Master Diomede gave her a tolerant, tired smile. "Don't try to pretend you don't know the back passages of the Lordican nearly as well as I do."

Eska looked down at her feet to hide her grin.

"I'm sure Albus would appreciate your attempt at covering for his decision to defy one of our most important rules."

Eska flushed a little. "The defiance was mine, Master Diomede, I assure you. Though Albus didn't put up much resistance."

The crease in between the old librarian's eyes returned. "I do hope you find him."

⸺ ◆ ⸺

Eska worked late into the night, submerging herself in Ardemis the

Deceiver's collection, trying to understand the workings of the mind of a woman who had burned innocent people in her effort to reach and destroy the palace of the Archon, who had conducted strange ceremonies in the ruins of Elysium and worshipped the Alescuans as gods. She had known the woman's story, but not the fascination for Godforged myths. It did not take Eska long to realize the collection of scrolls was likely the most comprehensive in existence.

The scrolls, most penned by anonymous hands, retold stories of fallen stars, of the island volcano and of the hands that had forged the discs and imbued them with power. The authors drew connections between the god discs, the Hands of Fate, and events throughout the world—wars and famines, plagues and tsunamis. Eska read them all.

The harrow root kept her awake, alert, and when Eska finished the last scroll, she began to pace the length of Albus's worktable—back and forth and back and forth.

The stories, for all their discrepancies and the frustrating lack of explanation as to *how* exactly the discs worked, agreed on one thing. One Godforged alone was a formidable thing, capable of sowing destruction. All six wielded by an individual of tremendous power and skill could shatter fate, destroy free will, and alter the very fabric of existence.

Which made Eska very glad she had never had both discs in the same place at the same time.

And yet, despite the dramatic nature of the stories, one thing was missing. There was nothing that might have sent Albus away from Arconia. Nothing that might have indicated he knew where a third disc was. Nothing that suggested immediate danger. Nothing, that is, except the fact that Master Diomede said Albus had removed one of the scrolls—and the second-most powerful man in Arconia, a man who happened to be the Archduke's closest friend, was looking for it.

"What did you find, Albus?"

The workstation wasn't going to tell her, that much was clear. But she could think of a place that might.

She went home first. Black silk and sapphires was not the sort of thing one wore when embarking on a midnight escapade. And though the harrow root wanted to convince her otherwise, she really did need to eat something.

The house was quiet when she returned, meaning one or both parents were sleeping or absent, which would not be unusual given their positions. Sorina might be playing host to foreign guests at the Varadome or one of the Archduke's other properties in the city, and Maximilian could be engaged in a council session that had extended far past a reasonable hour or barricaded in his offices studying up on a vexing or peculiar law.

As for Valentin, there was no sign, which was unsurprising. Though he considered the family home his primary residence, he kept a lavish suite of rooms at the city's most luxurious hotel. Certainly he would have had no wish to cross paths again with Eska.

Waving away the assistance of two sleepy maids, Eska went to the kitchen and put together an eclectic tray of food—pickles, bread (smothered in mustard), cold eggs, and half an apple and plum tart—then promptly abandoned the tray and ate standing in the middle of the kitchen. When she finished, she hurried to her chambers and traded the silk for slim black trousers, her most comfortable boots, and a loose black shirt. A moment's hesitation in front of her mirror resulted in the addition of a black waistcoat, which had the added benefit of pockets. Into the pockets went a pocket watch—naturally—and a slim leather case she had used only on rare occasions. On her way out of her rooms, Eska grabbed a slender black walking stick with a silver hawk handle from a rack by the door.

She was halfway down the stairs before she thought to turn back, and she quickly retraced her steps to the guest chamber in which she had situated Perrin. A gentle knock on the door elicited no response and Eska nearly turned away—she would have, in fact, if she had not noticed the small puddle of water trailing under the door.

For the first time since leaving the Varadome that afternoon, she paused, her mind slowing for an instant. And then she was turning the gilt handle and opening the door.

The room was ransacked. Chairs overturned, bed curtains hanging askew, a vase smashed on the floor, broken glass from an unknown source, nearly everything torn from the walls. The washbasin on the pedestal by the door lay in pieces at Eska's feet, the source of the water fleeing out into the hall.

Eska didn't bother to call out for Perrin. It was clear the room was empty. Her thoughts flew to her uncle, wondering if he had returned to harm the man with the name he so despised. Eska would not have believed it—and yet the evidence of anger and violence was all too obvious.

Eska rushed downstairs and through the kitchen to the servants' wing of the house. She hammered on Roscoe's door and was rewarded by hearing the captain of the de Caraval guards curse his way out of bed. There was no trace of sleep on his face, though, when he opened the door.

"My lady?"

"My friend has gone missing. Violently, it seems," Eska said. "The room has been overturned and there is no sign of him." Roscoe's face creased into a frown. "Question the servants. Surely someone heard or saw something. And then organize a search party."

"Of course, my lady." Roscoe retreated into his chambers and stepped into his boots. Grabbing a cloak off a peg, he followed Eska back down the hall. "Where should we begin the search? Where would he have been taken?"

Eska's stride hitched ever so slightly. She didn't have an answer. Hadn't even given it more than a cursory thought. The harrow root had shaped her into a compass capable of pointing in only one direction that night.

"I'm not sure," she said. "Check the Barca house. And you could enquire after my uncle's whereabouts at the Tamerlane."

"Your uncle?"

Eska rounded on the captain of the guard. "I don't know where he is," she said, the unexpected ire in her voice causing him to slow his steps. "That's why I'm asking you to look." She turned and made her way into the entry hall, Roscoe's footsteps trailing after her.

"My lady, what is this about?"

But Eska was already gone, slipping out of the house and into the dark.

To keep from being seen by any of the grooms, Eska scaled the garden wall—a skill honed as a child—and dropped into the narrow street behind the de Caraval house. She walked the first part of her journey, moving quickly through the wide lanes that ran between the grand houses in that part of the city. Carriages passed here and there, their lanterns swaying, wheels clattering over the cobblestones. A handful of other people on foot kept to themselves and Eska passed more than a few houses brilliantly lit from within, laughter and music streaming from windows open to the warm night air. She tried not to think of black sleeves embroidered with golden daggers.

As she moved into the trade districts, the night grew rowdier. Tavernas bursting with voices, intoxicated men and women calling to their friends, apprentices running late—or early—errands for their masters. Eska moved from street to street, keeping out of the way and out of the light as much as possible until she found herself standing in front of a tall, narrow home surrounded by other tall, narrow homes. This particular tall, narrow home with its flower boxes lining the windows and the porpoise shaped doorknocker belonged to a certain Lysander Montmere, captain of the *Argonex*.

Eska bypassed the door and its porpoise knocker, bypassed the house entirely, in fact, until she could turn down the nearest alley and approach from the rear. The wooden gate to the small back garden was unlocked.

"Shame on you, Captain," Eska murmured to the pair of horses sleeping in a two-stall stable. She chose the black one, admittedly for its appearance, and it stood compliantly as she saddled it. Only when she went for the bridle did the horse stir, staring at her reproachfully.

"You can sleep in the morning," Eska told it.

Before leading the horse through the gate, Eska took the pocket watch from her waistcoat and hung it on the latch to the now empty stall. It swung gently, revealing the engraved de Caraval hawk, a snake clutched in its talons, every time it touched the moonlight.

The rest of Eska's journey to the edge of the city passed quickly and it wasn't long before she was pulling the horse up alongside a tall hedge. The wide green park around her was quiet. The hedge smelled faintly of smoke.

The legality of what she was doing was up for debate.

Technically, the Varadome was both a private and public property. Private in the sense that it was the Archduke's home, public in that it was the seat of the Arconian government. As a citizen of Arconia, Eska had every right to enter a public property. As an employee of said government via her mother's position, one could even say it would be expected.

Whether she ought to visit it in the middle of the night, enter through a hedge rather than a door, and pay a discreet visit to the private—and most certainly locked—offices of Lord Sylvain de Ulyssey—well, in the end she had to admit there wasn't much to debate after all.

She didn't know what she would find in de Ulyssey's chambers. She knew only that he had them, granted to him by the Archduke. All she wanted to do was look around.

Eska dismounted and tied the horse's reins around a sturdy bit of hedge. She patted its nose. "If I come back at a run," she said, "be prepared to do your part." As escape plans go, it wasn't perhaps the most thorough, but better to have four legs at her disposal than her mere two, if it came to that.

The hedge was thinnest at the ground, so Eska dropped to her stomach and, after shoving the walking stick through, wormed her way to the other side. Branches snagged at the braids in her hair and pulled at her clothes and when she stood up, her sleeves and waistcoat were streaked with dirt. Eska tucked one particularly loosened strand of hair back into its braid, then, taking up her walking stick, strode across the charred Carrier training ground. There were fresh patches of ash and burned wood.

The statues on the other side gleamed white in the moonlight. Eska kept close to the hedge lining the wide lane, trying to stay in the shadows. When she reached the door, she found it unguarded but locked. Plucking the thin folded leather case from her pocket, Eska knelt, selected a pair of lock picks, and went to work.

Lock picking was not a skill she had mastered. After all, she wasn't a thief and it had hardly been part of her formal education. Nor did she have time to practice.

She broke two picks before she gave up and began to search for an alternative entry. She found it by looking up.

The second story terrace was draped with vines. None were conveniently long enough to climb from the ground, but the outstretched, pontificating arm of a tall statue was at the right height.

"I seem to be making a habit of climbing on statues."

Eska clambered up onto the statue's square base, tucked her walking stick through a belt loop, and reached up to take hold of the top of the statue's greave. It was a scramble at first, but as she reached the warrior's thighs, his armored skirt and well-defined leg muscles created sufficient handholds until she reached the relative safety of his chest. There, one arm held across his torso helped create a wide base for Eska to stand on and catch her breath. She eyed the outstretched arm, then inched her way up to the warrior's shoulder and crouched there for a moment.

"That's a long way."

It was the harrow root talking, and it was a challenge, not a warning.

Indeed, the distance between the statue's gesturing fingers and the vines clinging to the wall was not insignificant.

But she was invincible.

Eska stood slowly, found her balance on the marble muscles, and then ran. One, two, three steps—she leaped.

And crashed against the wall with enough force to knock the breath from her. Her hands clutched at the vines. One tore under her weight. Her left knee protested the collision. But she didn't fall.

Setting her feet against the wall and taking as deep a breath as her lungs could manage, Eska began to climb. When she reached the top, she had enough presence of mind to peer over the terrace's railing before vaulting it. She smiled at what the moonlight showed her. A set of glass double doors had been left open. Whatever room they led to was dark, so Eska pulled herself over the railing, her mind racing to locate herself on her—admittedly imperfect—mental map of the Varadome.

She had a vague notion that the Archduke had given his close friend and confidant a tower somewhere between the dome, which housed the Spectacle Hall, multiple ballrooms, an indoor pool large enough to hold mock naval battles, and an exotic animal garden, and the private palace. In other words, nowhere near her.

Undaunted, Eska moved from terrace to roof to hidden courtyard, working her way between the towers. When she saw guards, she ducked into stairwells or behind statues. Either an unknown deity was watching over her journey, or the harrow root made her every move perfect—either way, she remained undetected as she traversed the extensive government wing of the Varadome.

The dome itself presented an obstacle. The smooth surface made passage other than by the walkway just above ground level impossible. It ran around the entire dome and, given its proximity to the primary entrance to the Varadome, was more heavily patrolled.

But like everything about the Varadome, it was made to be beautiful, and beauty required alcoves and statues, fountains and walls of flowers—plenty of opportunities for concealment.

Eska raised her face to the star-filled sky above her. The air seemed clearer, the stars brighter, the spaces between darker. Eska filled her lungs, felt the winds of the earth swirl inside her, felt the power of storms surge around her. Smiling, she knew she could fly if she wanted, to the moon, even beyond.

Traversing the walkway around the northern side of the massive dome without being seen was like a dance, and Eska executed every step, every turn, every pause with perfection. She might as well have been invisible.

She was breathless with exhilaration by the time she reached the twin towers on the western side. She closed her eyes and pictured the interior of the Varadome once more. Eska had never entered the private palace, but she knew the halls and towers leading to it. There were three towers, not counting the tall ones she had just passed, between her and the Archduke's sanctum, three smaller towers that might house Sylvain de Ulyssey. One of the three was dedicated to servants, who were kept close but carefully out of the way of the private palace. That would be, Eska determined, the one with the most lights in the windows, leaving two, one to the north and one to the south.

Eska chose the southern tower, dark but for the ground level windows, and connected on her level to the main vein of the structure by a narrow, arched bridge, which led to a small doorway. Eska reached for her lock picks as she approached the door, then threw herself to the shadows as she heard footsteps on the other side.

Pressing herself against the white stone, Eska held her breath as the door opened, flung so hastily by a sprinting young man, hardly more than a boy, that it did not close completely behind him. The boy raced over the bridge, a leather case swinging from his back—a messenger, using the rooftops rather than the busy corridors below.

Eska ducked inside the door and stepped into a darkened stairwell. She climbed a short distance up, emerging into an entrance chamber sprouting three doors and lit by two lanterns casting long shadows. Tapestries hung from the walls, old, but finely wrought. One depicted mythical creatures fighting against unrealistically naked heroes. A second featured three maidens cavorting around a fountain. The third showed a man driving a chariot—a flying chariot, no less—across a sunbeam-strewn sky. And all three had identical tawny-colored mountain cats woven into the scenery. Each spouted gouts of fire from long-toothed jaws.

Eska smiled. The mountain cat was the old symbol of the de Ulyssey family, replaced after the fall of the Alescuan dynasty by the less bloodthirsty, more civilized—and far less interesting, as far as Eska was concerned—oak tree.

Eska waited a moment, listening for signs of life from behind the doors. The messenger boy had, after all, come from somewhere and would no doubt return. When she had stood in silence for longer than she could tolerate, Eska tucked the walking stick under her arm, removed one of the lanterns from its iron hook on the wall, and approached the middle door.

As she pulled the leather case from her pocket once more, Eska rested her free hand on the door. To her complete surprise, it swung open quietly.

"Really, Sylvain." Eska clapped a hand over her mouth and forced down the giggle rising in her chest. Retrieving the lantern from the floor, she crossed the threshold.

The chamber was part study, part smoking lounge, part boudoir. The putrid smell of de Ulyssey's favorite leaf clung to everything and Eska grimaced as she shut the door behind her. A desk sat close to one wall and, judging by the pristine emptiness of the writing surface, was clearly the least-used thing in the room. Though perhaps that distinction belonged to the built-in bookshelves hovering rather forlornly behind it. Opposite the desk and without a doubt the centerpiece of the room, a silk sling the length of a bed and lined with peacock feathers hung down from the ceiling. It was piled high with plush cushions.

"Really, Sylvain," Eska repeated—for entirely different reasons. She did laugh, then, not in condemnation of whatever fantasies had inspired the feathers and the cushions and the swinging bed, but at the thought of how best she could slip an innocent reference to peacock feathers into her next conversation with him.

Still smiling merrily, Eska began her search. It didn't matter that she didn't have the slightest clue what she might be searching for.

Though she didn't harbor much hope for it, she started with the desk. A quick riffling through the twin drawers revealed nothing more than discarded scraps of paper, a letter opener, a set of very fine quills (Albus would approve), ink, and a book with more than a few page corners turned down. Eska flipped through the book, an account of early de Ulyssey family history, causing a single sheet of paper folded in half to fall free. Eska opened it eagerly, only to discover it was a very poor attempt at poetry.

"*Really*, Sylvain." Eska read further. "Comparing her skin to that of a snake is not advisable. Thank all the dead librarians you saw the error of your ways and gave this up." Eska slipped the paper back inside the book and returned it to the drawer, then turned her attention to the large trunk positioned under the nearest window.

She was expecting clothes. Perhaps more peacock feathers.

She was not expecting the trunk to be empty but for a single object—a box of smooth ivory and shining gold.

———— ◆ ————

She had, Eska realized, now seen and held three of six Alescuan reliquaries.

This was followed closely by the realization that if the pattern held true, she was also holding a third Godforged.

The puzzle was obvious on this one. The top of the box, as ornately decorated with gold flowers and coiling snakes and luscious fruits as the other sides, was cut into small squares forming a grid. Eska brushed a finger along the lid, the slight give in the surface confirming her suspicion. There was a code built into the squares. When the correct squares were pressed in the correct order, the lock inside would release and the reliquary would open. What Eska did not wish to discover was whether the box would destroy the mechanism inside and lock itself forever if she guessed incorrectly.

Eska mulled over that thought for a moment, aware that she was likely running out of time. She had, she decided, two options. Attempt to open the box immediately, which would, if she succeeded, allow her to remove the contents of the reliquary, replace it in the trunk, and slip out of the Varadome. By the time Sylvain de Ulyssey discovered what was missing, if, indeed, he had even successfully opened the reliquary and knew what he possessed, she would be long gone and beyond suspicion.

The alternative was to take the reliquary with her. While that solution would limit the time she was exposed to discovery, it would also likely result in Sylvain knowing he had been robbed immediately. And if she was caught sneaking out of the Varadome with it, even she might have difficulty talking herself out of trouble.

As Eska stared at the chamber's empty hearth, debating her options, a third came to her.

It was a child born from the harrow root. Eska de Caraval would not normally consider it an option to use an iron poker to smash open a priceless artifact just to retrieve what might or might not be inside.

And yet that is exactly what she did.

Without hesitation, Eska got to her feet and strode over to the hearth. Seizing the poker with both hands, she brought it down on the reliquary. Chunks of gold skittered across the floor as the ivory splintered and shattered, revealing a silk interior, just like its siblings. Dropping the poker, Eska went to her knees and prodded at the wreckage.

No disc of bronze. Nothing.

She didn't have time for disappointment. Sweeping the pieces of the reliquary together as best she could, Eska gathered them into her cupped hands and poured them back into the bottom of the trunk. She had no illusions about the mess. The only thing that mattered then was not being seen.

Eska fled from the room on swift feet, returning the lantern to its hook as she went. All was quiet as she slipped back into the stairwell, but she had gone only two steps down when voices from below froze her in place. One hand went to the cane in her belt.

The voices lasted only the span of a few words, but it was the sound of a pair of boots on the stone that sent Eska careening down the stairs. She had to reach the door on the second level first.

And she did. But not fast enough. As she fled into the moonlit night, a shout told her she had been spotted.

Eska raced over the bridge, her pursuer only steps behind. She turned left, toward the private palace, only because right would bring her back toward the dome and the horde of armed guards there. The voice called after her, demanding she stop, but Eska paid it no mind.

For a moment she was back among the wild beeches and oaks behind the Lordican, horse hooves pounding behind her, a whip cracking the air—and then the harrow root squashed her fears and there was only the cool air in Eska's lungs and the colder stars above.

The rooftops and terraces passed by in a blur and Eska's feet remained sure, her legs strong—until she ran out of roof.

Eska skidded to a stop. The steps behind her slowed and halted. Her gaze darted right and left, searching for a way out.

She heard her pursuer take a deep breath, no doubt to proclaim her arrest. But the inhale hitched oddly and then there was only silence. She didn't dare turn.

"Eska?"

She exhaled sharply on the wake of that voice saying her name. And then she turned to face Alexandre de Minos.

"Sascha."

It was the harrow root that provided her composure, that kept her voice from trembling. But the squaring of her shoulders, the jutting of her jaw—that was all Eska.

Alexandre stared at her, his blue eyes hooded in confusion, the large rolled parchment clutched in his hand forgotten. "What are you doing here?" he managed.

"What does it look like?"

"You were in Lord de Ulyssey's private chambers."

"I was."

"Why?" He became the Arch-Commander with that single word, pushing whatever conflicting emotions he might have been feeling beneath the confidence in his position.

"I was looking for something, Sascha."

Alexandre's gaze narrowed. "What have you taken?"

Eska laughed and heard the stars laugh with her. "Nothing."

"This isn't amusing, Eska. I have to arrest you." The words came out reluctantly.

Eska's laughter faded into cold anger. "Don't try to walk the moral high ground with me, Sascha. You lied."

He drew back ever so slightly.

"You promised me Manon Barca would be brought to justice. But you lied. She's free as a songbird and playing a part in whatever schemes the Archduke is orchestrating. I saw her. I saw the training ground. Is that why you really came to Toridium? To collect her? How many Carriers have you collected for our beloved Arcturos?" Eska leaned close. "Tell me, Sascha, what have you been paid to forget that she tried to kill me and sink my ship? I hope it was worth the loss of your integrity and honor."

She might have expected a hint of shame. She saw none. Only sadness.

"Eska," he said quietly. "There is a lot we need to discuss."

She shook her head. "No, there isn't."

"Please." He took a step forward, his hand outstretched, his eyes fixed on hers.

Eska whipped the walking stick from her belt and freed the silver hawk handle, revealing a slender dagger. Alexandre didn't flinch, but he halted his forward momentum and spread both hands in front of his torso, palms out.

"I'm leaving, Sascha."

"How? There's nowhere for you to go Eska. Not unless you put that in my heart."

But he was wrong. Eska could fly.

Sheathing the dagger inside the cane, Eska turned on her heel and jumped.

Interlude 17

A letter from Eska de Caraval to Albus Courtenay, dated two years ago

My dear Albus,

You will be surprised, I think, to learn that I am writing to you from Vachon.

There. I have written it, so it must now be true. Strange that writing such seemingly inconsequential words can be an action that carries such meaning—and that words can somehow be more true than the act of being in a place.

Sascha asked me to marry him, Albus. And I have said I will not.

Though asking why is as natural to you as breathing, it would not be in your nature to ask why in regards to this matter. But I am going to carry on as though you have set aside your tome, propped one hand on your chin, and gazed expectantly at me.

And yet I find I do not quite know where to begin. You see, Albus, the reason I gave Sascha is not the same reason I am going to give you. And that is what hurts most of all—knowing that I could not tell him the truth.

I told him that expectation weighed too heavily on me, that I needed to focus on my diplomatic career. I told him, and watched something break within those blue eyes, that the long-standing, much discussed in Arconian ballrooms, expectation that one day the families of de Caraval and de Minos would be united by our marriage had made the very idea of marriage grow stale on my tongue.

I know you think Sascha to be a man armored in self-control, aloof even. And he is, in part. You respect him for my sake, but you were never destined be to great friends. His blunt, military manner and your meandering mind are not compatible. But know that he is more than that, that I have seen all of him, and that in the moment of my refusal I saw something in him I had never seen before.

Grief, I suppose. Though it seems an inadequate word. I have seen him grieve before—when confronted with bodies of comrades felled in battle, or, hardest of all, innocent lives among the casualties. This was different. I didn't give him the chance to change my mind. He could have. I know in that moment I was existing on a whisper of resolve.

So what, then, I hear you ask, was your true reason, Eska?

Alexandre de Minos is destined to be the next Arch-Commander of Arconia. He will not say it himself, but as much as any man or woman can be said to have a purpose, this is his. There is no rival among the other officers who can compete with his achievements and his strengths. And yet there was one obstacle that stood between him and that fate: me.

You see, Albus, our current Arch-Commander, the illustrious Domenico de Farenault, is a man who feeds a grudge with his blood and the blood of everyone he meets. And it just so happens that Domenico de Farenault has been nursing a grudge against my father for half his miserable life.

If Sascha and I were married, de Farenault would never name him as his successor. And I refuse to keep the man I love from being what he is meant to be. If I tell him this truth, he will throw away everything for me and he will regret it for the rest of his life.

You must never breathe a word of this to Sascha, to anyone. I do not believe you would, Albus. You know I trust you as I trust myself. And yet my heart demands this promise of you because my heart is crying out for shelter and you are the only harbor I have left.

I do not know how long I intend to stay here. I came to Vachon looking for peace, but I grow weary in that search. I will write again soon.

Yours, because I can no longer be his,
Eska

38

"That which is precious is not always valuable."

My dearest Eska-

I am directing this letter to your family home in Arconia. I can only hope it reaches you, wherever you are, in a timely manner.

And now I must beg pardon for my unexpected departure. I received word that my aunt had fallen ill and, as her only living family member, I have traveled to her bedside to do what I can for her. Her condition is serious and I expect to be here for some time. She speaks of strange things in her sleep, most often a masked eagle, and I find I can only give her small comforts. I ask that you pray to all seven gods for her recovery, though perhaps it would be better to pray for a painless and easy death.

Do not fear that I neglect my work. I have, however, left behind that treatise you and I spoke of, the one by the six monks of Altiere. Perhaps you can provide a better translation of the passage about the lettering and symbols on the Ulyssian tomb.

Messengers are hard to come by, as you know, in these small mountain villages, so I cannot anticipate when next I might be able to write to you.

Please pass along my greetings to our friend Val. I look forward to a time when we can all be together as we once were.

Fondly yours,
Albus

"Your aunt?"

Albus nodded.

Keleut frowned over the paper in her hands. "I granted you permission to write to this," she glanced back at the top of the page, "this Eska so that you might assuage any fears regarding your safety—not discuss monks and treatises."

Albus swallowed. "I thought the point of this letter was to make sure no one went looking for the kidnapped librarian." Keleut directed her frown at Albus, but he carried on. "Eska and I always discuss work within our letters. If I don't, it will be very suspicious."

Keleut kept her gaze trained on Albus for an interminably long moment. Surely she was about to call out one of the lies in the letter. There were many to choose from—though in the end he had not dared to include the one he most wished to write. How does one slip in a warning about an impending invasion when the invader is going to be examining it for that very thing? Whatever courage and boldness he had discovered on the sea wall of Onaxos had deserted him. But Eska would puzzle out the meaning of the letter. She had to.

After what felt like a lifetime, the Seycherran pirate looked down at the paper once more and refolded it. "Very well. You may send it immediately."

Albus nodded his thanks, not trusting himself to speak. Only when he had left the room did he allow himself to exhale fully. But he had little time to recover his nerves. Aurelia was waiting for him. The slender girl stood between two pillars at the end of the fountain room, the arched window behind her framing her in the golden light of the morning.

They had begun the past two mornings this way. Aurelia would take him to part of the city and explain something of Onaxos's heritage or customs. She had given no reason for these lessons, and Albus had submitted to them without question, more to satisfy his own curiosity than to avoid angering the strange, pale-haired twins. Not that he wanted to anger them or the large brute who seemed permanently attached to the shadow of whichever twin he was in the presence of.

"What will you show me today?" Albus asked as he put a pleasant expression on his face.

Aurelia smiled. "Today is a secret. But we are leaving the city. Are you ready?"

Albus made a show of looking around. "And your friend?"

The girl laughed. "Where we are going, I have no need of Manuba's protection. Though," she said, leaning toward Albus as though they were sharing a great secret, "he thinks otherwise, of course."

Albus matched her smile but his insides twisted in—guilt, shame? He wasn't sure. The twins fascinated him, but he was afraid of what they could do. More specifically, he was afraid of what those who believed in their divinity would be willing to do. To make it worse, he had searched in vain for any sign of an adult's guiding hand, an authority to whom Aurelia and her brother answered, who was dictating the course of their actions. The absence of any such figure was frightening and Albus was forced to attribute the twins' composure and competence to them alone. His mother had warned him against unsupervised children—for vastly different reasons, but Albus was fairly sure the principle still applied.

The fact that they often engaged in childlike behavior made it all the more confusing. Not petulance or tantrums or spite. But laughter and games and giggling.

As for the Wisdoms of Onaxos, they might as well have been nonexistent. After that day on the sea wall, Aurelia and Aurelian had taken Albus and Keleut to a vast house situated on the highest terrace of the city. They didn't rule—not as Albus would define it. They didn't settle disputes or give orders. They certainly didn't dictate law. But they were revered. They were adored. And they were far more visible than the Wisdoms.

It had only taken a day in the city with Aurelia for Albus to understand what he had glimpsed that moment in the garden with the statue of the divine Twins framed behind Aurelia and Aurelian—they had the power to attract followers and keep them. The Wisdoms might be the mind of the city. But Aurelian and Aurelia nox Macedonos were its heart.

If the Wisdoms had any sense, Albus had concluded, they would arrange for an expedient, tragic accident. But then, the Wisdoms of Onaxos had demonstrated none of that stuff for which they were named.

"I love a secret," Albus heard himself say. It earned him a delighted smile.

They took a litter as they had the other mornings—but not down through the city. Instead the servants trotted them upward. They passed across the sprawling white stone terrace and then under the shadow of the spire. Upon reaching a high wall spanning the entire width of the promontory and manned by trident-wielding warriors, the litter slowed, but only until Aurelia showed her face. A barked order followed and the iron gate set into the wall swung open to release them.

"The Plains of Naxos," Aurelia said, waving a hand through the sheer white curtain of the litter.

Onaxos, Albus realized, was situated between two seas. The first was the wet kind, of course, but this, this was a sea of grass the most remarkable shade of green. It flowed around the knees of the litter-bearers and crested in waves driven onward by the wind.

Aurelia gave him a moment to appreciate the beauty of the plains before asking, "Do you know why the grass is this color? It is unique to the Plains of Naxos."

"I do not. But I should like to."

"You'll have the answer soon enough." The girl shifted so she faced Albus squarely. Her face had turned serious. "Master Tarvonos," she began, using the false name Albus had given on a whim, "what you will see today are among two of the greatest secrets of my city. With our divine Twins' favor, one of those secrets will become known to the world soon enough, but for now, do I have your word that you will not

436 TL GREYLOCK & BRYCE O'CONNOR

divulge them to anyone?"

He was not, thanks to Keleut, likely to be divulging much of anything to anyone. The Seycherran captain had given no indication that she might be inclined to grant him his freedom. But Aurelia could not know that. As far as she was concerned, he was a Bellaran who had forsaken his home in favor of Seycherra. Keleut had fabricated some story about Albus feeling a connection of the heart to the people of Seycherra and choosing to abandon the woman he loved in favor of a life on a Seycherran ship.

Albus had been forced to cover his laughter with a coughing fit.

"You have my word," he said in his gravest voice.

Aurelia smiled and Albus took the opportunity of a captive audience to attempt to fish for information.

"You have, princess, shown me a great deal of your city." She had never demanded the use of a title, but neither had she rebuffed it. "But you have shared only a little of yourself. Your prestige and position are remarkable for your age."

"The name Macedonos is an old one. Many of my ancestors served as Wisdoms when Onaxos was a great and feared city on the Anerrean Sea."

"Forgive me, but that was many, many years ago."

Aurelia sighed a little. "It was. When the last of my ancestors was called to Wisdom, a rift grew between the occupants of the spire. In the end, one faction overruled the other and cast out the dissenters, my ancestor included. Not violently, for that was not the way they believed things should be done. But they forever changed this city. Our decline in influence and significance began that day."

"What caused this rift?" This was no history Albus knew. He had learned only of a gradual and natural decline as other cities on the Anerrean Sea rose to power—as had happened countless times before. The books did not speak of internal strife. But Albus had learned by then that Onaxos was very good at hiding things from the world.

Aurelia was quiet for a moment, her smooth face contemplating the waving grass. "You have seen our Wisdoms as they are today. You have seen how they look only inward, how they ask questions of the stars rather than seek answers among the people." She shifted her gaze to Albus. "No Wisdom has set foot outside the spire once entering it for a generation."

Albus frowned, his confusion genuine. "How do they rule?"

Aurelia shrugged elegantly. "The day to day work is done by faithful followers. They adhere to their tasks. The city functions. Barely."

"Can they not be reasoned with? Made to see the harm they cause?"

Aurelia smiled as though Albus were the child. "My dear Master Tarvonos, they are the product of generations upon generations of philosophy stating that the Wisdoms are the divine conduit of Taalo and Toora, that this is how they protect the city. Nothing else matters but their conversation with our gods. There is no reason in them."

"Protect the city. From what? I do not wish to offend, princess, but Onaxos is far from the minds of the conquerors of the world. Even the Alescus never thought it worth their time."

"You do not offend, Master Tarvonos. I am well aware of what the world thinks of us. My parents, the product of two of the remaining families who hold on to the memories of what Onaxos once was, taught me well. But I have not told you all there is to know about the rift that brought about our decline." Three slender fingers pushed aside the curtain and Aurelia glanced out the window. Albus sensed they were descending slightly.

"The Wisdoms argued over a prophecy. My ancestor and her followers believed the Twins were trying to tell us of a threat originating from within the city. The faction that won insisted the threat was external and that by turning inward, the city could be saved." She looked at Albus. "Remarkable, isn't it, how the world can hinge upon the interpretation of only a few words. But I don't need to tell you that, master interpreter." She sighed. "They fulfilled the prophecy themselves, you see. They drove the city in on itself. They shut the sea wall, they built the defenses behind the spire, they shunned visitors and any trade, they cast suspicion on their allies. You can see, I'm sure, how that might contribute to a once great city's downfall."

"Indeed," Albus murmured. "How is it that Onaxos wasn't swallowed up by a rival as she weakened?"

Aurelia laughed. "I think we owe that to the Peliades."

"Of course. The Anerrean Sea was in chaos. I hadn't thought of the timing."

The girl nodded. "By the time the Peliades were finished killing each other off, Onaxos's sea wall had been shut for decades. Most people who knew what might be gained from taking the city were dead or in chains. And so we were allowed to be forgotten."

Albus almost felt a pain of sadness. Almost. After all, as a historian, to learn that Onaxos had been shut off from the world, all on the words of a few god-addled minds, it was, in Albus's mind, an intolerable loss.

And yet, thanks to two children, that very city was contemplating conquering his own.

"We're here," Aurelia said.

The litter came to a halt and was lowered to the ground. Aurelia stepped nimbly through the sheer curtain. Albus followed.

The sea of grass waved around them, stretching as far as Albus could see, infinite and unblemished by manmade structure. He followed Aurelia a short distance from the litter, and only then did he see the narrow chasm splitting the sea in two.

The gorge ran north to south through the Plains of Naxos and carved deep into the earth. As Albus stepped as close to the edge as he dared, he was aware of Aurelia watching him with a proud smile. The bottom was a distant idea more than a reality Albus could see. He could hear water running, the sound amplified by the stone confines of the chasm, but only saw flashes of the buried river, the rest obscured by protrusions of rock and vegetation clinging to the canyon walls.

But Aurelia wasn't interested in the strange plants with their purple leaves or the beautifully layered formations of rock showcasing yellow limestone and blue granite and greenschist that featured a pale version of its namesake color. She was pointing south.

Albus shifted on the edge of the chasm, adjusting his perspective so he could see what Aurelia wanted to show him.

"Scaffolding," he murmured. It clung to the cliff face like a parasite, obscuring the layers of geological history, a skeleton sucking the earth of life—for Albus understood what he was standing over, what the gorge concealed.

"A mine," he said.

"Not just any mine, Master Tarvonos. You asked how Onaxos has survived. I told you the Wisdoms suspended all nonessential trade. Onaxians were expected to live off fish and the inadequate quantities of grain and vegetables they could grow in their small garden plots in the city. It is possible, but such a life prohibits growth or innovation, as you might imagine. Our people were so intent on surviving and feeding their children, they stopped inventing, they stopped making music and art and poetry. In time, as things stabilized, those beautiful talents resurfaced, but that time of darkness cost us." Aurelia's young face held a perfect expression of sorrow—and yet Albus could not find it genuine, and not just because of her youth.

"I digress," she said, smiling apologetically. "But other work suffered, too. A century ago, a discovery was accidentally made here on the Plains of Naxos, a discovery that once would have made Onaxos wealthy. But the Wisdoms forbade our finest minds from exploring it. My father finally convinced the Wisdoms to open this mine not long after my brother and I were born. It was his life's goal. And he sacrificed himself to it. But it worked. And thanks to the discreet assistance of our closest island neighbor, the contents of the mine flow out—in small quantities only—and in return, Onaxos once again has access to the finest lumber from Anderran forests, iron from Parphea, and grain from Umoria. Out of necessity, it is a slow process, for we do not wish to attract the greed of those who would like to lay claim to our greatest resource."

"And what is that resource, princess?"

"I'll show you." Aurelia beckoned Albus onward and they traversed the edge of the chasm until they reached a point where the scaffolding extended to the surface. A short descent on a wooden ladder anchored to the stone brought them to a platform and a great deal of rope and rigging. A man waited there, pale and skinny, dressed only in trousers cut off above his knee. He spoke not a word and did not so much as look at Aurelia, but he began to adjust several components of the rigging, then leaned over the railing of the platform and gave a sharp whistle. The platform jolted to life under Albus. He reached out a hand at empty air to steady himself and gritted his teeth as Aurelia maintained perfect balance, her arms behind her back, her face politely refusing to register Albus's wobble.

They descended perhaps halfway down the gorge, stopping when they reached a second platform, this one manned by two more shirtless men who, like bell ringers, had been taking turns heaving on the ropes. They, too, stood completely still as Aurelia passed, their gazes staring vacantly over the top of her head. Albus tarried behind her, unable to take his eyes away from the strange men.

She led Albus along a wooden walkway, one of many crisscrossing the walls of the chasm. Several hairpin turns later, they reached a tunnel boring into the rock. Albus expected Aurelia to enter, but instead she extended a hand toward one of two men waiting at the entrance to the tunnel. The second man held a burning torch. The first placed a small object in her palm, a vial, which she held up between thumb and forefinger to show Albus

It was empty.

Albus frowned.

Aurelia laughed.

"I'm not making a joke, Master Tarvonos," she said, "though your confusion is to be expected."

"I don't understand."

Aurelia returned the vial to the man, who clamped his fist around it, his posture still ramrod straight.

"What is the most valuable substance in the earth, Master Tarvonos?"

"Diamonds. Gold. Any number of precious things."

"A true statement, but I encourage you to think of it another way. That which is precious is not always valuable." Aurelia looked over her shoulder and gave a nod to the men.

The torchbearer, his gaze still as blank as an artist's canvas, held his torch out at an angle. The first man clamped the vial into a pair of iron pincers, extended the vial so it angled toward the torch, and, with a second pair of long pincers, twisted the cork stopper free.

The blast of flame and heat sent Albus stumbling backward. Aurelia, composed as ever, reached a hand out to steady him. As the cloud of fire billowed away, Albus stared at the shattered remnants of the vial at the feet of the two men. Their expressions had not changed, indeed, they seemed to look right through Albus, heedless of how close they had come to losing their eyebrows—or worse.

For a moment, as the last of the heat shimmered around Aurelia's face and his heart pounded in his chest, Albus could have been convinced of the power of her gods. But then his mind reasserted control. Albus, after all, was a man of science, of learning and knowledge— even if he had nearly jumped out of his skin.

"Would I be right, princess, in assuming this is the root explanation for the eternal flame at the temple on Mount Vierassos, sacred to the ancient sphinx goddess?"

"You know your history, master interpreter." Aurelia bestowed the praise like a teacher would to a student.

"For a long time now," Albus went on, "scholars have theorized that a substance, clear and undetectable, like air, emitting from the earth and sparked by lightning, could burn as the Sphinx's flame does. But the priests and priestesses do not grant access to the temple and the flame to outsiders. And no other instance of this has been recorded."

Aurelia smiled. "We call it aeras, which means like air, just as you said, and its presence in this soil is what gives the grass its unique color. Can you imagine, Master Tarvonos, a world lit by this instead of by candles that die out, wood that must be labored for, or oil that spills and leaves the air black with smoke?"

Albus could, in fact, imagine it.

"How is it gathered and stored?"

Aurelia waved a hand. "I will let one of our engineers explain the details, if you insist."

"But is it safe?"

She let out a little laugh. "It is a gift from Taalo and Toora. Of course it is safe."

Albus felt himself recoil and tried not to let the visceral reaction show. Her blithe dismissal was chilling. He hurried to turn the conversation before she noticed his discomfort.

"And the cities and kingdoms who have accepted it in trade? How are they using it?"

Aurelia shrugged. "The properties of the aeras is explained to them, but the rest is up to them, of course. I would not expect or allow them to tell Onaxos how to use iron. Would you?"

"Of course not. Tell me, princess," Albus said, "do you know if the Bellaran cities have traded for your aeras?"

Aurelia's mouth tightened in displeasure. "They have so far rebuffed our representatives. Your people seem intent on clinging to their beeswax and their oil."

Her words brought Albus some relief—to think of such a powerful substance in the hands of some hapless trade minister or curious chancellor made him shudder. Use of the aeras needed to be studied, and, if implementation was desired by the Archduke or the other six rulers, the Lordican and the other institutions of learning in the Seven Cities ought to be responsible for—or at the very least involved in—developing a plan to do so. But here, in Onaxos, he wasn't Bellaran. He was a self-imposed exile enamored with Seycherran culture.

"They will, I'm sure, see the error of their ways, princess."

Albus saw her smile, saw the way she beheld the world—already at her feet. He wondered if he could push her from the platform and if she would fall far enough to break her neck. And how long he would live after doing so. Albus lowered his gaze, afraid his thoughts might be written across his face as though in ink.

"And now, Master Tarvonos, it is time to show you the second secret," Aurelia said.

They rode the platform back to the surface, once again in the company of the first of the silent, shirtless workers. When Albus tried to thank him for his attentive care of the mechanism and the pulleys that kept them safe, he, as they had all done before, stared straight ahead and gave no sign that he had heard.

Aurelia turned sharp eyes on Albus. "They are not accustomed to being addressed." It was the first hint of anger he had seen from her. Under its influence, she seemed older.

"Forgive me, princess."

"And they do not speak."

Do not. Can not. Albus's mind made the jump from one to the next instantly and the slight twitch under Aurelia's right eye told him she had not intended to say as much as she had—and that he was right.

A sudden gust of wind caught up Aurelia's mane of straight white-blonde hair as they crested the top of the chasm and returned to the sea of grass, and when the breeze faded and her hair had settled once more about her face, her usual expression—pleasant, kind, just ever so slightly bored—had returned.

They continued their journey across the Plains of Naxos in silence, following the gorge south until the sea of grass swallowed it. What occupied Aurelia's mind, Albus could not begin to contemplate. For his part, he could not stop thinking about the aeras, his mind seizing upon methods of safely harnessing and controlling the substance to provide a new source of light. He could think of one or two scholars at the Lordican with whom he would very much like to consult on the subject—but the second secret of Onaxos served as a sharp reminder that he might never return to his beloved Lordican again, or if he did, it might be a smoking ruin.

When the litter halted for the second time, Aurelia's good humor had fully returned and the smile she gave Albus was bright and brilliant as she slipped through the curtain once more.

"I can't decide," she said, "which will be the greater surprise." She laughed and disappeared.

Albus could not quite imagine anything offering as great a shock as the aeras mine, but that was before he stepped out of the litter.

Aurelia was standing on yet another precipice. But instead of a gorge cutting through the sea of grass, she overlooked a valley—a massive, shallow bowl in the Plains of Naxos—filled with that same grass.

Albus gaped. He would freely admit it if Keleut were to ask him later.

"I must admit, princess, this is most spectacular," he finally managed, a very long silence later.

"The Second Spears of Naxos, Master Tarvonos," Aurelia said, sweeping one hand over the valley, as though she could contain the army in a single gesture. Perhaps she could.

Albus watched for a moment, trying to take in the very large quantity of warriors wielding tridents and long rectangular shields. Just below the precipice they stood on, a training ground had been marked out with white and blue flags. A cohort of warriors was drilling, moving in unison, their shields flashing, tridents arcing and stabbing in perfectly timed movements. Beyond the training field, pairs worked one on one. Even from that distance, Albus could see they were not gentle with their comrades. And beyond that, a small city had been built in that strange blue-green grass.

The structures were simple and impermanent, single story huts arranged in neat rows. Albus could see more figures milling between the buildings. They were all, as far as he could see, men.

"I don't understand," Albus said for the second time that day. They were not words he enjoyed. "Onaxos doesn't have this kind of population. Nor can it support it."

"Didn't," Aurelia said. "I have shown you my father's life work, now I show you my mother's."

"An army?"

"Not just any army. These men do not feel as you and I do, Master Tarvonos. They are immune to cold and pain, even to hunger. They can march longer, swim farther, climb higher. You met some of them at the mine, though those men are the ones who are not up to standard."

"Up to standard?"

Aurelia shrugged. "If they cannot meet certain specifications, they are sent to work the mines instead."

"But where do they come from?"

"They were not born as you or I were born, Master Tarvonos." She said these words as easily as Eska might casually remind Albus to stop reading for a moment and eat something. "They were crafted and bred in the waters of our most holy spring. They do not drain the city of resources. They have everything they need here. The Plains of Naxos provides game, and the river beyond," she said, pointing to where a ribbon of water gleamed near the horizon, "offers up fish and water for these warriors of Toora and Taalo."

Albus, a man of science, was not limited by views of men and women as creations of divine beings. But the notion of breeding men to die in war was abhorrent. And yet that was not what made him go pale as he looked out over Aurelia's army.

It was that moment, with the sea of grass whispering around him, with Aurelia next to him smiling out over her holy warriors, and as the horde roared at the sight of her, that he realized she and her brother were no different, not at the heart of things, than the Wisdoms they scorned. They were all fanatics. Cult-like in their convictions. The only difference that mattered was that the twins intended to act.

———— •‣ ————

"We need to leave this place."

Keleut frowned at Albus, though whether she was more irritated by being woken in the middle of the night or by the words he was speaking, he could not say. She made no move to open the door further and her face filled the narrow opening, braids clinking against the wood.

"Albus, go to bed."

She stifled a yawn and made to close the door, but Albus thrust a hand out. Grimacing as his knuckles ground against the frame, he begged Keleut to listen.

The pirate contemplated him for a moment and Albus was reminded of the day they met. Whatever understanding they had come to in the days since, whatever rapport they had established, he was reminded that she was still a pirate, grim and fierce and unafraid of bloodshed. He could still see the shock on the face of the man she had slid her knife into with such nonchalance. For an instant, Albus was once again standing on the deck of the merchant ship, feeling the swell of the ocean waves as a man bled out at his feet, and Keleut, daughter of Nestor, could decide his fate with a single word. But perhaps he could speak that word and decide hers.

"Please."

The hardness in her eyes remained, but Keleut opened the door just enough to let him inside the chamber—nearly identical to his own—in the Macedonos house. She wore a sleeveless tunic and trousers—and boots.

"Do you sleep in those?" Albus's question slipped out with a great deal of regret chasing after it. He very nearly clapped a hand over his mouth as she shut the door behind him.

Keleut's gaze narrowed further, if that was even possible.

Albus fumbled for words that might placate her. "I suppose it's practical to be dressed for action at all times." He tried to smile.

"What do you want?" Her voice was flat, her face closed off.

Albus swallowed and took a deep breath. "You ought to have come with us today. I do not think I can properly convey to you what Aurelia showed me."

"You know I had work to do here, letters to write so Seycherra can begin preparations."

Somehow the thought of Seycherra preparing for war was not nearly as frightening as it had been a matter of days ago—not after seeing Onaxos's preparations.

"Keleut. The twins have an army."

"Good. That is what I came for."

Albus shook his head, trying to order his thoughts into something that might persuade her. "The men, they are shells of men, they do not speak, they do not feel pain or hunger as you or I would. They have been bred like dogs for the purpose of dying for Taalo and Toora. They are enslaved to a divine cause."

Keleut raised an eyebrow at mention of the warriors' immunity to physical limitations, but not, Albus realized, for the reasons he had hoped. He shifted tactics.

"Do you remember trying to speak to the Wisdom Isopho or the acolyte who died? The single-mindedness? The strict adherence to beliefs? The inability to conceive of any thought or idea not born from their gods?"

Keleut nodded slowly.

"Aurelia and Aurelian are no different. They accept nothing but their own view of the world."

"Single-mindedness can serve a purpose, Albus," Keleut said. "If it means they will be unwavering allies, then I have no objection to whatever strange beliefs they hold."

Frantic now, feeling the tide of Keleut's need for vengeance pulling against him, Albus dropped to his knees. The Seycherran woman stiffened at the unexpected act of submission. "Please, Keleut. Please hear me. The twins mean to see Onaxos returned to the glory it knew in a more ancient, barbaric world. They will stop at nothing to achieve this. And your attack against the Seven Cities will serve as the ship from which they launch themselves upon the world. Do you want to see Seycherran children worshipping Taalo and Toora? Do you want to see your homeland turned into a city of white stone and mindless slaves? Do you want to answer to a pair of pale-haired demagogues who act on principles you cannot understand?"

As he spoke, he thought he saw something shift in Keleut's eyes, and in the silence that followed, he held out hope that she had not merely listened, but that she had truly heard him.

Keleut crushed that hope the moment she opened her mouth.

"I, too, am single-minded, Albus. The Seven Cities of Bellara must know that the world has not forgotten the Alescus."

She moved past him. Albus reached for her knees, willing to prostrate himself and beg if that was what it took. She sidestepped him neatly and Albus, on his hands and knees, felt the cool night air slip into the room as she opened the door.

Hopelessness was not a feeling Albus was accustomed to. In the Lordican, there was always a solution to a problem. Always a work-around or an alternative or an equation that made everything right. And yet as Albus struggled to his feet, his body suddenly too heavy, too cumbersome, he could see no solution. Never before had his mind felt so tired.

Keleut waited by the door. Albus's feet carried him there slowly, and as he stepped into the light beyond her chamber, he turned to look at her.

"Two things I will say to you now, Keleut, daughter of Nestor," he said, his voice soft. "You are not like them. You carry rage and pain and the burden of your people, but you are not like them." He took a breath, feeling again something of the certainty he had known on the sea wall. "The second is this. I may be your captive and I do not expect to survive this path to revenge, but know that I will fight you. With words, yes, but with tooth and nail if I must."

He expected an angry retort. Or at least grim dismissal. What he got was a smile tinged with something that might have been sadness as Keleut shut the door, leaving him alone to question his conviction.

39

"He's never been here in his life."

"I never imagined it would be beautiful."

The sprawling ruins of Elysium lay before Manon and Luca. It was not the dark-faced cliff looming behind that made it beautiful, nor the sparkling river that flowed swift and furious to the south, nor even the constant cloud of mist and spray created by the thunderous waterfall that joined cliff and river—though all these things played their part.

It was the way the once proud palace, razed by human hands, was now entangled so deeply with nature, as though it had always been thus. Soft moss crept across crumbled walls. Stalwart trees grew from cracked plazas, their exposed roots holding dominion over the stones. Twisting vines coiled down from broken arches, like a memory of the stones long destroyed.

Luca shifted next to Manon, his hand dropping to the hilt of the knife on his belt. She glanced over at him, alert to danger, but the look on the hunter's face did not indicate the presence of a threat. Instead, he looked out across the ruins of the Alescuan palace with trepidation. Reaching for the knife, she realized, was a reflection of his unease.

"What is it?"

"My gran's stories of stone circles and ancient things," he began. He flushed a little. "She spoke of folk wandering where they didn't belong, of the power of those places and what befell those who trespassed. I respected the stories because it seemed the right thing to do, not because

I ever felt any of that power."

Manon studied the young man's face, the way his brow creased, the way his eyes shifted over the ruined palace. She wondered if she ought to have found a way to make him remain in Arconia—or slipped away in the dead of night—but she withdrew the thought immediately. The dismissal startled her. Once she would have preferred to be alone because she found the presence of others a hindrance. Now she found she would not have wished to be in the shadow of the dead kings and queens without his steadiness beside her.

"And now?" she asked.

Luca didn't answer immediately and she could see him searching for the words to explain. "For all the beauty of this place, it's not a happy one." He looked at Manon. "Sometimes I can feel a Carrier's power. Not always. I didn't with you. But sometimes it's like there's a thread between us. Not tugging, not pulling, not painful. Just a connection." He returned his gaze to the ever-changing rainbow hues of the spray surging off the waterfall. "I feel that here. Stronger than I have ever felt it."

"Each of the thirteen kings and queens Carried," Manon said. "They were masters of their craft, among the most powerful Carriers of recorded history. I suppose some of that power could have leached into the stone and earth of Elysium."

Luca nodded, but, after the slightest hesitation, he looked at Manon once more. "By accident or deliberately?"

It was not a question Manon could answer—or wished to. Though her own Carrier talents paled in comparison, she had, since childhood, harbored conflicting feelings about the dynasty. The horrors and atrocities committed at their hands or on their orders were to be condemned. Of course. But Manon also knew the history that followed—the persecution of Carriers, driven by fear and a need to lash out at anything that bore resemblance to the hated despots who had ruled with cruelty in their left hands and insatiable hunger in their right. Even by Manon's lifetime, three centuries after the death of the last Alescuan ruler, those who Carried were often mistrusted, vilified, even sometimes forced to flee from homes their families had lived in since before the name of Alescu blackened the gift.

Manon had been fortunate. Her family's position and wealth, though recently acquired, and the cultured nature of the city of Arconia offered her a normal childhood. But she remembered listening at the door to her father's library, late at night, her ear pressed to the keyhole, and hearing of yet another attack in a small village, where superstition and ignorance could spark anger.

Manon shook off the silence. "Come. We might as well get this over with."

She urged her horse forward and crossed the final distance to Elysium, Luca trailing just behind.

"I still don't understand how your Archduke thinks there can be anything of value left here," Luca said when they dismounted in the middle of one of the large plazas. He looped his horse's reins over the branch of a thin, gnarled tree. "Looters would have stripped it bare long ago."

Manon shrugged. "I don't disagree with your theory. But I have my orders." She waited for him to start the argument—they'd had it once already on the journey from Arconia—about Manon's subservience to the Archduke. She had yet to mention her father to him, which left a gaping hole in any explanation she tried to form. But to her relief, Luca merely raised an eyebrow, more focused, Manon guessed, on the strange connection he was feeling to the ruins.

Manon, for her part, was trying—and failing—to determine the best way to start her search for the reliquary the Archduke believed to be somewhere in the ruins. "She would have known where to look," Manon muttered.

She had been unable to shake Eska de Caraval's face from her head since their brief, strained, and entirely unlooked for meeting at the Varadome—a fact that was just as irritating as the meeting itself had been.

"Who?"

"A self-centered bitch with more money than anyone ought to

have," Manon spat. "Not to mention the ability to pull strings to get her hands on anything." Luca raised an eyebrow again, but this time the look lingered. Manon sighed. "We crossed paths at the Varadome. Whenever I see her, I can't decide if I would rather burn her hair off or never set eyes on her again."

Luca smirked. "And yet you'd like her help right now."

"I didn't say that," Manon snapped. "Besides, she'd refuse."

"How do you know?" Luca asked the question softly.

Manon turned her back and began to stride across the shattered plaza, aiming toward the bulk of the remaining foundation—the throne room, or so the Archduke had said. Broken pillars wrapped in vines stretched no higher than Manon's head, crippled giants that had once reached to the sky and supported a ceiling of painted glass and slender, soaring arches of stone. Manon wondered if even a single shard of that famous glass survived in Elysium, buried under the weeds, or if every last piece had been taken by looters hoping for coin in exchange for something the Alescus had once touched—not that the kings and queens had raised so much as a finger to build their palace. It was said that all the slaves who labored over the palace for years, those that survived, that is, were slaughtered on the day of its completion.

Manon shook her head as though she could shake free the thoughts of the Alescuan kings and queens. They were dead, long dead, and there was no space for them, not when she had the Archduke laying a path before her feet, a path she couldn't see and a destination she didn't know.

And then there was Perrin. She had taken some solace in the Archduke's news and knowing Perrin was no longer in custody in Toridium—but what she longed to know the Archduke could not tell her. She tried to picture him, happy and carefree as he had once been, but always his face came to her as she had last seen it. And so his face joined the others—her father, Victor, even her mother—a silent host accompanying Manon everywhere.

The only indication the throne room had once deserved its name was the dais. It rose above the rest of the foundation, but only a step and a half survived. The rest was rubble, blocks of black stone veined with white. Manon closed her eyes and imagined the destruction—the dust, the noise, the angry triumph of those wielding two-handed hammers and driving long picks into the stones that had held the hated Alescus above everyone, above the world. Taking a deep breath, she opened her eyes and began an ordered search—not because she thought the care would yield a result but because it kept her from thinking of other things.

Luca joined her in silence but after a time the hunter stopped and straightened. He turned to the left and right, stretching his back muscles, and watched her. Manon could feel his gaze, but didn't look up and acknowledge him for fear it would spark further questions about Eska de Caraval.

"Manon," he said at length. She kept pulling up the tangle of vines in the northwest corner of the throne room. "Manon," he said again, louder the second time. "If you were Varin II and if you knew the rebellion was coming for you, what would you do?"

Frowning, Manon stopped pulling on the vines. She stood and glanced over at Luca, using one hand to shield her eyes from the sun. "He was waiting for them in the throne room. Everyone knows that."

"But why was he waiting here?"

Manon squinted at Luca. "Because he knew his forces were defeated. Because he wanted to die as a king on his throne?"

"You're a Carrier." Luca began to walk toward her. "Imagine you're Varin. You have powers most of us would never believe possible. You might know you'll die eventually, but your heart is full of wrath. What would you want to do?"

"I'd want to kill as many of them as possible before I died."

Luca came to a halt in front of her. He nodded slightly. "And would you choose the throne room as your last stand?"

Manon thought for a moment, trying to imagine the palace as it once had been. She couldn't, of course, not really. "I'd want to find high ground. Somewhere I could rain fire down on them like a storm of hail."

Luca nodded again. "Would anything prevent you from doing that?"

"No," she said, hesitating. "Unless it was more important that I protect something than kill a few weak enemies."

Luca smiled a little. "So you confront your enemy here, in this throne room, this place with no escape, with no cover, with no strategic importance. Because--"

"Because you don't want the enemy to go looking for you," Manon finished. "Because you don't want to risk them stumbling across something important."

The hunter's smile grew. "Exactly. We shouldn't be looking in here. If Varin had the reliquary when he died and if it was as important as your Archduke believes it was, it wouldn't be anywhere near his throne."

Manon gestured around them. "That still leaves us a lot of ground to cover."

Luca shrugged. "It would help if we knew more about the palace. And I wouldn't mind knowing what was so important to an Alescuan king that he would give up his chance to fight. I don't suppose we'll ever know either of those things."

Something in Luca's words flickered in Manon's mind, like a memory of a flame illuminating something important—but like a star in the night sky, the harder she looked for it, the faster it vanished. Shaking her head, Manon scanned the ruins around them. She had no desire to ponder the whims of dead kings. "I suppose we might as well start by looking on the outskirts of the ruins. We know the Tribunes and the rebel army approached from the west, just like we did. Varin would have seen them coming and the cliff might have offered a hiding place." She watched Luca's face for confirmation, knowing she was grasping at air.

"East, then," he said. "It's something."

They trudged through the ruins, weaving among walls no higher than their knees, dry fountains with the mosaics chiseled away, and endless piles of broken stone shrouded in moss and vines and small purple flowers. The mist grew heavier as they moved closer to the waterfall and Manon welcomed the cool water on her skin. The roar of the waterfall soon drowned out all hope of speech, so Manon and Luca communicated with gestures. As they reached the eastern-most edge of the ruins, where the walls had abutted the cliff, they separated, Luca heading north, Manon south toward the waterfall.

She wandered, abandoning the precision she had adopted in the throne room—but then, what really was she even looking for? A trap door in the stone? A cave in the cliff? What could she possibly see that had escaped the countless feet crossing the same stones in search of treasure for hundreds of years?

What she saw was another person.

A faint outline in the mist, nothing more than a shape that might have been a head with shoulders below it. The drifting spray swirled and Manon frowned, trying to decide if she had imagined it.

And then the mist parted, as though by an invisible hand, and Manon's heart stopped for a moment.

"Perrin?"

He appeared not to hear. He stood in profile to Manon, still as a statue. The waterfall spray gusted between them, threatening to swallow him from view. Manon took two hurried steps forward, but then hesitated, the memory of their last moments in Toridium wedging into the empty space between them.

"Perrin?" she tried again, but her voice was lost in the waterfall—or perhaps that was just the blood rushing in her own ears. He began to walk, his movement strangely uncoordinated, like a man still half asleep or hampered by injury. Manon hurried after him, calling his name repeatedly to no response. Stepping nimbly over a fallen pillar, she caught him quickly and reached a hand out to touch his shoulder.

He flinched at her touch but turned slowly, and his expression was guarded as he faced Manon, his eyes not quite meeting hers.

"Perrin? Are you all right?" Manon asked. Then the words that had sat like a stone in her heart since that day in Toridium tumbled forth. "I was trying to protect you. Please. Forgive me." He said nothing.

Indeed, he didn't seem to have heard her. "Perrin, I know you're angry," Manon went on, but her voice failed against the force of his empty expression. He turned away and continued walking in the same direction.

Not guarded, Manon realized. Not angry. Her brother wasn't avoiding her, wasn't punishing her. He didn't know her.

◄ ● ►

They had been following Perrin all afternoon. He wandered aimlessly through the ruins of Elysium, never stopping, never acknowledging their presence. He appeared to have traveled on foot without supplies, and his clothes were stained with sweat and dirt. Manon had not seen Perrin look so disheveled since he was a small boy.

Luca came to a halt and propped one foot up on a block of stone, his eyes following Perrin, who was circling a large pile of rubble for the fifth time.

"You're sure he wasn't wounded?" It was not the first time Luca had posed the question.

Manon didn't answer. She'd already answered it three times. The truth was she didn't know. There was no outward appearance of injury, no head wound. And though he hadn't met her gaze, Perrin hadn't appeared to be suffering from addled vision. And yet she could think of no other reason for his behavior.

"What do you want to do?" Luca asked.

That was a new question, but not one Manon wanted to answer, either. She certainly didn't want to leave Perrin there, but neither did she want to forcibly seize him. If he resisted, Luca was strong enough to inadvertently hurt him. If he was frightened, she feared they would only make it worse.

"I don't think he's lost," Luca said. "He might not be himself, but he knows where he is."

Manon glanced sharply at the hunter. "Why do you say that? He's never been here in his life."

Luca shifted his boot on the stone, that crease Manon was beginning to know so well forming between his eyes. He seemed reluctant to speak.

Manon folded her arms across her chest. "Tell me."

He sighed. "It reminds me of an animal whose home has been disturbed. A bird, maybe. I've seen it plenty of times. They'll fly from tree to tree, circling around the destroyed nest. I think they're looking for the baby birds. Or for signs of a predator. Or just trying to understand what happened." Luca glanced at Manon. "Foxes will do it, too."

"He's never been here," Manon repeated, more sharply than she intended. Luca stepped off the stone and held up both hands, as though warding off the anger that threatened to spill over.

"As you say." The mildness in his voice, the careful tone, was somehow worse than if he had taken offense. Luca nodded in Perrin's direction. "He's on the move."

They continued the strange game of follow the leader through the waning hours of the day. Manon only made one more attempt to interact with her brother, to reach him through whatever haze shrouded his mind. She approached as he studied the cracks in a small plaza that might have once been a courtyard—but that time the gentle touch on his arm earned her something other than a blank expression. He snapped his head around to look at her and Manon recoiled against the fury flashing in his eyes. It vanished almost immediately and the blank emptiness returned as his gaze slid beyond her, but Manon could not keep from trembling as she watched him walk away. Perrin's eyes had always been green, the irises ringed with a golden yellow. The savage rage she had seen in those eyes that ought to have been her brother's had burned in a sea of brilliant blue.

She had cried then, the tears rolling silently down her cheeks. Luca, who had watched her attempt at communication from a discreet distance, came close but stopped just out of reach, hovering, waiting.

"It's not him," she said at last. Her voice broke, but the words were like a barricade wrestled into place to stem the tears. She took a deep breath. Not to reach for calm or composure—the look in her brother's eyes had just pushed calm and composure off a cliff, leaving Manon teetering precariously close to the same fate. She took that breath to curse her father, to channel her fear and her pain into something she could blame. Julian Barca was an easy—and oft-used—target.

She didn't have the chance to get the words out.

A blinding flash of light streaked to the earth, a bolt of white fire from the sky. Manon looked away just as it struck somewhere deep in the ruins of Elysium—and sent a thunderous wave of air surging out in a perfect circle from the point of impact.

She never saw it coming.

The wave hit Manon and Luca, sending them flying through the air with such speed and force that they were thrown clear of the ruins of the palace—except there were no more ruins. Manon struck the ground, skidding through dirt and grass, her disoriented vision glimpsing the emptiness that had been Elysium. Every pillar, every wall, every stone had disintegrated to dust that still fell like dry rain. Gone. Nothing was left.

Nothing, that is, except the lone figure standing precisely where the bolt of fire had struck the earth.

Manon blinked, her mind a maelstrom of apprehension and pain. And then she slipped into that place between death and dreams.

Interlude 18

Excerpt from a decoded military report, now considered one of the keys to the Alescuan defeat, sent from a spy in the Alescu palace of Elysium to Titianus, Tribune of Vienisi, during the last days of the Great Rising—the spy's true name and fate are unknown

The prisoner has agreed to help. I have accepted her terms, as instructed, though I ask the good god Oru nightly how we shall make right on our part of the bargain. You know, Tribune, of my reluctance and my concern that allowing her everything she asks for will only see our moment of victory turn to ash—but I suppose we are far past reluctance and concern. It is done and I shall not look back or falter.

In addition to the Trueblade, I have at last discovered the location of the prisoners from the battles at Montalois and Anavairre. Those that have not been slaughtered for sport or for experimentation are being kept in an underground compound east of Elysium and I understand that more than two-thirds are still alive. You know as well as I do that these numbers could mean the difference between victory and defeat. I have included a map of sorts, which I trust you can decipher. Our time of opportunity is limited, however, as the prisoners are due to be moved to another location before the end of summer. You know how suspicious Varin is—this information was not easily obtained and I think it unlikely I'll be able to do so again after the move is made, not without drawing too much attention.

I have also, when time allows, been working on stockpiling the items requested by the Tribunes. Despite placing this message under code,

I dare not write the location at this time. Trust that you will know where to find them when the time comes—when you are ready to storm the walls of Elysium.

May the strong arm of Oru protect you and all our noble Tribunes. Though I know you do not share my faith, I hope you will allow me to beseech my god for your preservation. Elysium is a dark, mind-fouling place and I find myself in deep need of his presence. May our warriors remain stout of heart and mind. May the Seven Cities know freedom from tyranny.

Yours in all good faith,
Zachaire, Varin's Bane

40

*"I refuse to believe an evangelist has swayed you from
your palace of knowledge."*

"Everything hurts."

The horse didn't seem overly concerned but it did stand still as Eska draped her arms over the saddle and sank against it, her face buried in its warm black coat.

The journey back across the extensive Varadome gardens had been a painful one and Eska was sure every limping step would be her last. Surely dark figures were about to hurtle out of the night and tackle her to the ground. Surely Alexandre was about to emerge from behind every hedge, every statue, every fountain and arrest her. But her progress was unimpeded, save for the ankle that threatened to collapse underneath her.

She didn't regret jumping. And in the grand scheme of things, the look of shock on Alexandre de Minos's face as she vaulted off the roof was worth the painful landing—though she suspected she might feel differently by the time she made it home. The horse flicked its ears, reminding Eska not to linger, and she pulled herself up into the saddle.

They took the long way home, keeping to the outskirts of the city, and the eastern horizon was a pleasant shade of pink by the time she guided the horse up the de Caraval drive. By then, the harrow root was keeping her upright in the saddle and Eska wanted nothing more than to crawl into her bed—no, a bath. No, food. She settled on the idea of food in the bath—and mint tea to help the inflammation burgeoning in her ankle—and dismounted outside the stable. Despite her best efforts, her ankle jarred painfully against the ground, and Eska's fingers wrapped into the horse's mane were all that kept her from crumpling. She closed her eyes and swallowed down the pain as best she could.

"Rough night?"

The harrow root reacted and Eska whirled on her injured foot, pulling the handle free from the walking stick once more.

Eden San-Germain slid free from the shadow of a flowering tree and stepped into the grey light, concern spreading on his face as he moved. "Eska?"

"What are you doing here?" Eska tried to hold herself up right. At least the dagger was steady in her hand.

"Are you all right?"

Eska took a halting step forward, her face twisting with pain. "Answer me," she hissed through a locked jaw.

"Eska, you're hurt. Let me help you." He had the sense to stay where he was.

Eska shook her head. "No." A humorless laugh escaped her lips. "Do you know, you're the second man I've pointed this at tonight. Did you think to ambush me? Take me back to your Tribune? You might think again if you knew what I did this morning." The faces of the Iron Baron's dead men swam suddenly before her, surging back into her mind.

"By all the gods, Eska, I am not your enemy."

"I've already found enemies where I would not have expected them today. And you need something I have no intention of giving you. Walk away, Eden."

He did as she said, though only after a long silence, his eyes never wavering from hers. When he turned his back to her at last, Eska gasped in a breath, her ankle screaming at the weight it was being asked to bear. But she didn't move until he passed through the arched gate of the de Caraval complex and was out of sight. Only then did she drop the handle of the walking stick and sink to the ground, fighting back tears, willing the harrow root to take away her pain.

How long she remained there, she could not have said. But her cheeks were dry when she rose and both the house and stables were stirring with the first signs of morning activity. Steeling herself, Eska raised her voice and called for one of the grooms. A boy hurried out, tugging a cap over his hair as he went, and took the borrowed horse from Eska, leading it into the stable.

She limped into the house, using the glass-walled garden entrance and taking the spiral staircase to her chambers. She made it within an arm's length of her door before she vomited and collapsed.

— • —

Eska was desperately thirsty. The rain on the windowpanes wasn't helping.

She opened her eyes and turned on her side to reach for the glass of water she always kept by her bed. She found her father instead.

He was asleep, his chin hovering over his chest, a book splayed across one knee. Eska sank back against her pillows, her memories rushing back to her. With them came awareness of a stiffness in her limbs. It wasn't just the stiffness that sometimes lingers after a long period of heavy sleep. Eska stretched and curled her fingers against the blankets, but they remained heavy and cumbersome, as though they weren't quite connected to her body.

The sensation was consistent throughout her torso, hips, and legs, but Eska managed to push herself into a seated position. From there she surveyed the room. She had been dressed in a nightgown. A cup of tea sat on a tray at her father's feet. Judging by the lack of steam and the way the flecks of tealeaves were clustered at the bottom of the cup, it had been there for some time. Rain spattered against the tall windows of her bedchamber in fat drops. The sky beyond was dark with mottled grey clouds.

Eska shifted to the edge of her bed and swung her legs over. She came to her feet unsteadily and was immediately scolded by her ankle for her efforts. Grimacing, she limped her way to the bath chamber and relieved herself, then splashed water from the washbasin onto her face.

When she limped back to her bed, her father stirred, the book tumbling from his knee and landing with a loud thud on the floor.

"Eska!" He burst from the chair and took her hand. "You're awake." The tone of his voice gave Eska pause and she began to understand that she had been asleep for longer than a single night. Maximilian de Caraval helped her back under the blankets, his gaze flickering anxiously over her.

"Papa," Eska said, her voice dry and quiet, "you haven't sat at my bedside since I was a child." She reached for the glass of water and Maximilian held it out for her. Eska took a long drink. "Was it bad?" she asked at last.

Her father was trying, she could see, to answer her question as though she had asked after the weather. He didn't quite manage it. "Alize found you. Outside your door. You were unresponsive." He glanced away from Eska for a moment. "We put you to bed. The doctors didn't know what was wrong." She reached for his hand and squeezed it. "You slept for two days."

"A friend was ill recently," Eska said, thinking of Perrin. "Perhaps I was struck by the same thing he had." But that was a lie. She knew what had caused her collapse, what was still causing her muscles and tendons to function as though caught in molasses. But telling her father she had taken four spoonfuls of harrow root powder—four, when two was considered a strong dose—was out of the question. Sorina and Maximilian de Caraval had no knowledge of her occasional use of the powder.

Part of Eska's mind, the analytical part, was already cataloging the experience, her symptoms, the time it had taken the powder to act and then cause her to crash, the time it had taken her to recover—not to mention the way it had released her inhibitions. She could still feel the gaze of the stars and the rush of air as she leaped from the roof of the Varadome.

The other part of Eska was still very tired. She squeezed her father's hand again and then let go. "I'm sorry to have worried you, Papa. Mama, too."

"Your mother doesn't know. She was sent to Rhia."

Eska smiled. "Then maybe we don't have to tell her."

Maximilian didn't answer her smile. "There's something else, Eska." He sat on the edge of the bed. "Alexandre de Minos came. The first day of your illness. He said the matter was urgent. Naturally, I told him you were gravely ill and that speaking to you was impossible." Her father hesitated for a moment. "He's very good at not revealing his thoughts. You know that. But I had the impression that he didn't believe me."

"I may have given him a reason to doubt anything you chose to say in that moment."

Maximilian studied Eska, his expression hovering somewhere between absolution and censure, his indecision a product of her illness. She would, she knew, have to explain herself eventually.

Her father stood. "Two more things. I don't suppose you know what happened in the east guest room?"

Eska sighed. "Not exactly." She told him of Perrin, the strange illness, and his subsequent disappearance—taking care not to identify him by his family name, though her father was not likely to be as reactionary to the name Barca as her uncle. "I alerted Roscoe, but I didn't know what else to do." She glanced out the window. "I fear he has come to harm while I slept."

"You can hardly be faulted for your own illness," Maximilian said. False, but a necessary deception. "If he's truly missing, I can arrange a search using the Varadome's authority and resources."

He wasn't wrong. But Eska did not think she ought to get within sighting distance of the Varadome. "And the second?"

He withdrew a letter from his waistcoat pocket. "This arrived this morning." Eska reached for it, but Maximilian frowned and held it just beyond her reach. "If you're sure you're well enough."

"I'm well enough to read a letter. Perhaps it's from Perrin."

Her father nodded and handed it to her. He looked as though he wanted to say something else, but after a moment he pressed his lips together, nodded, and retreated from her chambers.

As the sound of his footsteps died away, Eska closed her eyes and let herself sink into the pillows for just a moment—a moment that turned into many. When she awoke again, the letter was still in her hand. Eska straightened, blinking away sleep. She took a drink of water and pulled the bell cord next to her bed, suddenly famished. Alize hurried into the room a moment later and Eska requested tea and a plate of bread, cheese, and fruit spreads.

Only after the maid left did Eska open the letter. The handwriting startled her into a seated position. Albus.

She began to devour his words eagerly, but each sentence deepened the furrow in her forehead. His words made only slightly more sense than if he had written them in another language, but taken as a whole, she would not have believed the letter a product of Albus's mind. She turned the paper over, thinking to find a continuation or at the very least a hastily scrawled note—but there was nothing on the reverse.

"What on earth are you going on about, Albus?" Eska murmured. She started again at the beginning.

I am directing this letter to your family home in Arconia. I can only hope it reaches you, wherever you are, in a timely manner.

That was simple enough. Albus had written to her weeks before in Toridium, but he couldn't know if she was still there.

And now I must beg pardon for my unexpected departure. I received word that my aunt had fallen ill and, as her only living family member, I have traveled to her bedside to do what I can for her.

"Albus, you haven't spoken to your family since you ran away from home. Forgive me if I don't understand why a sick aunt would be asking for you."

Her condition is serious and I expect to be here for some time. She speaks of strange things in her sleep, most often a masked eagle, and I find I can only give her small comforts. I ask that you pray to all seven gods for her recovery, though perhaps it would be better to pray for a painless and easy death.

Curious. Albus was politely but resolutely anti-divinity. "I refuse to believe an evangelist has swayed you from your palace of knowledge," Eska muttered.

Do not fear that I neglect my work. I have, however, left behind that treatise you and I spoke of, the one by the six monks of Altiere.

"Utter nonsense. We haven't spoken of any treatise recently, and certainly not one written by monks."

Perhaps you can provide a better translation of the passage about the lettering and symbols on the Ulyssian tomb.

Eska paused after that sentence, her mind hovering over the uncanny similarity between this unfamiliar tomb Albus mentioned and the de Ulyssey family name.

Messengers are hard to come by, as you know, in these small mountain villages, so I cannot anticipate when next I might be able to write to you. Please pass along my greetings to our friend Val. I look forward to a time when we can all be together as we once were.

"Val?" Albus had met Eska's uncle, but to refer to Valentin de Caraval as his friend—and by a shortened name only Maximilian used, and even then rarely—was absurd.

Her thoughts were interrupted by Alize's return and Eska used the distraction of cheese and tea to, well, distract her from Albus's cryptic words—for that was what they were, she decided. Deliberately ambiguous for reasons only Albus knew. When Alize departed for the second time, Eska got out of bed, desperate to do something other than lie still.

Her pacing was an embarrassment to the definition of the word, but Eska felt better for having her blood flowing once more, and so she limped slowly around the room, pausing at the rain-streaked windows every now and then, Albus's words running through her mind on endless repeat.

During one particularly painful turn on the floorboards, Eska's ankle gave out. As she caught herself on the edge of her writing desk, her gaze landed on the ivory and gold reliquary sitting on the mantel over her dormant fireplace.

The pieces of Albus's letter tumbled into place.

"Forget the aunt," Eska said. "That was for the benefit of whoever was reading your letter, so they knew you were trying to give me an excuse for your absence." The words flowed from her. "Six monks for six Godforged. You didn't leave a treatise behind. You hid a god disc before leaving Arconia. There is no Ulyssian tomb, you needed to warn me that de Ulyssey is involved." Eska laughed. "Would have saved me the need to trespass at the Varadome, but now I know without a doubt de Ulyssey is seeking the Hands of Fate—and so is our mutual friend Val, who is neither our friend nor likely to enjoy being called Val." Eska took a breath. "Valexi Arcturos de Vauquelin-Preux, Archduke of Arconia." Eska limped across the room and came to a halt in front of the reliquary. "But a masked eagle? Seven gods? And why a reference to Altiere, Albus? Where are you?"

Altiere was a region of Sandalese far north of the Anerrean Sea. Eska turned to the closest window and pressed her forehead against the glass, trying to comb through her brain for a reason the librarian would mention a remote place known for its wine and its fruit orchards.

She thought she might know the answer to the last question—well, not exactly. Albus had clearly been detained and prevented from contacting Eska sooner. There was no telling where he was that very moment. But perhaps he had been headed for Altiere.

It was a logical assumption, if not for the fact that Albus preferred the known to the unknown. His world was the Lordican, not the vastness that lay outside its walls. She could not imagine him choosing to undertake such a journey.

"What could have driven you from Arconia?" Eska whispered. The answer, she felt, lay in the missing scroll from Ardemis the Deceiver's collection on the Hands of Fate. Something had propelled the scholar to take action. It was a more disturbing realization than knowing the Archduke was hunting for Godforged.

Her breath fogged the glass, imitating how Eska's mind felt. Sighing, she pushed herself off the window and turned back to the reliquary.

Her fingers brushed the smooth ivory and she ran her thumb across the golden stag's back. Her thumb slipped below the stag's belly and she, entertaining the rather foolish notion that the markings on the god disc might at long last make sense, lifted the lid.

It was empty.

———•—•—•———

The conclusion—reluctantly arrived at but admittedly logical—was that Perrin had taken the disc.

Eska no longer suspected her uncle had returned to the house and dragged Perrin from his bed. Rather she began to suspect that perhaps Valentin had not been far off the mark when he had suggested Perrin and Manon Barca had schemed against Firenzia from the start.

And yet Eska could still hear the strain in Perrin's voice when he had spoken of Manon, could see the pain on his face at the thought that his sister had, like the rest of his family, abandoned him. Eska did not think that an act.

And yet—there were many and yets, she began to realize—what other reason could he have to abscond with the god disc, an artifact they still did not comprehend fully. Perhaps Perrin hoped to find Manon and offer the disc to her as a token of his forgiveness. Perhaps he had discovered something of the disc's power and had claimed it for himself. Perhaps he believed Manon and her Carrier skills could wield it. Perhaps he hoped to sell it and use the money to pull Barca Company back from the brink of collapse.

Perhaps this, perhaps that. Eska came to a sudden halt at the foot of her bed and pulled herself out of the maze of swirling possibilities made all the more alluring by the sting of Perrin's betrayal. She forced herself to focus on the facts, such as they were, and arrive at a course of action. And though she longed to seek out and confront Perrin, there was a larger problem.

"The Archduke must not be allowed to collect all six discs."

As Eska said the words out loud, the final piece of Albus's puzzle fell into place. Six discs. Seven gods, he'd written. Not six discs. Seven. And the seventh was in Altiere.

Eska resumed her pacing, the pain in her ankle a dull ache she refused to acknowledge. Albus had also hidden a disc, the one Eska had discovered in the Iron Baron's reliquary, which left Eska with a choice. Stay in Arconia, search for the hidden disc, and face the wrath of Thibault de Venescu and charges of trespassing from the Varadome and murder from Toridium. Or take inspiration from a librarian who had been frightened enough by whatever he had learned about the seventh disc to leave his beloved library, his work, and everything he knew and held dear to go in search of it.

She didn't expect she could do both. But then a knock on her door gave her the means and knowledge to do just that.

"My lady? A gift has arrived from your mother."

"Come in, Alize," Eska called, impatient and eager to be alone once more.

The maid entered and presented Eska with a large, slender box tied up with black ribbon.

Eska frowned. "From my mother?"

Alize nodded. "She mentioned it before leaving the city. Said she'd ordered you a mask for the masquerade."

"I'm not going to the masquerade," Eska said, then shook her head. "Very well, Alize, you can leave it."

When the maid had gone, Eska untied the ribbon and lifted the lid from the box. She pulled the tissue paper away, curious as to what her mother might have chosen.

"Oh," she said, when the mask was revealed.

It was astonishingly beautiful. Intricate. Luxurious. But that was not why Eska found herself speechless, her heart racing.

"A masked eagle," she breathed out, her fingers reaching to stroke the mask's glossy red hawk feathers and the sharp beak. "Albus, it seems you've planned for me to go to the midsummer masquerade after all."

41

"Because the world needs saving, apparently."

ONCE, THE SIGHT OF THE VARADOME'S SPECTACLE HALL DECORATED opulently and filled to the brim with the luxurious finery and alluring masks of the wealthy denizens of Arconia would have filled Eska with delight.

But as she disembarked from an unmarked carriage and slid her lion mask down onto her face—not the hawk that would so readily identify her—under the light of a slivered moon, Eska was feeling a great many things, none of which were delight.

Curiosity was perhaps the kindest of those feelings—curiosity as to who she would find in an eagle mask that night. But mostly she was a storm of harsher, harder emotions, calculation perhaps above all. After all, somewhere amid the masked faces would be the Archduke of Arconia, who was trying to frame her for a murder he arranged, and very likely Thibault de Venescu, who was trying to murder her himself. As much as she might wish it otherwise, meeting with Albus's mysterious eagle was not all she could concern herself with. She needed to stay alive.

Perrin's knife was strapped to her calf, beneath the red silk swirling around her legs. It seemed to Eska that it was not just a knife. That night it was sorrow and misplaced trust. The memory of a conversation about abandoning family lurked just below Eska's heart—and was why she had hastily swallowed a cold harrow tea moments before climbing into the carriage. Her sickness and ordeal was not forgotten. Hence the single spoonful added to the tea. But Eska had to face the Varadome alone that night—and the harrow root could very nearly convince her otherwise.

She wondered if Manon Barca was in the crowd.

And then there was Alexandre, who would be looking for her and who would, above all others, be most able to spot her beneath a disguise.

Eska adjusted the mask one last time, lifted her chin, and ascended the steps to the Varadome's grand entrance. When she was admitted and passed through the wide golden doors, she surveyed the Spectacle Hall from the top of the sweeping marble staircase.

There were, she realized with the sort of slow dawning she did not often experience, fountains on the ceiling.

Water jetted in graceful arcs across the massive dome—and nary a drop fell on the revelers below.

A quick glance along the balconies lining the dome just above Eska's head showed her the Carriers, three of them, controlling the streams. She wondered how long they could keep up the necessary concentration. The effect was, she had to admit, quite enchanting.

Eska undid the clasp of her cloak and let the black velvet fall away to reveal the red dress beneath. It was worthy of a lioness, unapologetically fierce, demanding of attention—perhaps not quite what one should wear when one does not wish to stand out, but Eska found she could not convincingly explain to Alize why, after suddenly changing her mind about the masquerade, she might not wish to wear a dress that would spark the imagination of all in attendance. The maid had prattled on about Arch-Commander de Minos—surely he wouldn't be able to take his eyes off her and didn't she long to see him again?—her mouth running faster than a mountain stream as she asked Eska questions Eska did not much care to answer.

The dress had the intended, if undesired, effect. Despite the masks shielding the many faces below, Eska could see eyes shift to take her in, and as the musicians struck up the next dance, a sedate, formal piece, and Eska descended the stairs, three men approached, each asking to dance with the lioness.

She chose the one wearing a heron mask, glad for the chance to slip into the dance and be less conspicuous in the crowd. He danced well enough and tried to make amusing conversation, but Eska was so intent on scanning the crowd for any sign of eagle feathers that the heron soon grew tired of her dull responses and they finished the dance in silence.

As the heron drifted away in obvious disappointment, Eska retreated from the dance floor in search of refreshment and a better vantage point. She had no sooner settled into relative obscurity between a golden elephant and a waterfall cascading down the side of the dome, than a voice, disembodied by Eska's compromised vision, appeared at her elbow.

"I knew I would not be disappointed tonight."

Eska froze, trying to place the muffled voice, certain for a moment that it was the Iron Baron.

"Surely it was fate that brought us here together."

And then a lion swung into sight and Eska could have laughed out loud. She smiled instead. "Never have I seen a lion with such a magnificent mane." This was no lie.

"Nor I a lioness so beautiful. Will you honor me with a dance?"

To refuse was another path to unwanted attention. And so Eska was whirled into the dancing throng once more. She was spared from speaking by the faster pace of the dance, and the lion was a lively partner with nimble feet and a pleasant laugh. By the time the music finished, Eska was aware she had very nearly enjoyed herself. But when the lion went in search of wine and failed to return within the span of the next two dances, Eska, after finding her own wine, abandoned the ballroom floor and claimed an unoccupied balcony for herself. She tucked herself into the corner of the balcony, just beyond the fringe of its velvet curtain, trying to observe without being observed.

Every feather called out to her. Every beak caught her eye. Peacocks, gulls, falcons, parrots—but no eagles.

As the night wore on, Eska became convinced of two things. That she had misinterpreted Albus's letter and that Alexandre de Minos was not in attendance at the midsummer masquerade. She was musing on the latter, her mind speculating, perhaps unfairly, that he was away from the city to collect more Carriers for the Archduke, when the woman screamed.

Eska saw a figure fall, saw the crowd below react in radiating circles outward, heard the musicians grind to a tentative halt, heard the silence before the whispers began. She also saw a knife flash and then vanish—or at least she thought she did.

The woman would live. This was the news put forth by a steward after the woman was carried away, called out in a loud, strong voice, as though the voice could imbue the words with truth. Eska wanted to believe it, but thought it just as likely the Archduke, wherever he was, wished his party to continue unmarred by the specter of death. The small smear of blood was quickly wiped from the floor, the musicians were ushered into a bawdy tune. No mention was made by the steward of a culprit brought to justice, no acknowledgment at all that the woman had almost certainly not plunged the knife into her own abdomen.

It was painfully obvious to Eska, and she was no doubt encouraged in this line of thinking by the harrow root, that the woman had been mistaken for her. She had been wearing a falcon mask, easily mistaken for a hawk if one was careless and not inclined to wonder about such things. The quality of her dress was unmistakable, her jewelry a stunning display. And the Iron Baron would not much care if he were wrong. Of this Eska was certain. She had eluded him for far too long. Thibault de Venescu would litter the Varadome with innocent dead if he got what he was seeking in the end.

Suddenly it seemed very foolish indeed to be alone at the Varadome, mask or no mask. Eska stood and turned to leave her balcony—only to stumble into a lion.

She made herself smile. "And here I thought I would never get that glass of wine."

The lion did not smile back, did not so much as move. Eska felt the hairs on her arms stand up. And then a hand was raised and the mask pushed back.

"I had to be sure it was you," Sylvain de Ulyssey said. "You can take off the mask, Lady de Caraval."

Eska did, if only to free her vision and her movement should she need to go for her knife. Perrin's knife.

"Much better," he said, smiling. "You're fortunate our mutual friend Thibault doesn't have as good an eye as I do."

Eska's sharp inhale made de Ulyssey laugh. "Have no fear, my dear, I'm not that sort of man and I certainly have no intention of turning you over to him."

"What do you want, then?" Eska asked, relieved to hear her voice was calm. Her mind was not. It was too busy trying to calculate if she could swing down from the balcony without hurting herself, or if she would be better off trying to push past de Ulyssey and escaping down the stairs. The fanciful notion that she might manage to throw him over the balcony was considered for more than a heartbeat.

"I'm looking for a librarian."

Eska fought to contain her surprise. This wasn't about her adventure in his private quarters. This was about Albus. If he knew about the smashed reliquary, he hadn't connected her to it.

"I know quite a few librarians, my lord."

"Yes, so I'm told. This one is called Courtenay. I believe you and he are quite close."

Denying it seemed fruitless. But she didn't have to give him everything. "We are acquainted."

Sylvain de Ulyssey narrowed his eyes—he was not, as it turned out, as composed as his friend the Archduke. He recovered quickly. "Master Courtenay, you see, was doing research for me and I'm afraid he's run off with something from my private collection." This gave Eska pause. Perhaps he did know about the smashed reliquary and suspected Albus of the crime. But the ivory box had been empty, the Godforged already removed. Surely de Ulyssey knew that? Or was he merely talking about the missing scroll from the collection of Ardemis the Deceiver? Eska forced her mind to stop whirling.

"I'm afraid I haven't seen Master Courtenay in weeks, my lord. I've been away from Arconia."

This was true. But Eska felt her heart leap into her throat because she had just seen an eagle.

The masked figure, cloak billowing behind, was disappearing down the stairwell over Sylvain de Ulyssey's shoulder. Eska could only hope her face was as empty as the mask in her hands.

"Understand, my lady," de Ulyssey was saying, "this is a serious matter. The Lordican has been extremely unsatisfying in their response. If the item is returned to me soon, I will be lenient on the young man, but if this goes on any longer, I will be forced to mete out harsher justice. We cannot be seen to allow those who answer to us to go unpunished." He appeared to be in no hurry to move out of her way.

"Of course not, my lord, but if you'll excuse me, I am expected below." Eska pulled the mask back over her face.

Sylvain de Ulyssey contemplated her for a long moment. "You will give Master Courtenay my message if you see him?"

"I will, my lord." And then she was gone, brushing past him as he shifted to let her pass.

Naturally, the eagle was nowhere to be found. Eska hurried down to the Spectacle Hall's main level as quickly as she could without drawing unwanted eyes. She scanned the crowd as she threaded her way along the outer edge of the dome, pushing past a disheveled goldfish, bumping into a monkey pontificating to a fern. She had just squeezed past a horse getting very friendly with a duck when she caught a glimpse of golden brown feathers and a sharp yellow beak through the crowd. The eyes behind the mask were staring straight at her.

Eska nodded toward an alcove to her right. The eagle disappeared in the crowd, then reappeared closer. They reached the alcove at the same moment, but the eagle didn't stop moving.

"Outside," the eagle said. A woman's voice. "The rose garden." And then she was gone.

She was waiting at the edge of a reflecting pool.

The mask was gone, discarded on a stone bench. The woman watched Eska approach.

"You know Albus?" Eska asked.

"Wouldn't be here if I didn't. Wouldn't know to look for you." The woman crossed her arms in front of her chest. She was older than Eska. Skinny with collarbones that jutted up above the neckline of her dress. The garment was an older style, Eska realized, the sort of thing a woman might have worn at the Varadome ten years before.

"I suppose that's true enough. Who are you?"

"A friend of Albus's." The woman's mouth quirked upward but no smile followed. "You're wondering if you can trust me. I could say the same of you. My lady." The woman added in the deferential address as an afterthought.

Eska spread her hands in front of her. "You have something for me. I don't need to know your name or how you know Albus or how you got here tonight. I just need what he left in your keeping."

"And what do I get in return?"

Eska studied her right hand for a moment and then removed a golden ring studded with tiny rubies. She held it up, letting what little light the garden offered catch the gold. She tossed it. The woman caught it deftly and peered at it.

"You won't be able to sell it without attracting attention," Eska said. "But if you bring it to a man named Gustini at the Firenzia Company offices, he'll see that you're properly compensated with coin in exchange for the ring." She could see the woman frown slightly over this proposition, but then the ring disappeared into her bodice and she reached behind her back. It took Eska a moment to understand that she was loosening the ties of her gown.

"Can I help?"

"You can stay right there." It was said without malice, but the warning was clear enough. Eska waited. At last the woman tugged free what she was searching for and held it out to Eska.

The disc was crumpled in on itself, a nebulous shape in the darkness. But Eska would know it anywhere.

"I take it you're satisfied."

"I am," Eska said, her voice quiet. The woman nodded and bent down to set the crumbled bronze on the bench next to the eagle mask.

"I hope he's all right, you know."

The words brought Eska's attention back to the woman's face. "Albus? Do you know where he is? What did he say?"

The woman shrugged. "Don't know anything. He just asked me to keep that thing until you came for it. Said it might be tonight and that I should wear that ridiculous mask. But he seemed worried."

Eska closed her eyes. "I hope he's all right, too." When she opened them, the woman was already moving away, retreating back into the light of the Varadome, the eagle mask forgotten. Eska went to the bench and knelt, her hand hovering over the disc. She plucked it from the cold stone.

"Seven," Eska whispered. "And I only have one."

———— ◆ ————

"I know this puts you in a difficult position. Just tell me if I am correctly interpreting the laws that govern the company."

The lawyer Pierro Gustini looked across the desk at Eska, his glasses magnifying the trepidation in his eyes. Morning light streamed through the windows of Maximilian de Caraval's library.

"My lady, there is no legal reason why you cannot do exactly as you say. You are, after all, an equal partner in Firenzia Company. Your uncle cannot stop you from doing any of these hypothetical things you have questioned me about. I might, however, argue that any number of other reasons might exist to act as counterpoint to that."

"I don't pay you for your other reasons, Master Gustini," Eska said, getting to her feet. "You're sure my uncle intends to depart this afternoon?"

The lawyer also stood, his hat caught in a death grip between his hands. "Yes, the weather is cooperating. He said he had no wish to delay any further."

Eska nodded. "Very well. That will be all, provided you have the information I asked you to bring regarding our friend the Iron Baron."

The lawyer reached down and produced a sheaf of papers from the case resting against his chair. "Indeed, my lady, I have what you requested. The evidence was abundant, if one knew where to look, and de Venescu has grown overconfident in his power."

Eska took the papers. "And your professional opinion of it?"

Pierro Gustini's lips pressed together in what passed for a smile. Eska knew it was as close to satisfaction as he ever came to expressing. "Watertight, my lady."

"Thank you, and thank you for your time, Master Gustini. You may go."

She left the lawyer in her father's great library—having received him there due to the skeleton arrayed on the floor of the room that served as her office and personal study—and returned to her chambers.

The bath was waiting for her, the air delightfully steamy and scented with orange. As she had requested, Alize was absent and Eska slipped into the bath, grateful for the silence. She thought it likely to be the last moment of peace she would enjoy for quite some time.

Though haste necessitated keeping her hair dry, she had just enough time to enjoy a soak and Eska reached for the jar of harrow root powder on a shelf next to the tub. She added a scoop to the water and breathed in the spicy steam that floated off the surface a moment later.

When she finished in the bath, Eska dressed in traveling clothes and then glanced around at the carefully organized disarray of her bedchamber, mentally checking off the items she could not do without as compared to the items she would take if space allowed. Much of it was exactly what she packed before every expedition. A good deal of it was not, most especially not the things inspired by Parisia of Mehatha. If Eska was honest with herself, she didn't quite know what she was going to do with the various artifacts she had set aside for the journey with her uncle to Anderra and Sandelese. She knew only that the objects had once called lands other than Bellara home—lands she would pass through after crossing the sea. And she also knew, thanks to Pierro Gustini, she had every right to do with the objects as she wished.

She began to fill two trunks and several leather cases and bags. When she finished, she turned to her desk and tucked the sheaf of papers from Master Gustini inside a satchel, added a hastily written note, then she summoned both a carriage and one of the stable boys. As the carriage was brought around and her trunks and bags loaded, Eska pulled the stable boy aside.

"Tobin, I have a very important task for you." Eska handed the dark-haired boy the satchel. "Bring this to the Varadome. Deliver it to the Arch-Commander. No one else, do you understand? He will see you immediately when he hears my name."

There were, perhaps, more fitting personages to receive the information in the satchel. The commander of the city guard, for instance, or the prefect. But she trusted Alexandre would act quickly on her word—if only because he would still be looking for an explanation regarding her midnight escapade at the Varadome. Not that he was going to get one—not yet, anyway.

The boy nodded and dashed off, vaulting onto the back of a waiting horse with ease. Eska watched him race down the drive and disappear around the corner, and then turned away as Roscoe announced that the carriage was ready.

"My lady?"

"I want you and four men to accompany me, Roscoe. Armed, all of you. To the teeth," Eska told the captain of the house guards, a small smile rising on her face. The captain raised an eyebrow—her habit of shunning an escort, armed or otherwise, was well known—but didn't question her motives and hurried off to collect four of his men from their quarters above the stable.

The troop, small as it was, followed Eska's directions perfectly. Led out by Roscoe, the five men bristled with weapons and their armor gleamed in the sun. Each man carried a spear and two swords, one long, one short. Roscoe wore a brace of knives across his chest, and one of the men had a crossbow slung over his back and a quiver of bolts on his belt.

"Are we to ride, my lady?" the captain asked.

Eska shook her head. "No, our pace will be quite sedate. But I need you to follow the carriage at a distance."

Roscoe frowned. "I don't understand, my lady."

Eska smiled and said, "Just keep us in sight." She turned and climbed into the open carriage, took one last surveying look at her trunks and bags, and then gave the order for the driver to proceed.

They were nearly halfway to the docks by the time Eska was quite certain they were being followed—which was considerably later than she had anticipated attracting the Iron Baron's attention. Nonetheless, amid the pedestrians, carts, and mounted travelers, she eventually caught sight of a few sleeves bearing the familiar ring of golden daggers. When she was confident of subtle pursuit, Eska indicated for Alfonse to alter the usual route slightly, taking the carriage onto smaller streets with less traffic, and waited.

She didn't have to wait long.

The golden daggers made their move as predicted, on a narrow stretch of road between Bartok Row and the parade grounds, closing in with a swiftness that set Eska's heart racing even though she had been expecting it. She stood up in the carriage as Alfonse reined in the horses and turned just as Thibault de Venescu emerged from behind four of his men.

The Iron Baron dropped his reins and held his palms up to the clear sky. "Like a gift from the gods dropped into my lap," he said. He lowered his hands and smiled widely at Eska. "We meet again, my lady. Just as I promised you. And my, my, isn't this awfully familiar."

Eska forced herself not to look over her shoulder in search of the de Caraval guards. They would be there. Any moment.

"Again you think to frighten me, my lord," Eska said. "And yet I remain unfrightened. Aren't you bored of this game yet?"

"On the contrary, my lady. How could I be bored when I am about to get what I want?"

"And what is it that you want, exactly?"

The smile on de Venescu's face deepened. "To see a thief justly punished."

"You mean to punish a woman who won't beg for mercy, a woman whom you have failed to kill twice now."

Splotches colored the Iron Baron's cheeks. He opened his mouth to reply, but Eska cut him off.

"Yes, I know what you like, my lord. You'll send me to a place where women are mutilated and raped until they no longer know their own names. If I'm lucky, you'll take a turn with me first, isn't that right?"

The flush spread to the baron's neck. "I know what you need, you bitch." His tongue darted out to wet his bottom lip. "How do you like the sound of a hot poker up your cunt?" His stallion leaped forward in the exact moment Eska heard Roscoe shout in the street behind her.

But it was the flash of white and crimson and steel in the alley to her right that drew Eska's eye.

Alexandre de Minos charged out of the alley, a host of soldiers in tight formation behind him, hooves thundering, his infamous pike poised to strike.

And for a moment, just a moment, Eska was back in the grove, the two men chasing her, the whip cracking behind her, her dagger plunging into flesh, and for that moment, she wished for the Arch-Commander to impale Thibault de Venescu on his pike.

He didn't, of course. Which was one of the reasons she had loved him once. But as Eska watched him strike the Iron Baron square across the jaw with the shaft of his spear, knocking de Venescu from the saddle, watched him dismount and drag the man to his knees as his officers surrounded the others, she saw the flash of rage in Alexandre's eyes as surely as she saw Thibault de Venescu throw his arms around the Arch-Commander's feet and plead his innocence.

In the aftermath, as de Venescu and his men were arrested and rounded up to be brought to the Varadome, Alexandre found her. Their eyes met over the heads of the men on their knees, and then he was standing in front of her. She dismissed Alfonse, telling him to drive on to the docks. Only then did she look up into Alexandre's face.

"Are you all right?" he asked.

She couldn't answer that. To do so would be to risk saying a great many things. She smiled. "Your timing was impeccable, Sascha."

He did not return the smile. "You took a great risk."

"It was worth it, to see him like this." Eska clenched her hands together behind her back, the face of the man she had killed floating in place of Alexandre's for an instant.

"How did you come by all that evidence against him?"

"I have a very talented lawyer," Eska said, the smile returning. "De Venescu has been threatening me since before I left for Toridium. He even sent a man to kill me at the excavation site on the Alencio, and two more just days ago here in the city. And given the stories about him, I knew some of it had to be true." She saw the disgust rise in Alexandre's face and knew it matched her own. "I never imagined the truth would be worse."

Alexandre nodded, his face sober. He opened his mouth, then hesitated, and Eska knew what would follow. "There's still the matter of that night at the Varadome," he said quietly.

"I know."

Whatever he might have said next, Eska would never know.

A shout from behind Alexandre drew his attention as de Venescu began to struggle as irons were clapped around his wrists. Alexandre turned to deal with the commotion—and Eska slipped away.

She took the Iron Baron's chestnut stallion. It seemed the least he could do for her after threatening to kill her. Eska mounted, glanced once more at Alexandre's back, at the way the short golden hairs on his head glowed, at the slope of his shoulders under his perfectly tailored military coat, at the line of his cheekbone and the curve of his ear, and then she turned the stallion and let him run.

Eska heard him call for her, his voice faint in the rush of wind flowing over her as she leaned over the horse's neck and they wove out of sight. She imagined him turning, imagined him moving to follow her only to call himself back to his duty. She could imagine the questions racing through his mind. But she could not imagine the look in his blue eyes.

By the time she reached the docks and caught sight of the *Argonex* at Firenzia Company's private wharf, there were tears drying on Eska's cheeks. She could not have said if they were true tears or merely a product of the wind—though she did not give herself leave to think on the question overly long. She wiped them away and approached the ship on foot.

The last of Eska's belongings were being lugged aboard. Eska handed off the stallion to Alfonse and directed him to return the horse to Alexandre. And then she scanned the ship, catching sight of him at last.

Valentin de Caraval stood at the stern, his hands folded in front of him, his gaze fixed on Eska. From that distance, she could read nothing in his expression. Nor could she, it turned out, after she walked up the gangplank and approached her uncle.

He said nothing, merely stared at her, his gaze narrowed, his posture unyielding, and so Eska spoke.

"I'm coming with you to Anderra and then on to Sandalese." Still Valentin did not move. "I'm not asking your permission, nor am I going to apologize for the actions and choices you believe have wronged you so greatly. There will be things I do on this journey that you will not approve of. Legally, you cannot stop me." Eska took a breath, feeling herself relent a little. "Uncle, for the sake of the niece I once was to you and the uncle you once were to me, let us both try to be kind."

Her uncle remained silent for a long moment, but Eska was content to wait him out. "Why are you coming, then?" he said at last.

"Because the world needs saving, apparently."

END OF BOOK ONE

Thank You All! Please Read!

After over a year of working back-and-forth, the first installment of The Godforged Chronicles has finally hit the shelves! We are so grateful to you—yes, you, reading this right now—for making the investment in and taking the time for Shadows of Ivory and joining us on this wild adventure. It's your support that makes it possible for writers like the pair of us to practice our craft, and your involvement that makes this journey so enjoyable.

On that subject, one very important note:

First: Please—please—rate and review Shadows of Ivory on Amazon, or any of your favorite book sites.

Many people don't know that there are thousands of books published every day, most of those in the USA alone. Over the course of a year, a quarter of a million authors will vie for a small place in the massive world of print and publishing. We fight to get even the tiniest traction, fight to climb upward one inch at a time towards the bright light of bestsellers, publishing contracts, and busy book signings.

Thing is, we need all the help we can get, and that's where wonderful readers like you come in!

Regardless of whether or not you choose to review, thank you again for taking the time to read Shadows of Ivory, and we will see you in the sequel!

Your biggest fans,

T L Greylock & Bryce O'Connor

Made in the USA
Monee, IL
31 March 2023